7 99

SCIENCE FICTION
OF THE FIFTIES

SCIENCE FICTION OF THE FIFTIES

Edited by:
Martin Harry Greenberg
Joseph Olander

AVON
PUBLISHERS OF BARD, CAMELOT AND DISCUS BOOKS

SCIENCE FICTION OF THE FIFTIES is an original publication of Avon Books. This work has never before appeared in book form.

AVON BOOKS
A division of
The Hearst Corporation
959 Eighth Avenue
New York, New York 10019
Copyright © 1979 by Martin H. Greenberg and Joseph D. Olander
Published by arrangement with the editors.
Library of Congress Catalog Card Number: 79-51349
ISBN: 0-380-46409-8

Cover design by Stanislaw Fernandes

First Avon Printing, September, 1979.

Avon Trademark Reg. U.S. Pat. Off. and in other countries, Marca Registrada, Hecho En U.S.A.

Printed in the U.S.A.

ACKNOWLEDGMENTS

"Spectator Sport," by John D. MacDonald, copyright © 1950 by Standard Magazines; copyright © 1978 renewed by John D. MacDonald. Reprinted by permission of the author.

"Feedback," by Katherine MacLean, copyright © 1951 by Street & Smith Publications, Inc.; copyright © 1962 renewed by Katherine MacLean. Reprinted by permission of the author.

"Bettyann," by Kris Neville, copyright © 1951 by Henry Holt & Co., Inc. Reprinted by permission of the author's agent, Forrest J Ackerman, 2495 Glendower Ave., Hollywood, CA 90027.

"Dark Interlude," by Fredric Brown and Mack Reynolds, copyright © 1951 by World Editions, Inc. Reprinted by permission of the author, the author's estate, and the author's agents, Scott Meredith Literary Agency, Inc., 845 Third Avenue, New York, New York 10022.

"What Have I Done?" by Mark Clifton, copyright © 1952 by Street & Smith Publications, Inc. (now Condé Nast Publications, Inc.). Reprinted by arrangement with Forrest J Ackerman, 2495 Glendower Ave., Hollywood, CA 90027, who is holding payment for the heir (please contact).

"DP!" by Jack Vance, copyright © 1953 by Stratford Novels, Inc. Reprinted by permission of the author and the author's agents, Scott Meredith Literary Agency, Inc., 845 Third Avenue, New York, New York 10022.

"The Liberation of Earth," by William Tenn, copyright © 1953 by Columbia Publications, Inc. Reprinted by permission of the author and Henry Morrison, Inc., his agents.

"A Bad Day for Sales," by Fritz Leiber, copyright © 1953 by Galaxy Publishing Corp. Reprinted by permission of the author and his agent, Robert P. Mills.

"Saucer of Loneliness," by Theodore Sturgeon, copyright © 1953 by Theodore Sturgeon. Reprinted by permission of the author and his agent, Kirby McCauley.

"Heirs Apparent," by Robert Abernathy, copyright © 1954 by Fantasy House, Inc. Reprinted by permission of the author.

"5,271,009," by Alfred Bester, from *The Magazine of Fantasy and Science Fiction*, copyright © 1954 by Mercury Press, Inc. and Alfred Bester. Reprinted by permission of the author.

"Short in the Chest," by Margaret St. Clair, copyright © 1954 by King-Size Publications. Reprinted by permission of the author.

"The Academy," by Robert Sheckley, copyright © 1954 by Robert Sheckley. Reprinted by permission of The Sterling Lord Agency, Inc.

"Nobody Bothers Gus," by Algis Budrys, copyright © 1955 by Street & Smith Publications, Inc. Reprinted by permission of the author.

"Happy Birthday, Dear Jesus," by Frederik Pohl, copyright © 1956 by Ballantine Books, Inc. Reprinted by permission of the author.

"A Work of Art," by James Blish, copyright © 1956 by James Blish. Reprinted by permission of Robert P. Mills, agent for the author's estate.

"The Country of the Kind," by Damon Knight, from *The Magazine of Fantasy and Science Fiction*, copyright © 1956 by Mercury Press, Inc. Reprinted by permission of the author.

"The Education of Tigress McCardle," by C. M. Kornbluth, from *Venture*, copyright © 1957 by Mercury Press, Inc. Reprinted by permission of Robert P. Mills, agent for the author's estate.

"The Cage," by A. Bertram Chandler, from *The Magazine of Fantasy and Science Fiction*, copyright © 1957 by Mercury Press, Inc. Reprinted by permission of the author and the author's agents, Scott Meredith Literary Agency, Inc., 845 Third Avenue, New York, New York 10022.

CONTENTS

PREFACE

by Frederik Pohl

ALTHOUGH I had nothing to do with selecting the stories for this volume, I jumped at the chance to say a few words as a Preface. It is a kind of nostalgia time for me, like a twenty-fifth anniversary class reunion, when you see how all those bright young classmates have grown bald or fat or rich.

I am glad to report that, as far as I can tell, time has been kind to these fellow alumni of the fifties. Alfie Bester is still brilliant, Fritz Leiber still moving, William Tenn still sardonically funny, Kornbluth and Knight and Budrys and all the others still a joy to read. In the early part of the fifties I was a literary agent, and about half the writers in this volume were at one time or another my clients. On and off in the decade I was editor of the *Star Science Fiction* series (where "Adrift on the Policy Level," for instance, was first published) and I was doing a lot of writing myself—for example, "Happy Birthday, Dear Jesus." So when I first read most of these stories they were in manuscript, and seeing them now, a couple of decades later—as antiquarian objects, archetypal of a whole decade of science-fictional literary history—is somewhat sobering. But the great thing is that the stories aren't! They wear their years well.

The ten years spanned by this volume encompassed drastic changes in the world of science fiction. Before 1950, there was almost nothing in the way of book publication of science fiction, barring a few semiprofessional, mostly fan outfits like Gnome Press, Shasta, and Fantasy Press. By the end of the decade the magazines were dwindling, and book publishing of sf had become big business. Television discovered science fiction in the fifties, with programs like *Captain Video* and that finest of all sf anthology series (ahead of its time, because filming and taping had not been perfected, so that the programs do not anymore exist in form suitable for reruns), *Tales of Tomorrow*. The film industry began to take notice, too, with movies like *Forbidden Planet* and *The Day the Earth Stood Still* and *The Thing*. And at least in the first part of the decade there was a perfect explosion of new science-fiction magazines, sparked by Horace Gold's *Galaxy* and Tony Boucher's and Mick McComas's *The Magazine of Fantasy and Science Fiction*; at one time there were three dozen separate sf magazines on the stands, until the winnowing-out that came with the demise of the American News Company. Markets create writers. In order to fill all those blank pages a host of new authors came into the field—Sheckley and Budrys and a great many others—and have permanently enriched it.

It was an interesting time to have been involved in science fiction.

It was not, however, a time in which science fiction was particularly well paid, or even very respectable.

The top rate in science-fiction magazines at the time was four cents a word, and usually a lot less—as little as a penny a word for many of the magazines. Living was cheaper then, but even so, in order to keep alive at a penny a word a writer needed to keep his fingers on the typewriter keyboard a good many hours of the day, most days of the year. Now and then there was a plum—Beaumont and Sheckley (and once in a while, I) managed to get a story into some mass-circulation magazine like *Playboy* at twenty times the usual sf magazine rate; occasionally there was a film sale, or a major book company bringing out a collection of short stories, or even a comic strip based on a story, and then for a while prosperity beamed. Usually, not.

It seems to me a curious fact that the frequent poverty of the writers was rarely reflected in the quality of the stories. Very few people write science fiction for money—even now, when sf books make the best-seller lists and sf films set world records for grosses. People write science fiction for exactly the same reasons as you and I read it: because they enjoy it. Because they want to. And I think it shows, particularly in the stories herein.

As to respectability—well, look at your present editors! A dean of one university and the acting president of another; how respectable can one get? The first bashful meetings between science fiction and academia began to occur along about the time some of these stories were being written, and nobody ever thought the relationship would last. But it has, and benefits have come to all concerned. For science-fiction writers, it has made it a lot easier for them to explain to chance-met acquaintances just what it is they do for a living. And to the world of academics, of literature in general, and even of the world of international relations, the relationship with science fiction has given some useful infusions of new ideas and new energy. I won't say they needed it . . . but I'm glad they have it!

FREDERIK POHL
Red Bank, New Jersey
February, 1979

INTRODUCTION

I

THE nineteen fifties were a momentous decade for America, one filled with many paradoxes. For example, a generation spawned by the Great Depression and World War II, aware of the sacrifices it had made, entered the fifties with expectations of finding the promised land of security and the good life. Instead, they found continued uncertainty, a still hostile world, and a strong feeling that somehow they had lost a great deal and would not be able to recover it.

This anxiety was caused by a number of factors, all of them interrelated. First, the world was still populated by villains despite the destruction of the Third Reich and the Japanese military machine, who were replaced in the public and governmental mind by Stalin and "International Communism." Indeed, the Cold War was in some ways more anxiety producing than World War II itself because the Atomic and then the Hydrogen Age meant that for the first time in history the proper elements were present to literally destroy mankind. These fears were preyed upon by a variety of individuals and movements. Some people sold fallout shelters; others sold dreams in the form of the United Nations Organization; and still others, like Senator Joseph McCarthy, sold half-truths and distortions.

There were other pressures as well. A number of trends that had been present in American society for some time reached public consciousness. One was urbanization, which saw the transfer of millions of people from rural areas and small towns into large metropolitan areas, continuing a trend that had begun with Depression farmers leaving the Dust Bowl for the promised land of California. At the same time large numbers of American city dwellers left the center city for the green lawns and "little boxes" of suburbia. But once there, the trouble remained—the mortgage had to be paid, monthly bills for household goods purchased on credit had to be met, and heavy taxes to pay for expanded services had to be imposed. And as the suburbs grew, the now vacated city dwellings were occupied by the newly arriving blacks, Hispanics, and poor and disadvantaged whites.

The rapid pace of technological change seemed to many to erode traditional values and institutions, leaving large vacuums where there once existed familiar supports. Almost anything could and was branded a threat to traditional values— even a cherubic man named Bill Haley who associated himself with others who called themselves the "Comets." Not even the affluence of the postwar boom years could allay the nervousness and anxiety. What was the problem?

Part of the problem was the fact that we lived in a world that no one foresaw and that nobody wanted. The optimism of the early years of the twentieth century evaporated with the destruction of part of a generation on the fields of Flanders. Moreover, none of the great political and social thinkers of the nineteenth and early twentieth centuries had foreseen the most basic side effect of industrialization on Western civilization— the rise of large bureaucratic structures that impinged upon people in a multitude of ways, depersonalizing them, dehumanizing them, and alienating men and women in a way and form unprecedented in human history. In earlier periods despots and tyrants of one kind or another were common enough, but if people kept their noses clean and didn't aspire to power, they were pretty much left alone. At least they did not have to worry about their daily lives being intruded upon. But the technological revolution of this century made possible some of the worst aspects of totalitarian movements—the invasion of privacy, the possibility of almost constant surveillance, and the feeling of vulnerability that goes without being able to really be alone.

II

The science-fiction field was also undergoing basic changes in the post-World War II period. The dominance of *Astounding Science Fiction* and its editor, John W. Campbell, Jr., was challenged on two fronts. Artistically, *The Magazine of Fantasy and Science Fiction*, under the leadership of Anthony Boucher and J. Francis McComas, proved that science fiction could stand the imposition of higher standards of style and character development than had heretofore been insisted upon. And in the area of ideas, H. L. Gold's entry, *Galaxy Science Fiction*, emphasized social content and social criticism with stories and novels written in a biting, satirical tone.

Science fiction emerged after World War II as a stronger, more dynamic, and more diversified field. Had not many science-fiction predictions come to pass during the war— radar, guided missiles—even atomic energy itself? This confidence found expression in the launching of numerous new science-fiction and fantasy magazines—*Future Science Fiction, Imagination, Worlds of If, Fantastic, Infinity Science Fiction*, and *Venture Science Fiction*, to mention only a few. Almost all of the several dozen new magazines would not live to see the sixties.

After a long, uphill struggle whose whole story is yet to be told, other areas of the publishing industry began to embrace science fiction. The socially conscious Ian and Betty Ballantine launched Ballantine Books in the early fifties and quickly established themselves as leaders in the field, as did Donald A. Wolheim and Ace Books. Through the efforts of Frederik Pohl and others, hardcover houses like Doubleday and Simon & Schuster entered the field, supplementing and then replacing fan-backed ventures such as Gnome Press and Shasta.

III

Although all types of science fiction were written during the fifties, a significant percentage of it reflected the currents and issues of the time. Among these were the following:

1. *Tendencies toward conformity and mobism.* Science fiction has a long and rich history of concern over man's loss of identity, depersonalization, and the annihilation of identity. Writers from Eugene Zamyatin to Aldous Huxley had written of the danger, but the experience of Nazism resulted in a resurgence of concern over the bureaucratization of life and the role of institutional forces in this process. There was an implicit and explicit feeling that the masses were easily led and misled, and that the "average citizen" simply did not have the will, intelligence, or drive to withstand the homogenizing forces of large structures. Emphasis was therefore placed on extolling the virtues of the *deviant*--the outcast who would not conform to the enforced norms of the societies portrayed in stories and novels. A stock setting in science fiction has been the revolution—movements led by individuals who either through accident or by virtue of superior intelligence understand the danger and find others who are willing to risk their lives in resistance. Ray Bradbury's *Fahrenheit 451* (1953) presented a society that repressed freedom even to the extent of banning books—a practice that was occurring when the book was being written.

2. *Cold War hysteria and its domestic repercussions.* The transformation of the Soviet Union from wartime ally to

monolithic enemy in less than five years provided the science-fiction writer with a wide variety of themes. In some works the Russians (or a surrogate, unnamed stand-in) have defeated the West and occupied the United States; an example would be C. M. Kornbluth's *Not This August* (1955). In others the competition between the United States and the Soviet Union was transferred to outer space. In these tales the stereotype of the resourceful American pitted against the humorless, true believer Communist appeared frequently, but in all fairness it must be said that many other stories were written that concentrated on the ways in which conflict between two sides could be resolved short of war—stories like "Brave New Word" by J. Francis McComas, "The Cave of Night" by James Gunn, and "Triggerman" by Jessie Bone. In some stories, Americans and Russians join forces *after* a war in a joint effort to rebuild civilization, as in Robert Abernathy's "Heirs Apparent," included in this volume.

American-Soviet animosities also affected domestic life in this country, and produced science-fiction stories and novels that reflected these tensions and concerns. The witch-hunts of the House Un-American Activities Committee, the Army-McCarthy hearings, and McCarthyism in general worked their way into a number of science-fiction stories, and it is to the credit of science fiction that the message of the vast majority of them supported individual freedom, the right to remain silent, and opposed guilt by association and "the naming of names."

3. *The post-holocaust story.* Fear of nuclear devastation peaked in this country in the fifties and science fiction shared in these fears. *Astounding Science Fiction*, in the decade after Hiroshima, featured stories of atomic destruction that seemed to despair of any viable alternative to war.[1] A number of

[1] Brian W. Aldiss, *Billion Year Spree: The True History of Science Fiction* (New York: Doubleday & Company, Inc., 1973) p. 246.

"near-future" novels like Nevil Shute's *On The Beach* spoke in gruesome detail of atomic war or its immediate aftermath.

But the most interesting development in this regard was the proliferation of novels and stories set in the relatively distant future *after* civilization has been destroyed by war or in a few cases, natural disaster. There had been novels on this theme before, including *Final Blackout* by L. Ron Hubbard (1948 in novel form, but the original appeared in *Astounding* around 1940) and *Earth Abides* by George Stewart (1949). However, the theme exploded in the fifties: Leigh Brackett's *The Long Tomorrow*; John Christopher's *No Blade of Grass*; Raymond F. Jones' *Renaissance*; Walter M. Miller, Jr.'s classic *A Canticle for Leibowitz*; Clifford D. Simak's *City*; and John Wyndham's aptly named *Re-birth*. Many more titles could be added to this list—what is important is not the number but the depth of concern for the possibility (for some the probability) that death and destruction were around the corner if mankind did not reverse the trend toward war.

4. *The anti-system story.* The fifties were also characterized by a large number of stories that featured highly developed and detailed societies based on specific tendencies visible in the present. The societies portrayed were almost uniformly awful to live in, especially if you had brains enough to recognize what was happening—a common device used by many writers was to construct what appeared to be utopias based on the existence of certain technologies which, on closer inspection, actually made them dystopias.

The targets of these stories were, as Albert Berger has pointed out,[2] the very things that made the modern world modern—large bureaucratic structures based on specializa-

---

[2] In Harold L. Berger, *Anti-Utopian Science Fiction of the Mid-Twentieth Century* (unpublished doctoral dissertation, University of Tennessee, 1970). This study is a fine piece of work and deserves wider circulation.

tion of function and the substitution of technology for human contact. Leading the charge were writers like Frederik Pohl, C. M. Kornbluth, William Tenn, and Robert Sheckley, mostly writing in H. L. Gold's *Galaxy Science Fiction*. The center of activity revolved around what the late James Blish has called[3] (in a different context) "the *Galaxy*-Pohl-Ballantine axis," one of the dominant science-fiction forces in the fifties—*Galaxy* as one of the "big three" magazines, Pohl as trend-setter with his social satire, and the Ballantines as a major publishing outlet.

The social science fiction of Frederik Pohl was particularly important, especially his novel (written with C. M. Kornbluth) *The Space Merchants*, which as *Gravy Planet* was serialized in *Galaxy* in 1952. It was one of the very few science-fiction books to receive recognition outside of science fiction, and its impact can be measured by the fact that it is still in print, has been translated into more than forty languages, and has sold in the millions. Pohl, who had worked as a copywriter for an advertising agency, projected a future in which advertising agencies had taken power. A number of writers of the fifties followed this pattern and portrayed societies controlled by forces that were personally distasteful to them. In fact, the extrapolation of current trends, whether they be the role of television, the increasing power of large corporate structures like the insurance industry, the growing influence of psychoanalysis, or others, to their logical or illogical conclusions became an art form during the fifties.

This attack upon what Brian Ash has called "the Admass Culture"[4] had a number of features, including a rather deep and profound distrust in the ability of "the masses" to resist

[3] James Blish (writing as William Atheling, Jr.) *More Issues at Hand* (Chicago: Advent: Publishers, Inc., 1970) p. 33.
[4] Brian Ash, *Faces of the Future: The Lessons of Science Fiction* (New York: Taplinger Publishing Company, Inc., 1975).

the traps and inducements offered them by their corporate enslavers. The docile nature of the common men and women depicted in the social science fiction written during this period can be shown by the ease with which they are distracted from the injustice and tyranny around them by bread and circus tactics (as in *Gladiator-at-Law* by Pohl and Kornbluth) and the tremendous success of advertising techniques. Indeed, the entire production-persuasion-consumption process became the focal point of attention for a variety of writers from William Tenn to Fritz Leiber. The creation of uncontrollable and insatiable desire for consumer goods and the role of advertising in this process was a feature of a large number of stories—for example, Pohl's "The Midas Plague," "Happy Birthday, Dear Jesus," and "The Man Who Ate the World"; Fritz Leiber's "A Bad Day for Sales"; and "Captive Audience" by Ann Warren Griffith.

In general, the social science fiction of the fifties was marked by a loss of confidence in the quality of life. In addition to widespread alienation in response to depersonalization, automation, and loss of identity, attention was given to uncontrolled population growth and its effects on small and large group behavior. Many novels and stories in the fifties depicted overpopulated societies, although in most this feature was incidental to the main story line. Another topic which received considerable attention was the future of race relations. It is interesting to note that while science fiction championed the cause of individual freedom and civil rights during the fifties the stories on racial themes very often employed alien surrogates, androids, or robots in place of minority group members. Blacks were extremely rare in these stories. Representative fiction from this period includes "The Big Stink" by Theodore Cogswell; "Made in U.S.A." by J. T. MacIntosh; "Love" by Richard Wilson; "Holdout" by Robert Sheckley; and "All the Colors of the Rainbow" by Leigh Brackett.

About the only thing that the science-fiction writers of the fifties did not extrapolate was human nature itself. That remained largely unchanged; men and women were still motivated by the old drives—power, a desire for wealth, the ego-fulfilling benefits of status—although these were often condemned. If these writers are correct, then the darkening visions of the fifties may well become the realities of the last quarter of the twentieth century.

Those of us who grew up reading the social science fiction of the fifties know that our values were shaped to a considerable extent by the authors who fill the following pages. We only regret that space limitations prevent us from including the work of numerous other writers, like James Blish and Theodore Sturgeon, and we urge you to use the bibliography at the end of the book and read and think about what they were and are telling us.

Let's return, then, to those days of beautiful Richard Powers covers—and discover some of the best science fiction ever written.

Spectator Sport

John D. MacDonald (1919-   )

JOHN D. MacDonald belongs to that small group of people who started out as science-fiction writers and then moved on to fame in other fields. This group includes such diverse individuals as John Jakes, one of the best-selling authors in the history of American publishing; Michael Shaara, winner of the Pulitzer Prize; and Kurt Vonnegut, Jr. (depending on your definition of science fiction and Kurt Vonnegut).

In science fiction, MacDonald is best known for his fifties novels Wine of the Dreamers (1951) and Ballroom of the Skies (1952) and especially for the complex and humorous The Girl, the Gold Watch, and Everything (1962). However, during the late forties and early fifties he produced fifty science-fiction short stories and novelettes, many like "A Child Is Crying," "The Big Contest," and "Game for Blondes," of considerable power and sophistication.

"Spectator Sport" captures the alienation and dreams of a decade in which many people discovered the reality of a postwar world that had difficulty living up to its promise.

From *Thrilling Wonder Stories*   February, 1950

Dr. Rufus Maddon was not generally considered to be an impatient man—or addicted to physical violence.

But when the tenth man he tried to stop on the street brushed by him with a mutter of annoyance Rufus Maddon grabbed the eleventh man, swung him around and held him with his shoulders against a crumbling wall.

He said, "You will listen to me, sir! I am the first man to travel into the future and I will not stand—"

The man pushed him away, turned around and said, "You got this dust on my suit. Now brush it off."

Rufus Maddon brushed mechanically. He said, with a faint uncontrollable tremble in his voice, "But nobody seems to care."

The man peered back over his shoulder. "Good enough, chum. Better go get yourself lobed. The first time I saw the one on time travel it didn't get to me at all. Too hammy for me. Give me those murder jobs. Every time I have one of those I twitch for twenty hours."

Rufus made another try. "Sir, I am physical living proof that the future is predetermined. I can explain the energy equations, redesign the warp projector, send myself from your day further into the future—"

The man walked away. "Go get a lobe job," he said.

"But don't I look different to you?" Rufus called after him, a plaintive note in his voice.

The man, twenty feet away, turned and grinned at him. "How?"

When the man had gone Rufus Maddon looked down at his neat grey suit, stared at the men and women in the street. It was not fair of the future to be so—so dismally normal.

Four hundred years of progress? The others had resented the experience that was to be his. In those last few weeks there had been many discussions of how the people four hundred years in the future would look on Rufus Maddon as a barbarian.

Once again he continued his aimless walk down the streets of the familiar city. There was a general air of disrepair. Shops were boarded up. The pavement was broken and potholed. A few automobiles traveled on the broken streets. They, at least, appeared to be of a slightly advanced design but they were dented, dirty and noisy.

The man who had spoken to him had made no sense. "Lobe job?" And what was "the one on time travel?"

He stopped in consternation as he reached the familiar park. His consternation arose from the fact that the park was all too familiar. Though it was a tangle of weeds the equestrian statue of General Murdy was still there in deathless bronze, liberally decorated by pigeons.

Clothes had not changed nor had common speech. He wondered if the transfer had gone awry, if this world were something he was dreaming.

He pushed through the knee-high tangle of grass to a wrought-iron bench. Four hundred years before he had sat on that same bench. He sat down again. The metal powdered and collapsed under his weight, one end of the bench dropping with a painful thump.

Dr. Rufus Maddon was not generally considered to be a man subject to fits of rage. He stood up rubbing his bruised elbow, and heartily kicked the offending bench. The part he kicked was all too solid.

He limped out of the park, muttering, wondering why the park wasn't used, why everyone seemed to be in a hurry.

It appeared that in four hundred years nothing at all had been accomplished. Many familiar buildings had collapsed. Others still stood. He looked in vain for a newspaper or a magazine.

One new element of this world of the future bothered him considerably. That was the number of low-slung white-panel delivery trucks. They seemed to be in better condition than the other vehicles. Each bore in fairly large gilt letters the legend WORLD SENSEWAYS. But he noticed that the smaller print underneath the large inscription varied. Some read, *Feeder Division*—others, *Hookup Division*.

The one that stopped at the curb beside him read, *Lobot-omy Division*. Two husky men got out and smiled at him and one said, "You've been taking too much of that stuff, Doc."

"How did you know my title?" Rufus asked, thoroughly puzzled.

The other man smiled wolfishly, patted the side of truck. "Nice truck, pretty truck. Climb in, bud. We'll take you down and make you feel wonderful, hey?"

Dr. Rufus Maddon suddenly had a horrid suspicion that he knew what a lobe job might be. He started to back away. They grabbed him quickly and expertly and dumped him into the truck.

The sign on the front of the building said WORLD SENSE-WAYS. The most luxurious office inside was lettered, *Regional Director—Roger K. Handriss*.

Roger K. Handriss sat behind his handsome desk. He was a florid grey-haired man with keen grey eyes. He was examining his bank book thinking that in another year he'd have enough money with which to retire and buy a permanent hookup. Permanent was so much better than the Temp stuff you could get on the home sets. The nerve ends was what did it, of course.

The girl came in and placed several objects on the desk in front of him. She said, "Mr. Handriss, these just came up from LD. They took them out of the pockets of a man reported as wandering in the street in need of a lobe job."

She had left the office door open. Cramer, deputy chief of LD, sauntered in and said, "The guy was really off. He was yammering about being from the past and not to destroy his mind."

Roger Handriss poked the objects with a manicured finger. He said, "Small pocket change from the twentieth century, Cramer. Membership cards in professional organizations of that era. Ah, here's a letter."

As Cramer and the girl waited, Roger Handriss read the letter through twice. He gave Cramer an uncomfortable smile and said, "This appears to be a letter from a technical publishing house telling Mr.—ah—Maddon that they intend to reprint his book, *Suggestions on Time Focus*, in February of nineteen hundred and fifty. Miss Hart, get on the phone and see if you can raise anyone at the library who can look this up for us. I want to know if such a book was published."

Miss Hart hastened out of the office.

As they waited, Handriss motioned to a chair. Cramer sat down. Handriss said, "Imagine what it must have been like in those days, Al. They had the secrets but they didn't begin to use them until—let me see—four years later. Aldous Huxley had already given them their clue with his literary invention of the Feelies. But they ignored them.

"All their energies went into wars and rumors of wars and random scientific advancement and sociological disruptions. Of course, with Video on the march at that time, they were beginning to get a little preview Millions of people were beginning to sit in front of the Video screens, content even with that crude excuse for entertainment."

Cramer suppressed a yawn. Handriss was known to go on like that for hours.

"Now," Handriss continued, "all the efforts of a world society are channeled into World Senseways. There is no waste of effort changing a perfectly acceptable status quo. Every man can have Temp and if you save your money you can have Permanent, which, they say, is as close to heaven as man can get. Uh—what was that, Miss Hart?"

"There is such a book, Mr. Handriss, and it was published at that time. A Dr. Rufus Maddon wrote it."

Handriss sighed and clucked. "Well," he said, "have Maddon brought up here."

Maddon was brought into the office by an attendant. He wore a wide foolish smile and a tiny bandage on his temple. He walked with the clumsiness of an overgrown child.

"Blast it. Al," Handriss said, "why couldn't your people

have been more careful! He looks as if he might have been intelligent."

Al shrugged. "Do they come here from the past every couple of minutes? He didn't look any different than any other lobey to me."

"I suppose it couldn't be helped," Handriss said. "We've done this man a great wrong. We can wait and reeducate, I suppose. But that seems to be treating him rather shabbily."

"We can't send him back," Al Cramer said.

Handriss stood up, his eyes glowing. "But it is within my authority to grant him one of the Perm setups given me. World Senseways knows that Regional Directors make mistakes. This will rectify any mistake to an individual."

"Is it fair he should get it for free?" Cramer asked. "And besides, maybe the people who helped send him up here into the future would like to know what goes on."

Handriss smiled shrewdly. "And if they knew, what would stop them from flooding in on us? Have Hookup install him immediately."

The subterranean corridor had once been used for underground trains. But with the reduction in population it had ceased to pay its way and had been taken over by World Senseways to house the sixty-five thousand Perms.

Dr. Rufus Maddon was taken, in his new shambling walk, to the shining cubicle. His name and the date of installation were written on a card and inserted in the door slot. Handriss stood enviously aside and watched the process.

The bored technicians worked rapidly. They stripped the unprotesting Rufus Maddon, took him inside his cubicle, forced him down onto the foam coach. They rolled him over onto his side, made the usual incision at the back of his neck, carefully slit the main motor nerves, leaving the senses, the heart and lungs intact. They checked the air conditioning and plugged him into the feeding schedule for that bank of Perms.

Next they swung the handrods and the footplates into position, gave him injections of local anesthetic, expertly flayed the palms of his hands and the soles of his feet, painted the raw flesh with the sticky nerve graft and held his hands closed around the rods, his feet against the plates until they adhered in the proper position.

Handriss glanced at his watch.

"Guess that's all we can watch, Al. Come along."

The two men walked back down the long corridor. Handriss said, "The lucky so and so. We have to work for it. I get my Perm in another year—right down here beside him. In the meantime we'll have to content ourselves with the hand sets, holding onto those blasted knobs that don't let enough through to hardly raise the hair on the back of your neck."

Al sighed enviously. "Nothing to do for as long as he lives except twenty-four hours a day of being the hero of the most adventurous and glamorous and exciting stories that the race has been able to devise. No memories. I told them to dial him in on the Cowboy series. There's seven years of that now. It'll be more familiar to him. I'm electing Crime and Detection. Eleven years of that now, you know."

Roger Handriss chuckled and jabbed Al with his elbow. "Be smart, Al. Pick the Harem series."

Back in the cubicle the technicians were making the final adjustments. They inserted the sound buttons in Rufus Maddon's ears, deftly removed his eyelids, moved his head into just the right position and then pulled down the deep concave shining screen so that Rufus Maddon's staring eyes looked directly into it.

The elder technician pulled the wall switch. He bent and peered into the screen. "Color okay, three dimensions okay. Come on, Joe, we got another to do before quitting."

They left, closed the metal door, locked it.

Inside the cubicle, Dr. Rufus Maddon was riding slowly down the steep trail from the mesa to the cattle town on the plains. He was trail-weary and sun-blackened. There was an old score to settle. Feeney was about to foreclose on Mary Ann's spread and Buck Hoskie, Mary Ann's crooked foreman, had threatened to shoot on sight.

Rufus Maddon wiped the sweat from his forehead on the back of a lean hard brown hero's hand.

Feedback

Katherine MacLean (1925–   )

THE *fifties witnessed the emergence of a small number of woman science-fiction writers who added immeasurably to the field. They included Zena Henderson, Margaret St. Clair, Mildred Clingerman, Andre Norton, and Katherine MacLean. Like Judith Merril, Catherine L. Moore, and Leigh Brackett before them, they sometimes encountered publishing difficulties because of their sex—problems which are not fully resolved to this day, although the situation is much improved over what it was.*

During the fifties a number of memorable social-science fiction stories were written by women, including "Captive Audience" by Ann Warren Griffith, "Created He Them" by Alice Eleanor Jones, and the present selection by Katherine MacLean, who often worked with social themes.

"Feedback" is a story of enforced conformism, of the feared deviant, and of the instinct to follow. It is also about what it means to be "subversive," "disloyal," unwilling to testify against others and to name names. In short, it was a powerful statement against one of the greatest evils of the fifties—McCarthyism.

From *Astounding Science Fiction*   1951

"Why did Leonardo write backward?" The year was 1991.

A pupil had asked the question. William Dunner switched on the lights suddenly, showing the class of ten- and twelve-year-olds blinking in the sudden glare.

"He was in danger of his life," he said seriously. "Here"— he tapped the pointer against the floor—"give that last slide again."

The pupil at the back of the room worked the slide lever, and Da Vinci's "Last Supper," which still showed dimly on the screen, vanished with a jerk and a click and was replaced by an enlarged sketch of a flying machine, with time-dimmed handwriting under it in oddly curled and abbreviated words. It was backward, as if the slide had been put in the wrong way.

"He was writing ideas that no one had ever written before," said William Dunner, "and he had seen things that should not have been there—the symmetry of sound waves—the perfect roundness of ripples spreading through each other, and high up on a mountain he had found sea shells, as if the sea and the land had not always been where they were, but had changed, and perhaps some day the sea would again close over the mountain top, and mountains rise from the depth of the sea. These thoughts were against the old beliefs, and he was afraid. Other men such as he saw new truths about nature, and risked their lives to teach and write them. And those men gave us the new world of science we have today. Leonardo had great thoughts, but he wrote them down in silence and hid them in code, for if the people guessed what he thought they might come and burn him, as they had burned some of his paintings. He was afraid."

He tapped the base of the pointer on the floor and the slide vanished and was replaced by the "Last Supper."

A chubby little girl put up her hand.

"Yes, Maralyn?"

"Were they Fascists?" It was an obvious identification: Fascists tortured people. Those who knew a little more history stirred and giggled to show that they knew better.

"Stand up, please," he said gently. She stood up. It did not matter what the question or answer was, as long as they stood up. That was the way they learned. Standing up while the class sat, being alone on the stage in the drama club he had formed for them; learning to stand and think alone; learning to grow past the fear.

"No, not Fascism. It wasn't their government which made them cruel." Mr. Dunner made a slight sad clumsy gesture with the hand that held the pointer. "You might say it is a democratic thing, for in defending the old ways people feel that they are defending something worthy and precious." He ran his eyes across their faces as though looking for something and said firmly, "Logically, of course, nothing is wrong which does not injure a neighbor, but if you attack a man's beliefs with logic he sometimes feels as if you are attacking his body, as if you are injuring him. In Leonardo's time they held very many illogical beliefs which were beginning to crumple, so they felt constantly insecure and attacked, and they burned many men, women, and children to death for being in league with Satan, the father of doubts."

In the painting on the screen the figure of Christ sat at the long table. The paint was blotched and cracked and his face almost hidden.

Mr. Dunner turned to it. "No, it need not be Fascism. The rulers of a venal government may have no beliefs or ideals left to defend. The Roman government would have pardoned Christ, but it was his own people who slew him, preferring to pardon a robber instead of a man of strange beliefs."

He pointed with his stick. "He is eating with his disciples. He has just said 'One of you will betray me.' Observe the composition of—"

There was a slight stirring and whispering of disapproval, and a question was passed in quick murmuring and agreement. A boy raised his hand.

"Yes, Johnny?"

"Why is it democratic?" He was almost defiant. "Burning people."

"Because it is an expression of the majority will. The majority of people have faith that the things they already believe are true, and so they will condemn anyone who teaches different things, believing them to be lies. All basic progress must start with the discovery of a truth not yet known and believed. Unless those who have new ideas and different thoughts be permitted to speak and are protected carefully by law, they will be attacked, for in all times men have confused difference with criminality."

The murmur began again, and the boy put up his hand.

"Yes, Johnny?"

"I *like* change. I *like* things different." He was speaking for the class. It was a question. The teacher hesitated oddly.

"Stand up, please."

The boy stood up. He had a thin oval face with large brown eyes which he narrowed now to hide nervousness. The class turned in their seats to look at him.

"You said you like things different," the teacher reminded him. "That's a good trait, but do you like to *be* different yourself? Do you like to stand up when the others are sitting down?" The boy licked his lips, glancing from the side of his eyes at the classmates seated around him, his nervousness suddenly increased.

Mr. Dunner turned to the blackboard and wrote "sameness." "Here is the sameness of mass production, and human equality, and shared tastes and dress and entertainment, and basic education equalized at a high level, and forgotten prejudices, and the blending of minorities, and all the other good things of democracy. The sameness of almost everybody doing the same thing at once. Some of the different ones who are left notice their difference and feel left out and alone. They try to be more like the others." He curved a chalk arrow, and wrote "conformity." Johnny, still standing, noticed that Mr. Dunner was nervous, too. The chalk line wavered.

The arrow curved through "conformity" and back to the first word in a swift circle. "And then those who are left feel more conspicuous and lonesome than ever. People stare and talk about them. So *they* try to be more like the others. And then everybody is so much like everybody else that even a very tiny necessary difference looks peculiar and wrong. The unknown and unfamiliar is feared or hated. All differences, becoming infrequent, look increasingly strange and unfamiliar, and shocking, and hateful. Those who want to be different hide themselves and pretend to be like the others."

He moved the chalk in swift strokes. The thickening circle of arrows passed through the words: sameness, conformity, sameness, conformity, sameness . . .

He stepped back and printed in the middle of the circle, very neatly. "STASIS."

He turned back to the class, smiling faintly. "They are trapped. And it is all unconscious. They don't know what has happened to them."

He turned back to the blackboard and drew another circle thoughtfully. This one wavered much more. "These are feedback circles. All positive feedbacks are dangerous. Not just man but other social animals have an instinct to follow, and can fall into the trap. Even the lowly tent caterpillars are in danger from it, for they crawl after each other in single file, and if the leader of a line happens to turn back and find before him the end of his own line, he will follow it, and the circle of caterpillars will keep crawling around and around, growing hungry and exhausted, following each until they die."

Johnny licked his lips nervously, wishing Mr. Dunner would let him sit down.

Miraculously the teacher's eyes met his.

"I stand up," said Mr. Dunner softly to him alone. "If everyone else went sledding, could you go skating alone, all by yourself?"

He could see that it was a real question: Mr. Dunner honestly wanted him to answer, as if he were an equal. Johnny nodded.

"It would take courage, wouldn't it? Sit down, Johnny."

Johnny sat down, liking the tall shy bony teacher more than ever. He was irritably aware of the stares and snickers of the others around him. As if he'd done something wrong! What did they think they were snickering at anyhow!

He leaned both elbows on the desk and looked at the teacher as if he were concentrating on the lecture.

The bell rang.

"Class dismissed," called Mr. Dunner unnecessarily and helplessly over the din of slamming desk tops and shouts as everybody rushed for the door.

Glancing back, Johnny saw the teacher still standing before the blackboard. Beside him the projected image of Leonardo's painting glowed dimly, forgotten, on the screen.

At his locker, Johnny slipped his arms into his jacket and grabbed his cap angrily. Why did they have to scare Leonardo? Grownups! People acted crazy!

Outside they were shouting, "Yeaaa-ahh yeaaa-ahh! Charlie put his cap on backward! Charlie put his cap on backward!" Charlie, one of his best pals, stood miserably pretending not to notice. His cap was frontward. He must have put it right as soon as they had started to call.

Johnny hunched his shoulders and walked through the ring as if he had not seen it, and it broke up unconcernedly in his wake into the scattering and clusters of kids going home. Johnny did not wait to get into a group. Stupid, they were all stupid! He wished he could have thought of something to tell them.

At home, stuffing down a sandwich in the kitchen he came to a conclusion. "Mother, does everyone have to be like everyone else? Why can't they be different?"

It's started again, she thought. *I can't let Johnny get that way*.

Aloud she said, "No, dear, everyone can be as different as they like. This is a free country, a democracy."

"Then can Charlie wear his cap backward?"

It was an insane concept. She was tempted to laugh. "No, dear. If he did, he would be locked up."

He grew more interested. "Why? Why would they lock him up?"

"Because it would be crazy—" Her breath caught in her throat but she kept the sound of her voice level, and busied herself at the stove, her head down so that he wouldn't notice anything wrong.

"Why? Why would it be crazy?" The clear voice seemed too clear, as if someone could hear it outside the room, outside the walls, as if the whole town could hear. "Why can't I wear my cap backward—"

"It's crazy!" she snapped. The pan clattered loudly on the stove under the violence of her stirring. Always answer a child's questions with a smile. She swallowed with a dry mouth, and tried.

"I mean it would be queer. It's odd. You don't want to be odd, do you?" He didn't answer, and she plunged on, trying desperately to make him see it. "Only crazy people want to be odd. Crazy people and seditioners." She swallowed again, turning her head covertly to see if he understood. He had to understand! He couldn't talk like this in front of her friends, they might not understand, they might think that she—

She remembered the seditioner who had moved into town three years ago, a plane and tractor mechanic. He had seemed such a nice man on the outside, but he had turned out to be a seditioner, wanting to change something. People from the town had gone to show him what they thought of it, and someone had hit him too hard, and he had died. Johnny mustn't—

He looked sulky and unconvinced. "Mr. Dunner said everybody could be as different as they liked," he said. "He said it doesn't matter what you wear." He kicked the edge of the sink defiantly, something like desperation welling up in his voice. "He said being like other people is stupid, like caterpillars."

She thought: *Mr. Dunner now, the history teacher, another seditioner. That tall shy man. And he had been teaching the children for five years! Other people's children too—* She turned off the stove and went numbly to telephone.

While she was telephoning the fourth house, Johnny came out of the kitchen with his cap on and his jacket zipped, ready to go out and play. She lowered her voice. While she talked on the phone he went to the hall mirror, looked into it and carefully took his cap off, rotated it and replaced it backward, with the visor to the back and the ear tabs on his forehead. His eyes met hers speculatively in the mirror.

For a moment she did not absorb what he had done. She had never seen anyone wearing a hat the wrong way before. It gave a horrible impression of a whole head turned backward, as if the back of his head were a featureless brown face watching her under the visor. The pale oval of his real face in the mirror seemed changed and alien.

Somehow a steel strength came to her. She remembered that the viewing screen was off. No one had seen. She said into the phone, as if starting a sentence, "Well, I think—" and putting her finger on the lever, cut the connection and hung up.

Johnny was watching her. Rising, she slapped his face. Seeing the white hand marks, she realized that she had slapped harder than she had intended, but she was not sorry. It was for his sake.

The phone began ringing.

"Go upstairs—" she whispered, breathing hard. "Go to your room—" He went. She picked up the phone. "Yes, Mrs. Jessups, I'm sorry . . . I guess we were cut off."

Three calls, four calls, five calls.

When Bruce Wilson arrived home he heard the story. He listened, his hand clutching the banister rail, the knuckles whitening.

When Pam finished he asked tightly, "Do you think a spanking would do any good?"

"No, he's all right now, he's frightened."

"Are you sure he's safe?"

"Yes." But she looked tired and worried. Johnny had been exposed to sedition. It remained to be seen if it would have any effect. Seditioners were always tarred and feathered, fired, driven out of their homes, beaten, hung, burned.

The telephone rang. Pam reached for it, then paused, glancing away from him. Her voice changed. "That will be the vigilantes, Bruce."

"I have to finish that report tonight. I'm tired, Pam."

"You didn't go last time. It wouldn't look right if you—"

"I guess I'd better go. It's my duty anyhow." They didn't look at each other. He answered the phone.

They screamed and shouted, pushing, making threatening gestures at the man on the platform, lashing at him with the noise, trying to build his fear to the point where it would be visible and cowering. Someone in the crowd was waving a noose, shouting for his attention. Someone else was waving a corkscrew. He saw it. They laughed at the comic horror of the threat, and laughed again at the man's expression as he realized what it was.

They were in a clearing among trees which was the town picnic grounds. At the center, before the mob, was the oration platform, built around the base of the giant picnic oak.

On the rear of the platform the judges of the occasion finished arranging themselves and were ready.

"Silence."

The mob quieted.

"William C. Dunner, you are accused of teaching sedition

—malign and unworthy doctrines—to our children, violating the trust placed in you." He did not reply.

"Have you anything to say in your defense?"

The fluorescent lamp shone on the people grouped on the platform. Below, the light gleamed across the upturned faces of the mob as they watched the tall, stooped man who stood disheveled in the light, his hands tied behind him and a smear of blood on one cheek. He shook his head in negation. "I wouldn't do anything against the children," he said. They heard the slightly faltering voice unclearly. "I'm sorry if it seems to you that—"

"Do you or do you not teach subversion?"

The reply was clearer. "Not by my definition of the term, although I have heard usages that—"

"Are you or are you not a seditioner?"

"You would have to define—"

A thick-armed young man standing by was given a nod by one of the judges and stepped forward and knocked the prisoner down. He started clumsily struggling to get to his feet again, hampered by his tied hands.

"Just like a seditioner, trying to hide behind words," said someone behind Bruce in the crowd. Bruce nodded.

Seditioners must all be skilled with words as their weapon, for, though it had been forty years since any hostile foreign power existed to assist and encourage treachery, there seemed to be more and more seditioners. It was impossible to open a paper without reading an item of their being tarred and feathered, beaten up or fired, of newer and stricter uniformity oaths with stricter penalties of jailing and fines for those who were found later expressing opinions different from those beliefs they had sworn to. Yet in spite of this the number of seditioners increased. Their creed must be terrifyingly seductive and persuasive.

And Johnny had been exposed to those words! The shy tall teacher who was supposed to be "so good with children," whom he and Pam had hospitably invited to dinner several times had repaid their hospitality with treachery.

Bruce felt the anger rising in him, and the fear. It must never happen again!

"We've got to find every crawling seditioner in Fairfield right now, and get rid of them! We've got to get the names of the others from this sneak!"

"Take it easy," said the man on his left, whose name he remembered vaguely as Gifford. "We're getting to that now." The teacher had regained his feet and stood up to face the judges.

The questioning began again.

Off to one side a man had climbed to the rail and was tossing the knotted end of a rope towards a liigh thick branch of the oak above.

"William Dunner, were you, or were you not, directed to teach subversion and disloyalty to our children?"

"I was not."

"Are you associated with other seditioners in any way?"

"I know other people of my own opinion. I wouldn't call them seditioners though."

"Are you directed by any subversive or disloyal organization?"

"I hold a great deal of love and loyalty for the people of the United States," he answered steadily. "But right now I think you people here are being extremely childish. You—" He was struck across the mouth.

"Answer the question!"

"I am a member of no subversive or disloyal organization."

"Will you give the names of those associated with you in subversion?"

The end of the rope was slung again, and passed over the limb this time, coming suddenly writhing down to be captured dexterously by the man holding the other end. He did not seem to be listening to the questions, or care what the answers would be.

"I will not. I'm sorry but it's impossible."

Gifford nudged Bruce. "He's sorry! He doesn't know how sorry he can get. He'll change his mind in a hurry."

Up on the platform the judges conferred ceremonially and Dunner waited, standing abnormally still. The finished noose was released, and swung down and past his face in a slow arc. In the crowd the man with the corkscrew waved it again, grinning. There was laughter.

The teacher's face was suddenly shiny with sweat.

The men who were the judges turned from their conferring.

"Our finding is treason; however, confess, throw yourself on the mercy of the court, give the names of your fellow traitors and we will extend clemency."

The disheveled tall man looked from one face to another for a time of silence. "Do you have to go through with this?" The voice barely reached the crowd. The judges said nothing. His eyes searched their faces.

"I have committed no crimes. I refuse to tell any names." His voice was clear and carrying, a teacher's voice, but he was terrified, they could see.

"The prisoner is remanded for questioning."

One of the judges made an imperious gesture and the teacher was seized roughly on either side by two guards, and his jacket and shirt stripped off roughly and cut free from the bound arms. As the slashed clothing was tossed to one side, the crowd chuckled at the effective brutality of the gesture, and at the reaction of the teacher.

"A good vicious touch," Bruce grinned. "He's impressed."

"Scared," Gifford laughed. "We'll have him talking like a dictaphone. Watch what's next."

Something small was handed up onto the platform. Walt Wilson, who had volunteered for the questioning, held it up for all to see. It was a card of thumbtacks.

The teacher was shoved against the trunk of the oak and secured to it rapidly. The rope was looped around his elbows, and his ankles fastened together with another loop. He faced the crowd upright, helpless and unable to struggle, with the harsh bright light of the lantern shining in his face and the noose dangling where he could see it.

"Scared green," commented somebody near Bruce. "He'll tell us."

Walt Wilson stood waiting to one side until all was quiet, then he extracted a tack and leaned forward with it pointed at the bare, bony chest.

"What are the names of the seditioners in Fairfield?"

The teacher closed his eyes and leaned back against the tree. The crowd waited, their breaths suspended unconsciously, waiting for the whimpers and apologies and confession, ready to laugh. The teacher was already afraid. Tacks are small things, but they hurt, and they held an aura of ruthlessness that spoke of tortures to come that would frighten him more. There was no sound from him yet, as Walt reached for another tack, but he jerked when it touched him. They laughed and waited, and waited with increasing impatience.

Walt's smile was fading. People in the crowd called encouragement. "Go on Walt, more." Walt put in more. He ran out of tacks and was handed another card of them.

"He's being a martyr," Bruce said, considering the shiny pale face and closed eyes with irritation. "A martyr with tacks. Trying to hold out long enough to seem noble."

"Go on, Walt!"

"He jumped that time," said someone behind Bruce. "He'll run out of nobility before we run out of tacks." They laughed.

Walt retired to a corner and the young guard took his place.

"Are you, or are you not, a seditioner?"

It went on.

The harsh bright light of the lantern beat on the figures on the platform: the cluster of people at the sides where it curved around the tree; in the middle, leaning back against the trunk, the bony ungainly figure of the teacher, dressed only in shoes and green slacks. The light caught a decorative glitter of metal from Dunner's chest.

"The names, Mr. Dunner, the names!"

One time he answered. "Nonsense," he said in his clear teacher's voice without opening his eyes.

There was no yielding in that answer, only an infuriating self-righteousness. They continued. The tacks were used up.

"Confess." Already he had wasted half an hour of their time.

He opened his eyes. "I have committed no crimes."

An angry sibilance of indrawn breath ran over the crowd. The questioner slapped his thick hand against the glittering chest, and Dunner's arms jerked, and he leaned his head back against the tree trunk watching them with an air of suffering and patience.

The hypocrisy was intolerable.

"Noble. He's being noble," Gifford growled. "Give him something to be noble about, why don't they?"

Someone handed up the corkscrew they had used to frighten the teacher with.

"Now we'll see," said someone on Bruce's left.

The tall bony teacher stood upright, looking with quick jerks of his head from the faces of the crowd to the man approaching with the thing in his hand. Without any pause or relenting the glittering small kitchen object was brought nearer to him. Suddenly he spoke, looking over their heads.

"If you will examine the term 'seditioner' semantically, you will discover that it has lost its original meaning and become a negatively charged label for the term referent 'innova—' "

A sudden blow stopped him.

"The names please, Mr. Dunner."

"The names, please."

"Mr. Dunner! Who are the seditioners?"

"There are a number of them." He had answered! A sudden hush fell.

He spoke again. *"They are here."*

The questioner asked, "Which ones?" People in the crowd stirred uneasily, not speaking. The names coming would be a shock. Bruce glanced around uneasily. Which ones?

The teacher raised his head sickly and looked at them, turning his face slowly to look across the crowd, with a wild smile touching his lips. They couldn't tell whose face his eyes touched— He spoke softly in that clear, carrying teacher's voice.

"Oh, I know you," he said. "I've talked to you and I know your minds, and how you've grown past the narrow boundaries of what was considered enlightened opinion and the right ways—forty years ago. I know how you hate against the unchanging limits, and fight yourselves to pretend to think like the contented ones around you, chaining and smothering half your mind, so that the stump will fit. And I know the flashes of insane rage that come to you from nowhere when you are talking and living like the others live; rage against the world that smothers you; rage against the United States; rage against all crowds; rage against whoever you are with—even if it is your own family; rage like being possessed!" Bruce suddenly felt that he couldn't breathe. *And it seemed to him that William Dunner was looking at him, at Bruce Wilson.* The gentle, inhumanly clear voice flowed on mercilessly.

"And how terror comes that the hatred will show, that the rage will escape into words and betray you. You force the rage down with the frenzy of terror and hide your thoughts from yourself, as a murderer conceals his reddened hands. You are comforted and reassured, moving with a crowd, pretending that you are one of them, as contented and foolish as they." He nodded slightly, smiling.

But Bruce felt as if the eyes were burning into his own, plunging deep with a torturing dagger of cold clear vision. He stood paralyzed, as if there were a needle in his brain—feeling it twist and go deeper with the words.

The man leaning against the tree nodded to himself, smiling. "I've had dinner with all of them one time or another. And I know you, oh hidden seditioners, and the fear of being known that drives you to act your savagery and hatred against those of us who become known." He smiled vaguely, leaning his head back against the tree, his voice lower. "I know you—"

The husky questioner jogged him, asking harshly—

"Who are they?"

Bruce Wilson waited for the names, and incredibly, impossibly, *the* name. It would come. He stood unmoving as if he were a long way away from himself, his eyes and ears dimmed by the cold weight of his knowledge. He waited. There was no use moving. There was no place to go. From all the multitude of the people of Fairfield there came no sound.

The teacher raised his head again and looked at them. He chuckled almost inaudibly in a teasing gentle chuckle that seemed to fill the world.

"All of you."

Bruce grasped at the words and found that they were nonsense, meaningless— Swaying slightly he let out a tiny hysterical chuckle.

Like a meaningless thing he saw the questioner swing an instantaneous blow that rammed the teacher's head against the tree and sent him toppling slowly forward to dangle from the ropes at his elbows.

Around him were strange noises. Gifford was clapping him on the back, shouting in his ear. "Isn't that funny! Ha ha! Isn't that crazy! The guy's insane!" Gifford's eyes stared out of a white face. He shouted and laughed.

"Crazy!" shouted Bruce back, and laughed loudly and shouted, "that crazy nonsense! We'll get the truth out of him yet." It had all been a dream, a lie. He could not remember why he was shaking. He had nothing to fear, he was one of the vigilantes, laughing with them, shouting against the teacher, hating him—

They revived William Dunner and he leaned back against the tree with his eyes closed, not speaking or answering, his body glittering with tacks. He must have been in pain. The crowd voices lashed at those on the platform. "Make him answer!" "Do something!" Bruce took out his pocket lighter and handed it up.

They took the pocket lighter.

The teacher leaned against the tree he was tied to, eyes closed with that infuriating attitude of unresentful patience, not seeing what was coming, probably very smug inside, laughing at how he had tricked them all, probably thinking—

Thinking—

Behind the closed eyes, vertigo, spinning fragments of the world. NAMES, MR. DUNNER. NAMES, MR. DUNNER. The yammering of insane voices shouting fear and hate and defensive rationalization. The faces which had been friendly, their mouths stretched open, shouting, their heavy fists coming— Impressions of changes of expression and mood passing over a crowded sea of upturned faces, marionettes being pulled by the nerve strings of one imbecile mind. Whirling and confusion—pain.

Somewhere far down in the whirlpool lay the quiet cool voice that would bring help.

He went down to it.

He was young, listening to the cool slow voice. The instructor standing before the class saying quietly: "It is easy. Your adult bodies have already learned subtle and precise associations of the cause and effect chains of sensations from within the body. The trick of making any activity voluntary is to bring one link of the chain to consciousness. We bring up the end link, by duplicating its sensations."

And a little later the instructor sitting on the edge of his cot with a tray of hypos, picking one up, saying softly, "This one is for you, Bill, because you're such a stubborn fool. We call it suspenser." The prick of the needle in his arm. The voice continuing. "One of your steroids. It can produce coma with no breathing or noticeable pulse. Remember the taste that will come on your tongue. Remember the taste. Remember the sensations. You can do this again." The voice was hypnotic. "If you ever need to escape, if you ever need to play possum to escape, you will remember."

The needle was withdrawn. After a time the voice of the instructor was at the next cot, speaking quietly while the blackness came closing in, his heart beat dimming, dwindling, the strange familiar taste—

Somewhere out of time came pain, searing and incredible.

Ignore it . . . ignore it— Concentrate on the taste. The taste— The heart beat dwindling— out of the dreaming distance a face swam close, twisted by some odd mixture of emotions.

"Confess. Get it over with."

Heart beat dwindling—

He managed a whisper: "Hello, Bruce." A ghost of laughter touched lightly. "I know . . . you—" A small boy taunt, mocking and then sad. The face jerked itself away and then pain came again, but it was infinitely distant now, and he was floating slowly farther and farther away down a long tunnel—

Night wind stirred across the empty picnic ground. It had been deserted a long time—the light and sound and trampling footsteps gone away, leaving a little whimper of wind. Stars glittered down coldly.

Up on the platform something moved.

When Dr. Bayard Rawling, general practitioner and police coroner, came home at five a.m., he saw the humped form of a man sitting on his doorstep in the dark. He approached and bent forward to see who it was.

"Hello, Bill."

Dunner stirred suddenly as if he had been over the edge of sleep. "Hello, Doc."

Rawling was a stoutish kindly man. He sat down beside Dunner and picked up his wrist between sensitive fingertips. He spoke quietly. "It happened tonight, eh?"

"Yes, tonight."

"How was it?" The doctor's voice roughened slightly.

"Pretty bad."

"I'm sorry. I would have been there if I could." In his bag he carried a small supply of cortocanan-oxidase, the life suspender, "death," and a small jet hypo, a flesh-colored rubber ball with a hollow needle which could be clenched in a fist with the needle between the fingers and injected with the appearance of a blow. Perhaps many doctors had carried such a thing as a matter of mercy since the hangings and burnings had begun.

"I know," Dunner smiled faintly in the dark.

"I was working on a hard delivery. No one told me about the trial."

" 'Sall right—I managed a trance. Took me a while though— Not very good at these things. Couldn't die fast enough." He whispered a chuckle. "Thought they'd kill me before I could die."

The doctor's fingertips listened to the thin steady pulse. "You're all right."

Dunner made an effort to get up. "Let's get back to the picnic grounds and tie me up to be dead." He mumbled apologetically. "Something wrong with my arms. Strained hanging from those ropes I guess. Took a while to get untied."

The doctor rose and gave him a hand up. "Make it to the 'copter?"

"Well enough." He made an obvious effort and the doctor helped him. Once in, the doctor started the blades with a quick jerky motion.

"You aren't in fit shape to be dead and have a lot of boobs pawing you over and taking your fingerprints for six hours," he said irritably. "We'll chance substituting another corpse and dub it up to look like you. I knew you'd be in trouble. Cox at State University has had one your size and shape in a spare morgue drawer for four months now. He set it aside for me from dissection class." The ground dropped away. The doctor talked with spasmodic nervous cheerfulness. "Had any fillings lately?"

"No."

"I have your fingerprint caps. We'll duplicate the bruises and give it a face make-up, and they won't know the difference. There's not much time to get there and get it back before morning." He talked rapidly. "I'll have to photograph your damage. I'm going to drop you with Brown."

Working with nervous speed, he switched on the automatic controls and took out a camera from the glove compartment. "Let's see what they've done to you. Watch that altimeter. The robot's not working well."

The 'copter droned on through the sky and Dunner watched the dials while Dr. Rawling opened the slit jacket and shirt and slid them off.

He stopped short and did not move for a moment: "What's that, burns?"

"Yes."

The doctor did not speak again until he had finished snapping pictures, slipped the tattered clothing back over Dunner's shoulders, turned off the light and returned to the controls. "Dig around in my bag and find the morphia ampoules. Give yourself a shot."

"Thanks." A tiny automatic light went on in the bag as it was opened and illuminated the neat array of instruments and drugs.

The doctor's voice was angry. "You know I'd treat you, Bill, if I had time."

"Sure." The light went out as the bag was closed.

"I've got to get that corpse back to the picnic grounds." The doctor handled the controls roughly. "People stink! Why bother trying to tell them anything."

"It's not them."

"I know, it's the conformity circle! But it's their own, not yours. Let 'em stew in it." He pounded the wheel. "Forty years with the same lousy type model 'copter, the same kind of clothes, the same talk, people repeating each other like parrots! They can't keep living in their own hell forever. It's bound to crack. Why not just ride it out?" He was plaintively vehement.

"It will end when enough people stand up in the open and try to end it." Dunner smiled. They landed with a slight jolt that made him suck in his breath suddenly.

"Don't preach at me," the doctor snarled, helping him out with gentle hands. "I'm just saying quit it, Bill, quit it. Stifle their kid's minds if that's what they want." They were out on the soft grass under the stars. Through the beginning pleasant distortion of the morphine Dunner saw that the doctor was shouting and waving his arms. "If they want to go back to the middle ages, let 'em go! Let 'em go back to the amoeba, if that's what they want! We don't have to tell 'em anything!"

Dunner smiled.

"Go on, laugh!" the doctor muttered. He climbed back into the 'copter abruptly. "If anyone wants to contact me, my 'copter number is ML 5346. Can you make it to the house?"

"Sure." Dunner located the source of the doctor's upset. "You've been a great help, Doc. Nobody expects you to do more than you've done."

"Sure," the doctor snarled, slamming the 'copter into gear. "Everything's just fine. And we've made a lot of progress since Nathan Hale's time. Remember what *he* was complaining of!" He slammed the door, the 'copter taxied away a little distance, and then lifted into the sky with a heavy whispering rush of wind.

The teacher walked towards Brown's house. The stars swung in pleasant blurred loops, and the memory of angry frightened screaming faces and blows seemed very distant. He pushed the doorbell and heard it ring far away in the house, and then remembered suddenly what Nathan Hale had complained of and laughed weakly until the friendly door opened.

Bettyann

Kris Neville (1925-   )

KRIS *Neville is one of the great unsung talents in science fiction, one of those authors who can be described (but not categorized) as a "magazine writer" since his novels have made little impact on the critics and fans. He is the author of one of the best psychological short stories ever published, the magnificent "Ballenger's People" (1967). His carefully crafted stories appeared throughout the fifties, most notably "Underground Movement," "Franchise," and "Hold Back Tomorrow."*

"Bettyann" was part of related group stories (novelized in 1970) that appeared during the first half of the fifties.

From *New Tales of Space and Time*   1951

It began to spit snow, and the car skidded slightly on the wet pavement.

"Please drive a little slower," the woman said, and the baby began to fret.

The man glanced at the luminous watch dial. "We've got to hurry," he said.

"They'll wait," the woman said. "Hush," she said softly to the baby.

The man bent forward slightly, his eyes staring out into the darkness. Snow splattered against the windshield to be smeared away by the fast-ticking windshield wiper.

"They'll think something's happened to us, and they'll go on," he said.

"No, they won't," she said. She petted the baby.

The man slowed the car for an upward curve that bent around a dripping cliff.

"What does the mileage gauge say?" he asked.

"Ten thousand, one hundred and . . . nine," the woman said, reading slowly by the dim dashlight.

"In about ten miles, then, we better start looking for the cutoff."

"We've got nearly half an hour, so please slow down," she said.

Reluctantly he eased up the footfeed.

The baby cried restlessly.

"She's in the body nicely," the woman said. "She wears it better than we do."

"We'll have trouble getting her out," he said. "It's all she knows."

They were silent for a moment, and the tires sizzled. Then the woman said, "Did you enjoy it?"

"It was interesting. Very pretty little world. Absorbing greens, I should say."

"There was one nice sunset."

"The planet near Elsini is better for sunsets: remember the one in which the cloud formations . . . ?"

"*Please* drive slower, dear! It makes me nervous."

Annoyed, he looked again at his watch.

"We've got plenty of time," she said.

"It's quite a distance down the cutoff. It's nearly a mile, remember, to that awful-looking white house; and they're far enough beyond so the ship will be out of sight."

The woman fondled the baby. "It's a nice planet, in its way; not all hard, not all soft. . . . She's actually growing in this body, have you noticed? She's gained several pounds, I imagine. Just look how fat her arms are!"

"After all, it's the only one she knows."

"Dear! This car is awkward on a road like this. So . . ."

"We're almost to the cutoff."

"Look out! Look out!" she screamed in terror.

It was a truck. It was jackknifed across the pavement. The car rushed up the steep grade to meet it. And the headlights of the car patterned briefly the outline of the truck driver, lying on his back on the wet concrete, tinkering with one of the multiple-tired rear wheels.

The driver of the car slammed in the brake pedal. The woman gasped. And the car swayed sickeningly. It leaped to the shoulder of the road, flashed by the stalled truck, and continued up the grade. The man fought the steering wheel, struggling to wrench the car back onto the pavement. The front wheels locked in a rut. Grunting explosively, the man jerked the steering wheel savagely to the left; it slipped from his hands, and the still hurtling car was free. The car leaped and bounced and teetered for an infinite second and crashed down sideways. It turned over and over until it half bent around a thick cedar tree nearly twenty yards down the slope. It lay quiet with one of its front wheels spinning leisurely.

The man had fallen across the woman; neither body moved; and slowly, second by second, life bled away, and the two bodies crumbled inward and dissolved, and all that was left was fine grayish powder.

Up on the road, the truck driver, white-faced, waved his flashlight beam in the direction of the wreck. For a long moment he heard nothing but the monotonous drip of water from a tree across the road.

Then he heard, very distinctly, a baby crying.

For a long time after the accident, for an eternity after the accident, Bettyann (although that was not yet her name) knew a puzzling progression of hands and faces and lights and shadows. At first, and for half her life and more than half, there had been a great, unlocalized pain. She cried whenever a nurse brushed her upper left side, but she could not associate the terrifying pain with the nurse's act, or ever quite understand the fear that came with a certain footstep.

At first the hands that touched her seemed no nearer than the far and dimly seen walls. Things existed, but they had no relation to each other and none to her.

Objects first began to order themselves when she became aware that the addition of something to her lips produced the cessation of a sharp, painlike pang not at her lips. Later, she found that the wall of the crib arrested the motion of her fist. And after that, as knowledge of space, bit by bit, became a part of her, she was acutely aware of the increasing rhythm of light and darkness.

Later still, she was able to localize the great pain, but by then it was not nearly so severe. It was in the left side of her body and eventually in the region of her left shoulder. Involuntarily, muscles seemed to want to exercise a second arm there; but the arm did not respond; it lay inert. One day she realized that the fist of the arm was tightly clenched. She tried to flex the fingers, but they would not flex. She cried herself to sleep.

Time began to move faster after she was transferred from the hospital to the State Home for Orphan Children, but the months were still long, because each was still so large a part of her total existence. At length there came the day when her routine of feeding, exercise, and sleep was broken by strange perfume and by new, quiet voices in kind-toned gabble, and soft, gentle hands. The hands most of all were pleasant.

"Isn't she a darling little girl?" the woman said, and the man agreed, and the nurse said, "Her arm was injured in an accident. She'll never have the use of it." And the man and woman murmured sympathetically.

Later, although Bettyann could not know this, the man and woman spoke with the gray-haired lady superintendent; and after that, they went away to think over all the implications of adopting a child with only one good arm.

The car in which Bettyann had been found lay rusting in a scrap heap. The dust on the seat was gone as thoroughly as yesterday's sunlight. The investigation of the accident was closed. And stranger things had happened before and will happen again in the memory of man than a demolished car and a deserted baby.

The soft hands remained in Bettyann's memory, and, vaguely discontent, she wanted them to return.

When finally the hands did return (and Bettyann was now her name), she gurgled happily, and upon being lifted, she kicked her feet in excitement.

Solemnly, as though Bettyann could understand the words, the superintendent said, "This is your new mother, Bettyann. Momma Jane and Daddy Dave."

And because she was pleased, Bettyann told them what the nurse who fed her always said: "Da da."

The woman blinked her eyes, looking down at the infant, and said, "Would you like to go home with us, Bettyann?" And the man cleared his throat.

The superintendent's eyes sparkled, and she smiled almost enviously. "I'm sure she'll be the kind of a daughter you deserve, Mrs. Seldon."

"Of course she will!" Mr. Seldon said. "And smart! She just said da da, didn't she? She's as smart as a tree full of owls already."

His wife said, "At first we'd half planned on a child a little older. In fact, we weren't even sure we wanted a girl at all. Until we saw Bettyann."

After more words, equally unintelligible to her, Bettyann felt a blanket being wrapped tightly over her body, and after that she felt bright sunshine on her face and then a sickening forward movement and strange noises. Soon the movement became mixed completely with the sound and everything was a hurrying purr except for the bobbing green tassel from Mother Jane's bonnet and the drowsy murmur of Daddy Dave's voice.

Jane studied Bettyann's fist with minute attention, and Bettyann liked the feeling of the warm palm around her hand.

"They're awfully small, the fingers," Jane said.

"Let's see," he said, glancing over quickly. "Hummm. They are, at that. When we get home, you know, we'll have to get a birthday cake for her. I forgot it."

"Isn't she a little young for that?"

"I wouldn't say so, no. I'm sure I had one, my first birthday. I had a cake every birthday. When I went to college, my great-aunt, Amelia, sent me a cake my freshman year, as I remember, and she'd wrapped up nineteen little candles in waxed paper and laid them right on top. Of course she'll have to have a cake."

Watching Bettyann, Jane said, "I think I'd rather not know her real birthday."

"Eh? And why not?"

"To make it the day we take her home, that makes it seem as if she's just been drifting around somewhere, waiting for us to come along."

Dave muttered happily to himself.

After a moment, she said, "Dave, dear. You don't really suppose the parents *will* turn up?"

"Of course they won't turn up!" he snapped, suddenly almost angry. "What the devil should they turn up for? After running off and leaving her in the wreck like that!"

"That's what I think, too. But you're not worried?"

He puffed his cheeks. "Even if they did, how could they get her back? What difference would it make?"

Bettyann was five, and it was her last spring before school, and she sat at the window staring longingly into the forbidden yard. She and Jane had had a postbreakfast clash about the toy doll. ("Bettyann, you simply must *not* leave your toys scattered about where someone's liable to stumble over them.") It was at least the tenth offense in the last two months, and Jane, at last becoming angry, had punished her.

All morning she sat at the window pensive and sad, and lunch eaten, she resumed her post. Her patience was rewarded when finally, relenting, as Bettyann intended she should, the severity of the confinement, Jane said, her voice slightly amused, "Very well. You may go outside now."

Bettyann slipped from the chair, her lips tucked into determined resistance. She went to the door without a word, and through it, proudly, into the sunshine. She was stubbornly indignant, and her childish jaw was set with unshakable resolve. She went directly from the porch, through the small cherry orchard, to the wealth of hollyhocks along the alley fence. She found a bee upon the lip of one of the flowers, a stunted plant within her reach, and with scarcely an instant's hesitation, she scooped up the bee and imprisoned it in her good right hand. She knew that Momma Jane would feel very sorry when she got stung. Daddy Dave, were he home, would chuckle not unkindly at the sting and say, "It'll feel better when it quits hurting"—his favorite statement for greeting her, oh so important scratches and bruises, a statement which infuriated her only to make her laugh through angry tears. But Momma Jane, seeing the savage hurt, would run to her and say, "Now, dear," kissing it, "let Mother put something on the nasty old pain right away."

The bee, when it finally stung her, hurt much worse than she had imagined it would, and she slapped her hand desperately against her dress to rid herself of the uncooperative insect. Then she ran toward the house crying, "I got stung! I got stung by a bee!"

The kitchen window faced the alley fence, and Jane stood beside it, waiting for her. She had her hands firmly planted on her hips, and when Bettyann rushed into the kitchen, she said, calmly, "I saw you deliberately pick up that bee, dear."

Bettyann blinked her eyes in surprise. "You did?"

"I most certainly did."

When she came to realize that the expected sympathy would not be forthcoming, Bettyann said, "I wish I hadn't, now." She left the kitchen and went to her room, and after crying a bit in frustration, she saw the humor of the situation, and she laughed about it, and eventually the bee sting stopped hurting.

Once more during the final, preschool summer, she received a bee sting, quite accidentally, this time. It was promptly administered to. And aside from the bees, of course, the summer was a pleasant one, and when fall finally came, as, she felt, it well might not have, Bettyann knew a touch of genuine sadness. Her question of the previous winter returned to puzzle her: Why must everything die in wintertime when we need the live greenness most of all? But as summer continued to fade away with quiet inevitability, she began to look forward, half fearful, half excited, to the new mystery into which she was shortly to be initiated.

On the first day, Jane walked with her to a foreboding white rock building from which she remembered having heard pleasant laughter the previous spring, and there introduced her to a not at all terrifying person who was to be her teacher for a whole, long year. She felt momentary fear, after Jane had gone, at being in a strange room, surrounded by strange and possibly hostile faces. She felt, for the briefest moment, as if she had broken away entirely from the certain security of the familiar home; the flower bed, the garden, the weathered oak, all solid and real, now seemed in memory, substanceless. She wanted desperately to rush after Momma Jane and run with her down the tree-lined walk, hurrying as fast as her feet would go, because the flower bed, the garden, and the weathered oak might not be there if she waited one endless hour. (Aunt Bessie had said to Momma Jane, "That's when you first begin to lose them. They're never quite the same after that. The teachers manage to take them away from you." To which Daddy Dave had said, "Nonsense, Bessie. She is, after all, only five." "But then, I suppose," Aunt Bessie had said, "it won't seem quite so bad for *you*, Jane, dear, as it would for—for, well you know . . ." At which Momma Jane's face had turned very red. And Bettyann had wanted to ask why that should be.)

After the initial shock of adjustment, Bettyann found the strange faces around her to be friendly. The first, bashful smiles of acquaintance came to be smiles of pleased recognition. Days began to hurry toward Christmas. And then, all at once, the holidays had come and gone, and bright, washed faces told with excited tongues of wonderful gifts from Santa Claus. And because there were so many new things to be done, it seemed that in no time at all sweet, lazy spring was back.

Just three weeks before school was dismissed, Miss Collier, the teacher, distributed finger-painting sets. "You'll get to play with sets like these all next year," she explained. And within fifteen minutes, she was standing over Bettyann's desk. Bettyann was working excitedly with brilliant colors on large, heavy paper. "What do you think your picture looks like, Bettyann? Is it supposed to be a big, brown cow or what?" Still working, Bettyann said, "It's a man in a tree." "Oh?" "Yes," Bettyann said, wrinkling her forehead, "the tree bark's all crum'led up, and the man's face is all crum'led up—right in the bark." "How very odd," Miss Collier said. "It looks as if you really painted it in, once I look for it." "I did." "No, child: I meant on purpose." "It *was* on purpose," Bettyann insisted, and Miss Collier laughed, rumpling her hair. "You should be a painter, then." After Miss Collier had gone, Bettyann, disappointed at being misunderstood, drew her fingers through the man in the tree and began to fashion the figure of a little girl. She tried to make the little girl's face seem as though you were looking at it from two directions at once.

During the final week of the school year, Miss Collier gave the children a series of simple aptitude tests. (Miss Collier was a recent college graduate.) Bettyann understood that the results would be very important throughout all the eight grades, so she tried as hard as she could. Later, when the principal was congratulating Miss Collier on her efficiency, while wondering what, exactly, should be done with the results of it, Miss Collier said, "This one, here, on Bettyann Seldon. She's certainly very intelligent, but I couldn't help feeling that the tests weren't getting at her real abilities; she seemed only half tested. I made a note about it on her form." "Oh, yes, I see," said the principal. "Of course," Miss Collier said, "I only had three units of elementary testing." And the principal, who had had none, remarked, uncomfortably, that he was sure it would be all very helpful and that he couldn't expect, after all, his teachers to know everything.

Bettyann was in the second grade for less than a month when one of her crayon pictures ("Almost good enough to be the work of an eighth grader") was posted on the big bulletin board in the main hall. Of another of her drawings, however, a semi-exploded view of a house with displaced hedge and chimney and furniture floating around the walls, her teacher said, "A little too unreal." And Bettyann resolved to be more careful in the future, for she did not want to be misunderstood.

She found the very elementary reading baffling until, midway through the year, she quit trying to associate the words with the pictures in the reader and began associating them with speech: and after that, reading was easy. She found in the group games and for ball passing in particular, that, with increasing familiarity, the shriveled arm presented scarcely any handicap.

But during the last part of that year and all of the next, her third, she came more and more to feel estranged from her classmates, and to a lesser degree, from her teachers, and even, but to a lesser degree still, from her parents. In class she came to fear that at any moment an unfortunate remark would elicit spasms of laughter; and at home she felt that there were things neither Jane nor Dave could understand, not in the way she understood, no matter how they might try, and failing to understand would, if she spoke of them, misunderstand not the thing itself but her for speaking. She withdrew inch by inch and became silent when others laughed and hesitant when others spoke boldly. ("She's a shy and sensitive child.")

Beginning her fourth year of school, no more than a week after the first session, one late autumn afternoon it was, when for the first parent-teachers' meeting, class was dismissed early and still unreacquainted children lingered in the schoolyard, Bettyann saw one of the older girls, a seventh or eighth grader, run from the empty teeters, kicking up white sand with flying tennis shoes, toward a vacant classroom, and she cried silently as she ran. Bettyann could see no reason for her action: the girl had been some distance from the nearest child. In that moment, Bettyann learned, and it was feeling more than thought, a second of certain insight, that each person was unique unto himself, and the memory of the tearful face told her that each, to his own degree, is misunderstood; and she, perhaps no more alone than the older girl, no more misunderstood than all the rest.

She was to have the same lesson repeated once more before she became a fifth grader. The second incident occurred not at school but while the class, under the supervision of Mrs. Fox, the eighth-grade teacher, who, Bettyann knew, went off by herself for a few minutes upon arrival to smoke a forbidden cigarette, was on a tour of the zoo some eighteen miles away in Joplin. The class went from Mark Twain School in a chartered bus, each child but Elmer carrying lunch in a brown paper bag. (Elmer carried a grown-up lunch box.) Within the park, for it was called a park rather than a zoo, there were many strange and wonderful and exciting animals. And when the eager class stopped beside the kangaroo, Willie, one of the smaller, less well-dressed boys, said, "Look! Bettyann's got a *kangaroo's* arm!" Bettyann, puzzled, looked at the kangaroo, frowned momentarily, and answered, "No, the kangaroo's arms are both all right; there's nothing wrong with either of them." Then she realized that the comparison was not based upon physical similarity. There had been resentment in Willie's voice, and viciousness, too. She knew of no offense that she had given him. She could not remember even speaking to him more than once or twice for he sat across the room from her and usually played by himself during recess. There was certainly no one-to-one cause-and-effect relationship. And, in thinking the incident over later, she wondered how it might be generalized in a picture of human relations: a group of people, perhaps, in pairs, each member of the pair chained to all the rest, with everyone pulling against the chains in an attempt to get closer to his partner.

She was supposed to skip the fifth grade; Dave, however, would not permit it. "She started school early as it is." And Jane agreed after the first excitement of her pride passed: "It wouldn't be fair for her to be almost two years younger than the others when she gets to high school." "And college," Dave added proudly. The parents nodded, and Dave held Bettyann on his lap and said, "She's as smart as a tree full of owls," and Jane said, "Be careful, Dave, or she'll grow too big for her britches." Dave said, "Nonsense. It gives her self-confidence."

All during her fifth year in school Bettyann made a special effort to accept the occasional strangeness of her playmates, to understand, as nearly as she could, their attitudes, and to adopt those attitudes for her own. At first it required conscious effort; later, it became automatic; and, as the school year drew to an end, she thought much as her playmates thought.

Spring came and then summer. And alone, one hot afternoon, she went to the flock of English sparrows on the lawn before the house and picked one up, gently, in her hand and

held it to her face and cheeped to it. Dave came out, letting
the screen door slam, and the birds flew in terror, and Dave
said, "How the devil did you manage to slip up that close to
them, Bettyann?" Laughing, she answered, "I just did." It occurred to her, then, to ask the question of herself; but there
was no answer other than the one she had given. "I must have
just been thinking right," she amplified, and Dave snorted,
"Damned sparrows'll have the whole country some day." She
turned to watch the sparrows fly from their tree limbs to settle
a safe distance away in the dust of the driveway. And watching them fly, it seemed that she could, if she only knew how,
join them and be as free to sail the skies as they. For an instant
she knew great longing, longing to be released from the narrow, confining space of her world; to float, as the song said,
where the south winds rise; to be, as the birds. . . . And the
feeling passed: she was content. Here, around her, the quiet,
sleepy afternoon. . . . She smiled, thinking of the light restric-
tions on her life: dishes to do, for which, of course, she was
paid; "helping around the house," Dave's inclusive phrase that
meant very little; attending the long, sleepy Sunday school,
which Jane said, "won't do any harm. . . ." No, here in the hot
afternoon she was free; and here, with the beat of town life
around her, exciting, she was happy, and she was at a loss to
understand the vast longing of a moment before.

The summer was unusually dry and she played outside a
great deal, went to one wiener roast, attended a blanket party
at Doris Heisten's house seven miles out in the country, and
spent one week with Aunt Bessie at Lakeside. When the rains
finally came they came in torrents that made the yard a welter
of mud and the outside an extremely unattractive place: the
rains flattened the dying hollyhocks, and later the first day,
savage hail sheared leaves and twigs from the cherry trees and
broke the glass front out of Al's Grocery across the street. She
located *David Copperfield* in Dave's haphazard collection of
books. There were perhaps twenty volumes in all, some left

over from college, some purchased during a half year of enlightenment when he was a member of The Book-of-the-Month Club. She was attracted by the name, a copperfield, in her imagination, being an endless stretch of copper stalks glistening in the sunlight, row on row, like tall corn. It took her several days of conscientious reading to finish the book, and all the while, for sleepy background, the rain drummed deliciously on the roof and dripped from the eaves and moved upon the windowpanes. She did not understand all of it, but she laughed with Mr. Micawber and cried when Dora died. And when the book was done, she felt glad and proud, although she could not understand why she should. It was a strange book, and unreal. But unreal in a different way than *Alice in Wonderland*, which she had read twice, each time feeling that she was missing something of the utmost importance.

Time hung poised with the rain, but finally sunny skies came and school and winter and then always-exciting spring again. But this spring, before her eighth year of school, was not the same as the ones that had gone before. The adults were quiet and waiting; and they seemed about to bubble over with some unexpected excitement. In early May the excitement broke, and the war in Europe was over. Everyone cheered and cried and was happy. But beneath that, Bettyann felt, sad and still, a little guilty perhaps because the war had eaten deep into men's hearts and burned there like a horrible conscience. Just before school began again, the other war, too, ended, and the people were deeply frightened at the way it had happened. But peace was a vast relief, and without fully knowing of war, Bettyann cried when she heard the news.

Bettyann's grade school teachers all agreed that she was not quite like the rest of the children. ("All *I* know," Mrs. Fox said, "is that she had an absolutely phenomenal grasp of historical time.") And her difference, whatever it was, was not altogether reflected in her superior grades. It was deeper than that, deeper, even, than her conduct: for she played as the others played, recited much as they recited but with occasional flashes of adult perspective, teased other girls about boy friends but was never teased in return, passed notes surreptitiously in class, and blushed whenever she was caught chewing gum. The deep difference, in the final analysis, it must have seemed to the teachers, was that she should be quiet and pensive and reserved, and that she completely refused to be.

As everyone expected, she graduated from the eighth grade at the top of her class. And then, during the pre-high school vacation, the frightening biological change came, and she became hurt and puzzled, and for the second time she withdrew into herself. (It was that summer that Jane and Dave told her of the adoption: and they attributed her new reserve as much to that as to anything else.)

The sense of having been unfairly imprisoned by nature, of having been tied in some vague way against her will to a new and not altogether likable body, persisted into her freshman year. There were flashes of acute embarrassment, not for any act, but, in surprising moments, perhaps while reciting at her desk, for existence itself. And always it seemed that just beneath the borderline of consciousness there lay a way for her to escape from everything that oppressed her.

Her art, so hopefully displayed and marveled at in grade school, no longer interested her; ambition lay dormant. Waiting, she instinctively realized, to be released by more knowledge and to be given direction by increased insight; and some day, in full maturation, many things would be possible for her; but not now. She was listless at her books; school bored her. She half wanted, more in daydream fantasy than anything else, to become a . . . an airplane pilot—or explorer—or gambler—or race car driver—or something else in revolt against this weak, feminine body. (Dave jokingly said, "A girl ought to know what she wants to be by the time she's in high school," and she answered, genuinely concerned, "I wish I did; I wish I did.")

The year wore on exasperatingly. Until, one day in late November (but almost a month beforehand!), the boy who sat across from her in general science class, Bill Northway, asked her to the holiday freshman prom, and she came home enthusiastic to announce: "I've got to learn to dance!"

Dave received the news with the false surprise of elevated eyebrows, and for a moment she was afraid he would refuse her request. But he nodded his head and said gravely, too gravely, "We'll have to see about it," which, she knew, meant, "Yes." The next Sunday afternoon, with a three o'clock appointment, she went to Zobel's Studio For The Dance. The studio was no more than one room above a bar, just off the Square, and the music was from a portable phonograph and scratchy fox trot records. Often the fox trots were only dimly heard above the stentorian bellow of the jukebox below. Mr. Zobel, a slender, effeminate man, had one assistant, a willowy blonde, Mrs. Hawkins, who danced with the older boys, those who objected to dancing with Mr. Zobel. It was the only studio in town, and Mr. Zobel taught tap and ballet as well as ballroom, and rumor said that he once danced in night clubs in the West and had a movie contract until something happened that led immediately to his return to his parents' home and the subsequent establishment of the studio. Bettyann had pliant movements, and she molded easily to Mr. Zobel's discreet lead, and after two private lessons, dancing, with an uncanny ability to anticipate his steps, became as natural for her as walking. And after the holiday prom, she was happy again, and reconciled to the no longer quite so new body.

Social science, as the elementary course in government was called, was first to prick her awakening interest, early in the second semester, and she began to read, avidly, the front page of the newspaper and ask puzzled questions, all of which, to the best of his ability, Dave tried to answer, and, when she appeared unduly depressed at some of the information, he quieted her with, "After all, honey, we don't live in the best of all possible worlds; it's just the best we have."

She checked out the two books on government from the school library, and, in further search in the public library, came across, quite accidentally, while browsing through the three hundreds (the assistant librarian had forgotten it was not to be filed in the stacks open to the public), *Das Kapital.* Miss Stemy, the librarian, said when Bettyann brought the book to the desk, "Aren't you a little young for such heavy reading, Bettyann? Wouldn't you like better an adventure novel or something like that?" But Bettyann said, "I'd like this, Miss Stemy, if you don't mind," and Miss Stemy, who was an old friend of the family and very fond of Bettyann, said, "Of course, my dear, if you wish it." And later she phoned Dave to say, "I thought you might like to know your daughter is taking up *Das Kapital.*" "She is, is she? She's a curious little devil, all right," Dave said. "Then you don't mind my letting her have it?" "Oh, I don't think it'll completely corrupt her mind," Dave said, "but please, Lee, if she comes in after Krafft-Ebing, don't let her have that. Not until her next birthday, at any rate."

Bettyann understood very little of *Das Kapital*; but the *Communist Manifesto* at the end of the book made her blood sing with enthusiasm. She felt she could do something for the workers immediately, and she went to Dave, who, after listening tolerantly to her excited speech, agreed that a sense of indignation at social injustice is invaluable, but, unfortunately, due to the absence of a revolutionary movement at the moment which had the people's welfare at heart, he was afraid there was very little one small girl could do; and that she'd have to content herself with such unexciting but necessary jobs as helping with the next Red Cross and Community Chest campaigns.

During the summer her enthusiasm for social science waned. By the beginning of the second year, she had taken up with almost crusading zeal the pursuit of a new occupation.

She was determined to become a doctor, or failing that, a nurse. She talked it over with Dave. Dave agreed that it was a worthwhile career and that it had many rewards. "But you've got lots of time to decide," he said, reversing, it seemed to Bettyann, his previous stand. And Jane, seeing her idealism, encouraged it soberly, but with equal restraint. Neither of them wanted to see the idealism expand unnaturally to the point where the world would crush it, and, disillusioned by asking too much, make Bettyann cynical and hard in automatic response.

"There's so much to do!" Bettyann cried. "So much that *needs* being done!" Dave said, "But it takes a long time and a hot oven even to hatch an ostrich egg." And Bettyann laughed, wanting to say, Of course, I know that. Dave said, "Society, I'm afraid, is pretty complex. Things that look simple frequently aren't." "Being a doctor's simple," Bettyann said. And Jane said, "It all depends on the kind of person you are."

She began to draw again, mostly pen-and-ink sketches, carefully, painstakingly wrought, but this time the drawings were abstract and personal, devoid of meaning for any save herself, and she burned them after they were completed. She could feel the growth of power, the technical mastery of line and perspective, a growth that would some day, when she was ready, permit her to do pictures that would say something to others as well, and something important, too, which, as yet, she had only the merest inkling of. She made the beginning tries at reading poetry (she liked best Emily Dickinson), and she discovered the adult short story in the O. Henry award volumes. She located them neatly arranged in dusty rows by the south window of the public library. The stories seemed to say a great deal about life, but it did not seem possible to put what was said in words other than the authors'. And society, she began to realize, *was* complex, and again she was lost and uncertain.

"Silly, romantic little fool!" she told herself, when she let her emotions be caught up and involved in something beyond her immediate life. She saw a picture of the Great Pyramid, and she was overcome by the grandeur of human effort and the sad, defiant presumption of a forgotten man, and she wanted to write poetry about the great ebb and swell of human life, something like Sandburg's *The People, Yes*. (She had read an excerpt from it, and the title haunted her, and later, when she learned that Hamilton called the people "the beast" she could not help thinking, Yes, but the people, yes!)

Toward spring of her second year, at the fourth all-school assembly in the auditorium after the holidays, the principal announced, to her complete surprise (she had been carrying on a whispered conversation with Bill Northway seated beside her), that she had been selected by the faculty as the Outstanding Sophomore and would be sent, all expenses paid, by the Federated Women's Clubs on a one-day trip to Jefferson City, the state capital, next Friday.

Friday came quickly. And she found herself in Jefferson City admiring Thomas Hart Benton's murals and Carthage Marble. She had tea in the Governor's Mansion and actually talked for a few moments, alone, with the governor's wife, an embarrassed sparrow of a woman who seemed flattered that Bettyann should notice her to say: "It must be tiresome to have so many strangers in your house like this," to which the governor's wife replied with an almost defeated sigh, "It is, sometimes, my dear," and then brightly, as if it were amusing and yet important, "Did you know the high school groups are the worst about the silverware? We lose thirty or forty spoons every time." Bettyann laughed and said, "I must take a spoon, then, mustn't I, to avoid being different?" So, conspiratorially, the governor's wife went to the table where the lemon ice was being served and took a silver spoon, wrapped it in a paper napkin, and carried it back to Bettyann. "Don't let them see you," she whispered. "Of course they wouldn't *say* anything. Votes, you know. But it's always best not to let them see you."

After that, the school year closed explosively, and Bettyann, over Jane's halfhearted opposition, got a job in Scot's

Five & Ten, where, for nearly three months, she waited on and came to know the townspeople. And as she came to know them, all of them, the petty and haggling, the self-consciously magnanimous over a dropped penny, the aggressive, the shy, the bold, the frightened, she knew that there was an infinite variety, and that very little was constant except, perhaps, the expression deep in their eyes, and nothing was certain but the multiplicity of ambitions, hopes, fears, desires.

There was much not to be forgotten: "Whistling" Red, a wizened man (a retired farmer, an ex-bootlegger, a renegade Catholic priest: there were many stories about his unknown past occupation) who whistled tunelessly to himself wherever he went and who attended every funeral and always cried into a big linen handkerchief. "I go for the music," he confided to Bettyann. And Ed Barnett, who fell four stories from the Drake Hotel to the sidewalk and walked away without even a bruise. And William Seiner, who shaved his head every Monday because he was afraid of dandruff. And Miss Leonard, who, it was said, got mad when her sister married, and stayed in bed for twenty years out of pique. She was a prim old maid with bright brown eyes, and she chuckled when she told Bettyann, "Get a man, child," winking, "get a *man*."

There were these, "Whistling" Red, Ed Barnett, William Seiner, and Miss Leonard, and a hundred more besides; and the days were warm and happy. Bill took her several times to the movies and once skating and twice swimming. And there were dates with other boys, and one of them, one evening, quoted a great deal of poetry of a man named Swinburne: the boy looked very soulful when he quoted it, and she wanted to laugh, but she was too polite.

In her junior year she had to write fiction for the English class. In her first composition, she used what she thought to be a new style for description. But as the teacher pointed out, in such passages as "Creeping moonlight genuflected at gaslight shadows, writhing," the style rather got in the way of the thought, making the whole more meaningless than necessary; and she agreed. (Always, at every turn, in painting, with prose, in conversation, there was the difficulty communicating.)

"Look at the yard," she said to Bill, while the two of them sat on her quiet front-porch swing, "and tell me what you see."

"Well, let's see," he said, pretending seriousness, as he frequently did, without, she knew, ever taking her seriously. "There's the grass. Yes, that. And there's the moonlight, of course. And the shadows from the old oak tree, and then there's the sidewalk with cracks in it, and the hedge. . . ."

Bettyann wanted to explain that one might, in addition to seeing the physical details, see also the relation between them, or one of the many relations between them, that caused everything to be ordered into a pattern. "There's first of all aliveness and deadness," she said. "Look how they're balanced against each other. See how soft the aliveness is and how hard the deadness is. Look at the aliveness of the grass and the oak; and the deadness of the sidewalk and the shadows. See how the leaves seem to suck at the moonlight and how the tree bark lies inert before it."

"Hummm," Bill said, only half serious, now, and then, no longer pretending, turned to her with catching laughter to say, "You've got a pretty head full of stars."

She knew that he did not understand. Or, more accurately, perhaps, he heard the words, understood the meaning, but did not feel as she felt the essential rightness and truth of them. But he did sympathize with her; he did not laugh coldly, but in friendship, and that made everything quite all right.

During the summer before her senior year, Bill went east to see his mother, who was divorced and lived in New York City, and, when Bettyann saw him again in early autumn, he was old and wise with travel, and deliciously she knew that she had been waiting for him.

The final year of high school opened, and together she and

Bill went to the movies and walked the quiet streets and drank Cokes in Gray-Reynold's Drugstore and laughed between classes. And his lean face was handsome.

But that he was soon to be drafted cast a net of dizzying uncertainty around their every handclasp and knit them together even as it promised to shear them apart. She wished desperately that this fact of divorcement might suddenly vanish. She wished—what nonsense she knew, even in the dream of it—that she might some way serve in his stead; or that a quick illness would come and pass and leave him with her to nurse back to health. Her other daydreams were quiet and contented and vaguely maternal; and surely, she thought, in close living, day to day, he will come to understand me as I must be understood.

Then, as spring came again and his draft date drew nearer, their lives became more desperate and frantic until, one evening, she knew with sudden insight that her dream was splintering. Her eyes were distant and angry and she was hurt and she reached out desperately after him, making, in memory, a perfect little idiot of herself and pushing him even further from her. Finally, to her shame, she cried bitterly and unfairly, "You've got to have a woman with *two* arms, haven't you?" and the dream lay at her feet, ruined forever, and even in the instant, the hot instant of the words, she knew that, for the first time, she had used her handicap to try to win advantage and that she could never again make that same mistake. And after he had gone, she remained weeping on the porch swing in hurt repentance, and mortification.

Sadness came in; she could never be happy again; resigned, never happy. As she sat in the darkness, staring out at the stars, she felt wave after wave of longing.

The world around her, silent, was quietly sad, and the air was quietly sad, and the leaves dripped quiet sadness; and life, too, was sad.

The first week afterward was endless: in her mind, a sad,

blue tune, low, minor, coloring her movements and humming behind her ordinary conversations.

Two weeks later still, three weeks to the day since Bill had left, left although daily she saw his faraway face in school, Dave called her into the living room and said without preamble: "How would you like to go to Smith next year?" She was stunned for a moment, and Dave explained that Lee Stemy, an alumna of Smith, herself, had been looking forward for the last several years to getting her a scholarship; and in view of her remarkable high school record and Miss Stemy's influence the scholarship was practically assured.

Bettyann's first thought was for Dave and Jane, and she tried stumblingly to argue that it would be unfair, after doing so much for her already, for them to give her the money for a school in the East; but Dave insisted quietly that she should go, and eventually when Jane said, "We've saved a little here and there for you to go to college on," she agreed, conditional upon the scholarship, and she felt proud and excited and happy, and it was fully fifteen minutes before she remembered that the world was a sad place.

Riding down on the train from Kansas City (she had flown there from Boston), a slow milk train that seemed to stop at every farm, Bettyann tried without success to sleep; and staring out the window, finally resigned to wakefulness, she slowly became aware of the extent to which less than one semester at Smith had changed the familiar countryside for her. When the train shrieked into a tiny depot, she could not help but notice the sense of isolation, the deadness, and the insularity of the station house and the somnolent main street.

Behind her in the East lay a different world. It was too new yet to be understood; but it was rich with promise like the sunrise. She caught glimpses of far horizons. New ideas from all directions, upon all subjects, were like keys unlocking doors to unexplored but exciting rooms, leaving her small and frustrated.

Her deeply hidden, latent talents were stirring under the impact. The promise of maturity was within her. Excitement trembled at her: at her fingertips lay an answer, and she could almost, but not quite, trace its outlines.

What am I to do with, how am I to fit into, this sad-funny world? What must I understand in order to be understood: and beyond that, in understanding, what then must I do? I wish I knew; I wish I knew.

And it was almost there on her mind's edge, almost, the answer. For one moment of utter loneliness (beyond the creeping train lay even, snow-splotched fields) she wanted most of all—as if that *were* the answer—to be completely understood. But that, she thought, would require complete identity; no, it is not that; the only one who can ever understand me completely is myself.

How can I fit into this sad-funny life: what is my role: what best can I do? The answer would be complex, as many-sided as life seemed, itself, to be, without easy definition. But this she knew, that she would be required to give unto them, the people, yes, of which she was a part and not a part, of her best talent so that, in return, they would give unto her that which she most needed. What did they want from her; what did she want from them? (I wish I knew; I wish I knew.)

And role, even that, was not enough. Beyond there was something more; perhaps some obscure branch of philosophy that she had never heard of dealt with that. Unless it was all on a purely local level, and need, where life and death seem senseless but through compulsive repetition gain meaning, need was the whole foundation: from complexity, vitality; from vitality, complex need: when the need dies, so, too, life: sleep, quiet, boredom, death. Role might be all. Could it be, she wondered, that beyond the role, I am always to seek because I have to, never to find because I cannot?

The answer, the lesser answer, trembled on her mind's edge, how can I fit into this sad-funny world? Not yet.

Someday, someday, someday, clicked the wheels.

And soon, sounded the whistle, soon.

Dave met her at the station, helped her from the coach, took her single bag. The air was crisp and wintry as they walked across the gravel, upon which snow had perished, to the waiting car.

Dave was silent after the greetings, and in sudden terror, feeling the strangeness between them, Bettyann cried, "There's something wrong!"

Helping her into the car, Dave said, "What makes you say that?"

"You're so . . ." She paused, seeking a word that expressed her conviction; seeking to name, for herself as well as for him, the quality from which the conviction sprang. A twitch of his mouth; the inflection of his greeting; the reservation she thought she saw behind his eyes? Not these; not entirely. It was as if she had heard, at the first moment, his secret thought, and now she could not remember it. In sudden panic she said, "Is Mom all right? Has something happened to her?"

Dave said, "Of course she's all right." He closed her door and came around the front of the car to the driver's side, and, getting in, said, "They've been giving you enough to eat? You certainly look healthy, but, I mean, you're getting *enough?*"

She laughed. "All I want."

"I went to the State University, you know. I was afraid in a private school maybe you wouldn't get enough. But it's good to see you. You look all right. . . . It's nice having you back."

"I was a little homesick," Bettyann admitted.

"How long do you have?" He set the cold motor snarling.

"Ten days."

"That doesn't seem very long. But you really like school? And what's it like to go to a big Eastern college? How are the other girls; do you have any trouble getting along with them? And . . ."

"Goodness! Not so fast! I've got ten days, Dad. If I tell you about everything now, I won't have anything to talk about tomorrow. Tomorrow I'll just have to be like some stick-in-the-mud of a farmer: 'Well, mighty cold today; looks like more snow; guess maybe the cold snap'll be pretty hard on the winter wheat.' "

The car made a U-turn away from the station.

She snuggled into the seat. "It's very exciting," she said. "It's different, too, than I imagined it." She paused to get her general impressions of Smith into words, and the silence, almost immediately, was uncomfortable. Puzzled by the feeling, she glanced out the window and said, "The courthouse looks cleaner."

"Didn't Jane write about that? They sand-blasted it last September. Just after you left."

"No. . . . She must have forgotten. . . . And what happened to Starke's Hardware Store? Isn't that a new front?"

"He sold the store. . . . They had a fire in the South End of town last month. It burned down the Castle Place."

"Mom wrote about the fire."

Dave turned right on Fifth toward Garrison.

She looked at him again. She tried to determine how to break through the hidden barrier newly between them. To forestall silence, she said, "It seems smaller. The town. More compressed . . . The houses aren't like New England houses. New England houses are all so old. They've been lived in so long that some of the aliveness has worn off on them. Our houses aren't like that."

Then to avoid giving the impression that because of three months in the East she was beginning to feel superior to the town, she said quickly, "But I guess, if you go out West, they're different out there, too. From pictures I've seen, you get an impression of isolated hostility. . . ." She bit her lip in annoyance, for the words seemed to increase rather than reduce the impression she had sought to dispel. She fell silent.

He drove to Maple; there he turned left.

The sense that something was wrong made Bettyann feel unsure of herself. She was half afraid to speak again for fear that the words would worsen the unknown difficulty.

"Is it something I've done or haven't done?" she said.

"What, honey? Haven't done what?"

"I *know* something's bothering you. I can feel it. Is it something I've done? Is it costing you too much money to keep me in school? If it's that . . ."

"It's nothing. It's . . ." Dave puffed his cheeks, a sign, Bettyann knew, that he was angry with himself. "All right," he said lamely. "Ever since you were so high you could see right through me, I guess . . . I promised Jane I wouldn't tell you."

"Oh, Lord!" she said. "I'm sure it's nothing so very solemn. I can't imagine anything that has to be kept a deep dark secret."

He seemed more relaxed now that the barrier was down. "It's probably not solemn at all. Jane just didn't want to tell you until you were ready to go back. . . . There was a man here to see you. He was from Boston or some place back East. Jane was afraid he might spoil your Christmas; and she's looked forward to it so much. So she asked him if he'd mind waiting until you went back to Smith and see you there . . ." Dave had bounced the car up the driveway into the front yard. He cut the motor.

Bettyann was puzzled and excited too. She could not quite understand the excitement. "What did he want?" she asked, and her voice surprisingly was tense.

"I'll get your bag," Dave said. "Don't mention what I told you. I'd better tell Jane first. He wanted to tell you—he had some information about—it was something about your . . . real parents. He didn't tell us very much."

Bettyann's heart was pounding.

"Don't say anything about it to Jane until I talk to her," Dave said.

And then Bettyann was running toward the porch where

Jane was waiting. Jane caught her, laughing, and she cried, "It's wonderful to be home, Mom!"

He came two days after she returned to Smith. She had been waiting with mounting suspense, and, when the house mother knocked on the door to say, "Bettyann? There's a young gentleman downstairs to see you. His name is Don Talley," she felt her heart jump violently.

"Don . . . Talley," she said slowly, letting the strange name melt into her mind. She did not like the name exactly. It was not the sort of name she had expected, and she wondered what face would go with it. "All right, Mrs. Reeves. Tell him I'll be right down."

As the house mother's footsteps sounded on the stairs, her roommate said, "Amherst?"

Bettyann shook her head uncertainly.

"Aggies? Williams?"

"I . . . don't think so."

"Well," the roommate said, disappointment in her voice. "Is he at least handsome?"

"I'm sure I don't know."

The roommate drew in her chin with amazement. "My God, you can't even tell whether he's *cute* or not?"

". . . I've never seen him before."

"And he's never seen you?" The roommate considered Bettyann's headshake. She blinked her eyes. "Now that I call real sex appeal: You've *got* it."

Bettyann smiled thinly.

"Gee, I wish. . . . Well, don't stand there. Go on down. Don't keep him waiting. Don't give the others a chance at him."

"I'm . . . going," Bettyann said.

"And you might ask him if he's got a friend who goes to Amherst or . . . Why, you're *white!* What's wrong? Are you scared?"

"No . . . Well, maybe I am, too, in a way."

"Are you in some kind of trouble? Can I help, Bettyann? Is there anything I can do?"

"I'm not in trouble . . . I guess I better go on down."

She left the room, and the door closed softly behind her. She walked down the wide stairs.

The crystal chandelier was tinkling musically. It had been moved by the wind when the huge, white door to the porch was last opened.

Bettyann stopped at the bottom of the stairs.

"He's the young gentleman talking to Mildred," Mrs. Reeves said when she saw Bettyann staring around the room. "He looks like a very nice young man."

"Yes," Bettyann said. "Thank you."

Bettyann crossed the room to where he was seated before the fireplace. Across the table from him, the brown-eyed Mildred was smiling with studied interest. Her hands lay quietly submissive in her lap; her lips were half parted.

When Bettyann reached his side he stood up and she felt a wave of uncanny recognition cross her mind. It seemed to come from outside herself.

"I'm Bettyann, Mr. Talley," she said.

"Bettyann . . . ah . . . Seldon?"

". . . Yes . . ."

Mildred leaned forward, her eyes aggressive. "Won't you join us? Don was just telling me he's from out West."

The fire threw a ruddy glare over his face. The face was still sharp from the cold outside; it was classically handsome, self-reliant, calm. Snowflakes glistened on his overcoat.

"Oh, Don, Don," Mildred said, standing and coming to his elbow. "Here," she said possessively, "let me take your over-coat, Don."

"No . . . Please . . . Don't bother . . ."

"I don't want you to think our house isn't hospitable. Let

me help you off with it." She fluttered at his collar. "I want you to feel perfectly at home here."

"Really, thank you, no," he said with a trace of annoyance in his voice.

"But . . ."

"I prefer to leave it on."

Bettyann looked at Mildred's suddenly lax face; childhood, sad childhood, perhaps, gleamed through on it for an instant, and then Mildred recovered her brittle defense and trying to keep injury from her voice, she said flippantly, "I—oh— Oh, well. I can see you two want to talk."

"If you don't mind," Don said.

"Not at all," Mildred said pleasantly and distantly. After a moment she said, "I have a damned test in Lit tomorrow and I have to be studying in a minute anyway."

When she was gone Don said, "She came over and sat down in front of me and started to play solitaire on this table. When I didn't say anything she looked up and said, 'I major in sociology.' When I didn't say anything, she said, 'When I graduate I'm going down to New York and hang out a red light and do firsthand research. Where do you come from?' So I told her I come from the West. She got my name from that woman over there, I think."

Bettyann said gravely, and her eyes were puzzled, "I thought you told my parents you came from somewhere around here."

He nodded at the fire. "It was convenient to say that." He turned to her. "Can you leave this building now?"

"I—I could, I guess, if I wanted to." For the first time she noticed that he had an accent; it was not heavy, scarcely noticeable, and she could not remember having ever heard one quite like it before.

"I want you to get your coat. I want you to come with me."

The curtness of the statements made her want to answer an

abrupt "No." But she held the refusal for there was something in his face—some indefinable tension—some almost sadness: some quality that drew her sympathy and excused his rudeness.

"Look at me," he said. "I have some things I must tell you about yourself. Look at me. Will you come?"

She looked into his eyes. She felt her heart flutter at the expression there. "I'll come." She reached out and touched his hand. "About my parents?"

"And about other things. Bettyann, I have a great deal to tell you."

"I'll get my coat."

"Please do."

He was waiting at the door when she came back downstairs. Mrs. Reeves nodded to her and said maternally, "Don't forget, dear. Eleven o'clock."

Wordlessly, Don opened the door, and the two of them stepped out from the bright warmth into the dark cold.

"Where are we going?"

"To the Draper."

Her feelings toward him were confused. She did not altogether like him; she felt that she should not trust him as fully as she seemed inclined to. And yet, beyond that, she felt a kinship with him that she could not define. ". . . they won't let me go up to any of the rooms," she said.

"Walk by the desk naturally. It will be all right."

She thrust her face into the snow. She should, perhaps, be afraid, but she was not. Or perhaps she was afraid—not of him but that he might tell her things she did not want to know about herself. They walked past the chapel. (Snow creaked under their feet.) They left the white campus. They turned onto the main street, and downtown Northampton lay before them.

Her teeth chattered, and she held on to his arm.

Neon lights made the drifting snow soft orange, and their

breath was frosty, and they heard laughter from a bar. They walked on. The town was readying for sleep.

At the Draper they stamped their feet free of clinging snow.

"Come. They won't notice you."

They walked up the outer steps, past the desk, and the drowsy clerk stared through her without interest, as if she were not there at all, and she looked at Don, whose face was relaxed.

Group voices, singing, drifted up from the Pilgrim's Room below. A girl laughed.

They walked up the worn carpet of the stairs leading from the lobby to the second floor. Don led the way to the room. He tapped lightly on the door. "Don," he said.

"Come in."

He opened the door and let Bettyann enter before him. He closed the door.

"Sit down, Bettyann," said the man on the bed. His face was old and lined and his eyes were deep set and his lips were thin and his hair was white.

She studied his face. "Why—why," she said in wonder. "*You're* not old!"

The man on the bed nodded.

"She's one of us," he said.

"You may call me Robin," the man on the bed said. "I'm going to tell you some very strange things, Bettyann."

Bettyann's eyes were wide.

"Don't be afraid."

Although her heart was beating wildly she said, "I'm not . . . afraid." And she wondered if that was strictly true.

Robin said, "Will you close your eyes, my dear?"

And his voice, like Don's, was a foreign voice; and beyond that, more than his voice was foreign. His face, everything about him, unreal. She could not pinpoint the unreality any more than she could explain how she knew that he was not old, any more than she could explain the feeling of kinship with him. She closed her eyes. Her lips moved silently. She stood upon the brink of something completely beyond all her experience. She waited.

"Listen carefully," Robin said. "Do you hear my thoughts?"

After a moment she breathed a tired sigh. "Yes." Inside her mind, not a part of it—terrifyingly, an intrusion upon it—she could feel words form and dissolve. They were indistinct and scattered, and beyond them there was an awareness of his presence. She felt revulsion, and she tried to fight against the words, but they continued, and then, after a moment, the revulsion passed.

"It is difficult to project this language. The symbols are too . . . heavy; not heavy, but . . . There's no word for it, here; *oxu*, in Fbun. You will see. You will learn many languages. Relax, my dear. I want to show you something more. Are you relaxed?"

"Yes," she said, but her body was tense.

"Try to follow this if you can. It may be difficult at first, so you must help me."

It was not words inside her mind, now, although she was aware of his presence. He was trying to guide her own thoughts. She put her hand to her forehead. He was making her . . . Her thoughts were . . . tugging . . . at a closed compartment, a new part of her mind, so strange a part that she tried to draw away from it, but he insisted . . .

"You must help," he said.

She moaned, finally, when she felt a sensation that was entirely different from any she had felt before: something like an electric shock, something like a fresh breeze, something like remembering pain.

"It's . . . it's . . . growing! I can feel it growing!" she cried.

She opened her eyes and looked at her left arm. She turned the hand over and over, holding it before her face. She felt of it uncertainly. "It's new," she said. "My arm is new." She turned her eyes, pleading, toward Robin. She wanted to cry; she felt tears well toward her eyes, and, with effort she blinked them back. Her skin prickled. *"Who are you?"*

Some part of her mind insisted, querulously, that this could not be happening. (Most real of all were the walls of the room: splotched wallpaper was so very stolid and prosaic that it shrieked refutation, but its presence insisted reality.) And the fingers of her new left hand, slim, delicate fingers, flexed in impossible freedom.

Robin stood and walked to the window. "You'll have to learn," he said. "Show her, Don."

Again she looked at Don. Instantly she felt her vague dislike dissolve into awe. She wanted to look away, to tremble, to, to . . . but she stood mute before him, unbelieving, over-powered, and her feelings, her thoughts, her whole body, were suspended in dull wonder. Slowly, before her eyes, he shimmered and changed. And after a moment he was not human.

"Oh!" she said, and her voice was weak and small.

"That's what we're like," Robin said. "That's what you're like, Bettyann."

"I'm like that?" she said. Don—what had been Don—was strange, compelling, not beautiful, but attractive in strangeness. She shuddered, scarcely able to think; to imagine that she, too, was like that was not to be believed, not in the moment, and belief and disbelief did not exist: merely wonder, mute.

"You'll get used to it," Robin said. "You will learn to take many shapes, to be, if you wish, something else: a bird, perhaps, an animal, or things with which you are not yet familiar. Once you learn you may take many forms."

She looked down at the new arm. Almost afraid to try to think, she let her mind explore the new compartment of its own accord. What happened seemed automatic reflex. Slowly the arm shrank to its original, withered shape. "Like that?" she said dully. "Like that?"

"You'll learn, Bettyann," Robin said.

Her heart seemed ready to burst. The very real—the oh, so real—walls of the room blurred, and the pattern of the wallpaper ran together, making her head ache with dry excitement. She expected them to crumble and dissolve, the walls, into flowing, rippling lines that would merge away in all directions leaving her alone on a little island of solid carpet surrounded by moving silence. "Where are you from?"

"The stars."

". . . the . . . stars . . ." she said. Odd words. She had seen stars at night. They were very far away (but sometimes they seemed farther away than at other times). Tensions were building up inside of her body. The stars. It would be very difficult to control the tensions, and she was going to be whipped back and forth in her mind, thoughts pulling this way and then that, for some time. (Eventually, her mind would quiet: she could sense that, but it was meaningless for now there was no quiet.) It would take time. For the stars were very far away.

"We are not from this planet. Surely, you, yourself, Bettyann, must have felt that you did not . . . entirely belong to this planet. Surely you must have seen that you were different from the rest."

She shook her head, feeling the curls move, and one dropped over her forehead, and she brushed it away. Different? Different? "Tell . . . tell me about it," she said. Tell me very slowly, she wanted to say, a little bit at a time, for I do not fully believe you, yet, and I would not like to hear more that I cannot believe, except slowly, so I can fit in pieces (like in a jigsaw puzzle). I remember a jigsaw Jane and I worked: it was a picture of two dogs, bird dogs, and we had lost the box top, and it was a very long time before we could imagine what the picture was about. (Jane at first thought it was a behemoth, and I thought it was a grizzly bear.)

"There's a great deal to tell," Robin said.

Bettyann thought of the bird dogs, and when Dave came home, he laughed and said, "Sure. It was on the box top." (And then she and Jane remembered, of course, and they said they'd really known it all along, now that he reminded them.) It seemed, suddenly, as if she had known forever: that here, finally, here were her people, people who could understand her as no one else had ever understood her, and she wanted to cry out with happiness, and then, not with happiness, but just surprise.

"We travel," Robin said. ". . . originally we came from a world that I suppose may have been much like this one. Our records show it was called Amio. We were already travelers when the race on this planet was still in its caves. It has been so long that our own planet is lost beyond the expanding horizon, perhaps twirls around a dead sun: I do not know. It has been very long. Our history . . . much of it . . . is forgotten. Who knows but perhaps all races pass through the same stages, and we may have been once like these new people among whom you have lived? But we travel now. We grew old . . . and wise on Amio, and after a long time, somehow, one of us discovered the *zeiui* effect, and we traveled far from Amio. And now we find a sunset here and the blue of waters a million-million miles away . . ."

As she listened the unshocked part of her mind realized that he was old, but not old in the sense she had used the word before, not as Earthmen are old; and it almost seemed as if his words were weary with age. The thought fluttered and died.

"When we came last to this planet," Robin said, "your parents were killed in an accident. I, myself, heard your father's thoughts just before he died, for I was waiting in a scout ship for him. I thought that you, too, were dead. . . . We returned a month ago. One of us thought he felt your presence on the planet. I was able to remember where the accident occurred; we computed the date from the Big Ship's log; we checked the files of a newspaper in the town nearest the accident. We found, indeed, that you had survived. From that, discreet inquiry led us to you."

"... go on ..."

"There are not many of us any more; not as many as we might prefer. It would be nice to have a new face again among us. There is ample room for you. And we have come for you, for you are one of us; we could not leave you here, lonely. We have come to ask you to come back to your own people, to travel with us. For you are one of us." He turned to stare out the window into the falling snow. "Many planets have more beautiful snow," he said.

"There are better snows on Lylo," Don said. "And better shadows, too. There are three moons there."

Bettyann knew they were giving her time to let the information settle into her mind. But it insisted on floating free, unmoored.

"This planet is famous for its greens," Robin said, more to himself than to Bettyann or Don. "There are some really startling greens in the tropical foliage, particularly Guam, for instance. But not here, not at this season, only this snow ..."

"These are not your people," Don said from the alien body.

Bettyann looked at him again. The form began already to lose some of its compelling strangeness. She was coming to accept it. And now familiarly her emotions went out to it, and she longed to assure herself of its reality and the reality of her own true body beneath the Earth flesh.

"Let me help you," Don said.

Trembling, Bettyann began to change. She reached back along unfamiliar paths toward the new compartment of her mind. Utter complexity there: a twisted skein of controls. Again unrealized patterns swirled her thoughts; and like birds southward in winter, the thoughts knew direction from instinct. It was slow and painful at first, and she bit her lip to keep from crying out. And then, as she felt her body move upon itself, she was stunned by the miracle, wonderful beyond belief, that vibrated on the edge of existence. Her thoughts were too overcome for understanding: there was only a sense of awe, of humbleness that here, within herself, she bore the great secret that could unlock the matter of her body and change it and release it and fashion it and mold it. She knew the new shape; she knew its lines; she knew its outward form: it was there in the compartment; and the compartment was not a second mind, not a greater mind at all, but something distinct from that, something apart from her personality, and wonderfully, wonderfully subservient to her thoughts. The transformation continued, with increasing speed, with increasing ease. And yet, she had never seen before; could hardly believe now, and they had shown her. It was too . . . alien.

It will take time, she thought, for the strangeness to leave. At first, so strange, and then, so new, and then (time is a wonderful thing) so natural after all. (And Dave had said, "If you walk over a path long enough, they'll pave it.")

"No," she said, her mind still quivering with the shock of the change and with the new (but not yet certain) freedom of her new form. "No," she said dully. There was the sense of belongingness: the absolute certainty of it, beyond everything, beyond feelings, thoughts: she belonged; it was right. "No," she said again. "They are not my people." She looked down to see how awkwardly her earth clothing draped on the alien body, and she tugged at the dress, and, for a moment, she felt sad and isolated.

"Then you will come with us?"

She started to say, "Yes. Yes, I will go. I must go, mustn't I? You are my people." But all the impressions, all the jumbled-together memories out of the past, rose within her, moaning. She tried to squeeze them away, tried to forget the now re-experienced excitement she had felt but two weeks ago at knowing she stood upon the brink of discovery (even now, still stood: still on the brink). My people are from the stars, she thought, unbelieving. And they go where they will, free and unbound. (And I told Doris I'd give her my history notes tomorrow, and I had an idea for an *Outlook* article.) She waited for her emotions to quiet.

"Give me a minute," she said. Emotions bubbled, frightfully out of control, and moved upward in her like furious hot water toward the top of a pan. (She stood feeling the strange body and watching Robin at the window staring into the snowfall.)

She had, once, a nightmare that her room was gone; above the stairs, at home, there was nothingness; and when she awakened, moonlight fell on the carpet, and there were Momma Jane's soft hands, hands that had been there, quieting, as long as she could remember and before she could remember. And downstairs there were lacy curtains and nine (she had counted them often) twelve-inch albums of music that Dave, sometimes, after supper, listened to, and some day she would put the music into a painting, along with how Dave felt and how she felt (and there was a new compartment in her mind that would help her mold paints to her will and show her many things to be done and to be shown). And there was once a family of mockingbirds nesting in the withered oak tree; in summer, they sang all night, and through the open windows she could listen until sleep came. She could taste the night summer air (with sweet hyacinth and mystic lily of the valley and polleny honeysuckle and spicy rose). And it was neither happy nor sad, the memory that came, wrapping up everything in a flash of the five senses colored by time, but strangely wonderful, and she remembered with quiet amazement until her blood tingled.

Don shuffled restlessly.

Watching the stars, ever so far away, sometimes before she entered school—very early, one of her first memories which merged into warm, assuring, nonmemories of the impalpable before. . . . They were hard and bright and intensely inviting, and she wanted to gather them like flowers. (Wasn't there a children's story about a little girl who wanted the moon, and one day she was gone, and her Daddy, pointing, said: "She's up there, she rowed away on a moonbeam," and the townspeople all shook their heads because it was sad?)

(Old man Starke was dying of cancer.)

But looking at Robin, old/young Robin, so very wise, she felt vast longing, longing more than earth longing, and the stars were spread out in a thousand excitements at her finger-tips, and the wonder of it, vast, eternally vast, overcame her. (A blazing sun to play with, and spin beyond, and a dead sun to make you ask never-to-be-answered questions; and a thousand planets, and blue water, and sound and movement, and love of space; and never understanding, until a comet comes from nowhere, and it makes you know, and know, forget, and try to remember again . . . later . . . in a quiet time.) She wanted to fall down on her knees before the thought and throw out her no longer arms in a gesture of gratitude for these, her people, and she wanted to cry: these are my people, and this strange body is my body, and these are the ones who will understand me because they are what I am. These are my people, and the sad-funny people and the world I have known, merely . . . human. . . . These, my people, and her blood raced with excitement, and she said, "Yes. Yes. I'll go. You are my people."

The words were said. And now she wanted to cry.

Robin was at her side. She looked up, and her heart raced with hope. "I've got to tell my parents good-bye first," she said. "I've got to tell them. I couldn't leave without telling them."

"I am sorry," Robin said after a moment. "I think I can imagine how you must feel. But that is impossible. To permit that would be to risk exposure. We ask only to be let alone; in return we let others alone. We waited for you here when your parents . . . seemed to want to question us. We did not want any trouble."

"But I just can't leave! I've got to see them again! I've got to tell them I'm going away!"

"The others will be waiting now," Don said. "We have de-layed departure for you. We cannot wait any longer."

"You must write your good-bye," Robin said.

"Please . . ." she said.

Robin shook his head. "It is the rule, Bettyann. It has al-ways been the rule. If this race were to discover our visits, if your parents found out. . . . No, the risk is too great. I cannot answer to the others. We ask only to be let alone; that is not too much to ask."

Slowly she changed back to the form of a college girl with a withered left arm, withered because it was more comfortable than the whole one which she would scarcely know how to use. (And she wondered idly with part of her mind, what would Bill say to see me with two arms, and where is Bill now—in the army somewhere—and does his handsome face, or the meaning of it, the memory of it, the . . . does it really matter what he would say or think? I could let the arm grow, a little at a time, a fraction of an inch a day, and get used to it, and tell everyone that some kind of exercise was making it grow again, and in a year when it was whole they would not think it strange, nor I. And I'm being a child to cry.)

"I'd . . . I'd like to be alone," she said. "I'll be all right after a bit. Please leave me alone for a few minutes."

"There is a pen and stationery on the desk," Don said.

When they came back, Robin said, "Do you feel better now?"

And she said, ". . . yes . . . I have written a letter to the college telling them that I have been called home by illness. They will not contact my parents and worry them about my absence." She looked at Don. "I wrote my parents a letter telling them I must go away." She looked at Robin, appealing for understanding. "It wasn't easy to write."

Robin said, "I am very sorry, believe me. But perhaps a letter will be best for you. I'll give them to the man at the desk downstairs."

Don said, "We'd better go."

"We have a car outside," Robin explained. "We have a scout ship several hours away."

They left the room, and, in the lobby, Robin roused the sleepy clerk and said, giving him the two letters and a bill, "Will you mail these first thing in the morning?"

(And Bettyann thought: It will take three days, maybe four days, for Jane to get it, and she will take it from the mailbox . . . and she will stand by the mailbox, perhaps open the letter before going back inside—if it isn't too cold on the porch that day. Open it by tearing neatly the right-hand edge, and shake out—or perhaps reach inside with thumb and forefinger after —the single page and the large-scrawled and few, pathetically few, words.)

They were in the car, and they drove through the cold night, and Bettyann trembled, sitting between Robin (driving) and Don, until finally noticing, Robin said, "Better turn on the heater, Don."

Robin drove slowly, and the night was long. Don dozed fitfully beside the window. At first Bettyann knew rising excitement that she could scarcely contain—not unmixed with sorrow but stronger. After a while she turned to Robin to ask him to hurry, and then, suddenly desperate, she wanted to talk to overcome the sickness of parting, but she could not find the words. Finally, her mind grew weary, and she wanted to sleep and forget (or perhaps dream a moment of flashing stars).

Night was endless. And then false dawn, gray and angry with snow clouds. And then the faint pink of real dawn, making her mouth feel dry and her head feel heavy.

Don roused, and after a while he consulted a map. "Turn right. The next road."

Slowly the world around them—flowing past them—awakened. They skirted a town.

". . . there's an odd red," Don said. "On that boy's cap, Robin."

Bettyann stared eagerly through the window. The boy,

pumping his bicycle, his breath steam, sailed a newspaper away in an arching curve to a porch, and Bettyann remembered how it was to hear the thump of a morning paper against the side of the house, when you were still half asleep, and it was winter outside.

Suddenly fully awake, Don said, "They don't see much, do they? Were you able to show them anything?"

". . . a little," Bettyann said.

"Their eyes are different from ours, I think. It must have been difficult," Don said.

Still looking out the window, she wanted to explain something of how she felt. "Old man Starke sold his hardware store and put all his affairs in order because the doctor told him he had cancer and was going to die before summer."

Don smiled, distantly. "You can tell us very much about the natives. Believe me, I'm sure we shall all enjoy listening to your experiences."

There was not indifference in his voice; indifference was too easy a word for it. It was as if he were agreeing politely to something he did not quite understand; or as if he thought a great fuss were being made over a trifle. But he did not know old man Starke, did not know that old man Starke kept candy suckers behind the counter to give to children when their parents made purchases. (To be sure, it was good business: but there was more than good business in his smile, and the candy was something more than good business, too: it was more complex than good business.) And she could remember the smile and the voice (where was the cancer? in the throat?) saying, "My, how she's grown, Mr. Seldon, and I think I have just the thing for her sweet tooth today." (Always as if this generosity were not his usual practice, but something highly special just for you.) And on that occasion, he waved the not-yet-wrapped paintbrush (Daddy Dave bought it to paint the sink drainboard with, and then reconsidering called in Mr. Olson to do the job instead), and the hardware store smell of oil and new iron, or how new iron *should* smell. But that was something Don could not know. And never having experienced, might not feel as she felt . . .

"Turn here," Don said. "We go straight ahead."

The houses began to fall away to be replaced by fields. The rocky ground seemed to protest cultivation. Everything was dead, and rich dirt showed through rifts in the snow. The air was crisp, and the sun was hard and bright.

The car purred on. A railway line circled in to parallel the road, and a train puffed at the grade. The train fell behind the car, and after a bit, Bettyann heard it whistle sadly for a crossing.

"Tell me about the planets," Bettyann said. "Tell me what I'm going to see."

"There's so much . . ."

"I'd like to paint. What can I paint?"

"Paint? Well, there's Oliki. It's a really beautiful blue lake."

"I'd like to paint something like that field there, I think," Bettyann said.

"But isn't it a bit colorless, don't you think?" Don said, and there was honest surprise in his voice, as if it had never occurred to him to paint a field.

"I guess you've seen so many things. . . . Yes, I guess it is. But don't you see how, in spite of all the rocks and the snow, how everything is all huddled up, waiting to come alive?"

Robin said helpfully, "Yes, that's a fact, all right."

And Don said, "Left, here."

They drove for several miles in silence. They came to a rambling, high-sided bridge over an icebound creek (the ice above the center current was no thicker than scum). The boards of the bridge rattled under the weight of the car. Once across it, Robin swung the car onto a fisherman's path. The path was closely pressed by dead tree branches which clawed at the metal roof with brittle fingers.

"We won't need the car any more," Don said. "We can leave it here."

Robin jolted the car to a halt, and the three of them got out, and Robin said, "You were right, Don. No one's come by. It was a safe place."

The ship rested thirty or forty yards into the forest. There was a dead, charred area around it.

"Well, can you change now, all right, Bettyann?" Robin said.

"I think I can," Bettyann said. She let her form waver and change, and now it was easier, and suddenly compelled to exact their approval, she felt of the power in the compartment and began to work with it.

"A little tree!" Don cried happily. "A little tree, Robin! Look how pretty the leaves are! She's a very good tree!"

(The air was chill. The sun, bright through hazy clouds.)

"She learns quickly," Robin said.

She changed again, this time not into anything that she knew, but as her feelings guided her.

Don stared deep into the grayness that had been, a moment before, a tiny tree in bright, full foliage, and then he turned away shuddering. "That isn't very pretty, whatever it is," he said.

She let her body relax into her real form, the form into which she belonged, and for a single instant, she seemed too tightly held and oddly uncomfortable, and earth words came difficultly from her new mouth, and she could not yet think to them, for she knew no language, and she realized that, on the long drive, they had been thinking in conversation beyond her. She said, "It was . . . sadness, I guess you'd say. How I feel about leaving."

"We'd better get in the ship now," Robin said.

And Don helped her up.

When they were in the air, looking down at the trees falling away and backward, Don said, "You must be very excited. You have a great deal to look forward to."

But her emotions, in the moment of severance, were too great to permit an answer. She stood quiet and the window fogged with low clouds. Already the forest was lost in swirling grayness. And the ship increased speed. She was caught and held by the cold metal walls, and she wanted to pound them futilely with her fists. Home was far away below, far away, and farther even as she thought, and farther still, and dwindling, dwindling, beyond her grasp.

"The Big Ship is not far off the coast of Mexico," Robin said. "We will be there soon."

Bettyann wanted to hold on to something, for she was sick with movement. It will pass, she told herself, it will pass. She thought of the stars, and of the body, her body, and the alien lips moved, and she thought: These are my people.

The ship rose. It turned slowly toward the west. And time passed, little or great, and the clouds lay behind them, the Great Lakes below, like fingers curled up from behind the horizon.

Then, after a while, new fields and new forests, new streams and wide plains (and a huge river gashing the red earth). And after that, shooting high, the young mountains with toothy sharp crags biting at storm clouds that were teasing their summits. And snow sparkled on the peaks.

The ship quivered with flight and sang good-bye to the land far below. (And now the West Coast below, which she saw for the first time, would never see again, and dawn was upon it.)

"Tell me about the planets," she pleaded. "Tell me quickly."

"You'll be able to see for yourself shortly," Don said.

"But tell me a little. Right now. Please."

"Well, there are the orange mountains of Kenu."

"What are they like?" she asked intently, trying to hold all of her attention together on his words.

"You'd just have to see them. We usually spend a whole day there."

"A . . . day?"

"That's not too long for the orange mountains," Don said.

"No," Bettyann said. "I meant how could you really see everything in a day?"

"I don't quite understand," Don said.

"I should like to *know* the orange mountains. Are there any streams there?"

". . . I can't say about that. Are there, Robin?"

Robin, at the controls, cleared his throat. "I can't say that I've ever noticed."

"But the colors, don't you see, Bettyann," Don said. "The texture of the colors."

"That's right," Robin said. "The colors. That's the important thing . . ."

Below lay the ocean, a tortured wash of deep green and gray: and white foam bounced like mad-dog slaver. The water changed to crystal sparkles and blue, deep blue, lighter blue, and then blue that was flat and waiting. A tiny steamer threw morning smoke. And night lay just ahead, for the ship outpaced the sun.

"There's always a great deal to see," Don said suddenly. "There are many sights," and Bettyann walked toward the rear of the ship.

Don thought to Robin, "She is a strange one."

Robin peered down, and moonlight was upon the water. "There's the Big Ship," he said. He dipped the scout toward it. Ocean roared up. He steadied the scout under his hands.

"The landing port's open, I see," Don remarked.

Bettyann looked down at the silver ship below. It lay upon the waves and rolled gently with them, and the landing port gaped like a hungry mouth, and the ship was a sleek, waiting prison.

If she were home now, she could tell Dave and Jane she had gotten sick at Smith and that she'd borrowed the money from June and hurried home because she was afraid to be sick among strangers. And then, after the letter came, after she had destroyed it, she could say she was well again and go back to Smith. She'd miss a week or so, but they'd let her back in after saying what a silly goose she'd been for not reporting to the dispensary instead of carrying a stomachache, that *might* have been appendicitis, halfway across the continent. It would be easy to pretend to be sick because she knew of her body now and she could counterfeit any symptom.

And then she realized the wonderful thing she bore within herself. So far, in the few hours of knowledge, she had only scratched the surface. What secrets were there? How much did she know that doctors never suspected? That artists never imagined? That . . . She thought of old man Starke, and what was the strange, rampant growth inside *his* body?

Did she know?

She became vastly excited at the thought of what it might mean to uncover the secret of herself. And now, for the first time, dimly but with overpowering certainty, she looked forward toward tomorrow knowing what her job would be and what her role was, and she was trembling.

But it was too late.

Below lay ocean in all directions, cutting her off from escape, and she looked at Don and Robin and felt a great sadness for them and for herself, and in all directions, bridgeless, the ocean rolled away to far horizons.

And Robin settled the scout inside the mother ship and berthed it.

Don walked back to her. "Do not cry," he said. "We are here." He smiled. "Let's get out. We're in the Big Ship. You're really home. Ready to travel at last."

"We are?" she said.

They climbed out into the huge hangar.

"I'll check the chart room before I close the port," Robin said. "There may be another scout out."

Don bent to inspect a pitted place in the hull of the scout.

After a moment, Robin came back. "No. They're all in. I'll close the port."

"I'll tell Bettyann. She'll want to watch the takeoff from the chart room."

Robin's feet pounded away. The port clanged shut. The feet came back. "What's wrong?"

"That's funny. She was here a moment ago. Bettyann! Oh, Bettyann! . . . I can't seem to find her . . . Bettyann!"

"I know she'll want to watch the takeoff," Robin said.

"Bettyann!" Don called, his voice echoing away unanswered.

Puzzled, they looked at each other and shook their heads.

"Bettyann!" Don called, and, "Where the devil is she?" Robin said.

And outside the mother ship the moon was low and the sea rolled lazily like an exhausted lover and the stars were far away in jet. Above the gentle sea, a lone, great bird flapped its powerful wings against the night.

Dark Interlude

Fredric Brown and Mack Reynolds
(1906–1972)   (1917–   )

THE *late Fredric Brown was a multi-talented man who was as at home with the detective story as he was in science fiction. He will always be remembered for the contributions he made to science fiction with his short-short stories, an extremely difficult literary form at which he excelled. He was also noted for bringing humor to science fiction, some of his best being collected in* Angels and Spaceships *(1954).*

Mack Reynolds has one of the most interesting personal backgrounds in the world of science fiction. The son of radical parents, he has worked as a lecturer for the Socialist Labor Party. His science fiction reflects his passion for and concern with political economy and his stories and novels are probably the mostly overtly political and social in the field. Reynolds has traveled widely and the locations of his fiction reflect his personal experience. For example, he is one of the few science-fiction writers to use the Third World as a setting for his work. Although he achieved his greatest fame during the sixties when he was voted the favorite science-fiction author of the readers of Galaxy, *he had been working in the genre much earlier, publishing his first story in 1950.*

In this collaboration, Brown and Reynolds addressed them-
selves to one of the oldest and most vicious problems in Ameri-
can and world history—racism. And in so doing, they pointed
out the fact that racism involves costs for the bigot as well as
for the victim of bigotry.

From *Galaxy Science Fiction*   1951

===

Sheriff Ben Rand's eyes were grave. He said, "Okay, boy.
You feel kind of jittery; that's natural. But if your story's
straight, don't worry. Don't worry about nothing. Everything'll
be all right, boy."

"It was three hours ago, Sheriff," Allenby said. "I'm sorry it
took me so long to get into town and that I had to wake you
up. But Sis was hysterical a while. I had to try and quiet her
down, and then I had trouble starting the jalopy."

"Don't worry about waking me up, boy. Being sheriff's a
full-time job. And it ain't late, anyway; I just happened to turn
in early tonight. Now let me get a few things straight. You say
your name's Lou Allenby. That's a good name in these parts,
Allenby. You kin of Rance Allenby, used to run the feed
business over in Cooperville? I went to school with Rance . . .
Now about the fella who said he come from the future . . ."

The Presidor of the Historical Research Department was
skeptical to the last. He argued, "I am still of the opinion that
the project is not feasible. There are paradoxes involved which
present insurmountable—"

Doctor Matthe, the noted physicist, interrupted politely,
"Undoubtedly, sir, you are familiar with the Dichotomy?"

The presidor wasn't, so he remained silent to indicate that
he wanted an explanation.

"Zeno propounded the Dichotomy. He was a Greek phi-
losopher of roughly five hundred years before the ancient
prophet whose birth was used by the primitives to mark the

beginning of their calendar. The Dichotomy states that it is impossible to cover any given distance. The argument: First, half the distance must be traversed, then half of the remaining distance, then again half of what remains, and so on. It follows that some portion of the distance to be covered always remains, and therefore motion is impossible."

"Not analogous," the presidor objected. "In the first place, your Greek assumed that any totality composed of an infinite number of parts must, itself, be infinite, whereas we know that an infinite number of elements make up a finite total. Besides—"

Matthe smiled gently and held up a hand. "Please, sir, don't misunderstand me. I do not deny that today we understand Zeno's paradox. But believe me, for long centuries the best minds the human race could produce could not explain it."

The presidor said tactfully, "I fail to see your point, Doctor Matthe. Please forgive my inadequacy. What possible connection has this Dichotomy of Zeno's with your projected expedition into the past?"

"I was merely drawing a parallel, sir. Zeno conceived the paradox proving that it was impossible to cover any distance, nor were the ancients able to explain it. But did that prevent them from covering distances? Obviously not. Today, my assistants and I have devised a method to send our young friend here, Jan Obreen, into the distant past. The paradox is immediately pointed out—suppose he should kill an ancestor or otherwise change history? I do not claim to be able to explain how this apparent paradox is overcome in time travel; all I know is that time travel *is* possible. Undoubtedly, better minds than mine will one day resolve the paradox, but until then we shall continue to utilize time travel, paradox or not."

Jan Obreen had been sitting, nervously quiet, listening to his distinguished superiors. Now he cleared his throat and said, "I believe the hour has arrived for the experiment."

The presidor shrugged his continued disapproval, but

dropped the conversation. He let his eyes scan doubtfully the equipment that stood in the corner of the laboratory.

Matthe shot a quick glance at the time piece, then hurried last minute instructions to his student.

"We've been all over this before, Jan, but to sum it up— You should appear approximately in the middle of the so-called Twentieth Century; exactly where, we don't know. The language will be Amer-English, which you have studied thoroughly; on that count you should have little difficulty. You will appear in the United States of North America, one of the ancient nations—as they were called—a political division of whose purpose we are not quite sure. One of the designs of your expedition will be to determine why the human race at that time split itself into scores of states, rather than having but one government.

"You will have to adapt yourself to the conditions you find, Jan. Our histories are so vague that we can help you but little in information on what to expect."

The presidor put in, "I am extremely pessimistic about this, Obreen, yet you have volunteered and I have no right to interfere. Your most important task is to leave a message that will come down to us; if you are successful, other attempts will be made to still other periods in history. If you fail—"

"He won't fail," Matthe said.

The presidor shook his head and grasped Obreen's hand in farewell.

Jan Obreen stepped to the equipment and mounted the small platform. He clutched the metal grips on the instrument panel somewhat desperately, hiding to the best of his ability the shrinking inside himself.

The sheriff said, "Well, this fella—you say he told you he came from the future?"

Lou Allenby nodded. "About four thousand years ahead. He said it was the year thirty-two hundred and something, but

*that it was about four thousand years from now; they'd
changed the numbering system meanwhile."*

"And you didn't figure it was hogwash, *boy? From the way
you talked, I got the idea that you kind of believed him."*

*The other wet his lips. "I kind of believed him," he said
doggedly. "There was something about him; he was different.
I don't mean physically, that he couldn't pass for being born
now, but there was . . . something different. Kind of, well, like
he was at peace with himself; gave the impression that where
he came from everybody was. And he was smart, smart as a
whip. And he wasn't crazy, either."*

*"And what was he doing back here, boy?" The sheriff's
voice was gently caustic.*

*"He was—some kind of student. Seems from what he said
that almost everybody in his time was a student. They'd solved
all the problems of production and distribution, nobody had to
worry about security; in fact, they didn't seem to worry about
any of the things we do now." There was a trace of wistfulness
in Lou Allenby's voice. He took a deep breath and went on.
"He'd come back to do research in our time. They didn't know
much about it, it seems. Something had happened in between
—there was a bad period of several hundred years—and most
books and records had been lost. They had a few, but not
many. So they didn't know much about us and they wanted to
fill in what they didn't know."*

"You believed all that, boy? Did he have any proof?"

It was the dangerous point; this was where the prime risk lay.
They had had, for all practical purposes, no knowledge of the
exact contours of the land, forty centuries back, nor knowledge of the presence of trees or buildings. If he appeared at
the wrong spot, it might well mean instant death.

Jan Obreen was fortunate; he didn't hit anything. It was, in
fact, the other way around. He came out ten feet in the air
over a plowed field. The fall was nasty enough, but the soft

earth protected him; one ankle seemed sprained, but not too badly. He came painfully to his feet and looked around.

The presence of the field alone was sufficient to tell him that the Matthe process was at least partially successful. He was far before his own age. Agriculture was still a necessary component of human economy, indicating a definitely earlier civilization than his own.

Approximately half a mile away was a densely wooded area; not a park, nor even a planned forest to house the controlled wild life of his time. A haphazardly growing wooded area—almost unbelievable. But, then, he must grow used to the unbelievable; of all the historic periods, this was the least known. Much would be strange.

To his right, a few hundred yards away, was a wooden building. It was, undoubtedly, a human dwelling despite its primitive appearance. There was no use putting it off; contact with his fellow man would have to be made. He limped awkwardly toward his meeting with the Twentieth Century.

The girl had evidently not observed his precipitate arrival, but by the time he arrived in the yard of the farm house, she had come to the door to greet him.

Her dress was of another age, for in his era the clothing of the feminine portion of the race was not designed to lure the male. Hers, however, was bright and tasteful with color, and it emphasized the youthful contours of her body. Nor was it her dress alone that startled him. There was a touch of color on her lips that he suddenly realized couldn't have been achieved by nature. He had read that primitive women used colors, paints and pigments of various sorts, upon their faces— somehow or other, now that he witnessed it, he was not repelled.

She smiled, the red of her mouth stressing the even whiteness of her teeth. She said, "It would've been easier to come down the road 'stead of across the field." Her eyes took him in, and, had he been more experienced, he could have read interested approval in them.

He said, studiedly, "I am afraid that I am not familiar with your agricultural methods. I trust I have not irrevocably damaged the products of your horticultural efforts."

Susan Allenby blinked at him. "My," she said softly, a distant hint of laughter in her voice, "somebody sounds like maybe they swallowed a dictionary." Her eyes widened suddenly, as she noticed him favoring his left foot. "Why, you've hurt yourself. Now you come right on into the house and let me see if I can't do something about that. Why—"

He followed her quietly, only half hearing her words. Something—something phenomenal—was growing within Jan Obreen, affecting oddly and yet pleasantly his metabolism.

He knew now what Matthe and the presidor meant by paradox.

The sheriff said, "Well, you were away when he got to your place—however he got there?"

Lou Allenby nodded. "Yes, that was ten days ago. I was in Miami taking a couple of weeks' vacation. Sis and I each get away for a week or two every year, but we go at different times, partly because we figure it's a good idea to get away from one another once in a while anyway."

"Sure, good idea, boy. But your Sis, she believed this story of where he came from?"

"Yes. And, Sheriff, she had proof. I wish I'd seen it too. The field he landed in was fresh plowed. After she'd fixed his ankle she was curious enough, after what he'd told her, to follow his footsteps through the dirt back to where they'd started. And they ended, or, rather, started, right smack in the middle of a field, with a deep mark like he'd fallen there."

"Maybe he came from an airplane, in a parachute, boy. Did you think of that?"

"I thought of that, and so did Sis. She says that if he did he must've swallowed the parachute. She could follow his steps every bit of the way—it was only a few hundred yards—and

there wasn't any place he could've hidden or buried a para-chute."

The sheriff said, "They got married right away, you say?"

"Two days later. I had the car with me, so Sis hitched the team and drove them into town—he didn't know how to drive horses—and they got married."

"See the license, boy? You sure they was really—"

Lou Allenby looked at him, his lips beginning to go white, and the sheriff said hastily, "All right, boy, I didn't mean it that way. Take it easy, boy."

Susan had sent her brother a telegram telling him all about it, but he'd changed hotels and somehow the telegram hadn't been forwarded. The first he knew of the marriage was when he drove up to the farm almost a week later.

He was surprised, naturally, but John O'Brien—Susan had altered the name somewhat—seemed likable enough. Handsome, too, if a bit strange, and he and Susan seemed head over heels in love.

Of course, he didn't have any money, they didn't use it in his day, he had told them, but he was a good worker, not at all soft. There was no reason to suppose that he wouldn't make out all right.

The three of them planned, tentatively, for Susan and John to stay at the farm until John had learned the ropes somewhat. Then he expected to be able to find some manner in which to make money—he was quite optimistic about his ability in that line—and spending his time traveling, taking Susan with him. Obviously, he'd be able to learn about the present that way.

The important thing, the all-embracing thing, was to plan some message to get to Doctor Matthe and the presidor. If this type of research was to continue, all depended upon him.

He explained to Susan and Lou that it was a one-way trip. That the equipment worked only in one direction, that there was travel to the past, but not to the future. He was a voluntary exile, fated to spend the rest of his life in this era. The idea was that when he'd been in this century long enough to describe it well, he'd write up his report and put it in a box he'd have especially made to last forty centuries and bury it where it could be dug up—in a spot that had been determined in the future. He had the exact place geographically.

He was quite excited when they told him about the time capsules that had been buried elsewhere. He knew that they had never been dug up and planned to make it part of his report so the men of the future could find them.

They spent their evenings in long conversations, Jan telling of his age and what he knew of all the long centuries in between. Of the long fight upward and man's conquests in the fields of science, medicine and in human relations. And they telling him of theirs, describing the institutions, the ways of life which he found so unique.

Lou hadn't been particularly happy about the precipitate marriage at first, but he found himself warming to Jan. Until . . .

The sheriff said, "And he didn't tell you what he was till this evening?"

"That's right."

"Your sister heard him say it? She'll back you up?"

"I . . . I guess she will. She's upset now, like I said, kind of hysterical. Screams that she's going to leave me and the farm. But she heard him say it, Sheriff. He must of had a strong hold on her, or she wouldn't be acting the way she is."

"Not that I doubt your word, boy, about a thing like that, but it'd be better if she heard it too. How'd it come up?"

"I got to asking him some questions about things in his time and after a while I asked him how they got along on race problems and he acted puzzled and then he said he remembered something about races from history he'd studied, but that there weren't any races then.

"He said that by his time—starting after the war of something-or-other, I forget its name—all the races had blended into one. That the whites and the yellows had mostly killed one another off and that Africa had dominated the world for a while, and then all the races had begun to blend into one by colonization and intermarriage and that by his time the process was complete. I just stared at him and asked him, 'You mean you got nigger blood in you?' and he said, just like it didn't mean anything, 'At least one-fourth.'"

"Well, boy, you did just what you had to," the sheriff told him earnestly, "no doubt about it."

"I just saw red. He'd married Sis; he was sleeping with her. I was so crazy-mad I don't even remember getting my gun."

"Well, don't worry about it, boy. You did right."

"But I feel like hell about it. He didn't know."

"Now that's a matter of opinion, boy. Maybe you swallowed a little too much of this hogwash. Coming from the future—huh! These niggers'll think up the damnedest tricks to pass themselves off as white. What kind of proof for his story is that mark on the ground? Hogwash, boy. Ain't nobody coming from the future or going there neither. We can just quiet this up so it won't never be heard of nowhere. It'll be like it never happened."

What Have I Done?

Mark Clifton (1906-1963)

MARK *Clifton was one of several fine science-fiction writers to die young between 1955 and 1965. He is perhaps best remembered as the coauthor (with Frank Riley) of* They'd Rather Be Right *which won the Hugo Award in 1955.*

Clifton worked for many years as a personnel specialist, interviewing over two hundred thousand people. In this story, which was the first he ever published, he drew upon his experience in this field to produce a subtle tale of what it means to be a human being and the nature of the societies that human beings create. We hope that he was wrong.

From *Astounding Science Fiction*   1952

It had to be I. It would be stupid to say that the burden should have fallen to a great statesman, a world leader, a renowned scientist. With all modesty, I think I am one of the few who could have caught the problem early enough to avert disaster. I have a peculiar skill. The whole thing hinged on that. I have learned to know human beings.

The first time I saw the fellow, I was at the drug-store counter buying cigarettes. He was standing at the magazine rack. One might have thought from the expression on his face that he had never seen magazines before. Still, quite a number of people get that rapt and vacant look when they can't make up their minds to a choice.

The thing which bothered me in that casual glance was that I couldn't recognize him.

There are others who can match my record in taking case histories. I happened to be the one who came in contact with this fellow. For thirty years I have been listening to, talking with, counseling people—over two hundred thousand of them. They have not been routine interviews. I have brought intelligence, sensitivity and concern to each of them.

Mine has been a driving, burning desire to know people. Not from the western scientific point of view of devising tools and rules to measure animated robots and ignoring the man beneath. Nor from the eastern metaphysical approach to painting a picture of the soul by blowing one's breath upon a fog to be blurred and dispersed by the next breath.

Mine was the aim to know the man by making use of both. And there was some success.

A competent geographer can look at a crude sketch of a map and instantly orient himself to it anywhere in the world— the bend of a river, the angle of a lake, the twist of a mountain range. And he can mystify by telling in finest detail what is to be found there.

After about fifty thousand studies where I could predict and then observe and check, with me it became the lift of a brow, the curve of a mouth, the gesture of a hand, the slope of a shoulder. One of the universities became interested, and over a long, controlled period they rated me 92 per cent accurate. That was fifteen years ago. I may have improved some since.

Yet standing there at the cigarette counter and glancing at the young fellow at the magazine rack, I could read nothing. Nothing at all.

If this had been an ordinary face, I would have catalogued it and forgotten it automatically. I see them by the thousands.

But this face would not be catalogued nor forgotten, because there was nothing in it.

I started to write that it wasn't even a face, but of course it was. Every human being has a face—of one sort or another.

In build he was short, muscular, rather well proportioned. The hair was crew cut and blond, the eyes were blue, the skin fair. All nice and standard Teutonic—only it wasn't.

I finished paying for my cigarettes and gave him one more glance, hoping to surprise an expression which had some meaning. There was none. I left him standing there and walked out on the street and around the corner. The street, the store fronts, the traffic cop on the corner, the warm sunshine were all so familiar I didn't see them. I climbed the stairs to my office in the building over the drug store. My employment-agency waiting room was empty. I don't cater to much of a crowd because it cuts down my opportunity to talk with people and further my study.

Margie, my receptionist, was busy making out some kind of a report and merely nodded as I passed her desk to my own office. She is a good, conscientious girl who can't understand why I spend so much time working with bums and drunks and other psychos who obviously won't bring fees into the some-times too small bank account.

I sat down at my desk and said aloud to myself, "The guy is a fake! As obvious as a high-school boy's drafting of a dollar bill."

I heard myself say that and wondered if I was going nuts, myself. What did I mean by fake? I shrugged. So I happened to see a bird I couldn't read, that was all.

Then it struck me. But that would be unique. I hadn't had that experience for twenty years. Imagine the delight, after all these years, of exploring an unreadable!

I rushed out of my office and back down the stairs to the street. Hallahan, the traffic cop, saw me running up the street and looked at me curiously. I signaled to him with a wave of a hand that everything was all right. He lifted his cap and scratched his head. He shook his head slowly and settled his cap back down. He blew a whistle at a woman driver and went back to directing traffic.

I ran into the drug store. Of course the guy wasn't there. I looked all around, hoping he was hiding behind the pots and pans counter, or something. No guy.

I walked quickly back out on the street and down to the next corner. I looked up and down the side streets. No guy.

I dragged my feet reluctantly back toward the office. I called up the face again to study it. It did no good. The first mental glimpse of it told me there was nothing to find. Logic told me there was nothing to find. If there had been, I wouldn't be in such a stew. The face was empty—completely void of human feelings or character.

No, those weren't the right words. Completely void of human—being!

I walked on past the drug store again and looked in curiously, hoping I would see him. Hallahan was facing my direction again, and he grinned crookedly at me. I expect around the neighborhood I am known as a character. I ask the queerest questions of people, from a layman's point of view. Still, applicants sometimes tell me that when they asked a cop where was an employment agent they could trust they were sent to me.

I climbed the stairs again, and walked into my waiting room. Margie looked at me curiously, but she only said, "There's an applicant. I had him wait in your office." She looked like she wanted to say more, and then shrugged. Or maybe she shivered. I knew there was something wrong with the bird, or she would have kept him in the waiting room.

I opened the door to my office, and experienced an overwhelming sense of relief, fulfillment. It was he. Still, it was logical that he should be there. I run an employment agency.

People come to me to get help in finding work. If others, why not he?

My skill includes the control of my outward reactions. That fellow could have no idea of the delight I felt at the opportunity to get a full history. If I had found him on the street, the best I might have done was a stock question about what time is it, or have you got a match, or where is the city hall. Here I could question him to my heart's content.

I took his history without comment, and stuck to routine questions. It was all exactly right.

He was an ex-G.I., just completed college, major in astronomy, no experience, no skills, no faintest idea of what he wanted to do, nothing to offer an employer—all perfectly normal for a young grad.

No feeling or expression, either. Not so normal. Usually they're petulantly resentful that business doesn't swoon at the chance of hiring them. I resigned myself to the old one-two of attempting to steer him toward something practical.

"Astronomy?" I asked. "That means you're heavy in math. Frequently we can place a strong math skill in statistical work." I was hopeful I could get a spark of something.

It turned out he wasn't very good at math. "I haven't yet reconciled my math to . . ." he stopped. For the first time he showed a reaction—hesitancy. Prior to that he had been a statue from Greece—the rounded, expressionless eyes, the too-perfect features undisturbed by thought.

He caught his remark and finished, "I'm just not very good at math, that's all."

I sighed to myself. I'm used to that, too. They give degrees nowadays to get rid of the guys, I suppose. Sometimes I'll go for days without uncovering any usable knowledge. So in a way, that was normal.

The only abnormal part of it was he seemed to think it didn't sound right. Usually the lads don't even realize they should know something. He seemed to think he'd pulled a boner by admitting that a man can take a degree in astronomy without learning math. Well, I wouldn't be surprised to see them take their degrees without knowing how many planets there are.

He began to fidget a bit. That was strange, also. I thought I knew every possible combination of muscular contractions and expansions. This fidget had all the reality of a puppet activated by an amateur. And the eyes—still completely blank.

I led him up one mental street and down the next. And of all the false-fronted stores and cardboard houses and paper lawns, I never saw the like. I get something of that once in a while from a fellow who has spent a long term in prison and comes in with a manufactured past—but never anything as phony as this one was.

Interesting aspect to it. Most guys, when they realize you've spotted them for a phony, get out as soon as they can. He didn't. It was almost as though he were—well, testing to see if his answers would stand up.

I tried talking astronomy, of which I thought I knew a little. I found I didn't know anything, or he didn't. This bird's astronomy and mine had no point of reconciliation.

And then he had a slip of the tongue—yes he did. He was talking, and said, "The ten planets . . ."

He caught himself, "Oh that's right. There are only nine."

Could be ignorance, but I didn't think so. Could be he knew of the existence of a planet we hadn't yet discovered.

I smiled. I opened a desk drawer and pulled out a couple science-fiction magazines. "Ever read any of these?" I asked.

"I looked through several of them at the newsstand a while ago," he answered.

"They've enlarged my vision," I said. "Even to the point where I could believe that some other star system might hold intelligence." I lit a cigarette and waited. If I was wrong, he would merely think I was talking at random.

His blank eyes changed. They were no longer Greek-statue eyes. They were no longer blue. They were black, deep bottomless black, as deep and cold as space itself.

"Where did I fail in my test?" he asked. His lips formed a smile which was not a smile—a carefully painted-on-canvas sort of smile.

Well, I'd had my answer. I'd explored something unique, all right. Sitting there before me, I had no way of determining whether he was benign or evil. No way of knowing his motive. No way of judging—anything. When it takes a lifetime of learning how to judge even our own kind, what standards have we for judging an entity from another star system?

At that moment I would like to have been one of those space-opera heroes who, in similar circumstances, laugh casually and say, "What ho! So you're from Arcturus. Well, well. It's a small universe after all, isn't it?" And then with linked arms they head for the nearest bar, bosom pals.

I had the almost hysterical thought, but carefully suppressed, that I didn't know if this fellow would like beer or not. I will not go through the intermuscular and visceral reactions I experienced. I kept my seat and maintained a polite expression. Even with humans, I know when to walk carefully.

"I couldn't feel anything about you," I answered his question. "I couldn't feel anything but blankness."

He looked blank. His eyes were nice blue marble again. I liked them better that way.

There should be a million questions to be asked, but I must have been bothered by the feeling that I held a loaded bomb in my hands. And not knowing what might set it off, or how, or when. I could think of only the most trivial.

"How long have you been on Earth?" I asked. Sort of a when did you get back in town, Joe, kind of triviality.

"For several of your weeks," he was answering. "But this is my first time out among humans."

"Where have you been in the meantime?" I asked.

"Training." His answers were getting short and his muscles began to fidget again.

"And where do you train?" I kept boring in.

As an answer he stood up and held out his hand, all quite correctly. "I must go now," he said. "Naturally you can cancel my application for employment. Obviously we have more to learn."

I raised an eyebrow. "And I'm supposed to just pass over the whole thing? A thing like this?"

He smiled again. The contrived smile which was a symbol to indicate courtesy. "I believe your custom on this planet is to turn your problems over to your police. You might try that." I could not tell whether it was ironic or logic.

At that moment I could think of nothing else to say. He walked out of my door while I stood beside my desk and watched him go.

Well, what was I supposed to do? Follow him?

I followed him.

Now I'm no private eye, but I've read my share of mystery stories. I knew enough to keep out of sight. I followed him about a dozen blocks into a quiet residential section of small homes. I was standing behind a palm tree, lighting a cigarette, when he went up the walk of one of these small houses. I saw him twiddle with the door, open it, and walk in. The door closed.

I hung around a while and then went up to the door. I punched the doorbell. A motherly, gray-haired woman came to the door, drying her hands on her apron. As she opened the door she said, "I'm not buying anything today."

Just the same, her eyes looked curious as to what I might have.

I grinned my best grin for elderly ladies. "I'm not selling anything, either," I answered. I handed her my agency card. She looked at it curiously and then looked a question at me.

"I'd like to see Joseph Hoffman," I said politely.

She looked puzzled. "I'm afraid you've got the wrong address, sir," she answered.

I got prepared to stick my foot in the door, but it wasn't necessary. "He was in my office just a few minutes ago," I said. "He gave that name and this address. A job came in right after he left the office, and since I was going to be in this neighborhood anyway, I thought I'd drop by and tell him in person. It's sort of rush," I finished. It had happened many times before, but this time it sounded lame.

"Nobody lives here but me and my husband," she insisted. "He's retired."

I didn't care if he hung by his toes from trees. I wanted a young fellow.

"But I saw the young fellow come in here," I argued. "I was just coming around the corner, trying to catch him. I saw him."

She looked at me suspiciously. "I don't know what your racket is," she said through thin lips, "but I'm not buying anything. I'm not signing anything. I don't even want to talk to you." She was stubborn about it.

I apologized and mumbled something about maybe making a mistake.

"I should say you have," she rapped out tartly and shut the door in righteous indignation. Sincere, too. I could tell.

An employment agent who gets the reputation of being a right guy makes all kinds of friends. That poor old lady must have thought a plague of locusts had swept in on her for the next few days.

First the telephone repair man had to investigate an alleged complaint. Then a gas service man had to check the plumbing. An electrician complained there was a power short in the block and he had to trace their house wiring. We kept our fingers crossed hoping the old geezer had never been a construction man. There was a mistake in the last census, and a guy asked her a million questions.

That house was gone over rafter by rafter and sill by sill, attic and basement. It was precisely as she said. She and her husband lived there; nobody else.

In frustration, I waited three months. I wore out the sidewalks haunting the neighborhood. Nothing.

Then one day my office door opened and Margie ushered a young man in. Behind his back she was radiating heart throbs and fluttering her eyes.

He was the traditionally tall, dark and handsome young fellow, with a ready grin and sparkling dark eyes. His personality hit me like a sledge hammer. A guy like that never needs to go to an employment agency. Any employer will hire him at the drop of a hat, and wonder later why he did it.

His name was Einar Johnson. Extraction, Norwegian. The dark Norse strain, I judged. I took a chance on his thinking he had walked into a booby hatch.

"The last time I talked with you," I said, "your name was Joseph Hoffman. You were Teutonic then. Not Norse."

The sparkle went out of his eyes. His face showed exasperation and there was plenty of it. It looked real, too, not painted on.

"All right. Where did I flunk this time?" he asked impatiently.

"It would take me too long to tell you," I answered. "Suppose you start talking." Strangely, I was at ease. I knew that underneath he was the same incomprehensible entity, but his surface was so good that I was lulled.

He looked at me levelly for a long moment. Then he said, "I didn't think there was a chance in a million of being recognized. I'll admit that other character we created was crude. We've learned considerably since then, and we've concentrated everything on this personality I'm wearing."

He paused and flashed his teeth at me. I felt like hiring him, myself. "I've been all over Southern California in this one," he said. "I've had a short job as a salesman. I've been to dances and parties. I've got drunk and sober again. Nobody, I say nobody, has shown even the slightest suspicion."

"Not very observing, were they?" I taunted.

"But you are," he answered. "That's why I came back here for the final test. I'd like to know where I failed." He was firm.

"We get quite a few phonies," I answered. "The guy drawing unemployment and stalling until it is run out. The geezik whose wife drives him out and threatens to quit her job if he doesn't go to work. The plain-clothes detail smelling around to see if maybe we aren't a cover for a bookie joint or something. Dozens of phonies."

He looked curious. I said in disgust, "We know in the first two minutes they're phony. You were phony also, but not of any class I've seen before. And," I finished dryly, "I've been waiting for you."

"Why was I phony?" he persisted.

"Too much personality force," I answered. "Human beings just don't have that much force. I felt like I'd been knocked flat on my . . . well . . . back."

He sighed. "I've been afraid you would recognize me one way or another. I communicated with home. I was advised that if you spotted me, I was to instruct you to assist us."

I lifted a brow. I wasn't sure just how much authority they had to instruct me to do anything.

"I was to instruct you to take over the supervision of our final training, so that no one could ever spot us. If we are going to carry out our original plan that is necessary. If not, then we will have to use the alternate." He was almost didactic in his manner, but his charm of personality still radiated like an infrared lamp.

"You're going to have to tell me a great deal more than that," I said.

He glanced at my closed door.

"We won't be interrupted," I said. "A personnel history is private."

"I come from one of the planets of Arcturus," he said.

I must have allowed a smile of amusement to show on my face, for he asked, "You find that amusing?"

"No," I answered soberly, and my pulses leaped because the question confirmed my conclusion that he could not read my thoughts. Apparently we were as alien to him as he to us. "I was amused," I explained, "because the first time I saw you I said to myself that as far as recognizing you, you might have come from Arcturus. Now it turns out that accidentally I was correct. I'm better than I thought."

He gave a fleeting polite smile in acknowledgment. "My home planet," he went on, "is similar to yours. Except that we have grown overpopulated."

I felt a twinge of fear.

"We have made a study of this planet and have decided to colonize it." It was a flat statement, without any doubt behind it.

I flashed him a look of incredulity. "And you expect me to help you with that?"

He gave me a worldly wise look—almost an ancient look. "Why not?" he asked.

"There is the matter of loyalty to my own kind, for one thing," I said. "Not too many generations away and we'll be overpopulated also. There would hardly be room for both your people and ours on Earth."

"Oh that's all right," he answered easily. "There'll be plenty of room for us for quite some time. We multiply slowly."

"We don't," I said shortly. I felt this conversation should be taking place between him and some great statesman—not me.

"You don't seem to understand," he said patiently. "Your race won't be here. We have found no reason why your race should be preserved. You will die away as we absorb."

"Now just a moment," I interrupted. "I don't want our race

to die off." The way he looked at me I felt like a spoiled brat who didn't want to go beddie time.

"Why not?" he asked.

I was stumped. That's a good question when it is put logically. Just try to think of a logical reason why the human race should survive. I gave him at least something.

"Mankind," I said, "has had a hard struggle. We've paid a tremendous price in pain and death for our growth. Not to have a future to look forward to would be like paying for something and never getting the use of it."

It was the best I could think of, honest. To base argument on humanity and right and justice and mercy would leave me wide open. Because it is obvious that man doesn't practice any of these. There is no assurance he ever will.

But he was ready for me, even with that one. "But if we are never suspected, and if we absorb and replace gradually, who is to know there is no future for humans?"

And as abruptly as the last time, he stood up suddenly. "Of course," he said coldly, "we could use our alternative plan: Destroy the human race without further negotiation. It is not our way to cause needless pain to any life form. But we can.

"If you do not assist us, then it is obvious that we will eventually be discovered. You are aware of the difficulty of even blending from one country on Earth to another. How much more difficult it is where there is no point of contact at all. And if we are discovered, destruction would be the only step left."

He smiled and all the force of his charm hit me again. "I know you will want to think it over for a time. I'll return."

He walked to the door, then smiled back at me. "And don't bother to trouble that poor little woman in that house again. Her doorway is only one of many entrances we have opened. She doesn't see us at all, and merely wonders why her latch doesn't work sometimes. And we can open another, anywhere, anytime. Like this . . ."

He was gone.

I walked over and opened the door. Margie was all prettied up and looking expectant and radiant. When she didn't see him come out she got up and peeked into my office. "But where did he go?" she asked with wide eyes.

"Get hold of yourself, girl," I answered. "You're so dazed you didn't even see him walk right by you."

"There's something fishy going on here," she said.

Well, I had a problem. A first-rate, genuine, dyed-in-the-wool dilemma.

What was I to do? I could have gone to the local authorities and got locked up for being a psycho. I could have gone to the college professors and got locked up for being a psycho. I could have gone to maybe the FBI and got locked up for being a psycho. That line of thinking began to get monotonous.

I did the one thing which I thought might bring help. I wrote up the happenings and sent it to my favorite science-fiction magazine. I asked for help and sage counsel from the one place I felt awareness and comprehension might be reached.

The manuscript bounced back so fast it might have had rubber bands attached to it, stretched from California to New York. I looked the little rejection slip all over, front and back, and I did not find upon it those sage words of counsel I needed. There wasn't even a printed invitation to try again some time.

And for the first time in my life I knew what it was to be alone—genuinely and irrevocably alone.

Still, I could not blame the editor. I could see him cast the manuscript from him in disgust, saying, "Bah! So another evil race comes to conquer Earth. If I gave the fans one more of those, I'd be run out of my office." And like the deacon who saw the naughty words written on the fence, saying, "And misspelled, too."

The fable of the boy who cried "Wolf! Wolf!" once too

often came home to me now. I was alone with my problem. The dilemma was my own. On one hand was immediate extermination. I did not doubt it. A race which can open doors from one star system to another, without even visible means of mechanism, would also know how to—disinfect.

On the other hand was extinction, gradual, but equally certain, and none the less effective in that it would not be perceived. If I refused to assist, then, acting as one lone judge of all the race, I condemned it. If I did assist, I would be arch traitor, with an equal final result.

For days I sweltered in my miasma of indecision. Like many a man before me, uncertain of what to do, I temporized. I decided to play for time. To play the role of traitor in the hopes I might learn a way of defeating them.

Once I had made up my mind, my thoughts raced wildly through the possibilities. If I were to be their instructor on how to walk unsuspected among men, then I would have them wholly in my grasp. If I could build traits into them, common ordinary traits which they could see in men all about them, yet which would make men turn and destroy them, then I would have my solution.

And I knew human beings. Perhaps it was right, after all, that it became my problem. Mine alone.

I shuddered now to think what might have happened had this being fallen into less skilled hands and told his story. Perhaps by now there would be no man left upon Earth.

Yes, the old and worn-out plot of the one little unknown guy who saved Earth from outer evil might yet run its course in reality.

I was ready for the Arcturan when he returned. And he did return.

Einar Johnson and I walked out of my office after I had sent a tearful Maggie on a long vacation with fancy pay. Einar had plenty of money, and was liberal with it. When a fellow can open some sort of fourth-dimensional door into a bank vault and help himself, money is no problem.

I had visions of the poor bank clerks trying to explain things to the examiners, but that wasn't my worry right now.

We walked out of the office and I snapped the lock shut behind me. Always conscious of the cares of people looking for work, I hung a sign on the door saying I was ill and didn't know when I would be back.

We walked down the stairs and into the parking lot. We got into my car, my own car, please note, and I found myself sitting in a sheltered patio in Beverly Hills. Just like that. No awful wrenching and turning my insides out. No worrisome nausea and emptiness of space. Nothing to dramatize it at all. Car—patio, like that.

I would like to be able to describe the Arcturans as having long snaky appendages and evil, slobbering maws, and stuff like that. But I can't describe the Arcturans, because I didn't see any.

I saw a gathering of people, roughly about thirty of them, wandering around the patio, swimming in the pool, going in and out of the side doors of the house. It was a perfect spot. No one bothers the big Beverly Hills home without invitation.

The natives wouldn't be caught dead looking toward a star's house. The tourists see the winding drive, the trees and grass, and perhaps a glimpse of a gabled roof. If they can get any thrill out of that, then bless their little spending money hearts, they're welcome to it.

Yet if it should become known that a crowd of strange-acting people are wandering around in the grounds, no one would think a thing about it. They don't come any more zany than the Hollywood crowd.

Only these were. These people could have made a fortune as life-size puppets. I could see now why it was judged that the lifeless Teutonic I had first interviewed was thought adequate to mingle with human beings. By comparison with these, he was a snappy song and dance man.

But that is all I saw. Vacant bodies wandering around, going through human motions, without human emotions. The job looked bigger than I had thought. And yet, if this was their idea of how to win friends and influence people, I might be successful after all.

There are dozens of questions the curious might want answered—such as how did they get hold of the house and how did they get their human bodies and where did they learn to speak English, and stuff. I wasn't too curious. I had important things to think about. I supposed they were able to do it, because here it was.

I'll cut the following weeks short. I cannot conceive of what life and civilization on their planet might be like. Yardsticks of scientific psychology are used to measure a man, and yet they give no indication at all of the inner spirit of him, likewise, the descriptive measurements of their civilization are empty and meaningless. Knowing about a man, and knowing a man are two entirely different things.

For example, all those thalamic urges and urgencies which we call emotion were completely unknown to them, except as they saw them in antics on TV. The ideals of man were also unknown—truth, honor, justice, perfection—all unknown. They had not even a division of sexes, and the emotion we call love was beyond their understanding. The TV stories they saw must have been like watching a parade of ants.

What purpose can be gained by describing such a civilization to man? Man cannot conceive accomplishment without first having the dream. Yet it was obvious that they accomplished, for they were here.

When I finally realized there was no point of contact between man and these, I knew relief and joy once more. My job was easy. I knew how to destroy them. And I suspected they could not avoid my trap.

They could not avoid my trap because they had human bodies. Perhaps they conceived them out of thin air, but the veins bled, the flesh felt pain and heat and pressure, the glands secreted.

Ah yes, the glands secreted. They would learn what emotion could be. And I was a master of wielding emotion. The dream of man has been to strive toward the great and immortal ideals. His literature is filled with admonishments to that end. In comparison with the volume of work which tells us what we should be, there is very little which reveals us as we are.

As part of my training course, I chose the world's great literature, and painting, and sculpture, and music—those mediums which best portray man lifting to the stars. I gave them first of all, the dream.

And with the dream, and with the pressure of the glands as kicker, they began to know emotion. I had respect for the superb acting of Einar when I realized that he, also, had still known no emotion.

They moved from the puppet to the newborn babe—a newborn babe in training, with an adult body, and its matured glandular equation.

I saw emotions, all right. Emotions without restraint, emotions unfettered by taboos, emotions uncontrolled by ideals. Sometimes I became frightened and all my skill in manipulating emotions was needed. At other times they became perhaps a little too Hollywood, even for Hollywood. I trained them into more ideal patterns.

I will say this for the Arcturans. They learned—fast. The crowd of puppets to the newborn babes, to the boisterous boys and girls, to the moody and unpredictable youths, to the matured and balanced men and women. I watched the metamorphosis take place over the period of weeks.

I did more.

All that human beings had ever hoped to be, the brilliant, the idealistic, the great in heart, I made of these. My little 145 I.Q. became a moron's level. The dreams of the greatness of man which I had known became the vaguest of wisps of fog before the reality which these achieved.

My plan was working.

Full formed, they were almost like gods. And training these things into them, I trained their own traits out. One point I found we had in common. They were activated by logic, logic carried to heights of which I had never dreamed. Yet my poor and halting logic found point of contact.

They realized at last that if they let their own life force and motivation remain active they would carry the aura of strangeness to defeat their purpose. I worried, when they accepted this. I felt perhaps they were laying a trap for me, as I did for them. Then I realized that I had not taught them deceit.

And it was logical, to them, that they follow my training completely. Reversing the position, placing myself upon their planet, trying to become like them, I must of necessity follow my instructor without question. What else could they do?

At first they saw no strangeness that I should assist them to destroy my race. In their logic the Arcturan was most fit to survive, therefore he should survive. The human was less fit, therefore he should perish.

I taught them the emotion of compassion. And when they began to mature their human thought and emotion, and their intellection was blended and shaded by such emotion, at last they understood my dilemma.

There was irony in that. From my own kind I could expect no understanding. From the invaders I received sympathy and compassion. They understood at last my traitorous action to buy a few more years for man.

Yet their Arcturan logic still prevailed. They wept with me, but there could be no change of plan. The plan was fixed, they were merely instruments by which it was to be carried out.

Yet, through their compassion, I did get the plan modified. This was the conversation which revealed that modification.

Einar Johnson, who as the most fully developed had been my constant companion, said to me one day, "To all intents and purposes we have become human beings." He looked at me and smiled with fondness, "You have said it is so, and it must be so. For we begin to realize what a great and glorious thing a human is."

The light of nobility shone from him like an aura as he told me this. "Without human bodies, and without the emotion-intelligence equation which you call soul, our home planet cannot begin to grasp the growth we have achieved. We know now that we will never return to our own form, for by doing that we would lose what we have gained.

"Our people are logical, and they must of necessity accept our recommendation, as long as it does not abandon the plan entirely. We have reported what we have learned, and it is conceived that both our races can inhabit the universe side by side.

"There will be no more migration from our planet to yours. We will remain, and we will multiply, and we will live in honor, such as you have taught us, among you. In time perhaps we may achieve the greatness which all humans now have.

"And we will assist the human kind to find their destiny among the stars as we have done."

I bowed my head and wept. For I knew that I had won.

Four months had gone. I returned to my own neighborhood. On the corner Hallahan left the traffic to shift for itself while he came over to me with the question, "Where have you been?"

"I've been sick," I said.

"You look it," he said frankly. "Take care of yourself, man. Hey . . . Lookit that fool messing up traffic." He was gone, blowing his whistle in a temper.

I climbed the stairs. They still needed repairing as much as ever. From time to time I had been able to mail money to

Margie, and she had kept the rent and telephone paid. The sign was still on my door. My key opened the lock.

The waiting room had that musty, they've-gone-away look about it. The janitor had kept the windows tightly closed and there was no freshness in the air. I half-hoped to see Margie sitting at her desk, but I knew there was no purpose to it. When a girl is being paid for her time and has nothing to do, the beach is a nice place to spend it.

There was dust on my chair, and I sank down into it without bothering about the seat of my pants. I buried my head in my arms and I looked into the human soul.

Now the whole thing hinged on that skill. I know human beings. I know them as well as anyone in the world, and far better than most.

I looked into the past and I saw a review of the great and fine and noble and divine torn and burned and crucified by man.

Yet my only hope of saving my race was to build these qualities, the fine, the noble, the splendid, into these thirty beings. To create the illusion that all men were likewise great. No less power could have gained the boon of equality for man with them.

I look into the future. I see them, one by one, destroyed. I gave them no defense. They are totally unprepared to meet man as he genuinely is—and they are incapable of understanding.

For these things which man purports to admire the most— the noble, the brilliant, the splendid—these are the very things he cannot tolerate when he finds them.

Defenseless, because they cannot comprehend, these thirty will go down beneath the ravening fury of rending and destroying man always displays whenever he meets his ideal face to face.

I bury my head in my hands.

What have I done?

DP!

Jack Vance (1920–   )

Jack Vance *is one of those rare writers who is equally at home with fantasy and science fiction, although he has been concentrating on the former in recent years. He wrote* To Live Forever *(1956), a minor science-fiction classic, but he is best known as the Hugo and Nebula Award winning author of* The Last Castle *and* The Dragon Masters.

The convulsions of the World War II period affected science fiction profoundly. The intense feelings of guilt and incomprehension which swept across Western civilization upon the realization of the atrocities of Nazism soon found expression in the work of science-fiction writers. "DP!" is an expression of that feeling. It is a powerful statement on the human fear of those who are different because of their customs, religion, appearance, or status. There were still millions of displaced persons in the real world when Vance was writing this story.

"DP!" skillfully blends the reactions of governments (large and small), the media, the scientific elite, and the "people," to the logistical, moral, economic, and political problems posed by the appearance of the troglodytes. It also examines the

111

ways in which distrust between nations can turn refugees into pawns, a practice that has not changed since 1953.

From *Avon Science Fiction Reader*   1953

═══════════════════════════════════════

An old woodcutter woman, hunting mushrooms up the north fork of the Kreuzberg, raised her eyes and saw the strangers. They came step by step through the ferns, arms extended, milk-blue eyes blank as clam shells. When they chanced into patches of sunlight, they cried out in hurt voices and clutched at their naked scalps, which were white as ivory, and netted with pale blue veins.

The old woman stood like a stump, the breath scraping in her throat. She stumbled back, almost falling at each step, her legs moving back to support her at the last critical instant. The strange people came to a wavering halt, peering through sunlight and dark-green shadow. The woman took an hysterical breath, turned, and put her gnarled old legs to flight.

A hundred yards downhill she broke out on a trail; here she found her voice. She ran, uttering cracked screams and hoarse cries, lurching from side to side. She ran till she came to a wayside shrine, where she flung herself into a heap to gasp out prayer and frantic supplication.

Two woodsmen, in leather breeches and rusty black coats, coming up the path from Tedratz, stared at her in curiosity and amusement. She struggled to her knees, pointed up the trail. "Fiends from the pit! Walking in all their evil; with my two eyes I've seen them!"

"Come now," the older woodsman said indulgently. "You've had a drop or two, and it's not reverent to talk so at a holy place."

"I saw them," bellowed the old woman. "Naked as eggs and white as lard; they came running at me waving their arms, crying out for my very soul!"

"They had horns and tails?" the younger man asked jocu-larly. "They prodded you with their forks, switched you with their whips?"

"Ach, you blackguards! You laugh, you mock; go up the slope, and see for yourself. . . . Only five hundred meters, and then perhaps you'll mock!"

"Come along," said the first. "Perhaps someone's been plaguing the old woman; if so, we'll put him right."

They sauntered on, disappeared through the firs. The old woman rose to her feet, hobbled as rapidly as she could toward the village.

Five quiet minutes passed. She heard a clatter; the two woodsmen came running at breakneck speed down the path. "What now?" she quavered, but they pushed past her and ran shouting into Tedratz.

Half an hour later fifty men armed with rifles and shotguns stalked cautiously back up the trail, their dogs on leash. They passed the shrine; the dogs began to strain and growl.

"Up through here," whispered the older of the two woods-men. They climbed the bank, threaded the firs, crossed sun-flooded meadows and balsam-scented shade.

From a rocky ravine, tinkling and chiming with a stream of glacier water, came the strange, sad voices.

The dogs snarled and moaned; the men edged forward, peered into the meadow. The strangers were clustered under an overhanging ledge, clawing feebly into the dirt.

"Horrible things!" hissed the foremost man, "Like great potato-bugs!" He aimed his gun, but another struck up the barrel. "Not yet! Don't waste good powder; let the dogs hunt them down. If fiends they be, their spite will find none of us!"

The idea had merit; the dogs were loosed. They bounded forward, full of hate. The shadows boiled with fur and fangs and jerking white flesh.

One of the men jumped forward, his voice thick with rage.

"Look, they've killed Tupp, my good old Tupp!" He raised his gun and fired, an act which became the signal for further shooting. And presently, all the strangers had been done to death, by one means or another.

Breathing hard, the men pulled off the dogs and stood looking down at the bodies. "A good job, whatever they are, man, beast, or fiend," said John Kirchner, the innkeeper. "But there's the point! What are they? When have such creatures been seen before?"

"Strange happenings for this earth; strange events for Austria!"

The men stared at the white tangle of bodies, none pushing too close, and now with the waning of urgency their mood became uneasy. Old Alois, the baker, crossed himself and, furtively examining the sky, muttered about the Apocalypse. Franz, the village atheist, had his reputation to maintain. "Demons," he asserted, "presumably would not succumb so easily to dog-bite and bullet; these must be refugees from the Russian zone, victims of torture and experimentation." Neinrich, the village Communist, angrily pointed out how much closer lay the big American lager near Innsbruck; this was the effect of Coca-Cola and comic books upon decent Austrians.

"Nonsense," snapped another. "Never an Austrian born of woman had such heads, such eyes, such skin. These things are something else. Salamanders!"

"Zombies," muttered another. "Corpses, raised from the dead."

Alois held up his hand. "Hist!"

Into the ravine came the pad and rustle of aimless steps, the forlorn cries of the troglodytes.

The men crouched back into the shadows; along the ridge appeared silhouettes, crooked, lumpy shapes feeling their way forward, recoiling from the shafts of sunlight.

Guns cracked and spat; once more the dogs were loosed. They bounded up the side of the ravine and disappeared.

Panting up the slope, the men came to the base of a great overhanging cliff, and here they stopped short. The base of the cliff was broken open. Vague pale-eyed shapes wadded the gap, swaying, shuddering, resisting, moving forward inch by inch, step by step.

"Dynamite!" cried the men. "Dynamite, gasoline, fire!"

These measures were never put into effect. The commandant of the French occupation garrison arrived with three platoons. He contemplated the fissure, the oyster-pale faces, the oyster-shell eyes and threw up his hands. He dictated a rapid message for the Innsbruck headquarters, then required the villagers to put away their guns and depart the scene.

The villagers sullenly retired; the French soldiers, brave in their sky-blue shorts, gingerly took up positions; and with a hasty enclosure of barbed wire and rails restrained the troglodytes to an area immediately in front of the fissure.

The April 18 edition of the *Innsbruck Kurier* included a skeptical paragraph: "A strange tribe of mountainside hermits, living in a Kreuzberg cave near Tedratz, was reported today. Local inhabitants profess the deepest mystification. The Tedratz constabulary, assisted by units of the French garrison, is investigating."

A rather less cautious account found its way into the channels of the wire services: "Innsbruck, April 19. A strange tribe has appeared from the recesses of the Kreuzberg near Innsbruck in the Tyrol. They are said to be hairless, blind, and to speak an incomprehensible language.

"According to unconfirmed reports, the troglodytes were attacked by terrified inhabitants of nearby Tedratz, and after bitter resistance were driven back into their caves.

"French occupation troops have sealed off the entire Kreuzertal. A spokesman for Colonel Courtin refuses either to confirm or deny that the troglodytes have appeared."

Bureau chiefs at the wire services looked long and carefully at the story. Why should French occupation troops interfere in what appeared on the face a purely civil disturbance? A secret colony of war criminals? Unlikely. What then? Mysterious race of troglodytes? Clearly hokum. What then? The story might develop, or it might go limp. In any case, on the late afternoon of April 19, a convoy of four cars started up the Kreuzertal, carrying reporters, photographers, and a member of the U.N. Minorities Commission, who by chance happened to be in Innsbruck.

The road to Tedratz wound among grassy meadows, story-book forests, in and out of little Alpine villages, with the massive snow-capped knob of the Kreuzberg gradually pushing higher into the sky.

At Tedratz, the party alighted and started up the now notorious trail, to be brought short almost at once at a barricade manned by French soldiers. Upon display of credentials the reporters and photographers were allowed to pass; the U.N. commissioner had nothing to show, and the NCO in charge of the barricade politely turned him back.

"But I am an official of the United Nations!" cried the outraged commissioner.

"That may well be," assented the NCO. "However, you are not a journalist, and my orders are uncompromising." And the angry commissioner was asked to wait in Tedratz until word would be taken to Colonel Courtin at the camp.

The commissioner seized on the word. " 'Camp'? How is this? I thought there was only a cave, a hole in the mountainside?"

The NCO shrugged. "Monsieur le Commissionaire is free to conjecture as he sees best."

A private was told off as a guide; the reporters and photographers started up the trail, with the long, yellow afternoon light slanting down through the firs.

It was a jocular group; repartee and wise cracks were freely exchanged. Presently the party became winded, as the trail was steep and they were all out of condition. They stopped by the wayside shrine to rest. "How much farther?" asked a photographer.

The soldier pointed through the firs toward a tall buttress of granite. "Only a little bit; then you shall see."

Once more they set out and almost immediately passed a platoon of soldiers stringing barbed wire from tree to tree.

"This will be the third extension," remarked their guide over his shoulder. "Every day they come pushing up out of the rock. It is"—he selected a word—*"formidable."*

The jocularity and wise cracks died; the journalists peered through the firs, aware of the sudden coolness of the evening.

They came to the camp, and were taken to Colonel Courtin, a small man full of excitable motion. He swung his arm. "There, my friends, is what you came to see; look your fill, since it is through your eyes that the world must see."

For three minutes they stared, muttering to one another, while Courtin teetered on his toes.

"How many are there?" came an awed question.

"Twenty thousand by latest estimate, and they issue ever faster. All from that little hole." He jumped upon tiptoe, and pointed "It is incredible; where do they fit? And still they come, like the objects a magician removes from his hat."

"But—do they eat?"

Courtin held out his hands. "Is it for me to ask? I furnish no food; I have none; my budget will not allow it. I am a man of compassion. If you will observe, I have hung the tarpaulins to prevent the sunlight."

"With that skin, they'd be pretty sensitive, eh?"

"Sensitive!" Courtin rolled up his eyes. "The sunlight burns them like fire."

"Funny that they're not more interested in what goes on."

"They are dazed, my friend. Dazed and blinded and completely confused."

"But—what *are* they?"

"That, my friend, is a question I am without resource to answer."

The journalists regained a measure of composure, and swept the enclosure with studiously impassive glances calculated to suggest, *we have seen so many strange sights that now nothing can surprise us.* "I suppose they're men," said one.

"But of course. What else?"

"What else indeed? But where do they come from? Lost Atlantis? The land of Oz?"

"Now then," said Colonel Courtin, "you make jokes. It is a serious business, my friends; where will it end?"

"That's the big question, Colonel. Whose baby is it?"

"I do not understand."

"Who takes responsibility for them? France?"

"No, no," cried Colonel Courtin. "You must not credit me with such a statement."

"Austria, then?"

Colonel Courtin shrugged. "The Austrians are a poor people. Perhaps—of course I speculate—your great country will once again share of its plenitude."

"Perhaps, perhaps not. The one man of the crowd who might have had something to say is down in Tedratz—the chap from the Minorities Commission."

The story pushed everything from the front pages, and grew bigger day by day.

From the U.P. wire:

Innsbruck, April 23 (UP): The Kreuzberg miracle continues to confound the world. Today a record number of troglodytes pushed through the gap, bringing the total surface population up to forty-six thousand. . . .

From the syndicated column, *Science Today* by Ralph Dunstaple, for April 28:

"The scientific world seethes with the troglodyte controversy. According to the theory most frequently voiced, the trogs are descended from cavemen of the glacial eras, driven underground by the advancing wall of ice. Other conjectures, more or less scientific, refer to the lost tribes of Israel, the fourth dimension, Armageddon, and Nazi experiments.

"Linguistic experts meanwhile report progress in their efforts to understand the language of the trogs. Dr. Allen K. Mendelson of the Princeton Institute of Advanced Research, spokesman for the group, classifies the trog speech as "one of the agglutinatives, with the slightest possible kinship to the Basque tongue—so faint as to be highly speculative, and it is only fair to say that there is considerable disagreement among us on this point. The trogs, incidentally, has no words for 'sun,' 'moon,' 'fight,' 'bird,' 'animal,' and a host of other concepts we take for granted. 'Food' and 'fungus,' however, are the same word."

From the *New York Herald Tribune:*

TROGS HUMAN, CLAIM SAVANTS; INTERBREEDING POSSIBLE
by Mollie Lemmon

Milan, April 30: Trogs are physiologically identical with surface humanity, and sexual intercourse between man and trog might well be fertile. Such was the opinion of a group of doctors and geneticists at an informal poll I conducted yesterday at the Milan Genetical Clinic, where a group of trogs are undergoing examination.

From *The Trog Story*, a daily syndicated feature by Harlan B. Temple, April 31:

"Today I saw the hundred thousandth trog push his way up out of the bowels of the Alps; everywhere in the world people are asking, where will it stop? I certainly have no answer. This tremendous migration, unparalleled since the days of Alaric the Goth, seems only just now shifting into high gear. Two new rifts have opened into the Kreuzberg; the trogs come shoving out in close ranks, faces blank as custard, and only God knows what is in their minds.

The camps—there are now six, interconnected like knots on a rope—extend down the hillside and into the Kreuzertal. Tarpaulins over the treetops give the mountainside, seen from a distance, the look of a lawn with handkerchiefs spread out to dry.

The food situation has improved considerably over the past three days, thanks to the efforts of the Red Cross, CARE, and FAO. The basic ration is a mush of rice, wheat, millet or other cereal, mixed with carrots, greens, dried eggs, and reinforced with vitamins; the trogs appear to thrive on it.

I cannot say that the trogs are a noble, enlightened, or even ingratiating race. Their cultural level is abysmally low; they possess no tools, they wear neither clothing nor ornaments. To their credit it must be said that they are utterly inoffensive and mild; I have never witnessed a quarrel or indeed seen a trog exhibit anything but passive obedience.

Still they rise in the hundreds and thousands. What brings them forth? Do they flee a subterranean Attila, some pandemonic Stalin? The linguists who have been studying the trog speech are close-mouthed, but I have it from a highly informed source that a report will be published within the next day or so. . . ."

Report to the Assembly of the U.N., May 4, by V. G. Hendlemann, Coordinator for the Committee of Associated Anthropologists:

"I will state the tentative conclusions at which this committee has arrived. The processes and inductions which have led to these conclusions are outlined in the appendix to this report.

"Our preliminary survey of the troglodyte language has convinced a majority of us that the trogs are probably the descendants of a group of European cave-dwellers who either by choice or by necessity took up underground residence at least fifty thousand, at most two hundred thousand, years ago.

"The trog which we see today is a result of evolution and mutation, and represents adaptation to the special conditions under which the trogs have existed. He is quite definitely of the species *homo sapiens*, with a cranial capacity roughly identical to that of surface man.

"In our conversations with the trogs we have endeavored to ascertain the cause of the migration. Not one of the trogs makes himself completely clear on the subject, but we have been given to understand that the great caves which the race inhabited have been stricken by a volcanic convulsion and are being gradually filled with lava. If this be the case the trogs are soon to become literally 'displaced persons.'

"In their former home the trogs subsisted on fungus grown in shallow 'paddies,' fertilized by their own wastes, finely pulverized coal, and warmed by volcanic heat.

"They have no grasp of 'time' as we understand the word. They have only the sparsest traditions of the past and are unable to conceive of a future further removed than two minutes. Since they exist in the present, they neither expect, hope, dread, nor otherwise take cognizance of what possibly may befall them.

"In spite of their deficiencies of cultural background, the trogs appear to have a not discreditable native intelligence. The committee agrees that a troglodyte child reared in ordinary surface surroundings, and given a typical education, might well become a valuable citizen, indistinguishable from any other human being except by his appearance."

Excerpt from a speech by Porfirio Hernandez, Mexican delegate to the U.N. Assembly, on May 17:

". . . We have ignored this matter too long. Far from being a scientific curiosity or a freak, this is a very human problem, one of the biggest problems of our day and we must handle it as such. The trogs are pressing from the ground at an ever-increasing rate; the Kreuzertal, or Kreuzer Valley, is inundated with trogs as if by a flood. We have heard reports, we have deliberated, we have made solemn noises, but the fact remains that every one of us is sitting on his hands. These people—we must call them people—must be settled somewhere permanently; they must be made self-supporting. This hot iron must be grasped; we fail in our responsibilities otherwise. . . ."

Excerpt from a speech, May 19, by Sir Lyandras Chandryasam, delegate from India:

". . . My esteemed colleague from Mexico has used brave words; he exhibits a humanitarianism that is unquestionably praiseworthy. But he puts forward no positive program. May I ask how many trogs have come to the surface, thus to be cared for? Is not the latest figure somewhere short of a million? I would like to point out that in India alone five million people yearly die of malnutrition or preventable disease; but no one jumps up here in the assembly to cry for a crusade to help these unfortunate victims of nature. No, it is this strange race, with no claim upon anyone, which has contributed nothing to the civilization of the world, which now we feel has first call upon our hearts and purse-strings. I say, is not this a paradoxical circumstance. . . ."

From a speech, May 20, by Dr. Karl Byrnisted, delegate from Iceland:

". . . Sir Lyandras Chandryasam's emotion is understandable, but I would like to remind him that the streets of India swarm with millions upon millions of so-called sacred cattle and apes, who eat what and where they wish, very possibly the food to keep five million persons alive. The recurrent famines in India could be relieved, I believe, by a rationalistic dealing with these parasites, and by steps to make the new birth-control clinics popular, such as a tax on babies. In this way, the Indian government, by vigorous methods, has it within its power to cope with its terrible problem. These trogs, on the other hand, are completely unable to help themselves; they are like babies flung fresh into a world where even the genial sunlight kills them. . . ."

From a speech, May 21, by Porfirio Hernandez, delegate from Mexico:

"I have been challenged to propose a positive program for dealing with the trogs. . . . I feel that as an activating principle, each member of the U.N. agree to accept a number of trogs proportionate to its national wealth, resources, and density of population. . . . Obviously the exact percentages will have to be thrashed out elsewhere. . . . I hereby move the President of the Assembly appoint such a committee, and instruct them to prepare such a recommendation, said committee to report within two weeks.

(Motion defeated, 20 to 35)

The Trog Story, June 2, by Harlan B. Temple:

"No matter how many times I walk through Trog Valley, the former Kreuzertal, I never escape a feeling of the profoundest bewilderment and awe. The trogs number now well over a million; yesterday they chiseled open four new openings into the outside world, and they are pouring out at the rate of thousands every hour. And everywhere is heard the question, where will it stop? Suppose the earth is a honeycomb, a hive, with more trogs than surface men?

"Sooner or later our organization will break down; more trogs will come up than it is within our power to feed. Organization already has failed to some extent. All the trogs are getting at least one meal a day, but not enough clothes, not enough shelter is being provided. Every day hundreds die from sunburn. I understand that the Old-Clothes-for-Trogs drive has nowhere hit its quota; I find it hard to comprehend. Is there no feeling of concern or sympathy for these people merely because they do not look like so many chorus boys and screen starlets?"

From the *Christian Science Monitor:*
CONTROVERSIAL TROG BILL
PASSES U.N. ASSEMBLY

New York, June 4: By a 35 to 20 vote—exactly reversing its first tally on the measure—the U.N. Assembly yesterday accepted the motion of Mexico's Hernandez to set up a committee for the purpose of recommending a percentage-wise distribution of trogs among member states.

Tabulation of voting on the measure found the Soviet bloc lined up with the United States and the British Commonwealth in opposition to the measure—presumably the countries which would be awarded large numbers of the trogs.

Handbill passed out at rally of the Socialist Reich (Neo-Nazi) party at Bremen, West Germany, June 10:

A NEW THREAT

COMRADES! It took a war to clean Germany of the Jews; must we now submit to an invasion of troglodyte filth? All Germany cries *no!* All Germany cries, hold our borders firm against these cretin moles! Send them to Russia; send them to the Arctic wastes! Let them return to their burrows; let them perish! But guard the Fatherland; guard the sacred German Soil!

(Rally broken up by police, handbills seized.)

Letter to the *London Times*, June 18:

To the Editor:

I speak for a large number of my acquaintances when I say that the prospect of taking to ourselves a large colony of "troglodytes" awakens in me no feeling of enthusiasm. Surely England has troubles more than enough of its own, without the added imposition of an unassimilable and non-productive minority to eat our already meager rations and raise our already sky-high taxes.

Yours, etc.,
Sir Clayman Winifred, Bart.
Lower Ditchley, Hants.

Letter to the *London Times*, June 21:

To the Editor:

Noting Sir Clayman Winifred's letter of June 18, I took a

quick check-up of my friends and was dumfounded to find how closely they hew to Sir Clayman's line. Surely this isn't our tradition, not to get under the load and help lift with everything we've got? The troglodytes are human beings, victims of a disaster we have no means of appreciating. They must be cared for, and if a qualified committee of experts sets us a quota, I say, let's bite the bullet and do our part.

The Ameriphobe section of our press takes great delight in baiting our cousins across the sea for the alleged denial of civil rights to the Negroes—which, may I add, is present in its most violent and virulent form in a country of the British Commonwealth: the Union of South Africa. What do these journalists say to evidences of the same unworthy emotion here in England?

Yours, etc.,
J. C. T. Harrodsmere
Tisley-on-Thames, Sussex.

Headline in the *New York Herald Tribune*, June 22:

FOUR NEW TROG CAMPS OPENED;
POPULATION AT TWO MILLION

Letter to the *London Times*, June 24:

To the Editor:

I read the letter of J. C. T. Harrodsmere in connection with the trog controversy with great interest. I think that in his praiseworthy efforts to have England do its bit, he is overlooking a very important fact: namely, we of England are a close-knit people, of clear clean vigorous blood, and admixture of any nature could only be for the worse. I know Mr. Harrodsmere will be quick to say, no admixture is intended. But mistakes occur, and as I understand a man-trog union to be theoretically fertile, in due course there would be a number of little half-breeds scampering like rats around our gutters, a bad show all around. There are countries where this type of mongrelization is accepted: the United States, for instance, boasts that it is the "melting pot." Why not send the trogs to the wide open spaces of the U.S. where there is room and to spare, and where they can "melt" to their heart's content?

Yours, etc.,

Col. G. P. Barstaple (Ret.), Queens Own Hussars.
Mide Hill, Warwickshire.

Letter to the *London Times*, June 28:

To the Editor:

Contrasting the bank accounts, the general air of aliveness of mongrel U.S.A. and non-mongrel England, I say, maybe it might do us good to trade off a few retired colonels for a few trogs extra to our quota. Here's to more and better mongrelization!

Yours, etc.,

(Miss) Elizabeth Darrow Brown
London, S.W.

The Trog Story, June 30, by Harlan B. Temple:

"Will it come as a surprise to my readers if I say the trog situation is getting out of hand? They are coming not slower but faster; every day we have more trogs and every day we have more at a greater rate than the day before. If the sentence sounds confused it only reflects my state of mind.

"Something has got to be done.

"Nothing is being done.

"The wrangling that is going on is a matter of public record. Each country is liberal with advice but with little else. Sweden says, send them to the center of Australia; Australia points to Greenland; Denmark would prefer the Ethiopian uplands; Ethiopia politely indicates Mexico; Mexico says, much more room in Arizona; and at Washington senators from below the Mason-Dixon Line threaten to filibuster from now till Kingdom Come rather than admit a single trog to the continental limits of the U. S. Thank the Lord for an efficient food administration! The U. N. and the world at large can be proud of the organization by which the trogs are being fed.

"Incidental Notes: trog babies are being born—over fifty yesterday."

From the *San Francisco Chronicle:*

REDS OFFER HAVEN TO TROGS
PROPOSAL STIRS WORLD

New York, July 3: Ivan Pudestov, the USSR's chief delegate to the U. N. Assembly, today blew the trog question wide open with a proposal to take complete responsibility for the trogs.

The offer startled the U.N. and took the world completely by surprise, since heretofore the Soviet delegation has held itself aloof from the bitter trog controversy, apparently in hopes that the free world would split itself apart on the problem. . . .

Editorial in the *Milwaukee Journal*, July 5, headed "A Question of Integrity":

"At first blush the Russian offer to take the trogs appears to ease our shoulders of a great weight. Here is exactly what we have been grasping for, a solution without sacrifice, a sop to our consciences, a convenient carpet to sweep our dirt under. The man in the street, and the responsible official, suddenly are telling each other that perhaps the Russians aren't so bad after all, that there's a great deal of room in Siberia, that the Russians and the trogs are both barbarians and really not so much different, that the trogs were probably Russians to begin with, etc.

"Let's break the bubble of illusion, once and for all. We can't go on forever holding our Christian integrity in one hand and our inclinations in the other. . . . Doesn't it seem an odd coincidence that while the Russians are desperately short of uranium miners at the murderous East German and Ural pits, the trogs, accustomed to life underground, might be expected to make a good labor force? . . . In effect, we would be turning over to Russia millions of slaves to be worked to death. We have rejected forced repatriation in West Europe and Korea, let's reject forced patriation and enslavement of the trogs."

Headline in the *New York Times*, July 20:

REDS BAN U. N. SUPERVISION OF TROG COMMUNITIES
SOVEREIGNTY ENDANGERED, SAYS PUDESTOV ANGRILY WITHDRAWS TROG OFFER

Headline in the *New York Daily News*, July 26:

BELGIUM OFFERS CONGO FOR TROG HABITATION ASKS FUNDS TO RECLAIM JUNGLE U.N. GIVES QUALIFIED NOD

From *The Trog Story*, July 28, by Harlan B. Temple:

"Four million (give or take a hundred thousand) trogs now breathe surface air. The Kreuzertal camps now constitute one of the world's largest cities, ranking under New York, London, Tokyo. The formerly peaceful Tyrolean valley is now a vast array of tarpaulins, circus tents, quonset huts, water tanks, and general disorder. Trog City doesn't smell too good either.

"Today might well mark the high tide in what the Austrians are calling 'the invasion from hell.' Trogs still push through a dozen gaps ten abreast, but the pressure doesn't seem so intense. Every once in a while a space appears in the ranks, where formerly they came packed like asparagus in crates. Another difference: the first trogs were meaty and fairly well nourished. These late arrivals are thin and ravenous. Whatever strange subterranean economy they practiced, it seems to have broken down completely. . . ."

From *The Trog Story*, August 1, by Harlan B. Temple:

"Something horrible is going on under the surface of the earth. Trogs are staggering forth with raw stumps for arms, with great wounds. . . ."

From *The Trog Story*, August 8, by Harlan B. Temple:

"Operation Exodus got under way today. One thousand Trogs departed the Kreuzertal bound for their new home near Cabinda, at the mouth of the Congo River. Trucks and buses took them to Innsbruck, where they will board special trains to Venice and Trieste. Here ships supplied by the U. S. Maritime Commission will take them to their new home.

"As one thousand trogs departed Trog City, twenty thousand pushed up from their underground homeland, and camp officials are privately expressing concern over conditions. Trog City has expanded double, triple, ten times over the original estimates. The machinery of supply, sanitation and housing is breaking down. From now on, any attempts to remedy the situation are at best stopgaps, like adhesive tape on a rotten hose, when what is needed is a new hose or, rather, a four-inch pipe.

"Even to maintain equilibrium, thirty thousand trogs per day will have to be siphoned out of the Kreuzertal camps, an obvious impossibility under present budgets and efforts. . . ."

From *Newsweek*, August 14:

Camp Hope, in the bush near Cabinda, last week took on the semblance of the Guadalcanal army base during World War II. There was the old familiar sense of massive confusion, the grind of bulldozers, sweating white, beet-red, brown and black skins, the raw earth dumped against primeval vegetation, bugs, salt tablets, Atabrine. . . .

From the U.P. wire:

Cabinda, Belgian Congo, August 20 (UP): The first contingent of trogs landed last night under shelter of dark, and marched to temporary quarters, under the command of specially trained group captains.

Liaison officers state that the trogs are overjoyed at the prospect of a permanent home, and show an eagerness to get to work. According to present plans, they will till collective farms, and continuously clear the jungle for additional settlers.

On the other side of the ledger, it is rumored that the native tribesmen are showing unrest. Agitators, said to be Communist-inspired, are preying on the superstitious fears of a people themselves not far removed from savagery. . . .

Headline in the *New York Times*, August 22:

CONGO WARRIORS RUN AMOK AT CAMP HOPE KILL 800 TROG SETTLERS IN SINGLE HOUR

Military Law Established
Belgian Governor Protests
Says Congo Unsuitable

From the U.P. Wire:

Trieste, August 23 (UP): Three shiploads of trogs bound for Trogland in the Congo today marked a record number of embarkations. The total number of trogs to sail from European ports now stands at 24,965.

Cabinda, August 23 (UP): The warlike Matemba Confederation is practically in a stage of revolt against further trog immigration, while Resident-General Bernard Cassou professes grave pessimism over eventualities.

Mont Blanc, August 24 (UP): Ten trogs today took up experimental residence in a ski-hut to see how well trogs can cope with the rigors of cold weather.

Announcement of this experiment goes to confirm a rumor that Denmark has offered Greenland to the trogs if it is found that they are able to survive Arctic conditions.

Cabinda, August 28 (UP): The Congo, home of witch-doctors, tribal dances, cannibalism and Tarzan, seethes with native unrest. Sullen anger smolders in the villages, riots are frequent and dozens of native workmen at Camp Hope have been killed or hospitalized.

Needless to say, the trogs, whose advent precipitated the crisis, are segregated far apart from contact with the natives, to avoid a repetition of the bloodbath of August 22. . . .

Cabinda, August 29 (UP): Resident-General Bernard Cassou today refused to allow debarkation of trogs from four ships standing off Cabinda roadstead.

Mont Blanc, September 2 (UP): The veil of secrecy at the experimental trog home was lifted a significant crack this morning, when the bodies of two trogs were taken down to Chamonix via the ski-lift.

From *The Trog Story*, September 10, by Harlan B. Temple:

"It is one A.M.; I've just come down from Camp No. 4. The trog columns have dwindled to a straggle of old, crippled, diseased. The stench is frightful. . . . But why go on? Frankly, I'm heartsick. I wish I had never taken on this assignment. It's doing something terrible to my soul; my hair is literally turning gray. I pause a moment, the noise of my typewriter stops, I listen to the vast murmur through the Kreuzertal; despondency, futility, despair come at me in a wave. Most of us here at Trog City, I think, feel the same.

"There are now five or six million trogs in the camp; no one knows the exact count; no one even cares. The situation has passed that point. The flow has dwindled, one merciful dispensation—in fact, at Camp No. 4 you can hear the rumble of the lava rising into the trog caverns.

"Morale is going from bad to worse here at Trog City. Every day a dozen of the unpaid volunteers throw up their hands, and go home. I can't say as I blame them. Lord knows they've given the best they have, and no one backs them up. Everywhere in the world it's the same story, with everyone pointing to someone else. It's enough to make a man sick. In fact it has. I'm sick—desperately sick.

"But you don't read *The Trog Story* to hear me gripe. You want factual reporting. Very well, here it is. Big news today was that movement of trogs out of the camp to Trieste has been held up pending clarification of the Congo situation. Otherwise, everything's the same here—hunger, smell, careless trogs dying of sunburn. . . ."

Headline in the *New York Times*, September 20:

**TROG QUOTA PROBLEM RETURNED TO
STUDY GROUP FOR ADJUSTMENT**

From the U. P. Wire:

Cabinda, September 25 (UP): Eight ships, loaded with 9,462 trog refugees, still wait at anchor, as native chieftains reiterated their opposition to trog immigration. . . .

Trog City, October 8 (UP): The trog migration is at its end. Yesterday for the first time no new trogs came up from below, leaving the estimated population of Trog City at six million.

New York, October 13 (UP): Deadlock still grips the Trog Resettlement Committee, with the original positions, for the most part, unchanged. Densely populated countries claim they have no room and no jobs; the underdeveloped states insist that they have not enough money to feed their own mouths. The U.S., with both room and money, already has serious minority headaches and doesn't want new ones. . . .

Chamonix, France, October 18 (UP): The Trog Experimental Station closed its doors yesterday, with one survivor of the original ten trogs riding the ski-lift back down the slopes of Mont Blanc.

Dr. Sven Emeldson, director of the station, released the following statement: "Our work proves that the trogs, even if provided shelter adequate for a European, cannot stand the rigors of the North; they seem especially sensitive to pulmonary ailments. . . ."

New York, October 26 (UP): After weeks of acrimony, a revised set of trog immigration quotas was released for action by the U.N. Assembly. Typical figures are: USA 31%, USSR 16%, Canada 8%, Australia 8%, France 6%, Mexico 6%.

New York, October 30 (UP): The USSR adamantly rejects the principle of U.N. checking of the trog resettlement areas inside the USSR. . . .

New York, October 31 (UP): Senator Bullrod of Mississippi today promised to talk till his "lungs came out at the elbows" before he would allow the Trog Resettlement Bill to come to a vote before the Senate. An informal check revealed insufficient strength to impose cloture. . . .

St. Arlberg, Austria, November 5 (UP): First snow of the season fell last night. . . .

Trog City, November 10 (UP): Last night, frost lay a sparkling sheath across the valley. . . .

Trog City, November 15 (UP): Trog sufferers from influenza have been isolated in a special section. . . .

Buenos Aires, November 23 (UP): Dictator Peron today flatly refused to meet the Argentine quota of relief supplies to Trog City until some definite commitment has been made by the U.N. . . .

Trog City, December 2 (UP): Influenza following the snow and rain of the last week has made a new onslaught on the trogs; camp authorities are desperately trying to cope with the epidemic. . . .

Trog City, December 8 (UP): Two crematoriums, fired by fuel oil, are roaring full time in an effort to keep ahead of the mounting influenza casualties. . . .

From *The Trog Story*, December 13, by Harlan B. Temple:

"This is it. . . ."

From the U. P. Wire:

Los Angeles, December 14 (UP): The Christmas buying rush got under way early this year, in spite of unseasonably bad weather. . . .

Trog City, December 15 (UP): A desperate appeal for penicillin, sulfa, blankets, kerosene heaters, and trained personnel was sounded today by Camp Commandant Howard Kerkovits. He admitted that disease among the trogs was completely out of control, beyond all human power to cope with. . . .

From *The Trog Story*, December 23, by Harlan B. Temple:

"I don't know why I should be sitting here writing this, because—since there are no more trogs—there is no more trog story. But I am seized by an irresistible urge to 'tell-off' a rotten, inhumane world. . . ."

The Liberation of Earth

William Tenn (1920-)

WILLIAM *Tenn was one of the bright stars of the fifties and a master of the short story form. His stories featured biting social satire, often on political themes, but no aspect of contemporary Western society was safe from his wit. Fortunately for science fiction fans, the great bulk of his short fiction is available to us in the form of short story collections, including* The Human Angle *(1956) and* Of All Possible Worlds *(1955). Unfortunately however, Tenn severely cut back on his science fiction after the early sixties when under his real name, Philip J. Klass, he became a professor of English at Pennsylvania State University. Recently, he has returned to science fiction with the wonderfully funny "On Venus, Have We Got a Rabbi" in Jack Dann's anthology* Wandering Stars *(1974).*

"The Liberation of Earth" shows Tenn at the top of his form. In some ways it is prophetic in that it preceded the Vietnam War, which brought home the question of just how high the price of "liberation" should be. Destroying a society in

order to save it proved too high a cost for us or the Vietnamese to bear. Tenn's story is a savage attack on the arrogance of power, from "making the world safe for democracy" to the "liberation" of Eastern Europe after World War II by Soviet forces, which may have been what he was writing about.

From *Future Science Fiction* 1953

This then, is the story of our liberation. Suck air and grab clusters. Heigh-ho, here is the tale.

August was the month, a Tuesday in August. These words are meaningless now, so far have we progressed; but many things known and discussed by our primitive ancestors, our unliberated, unreconstructed forefathers, are devoid of sense to our free minds. Still the tale must be told, with all of its incredible place-names and vanished points of reference.

Why must it be told? Have any of you a *better* thing to do? We have had water and weeds and lie in a valley of gusts. So rest, relax and listen. And suck air, suck air.

On a Tuesday in August, the ship appeared in the sky over France in a part of the world then known as Europe. Five miles long the ship was, and word has come down to us that it looked like an enormous silver cigar.

The tale goes on to tell of the panic and consternation among our forefathers when the ship abruptly materialized in the summer-blue sky. How they ran, how they shouted, how they pointed!

How they excitedly notified the United Nations, one of their chiefest institutions, that a strange metal craft of incredible size had materialized over their land. How they sent an order *here* to cause military aircraft to surround it with loaded weapons, gave instructions *there* for hastily grouped scientists, with signaling apparatus, to approach it with friendly gestures. How, under the great ship, men with cameras took pictures of it; men with typewriters wrote stories about it; and men with concessions sold models of it.

All these things did our ancestors, enslaved and unknowing, do.

Then a tremendous slab snapped up in the middle of the ship and the first of the aliens stepped out in the complex tripodal gait that all humans were shortly to know and love so well. He wore a metallic garment to protect him from the effects of our atmospheric peculiarities, a garment of the opaque, loosely folded type that these, the first of our liberators, wore throughout their stay on Earth.

Speaking in a language none could understand, but booming deafeningly through a huge mouth about halfway up his twenty-five feet of height, the alien discoursed for exactly one hour, waited politely for a response when he had finished, and receiving none, retired into the ship.

That night, the first of our liberation! Or the first of our first liberation, should I say? *That* night, anyhow! Visualize our ancestors scurrying about their primitive intricacies: playing ice-hockey, televising, smashing atoms, red-baiting, conducting giveaway shows and signing affidavits—all the incredible minutiae that made the olden times such a frightful mass of cumulative detail in which to live—as compared with the breathless and majestic simplicity of the present.

The big question, of course, was—what had the alien said? Had he called on the human race to surrender? Had he announced that he was on a mission of peaceful trade and, having made what he considered a reasonable offer—for, let us say, the north polar ice-cap—politely withdrawn so that we could discuss his terms among ourselves in relative privacy? Or, possibly, had he merely announced that he was the newly appointed ambassador to Earth from a friendly and intelligent race—and would we please direct him to the proper authority so that he might submit his credentials?

Not to know was quite maddening.

Since decision rested with the diplomats, it was the last possibility which was held, very late that night, to be most likely; and early the next morning, accordingly, a delegation from the United Nations waited under the belly of the motionless star-ship. The delegation had been instructed to welcome the aliens to the outermost limits of its collective linguistic ability. As an additional earnest of mankind's friendly intentions, all military craft patrolling the air about the great ship were ordered to carry no more than one atom-bomb in their racks, and to fly a small white flag—along with the U.N. banner and their own national emblem. Thus did our ancestors face this, the ultimate challenge of history.

When the alien came forth a few hours later, the delegation stepped up to him, bowed, and, in the three official languages of the United Nations—English, French and Russian—asked him to consider this planet his home. He listened to them gravely, and then launched into his talk of the day before—which was evidently as highly charged with emotion and significance to him as it was completely incomprehensible to the representatives of world government.

Fortunately, a cultivated young Indian member of the secretariat detected a suspicious similarity between the speech of the alien and an obscure Bengali dialect whose anomalies he had once puzzled over. The reason, as we all know now, was that the last time Earth had been visited by aliens of this particular type, humanity's most advanced civilization lay in a moist valley in Bengal; extensive dictionaries of that language had been written, so that speech with the natives of Earth would present no problem to any subsequent exploring party.

However, I move ahead of my tale, as one who would munch on the succulent roots before the drier stem. Let me rest and suck air for a moment. Heigh-ho, truly those were tremendous experiences for our kind.

You, sir, now you sit back and listen. You are not yet of an age to Tell the Tale. I remember, *well enough do I remember* how my father told it, and his father before him. You will wait your turn as I did; you listen until too much high land between water holes blocks me off from life.

Then *you* may take your place in the juiciest weed patch and, reclining gracefully between sprints, recite the great epic of our liberation to the carelessly exercising young.

Pursuant to the young Hindu's suggestions, the one professor of comparative linguistics in the world capable of understanding and conversing in this peculiar version of the dead dialect was summoned from an academic convention in New York where he was reading a paper he had been working on for eighteen years: *An Initial Study of Apparent Relationships Between Several Past Participles in Ancient Sanskrit and an Equal Number of Noun Substantives in Modern Szechuanese.*

Yea, verily, all these things—and more, many more—did our ancestors in their besotted ignorance contrive to do. May we not count our freedoms indeed?

The disgruntled scholar, minus—as he kept insisting bitterly—some of his most essential word lists, was flown by fastest jet to the area south of Nancy which, in those long-ago days, lay in the enormous black shadow of the alien spaceship.

Here he was acquainted with his task by the United Nations delegation, whose nervousness had not been allayed by a new and disconcerting development. Several more aliens had emerged from the ship carrying great quantities of immense, shimmering metal which they proceeded to assemble into something that was obviously a machine—though it was taller than any skyscraper man had ever built, and seemed to make noises to itself like a talkative and sentient creature. The first alien still stood courteously in the neighborhood of the profusely perspiring diplomats; ever and anon he would go through his little speech again, in a language that had been almost forgotten when the cornerstone of the library of Alexandria was laid. The men from the U.N. would reply, each one hoping desperately to make up for the alien's lack of familiarity with his own tongue by such devices as hand gestures and facial expressions. Much later, a commission of anthropologists and psychologists brilliantly pointed out the difficulties of such physical, gestural communication with creatures possessing—as these aliens did—five manual appendages and a single, unwinking compound eye of the type the insects rejoice in.

The problems and agonies of the professor as he was trundled about the world in the wake of the aliens, trying to amass a usable vocabulary in a language whose peculiarities he could only extrapolate from the limited samples suppled him by one who must inevitably speak it with the most outlandish of foreign accents—these vexations were minor indeed compared to the disquiet felt by the representatives of world government. They beheld the extra-terrestrial visitors move every day to a new site on their planet and proceed to assemble there a titanic structure of flickering metal which muttered nostalgically to itself, as if to keep alive the memory of those faraway factories which had given it birth.

True, there was always the alien who would pause in his evidently supervisory labors to release the set little speech; but not even the excellent manners he displayed, in listening to upward of fifty-six replies in as many languages, helped dispel the panic caused whenever a human scientist, investigating the shimmering machines, touched a projecting edge and promptly shrank into a disappearing pinpoint. This, while not a frequent occurrence, happened often enough to cause chronic indigestion and insomnia among human administrators.

Finally, having used up most of his nervous system as fuel, the professor collated enough of the language to make conversation possible. He—and, through him, the world—was thereupon told the following:

The aliens were members of a highly advanced civilization

which had spread its culture throughout the entire galaxy. Cognizant of the limitations of the as-yet-underdeveloped animals who had latterly become dominant upon Earth, they had placed us in a sort of benevolent ostracism. Until either we or our institutions had evolved to a level permitting, say, at least *associate* membership in the galactic federation (under the sponsoring tutelage, for the first few millennia, of one of the older, more widespread and more important species in that federation)—until that time, all invasions of our privacy and ignorance—except for a few scientific expeditions conducted under conditions of great secrecy—had been strictly forbidden by universal agreement.

Several individuals who had violated this ruling—at great cost to our racial sanity, and enormous profit to our reigning religions—had been so promptly and severely punished that no known infringements had occurred for some time. Our recent growth-curve had been satisfactory enough to cause hopes that a bare thirty or forty centuries more would suffice to place us on applicant status with the federation.

Unfortunately, the peoples of this stellar community were many, and varied as greatly in their ethical outlook as their biological composition. Quite a few species lagged a considerable social distance behind the Dendi, as our visitors called themselves. One of these, a race of horrible, worm-like organisms known as the Troxxt—almost as advanced technologically as they were retarded in moral development—had suddenly volunteered for the position of sole and absolute ruler of the galaxy. They had seized control of several key suns, with their attendant planetary systems, and, after a calculated decimation of the races thus captured, had announced their intention of punishing with a merciless extinction all species unable to appreciate from these object-lessons the value of unconditional surrender.

In despair, the galactic federation had turned to the Dendi, one of the oldest, most selfless, and yet most powerful of races in civilized space, and commissioned them—as the military arm of the federation—to hunt down the Troxxt, defeat them wherever they had gained illegal suzerainty, and destroy forever their power to wage war. This order had come almost too late. Everywhere the Troxxt had gained so much the advantage of attack, that the Dendi were able to contain them only by enormous sacrifice. For centuries now, the conflict had careened across our vast island universe. In the course of it, densely populated planets had been disintegrated; suns had been blasted into novae; and whole groups of stars ground into swirling cosmic dust.

A temporary stalemate had been reached a short while ago, and—reeling and breathless—both sides were using the lull to strengthen weak spots in their perimeter.

Thus, the Troxxt had finally moved into the till-then peaceful section of space that contained our solar system—among others. They were thoroughly uninterested in our tiny planet with its meager resources; nor did they care much for such celestial neighbors as Mars or Jupiter. They established their headquarters on a planet of Proxima Centaurus—the star nearest our own sun—and proceeded to consolidate their offensive-defensive network between Rigel and Aldebaran. At this point in their explanation, the Dendi pointed out, the exigencies of interstellar strategy tended to become too complicated for anything but three-dimensional maps; let us here accept the simple statement, they suggested, that it became immediately vital for them to strike rapidly, and make the Troxxt position on Proxima Centaurus untenable—to establish a base inside their lines of communication.

The most likely spot for such a base was Earth.

The Dendi apologized profusely for intruding on our development, an intrusion which might cost us dear in our delicate developmental state. But, as they explained—in impeccable pre-Bengali—before their arrival we had, in effect, become (all unknowingly) a satrapy of the awful Troxxt. We could now consider ourselves liberated.

We thanked them much for that.

Besides, their leader pointed out proudly, the Dendi were engaged in a war for the sake of civilization itself, against an enemy so horrible, so obscene in its nature, and so utterly filthy in its practices, that it was unworthy of the label of intelligent life. They were fighting, not only for themselves, but for every loyal member of the galactic federation; for every small and helpless species; for every obscure race too weak to defend itself against a ravaging conqueror. Would humanity stand aloof from such a conflict?

There was just a slight bit of hesitation as the information was digested. Then—"No!" humanity roared back through such mass-communication media as television, newspapers, reverberating jungle drums, and mule-mounted backwoods messenger. *"We will not stand aloof! We will help you destroy this menace to the very fabric of civilization! Just tell us what you want us to do!"*

Well, nothing in particular, the aliens replied with some embarrassment. Possibly in a little while there might be something—several little things, in fact—which could be *quite* useful; but, for the moment, if we would concentrate on not getting in their way when they serviced their gun mounts, they would be very grateful, really. . . .

This reply tended to create a large amount of uncertainty among the two billion of Earth's human population. For several days afterward, there was a planet-wide tendency—the legend has come down to us—of people failing to meet each other's eyes.

But then Man rallied from this substantial blow to his pride. He would be useful, be it ever so humbly, to the race which had liberated him from potential subjugation by the ineffably ugly Troxxt. For this, let us remember well our ancestors! Let us hymn their sincere efforts amid their ignorance!

All standing armies, all air and sea fleets, were reorganized into guard-patrols around the Dendi weapons: no human might approach within two miles of the murmuring machinery, without a pass countersigned by the Dendi. Since they were never known to sign such a pass during the entire period of their stay on this planet, however, this loophole-provision was never exercised as far as is known; and the immediate neighborhood of the extra-terrestrial weapons became and remained henceforth wholesomely free of two-legged creatures.

Cooperation with our liberators took precedence over all other human activities. The order of the day was a slogan first given voice by a Harvard professor of government in a querulous radio round table on "Man's Place in a Somewhat Over-Civilized Universe."

"Let us forget our individual egos and collective conceits," the professor cried at one point. "Let us subordinate everything—to the end that the freedom of the solar system in general, and Earth in particular, must and shall be preserved!"

Despite its mouth-filling qualities, this slogan was repeated everywhere. Still, it was difficult sometimes to know exactly what the Dendi wanted—partly because of the limited number of interpreters available to the heads of the various sovereign states, and partly because of their leader's tendency to vanish into his ship after ambiguous and equivocal statements—such as the curt admonition to "Evacuate Washington!"

On that occasion, both the Secretary of State and the American President perspired fearfully through five hours of a July day in all the silk-hatted, stiff-collared, dark-suited diplomatic regalia that the barbaric past demanded of political leaders who would deal with the representatives of another people. They waited and wilted beneath the enormous ship—which no human had ever been invited to enter, despite the wistful hints constantly thrown out by university professors and aeronautical designers—they waited patiently and wetly for the Dendi leader to emerge and let them know whether he had meant the State of Washington or Washington, D.C.

The tale comes down to us at this point as a tale of glory. The capitol building taken apart in a few days, and set up almost intact in the foothills of the Rocky Mountains; the missing Archives, that were later to turn up in the Children's Room of a Public Library in Duluth, Iowa; the bottles of Potomac River water carefully borne westward and ceremoniously poured into the circular concrete ditch built around the President's mansion (from which unfortunately it was to evaporate within a week because of the relatively low humidity of the region)—all these are proud moments in the galactic history of our species, from which not even the later knowledge that the Dendi wished to build no gun site on the spot, nor even an ammunition dump, but merely a recreation hall for their troops, could remove any of the grandeur of our determined cooperation and most willing sacrifice.

There is no denying, however, that the ego of our race was greatly damaged by the discovery, in the course of a routine journalistic interview, that the aliens totaled no more powerful a group than a squad; and that their leader, instead of the great scientist and key military strategist that we might justifiably have expected the Galactic Federation to furnish for the protection of Terra, ranked as the interstellar equivalent of a buck sergeant.

That the President of the United States, the Commander-in-Chief of the Army and the Navy, had waited in such obeisant fashion upon a mere noncommissioned officer was hard for us to swallow; but that the impending Battle of Earth was to have a historical dignity only slightly higher than that of a patrol action was impossibly humiliating.

And then there was the matter of "lendi."

The aliens, while installing or servicing their planet-wide weapon system, would occasionally fling aside an evidently unusable fragment of the talking metal. Separated from the machine of which it had been a component, the substance seemed to lose all those qualities which were deleterious to mankind and retain several which were quite useful indeed. For example, if a portion of the strange material was attached to any terrestrial metal—and insulated carefully from contact with other substances—it would, in a few hours, itself become exactly the metal that it touched, whether that happened to be zinc, gold, or pure uranium.

This stuff—"lendi," men have heard the aliens call it—was shortly in frantic demand in an economy ruptured by constant and unexpected emptyings of its most important industrial centers.

Everywhere the aliens went, to and from their weapon sites, hordes of ragged humans stood chanting—well outside the two-mile limit—"Any lendi, Dendi?" All attempts by law-enforcement agencies of the planet to put a stop to this shameless, wholesale begging were useless—especially since the Dendi themselves seemed to get some unexplainable pleasure out of scattering tiny pieces of lendi to the scrabbling multitude. When policemen and soldiery began to join the trampling, murderous dash to the corner of the meadows wherein had fallen the highly versatile and garrulous metal, governments gave up.

Mankind almost began to hope for the attack to come, so that it would be relieved of the festering consideration of its own patent inferiorities. A few of the more fanatically conservative among our ancestors probably even began to regret liberation.

They did, children; they did! Let us hope that these would-be troglodytes were among the very first to be dissolved and melted down by the red flame-balls. One cannot, after all, turn one's back on progress!

Two days before the month of September was over, the aliens announced that they had detected activity upon one of the moons of Saturn. The Troxxt were evidently threading their treacherous way inward through the solar system. Considering their vicious and deceitful propensities, the Dendi warned, an attack from these worm-like monstrosities might be expected at any moment.

Few humans went to sleep as the night rolled up to and past the meridian on which they dwelt. Almost all eyes were lifted to a sky carefully denuded of clouds by watchful Dendi. There was a brisk trade in cheap telescopes and bits of smoked glass in some sections of the planet; while other portions experienced a substantial boom in spells and charms of the all-inclusive, or omnibus, variety.

The Troxxt attacked in three cylindrical black ships simultaneously; one in the Southern Hemisphere, and two in the Northern. Great gouts of green flame roared out of their tiny craft; and everything touched by this imploded into a translucent, glass-like sand. No Dendi was hurt by these, however, and from each of the now-writhing gun mounts there bubbled forth a series of scarlet clouds which pursued the Troxxt hungrily, until forced by a dwindling velocity to fall back upon Earth.

Here they had an unhappy after-effect. Any populated area into which these pale pink cloudlets chanced to fall was rapidly transformed into a cemetery—a cemetery, if the truth be told as it has been handed down to us, that had more the odor of the kitchen than the grave. The inhabitants of these unfortunate localities were subjected to enormous increases of temperature. Their skin reddened, then blackened; their hair and nails shriveled; their very flesh turned into liquid and boiled off their bones. Altogether a disagreeable way for one-tenth of the human race to die.

The only consolation was the capture of a black cylinder by one of the red clouds. When, as a result of this, it had turned white-hot and poured its substance down in the form of a metallic rainstorm, the two ships assaulting the Northern Hemisphere abruptly retreated to the asteroids into which the

Dendi—because of severely limited numbers—steadfastly re-fused to pursue them.

In the next twenty-four hours the aliens—*resident* aliens, let us say—held conferences, made repairs to their weapons and commiserated with us. Humanity buried its dead. This last was a custom of our forefathers that was most worthy of note; and one that has not, of course, survived into modern times.

By the time the Troxxt returned, Man was ready for them. He could not, unfortunately, stand to arms as he most ardently desired to do; but he could and did stand to optical instrument and conjurer's oration.

Once more the little red clouds burst joyfully into the upper reaches of the stratosphere; once more the green flames wailed and tore at the chattering spires of lendi; once more men died by the thousands in the boiling backwash of war. But this time, there was a slight difference: the green flames of the Troxxt abruptly changed color after the engagement had lasted three hours; they became darker, more bluish. And, as they did so, Dendi after Dendi collapsed at his station and died in convulsions.

The call for retreat was evidently sounded. The survivors fought their way to the tremendous ship in which they had come. With an explosion from her stern jets that blasted a red-hot furrow southward through France, and kicked Marseilles into the Mediterranean, the ship roared into space and fled home ignominiously.

Humanity steeled itself for the coming ordeal of horror under the Troxxt.

They were truly worm-like in form. As soon as the two night-black cylinders had landed, they strode from their ships, their tiny segmented bodies held off the ground by a complex harness supported by long and slender metal crutches. They erected a dome-like fort around each ship—one in Australia and one in the Ukraine—captured the few courageous indi-viduals who had ventured close to their landing sites, and disappeared back into the dark craft with their squirming prizes.

While some men drilled about nervously in the ancient military patterns, others pored anxiously over scientific texts and records pertaining to the visit of the Dendi—in the desperate hope of finding a way of preserving terrestrial independence against this ravening conqueror of the star-spattered galaxy.

And yet all this time, the human captives inside the artificially darkened space-ships (the Troxxt, having no eyes, not only had little use for light but the more sedentary individuals among them actually found such radiation disagreeable to their sensitive, unpigmented skins) were not being tortured for information—nor vivisected in the earnest quest of knowledge on a slightly higher level—but educated.

Educated in the Troxxtian language, that is.

True it was that a large number found themselves utterly inadequate for the task which the Troxxt had set them, and temporarily became servants to the more successful students. And another, albeit smaller, group developed various forms of frustration hysteria—ranging from mild unhappiness to complete catatonic depression—over the difficulties presented by a language whose every verb was irregular, and whose myriads of prepositions were formed by noun-adjective combinations derived from the subject of the previous sentence. But, eventually, eleven human beings were released, to blink madly in the sunlight as certified interpreters of Troxxt.

These liberators, it seemed, had never visited Bengal in the heyday of its millennia-past civilization.

Yes, these *liberators*. For the Troxxt had landed on the sixth day of the ancient, almost mythical month of October. And October the Sixth is, of course, the Holy Day of the second Liberation. Let us remember, let us revere. (If only we could figure out which day it is on our calendar!)

The tale the interpreters told caused men to hang their heads in shame and gnash their teeth at the deception they had allowed the Dendi to practice upon them.

True, the Dendi had been commissioned by the Galactic Federation to hunt the Troxxt down and destroy them. This was largely because the Dendi *were* the Galactic Federation. One of the first intelligent arrivals on the interstellar scene, the huge creatures had organized a vast police force to protect them and their power against any contingency of revolt that might arise in the future. This police force was ostensibly a congress of all thinking life forms throughout the galaxy; actually, it was an efficient means of keeping them under rigid control.

Most species thus-far discovered were docile and tractable, however; the Dendi had been ruling from time immemorial, said they—very well, then, let the Dendi continue to rule. Did it make that much difference?

But, throughout the centuries, opposition to the Dendi grew —and the nuclei of the opposition were the protoplasm-based creatures. What, in fact, had come to be known as the Protoplasmic League.

Though small in number, the creatures whose life cycles were derived from the chemical and physical properties of protoplasm varied greatly in size, structure, and specialization. A galactic community deriving the main wells of its power from them would be a dynamic instead of a static place, where extra-galactic travel would be encouraged, instead of being inhibited, as it was at present because of Dendi fears of meeting a superior civilization. It would be a true democracy of species—a real biological republic—where all creatures of adequate intelligence and cultural development would enjoy a control of their destinies at present experienced by the silicon-based Dendi alone.

To this end, the Troxxt—the only important race which had steadfastly refused the complete surrender of armaments demanded of all members of the Federation—had been implored by a minor member of the Protoplasmic League to rescue it from the devastation which the Dendi intended to visit upon it, as punishment for an unlawful exploratory excursion outside the boundaries of the galaxy.

Faced with the determination of the Troxxt to defend their cousins in organic chemistry, and the suddenly aroused hostility of at least two-thirds of the interstellar peoples, the Dendi had summoned a rump meeting of the Galactic Council; declared a state of revolt in being; and proceeded to cement their disintegrating rule with the blasted life-forces of a hundred worlds. The Troxxt, hopelessly outnumbered and out-equipped, had been able to continue the struggle only because of the great ingenuity and selflessness of other members of the Protoplasmic League, who had risked extinction to supply them with newly developed secret weapons.

Hadn't we guessed the nature of the beast from the enormous precautions it had taken to prevent the exposure of any part of its body to the intensely corrosive atmosphere of Earth? Surely the seamless, barely translucent suits which our recent visitors had worn for every moment of their stay on our world should have made us suspect a body chemistry developed from complex silicon compounds rather than those of carbon?

Humanity hung its collective head and admitted that the suspicion had never occurred to it.

Well, the Troxxt admitted generously, we were extremely inexperienced and possibly a little too trusting. Put it down to that. Our naiveté, however costly to them—our liberators—would not be allowed to deprive us of that complete citizenship which the Troxxt were claiming as the birthright of all.

But as for our leaders, our probably corrupted, certainly irresponsible leaders. . . .

The first executions of U.N. officials, heads of states, and pre-Bengali interpreters as "Traitors to Protoplasm"—after some of the lengthiest and most nearly-perfectly-fair trials in the history of Earth—were held a week after G-J Day, the inspiring occasion on which—amidst gorgeous ceremonies—Humanity was invited to join, first the Protoplasmic League and thence the New and Democratic Galactic Federation of All Species, All Races.

Nor was that all. Whereas the Dendi had contemptuously shoved us to one side as they went about their business of making our planet safe for tyranny, and had—in all probability—built special devices which made the very touch of their weapons fatal for us, the Troxxt—with the sincere friendliness which had made their name a byword for democracy and decency wherever living creatures came together among the stars—our Second Liberators, as we lovingly called them, actually *preferred* to have us help them with the intensive, accelerating labor of planetary defense.

So men's intestines dissolved under the invisible glare of the forces used to assemble the new, incredibly complex weapons; men sickened and died, in scrabbling hordes, inside the mines which the Troxxt had made deeper than any we had dug hitherto; men's bodies broke open and exploded in the undersea oil-drilling sites which the Troxxt had declared were essential.

Children's schooldays were requested, too, in such collecting drives as "Platinum Scrap for Procyon" and "Radioactive Debris for Deneb." Housewives also were implored to save on salt whenever possible—this substance being useful to the Troxxt in literally dozens of incomprehensible ways—and colorful posters reminded: "*Don't salinate—sugarfy!*"

And over all—courteously caring for us like an intelligent parent—were our mentors, taking their giant supervisory strides on metallic crutches, while their pale little bodies lay curled in the hammocks that swung from each paired length of shining leg.

Truly, even in the midst of a complete economic paralysis caused by the concentration of all major productive facilities on other-worldly armaments, and despite the anguished cries of those suffering from peculiar industrial injuries which our medical men were totally unequipped to handle, in the midst

of all this mind-wracking disorganization, it was yet very ex-
hilarating to realize that we had taken our lawful place in the
future government of the galaxy and were even now helping
to make the Universe Safe for Democracy.

But the Dendi returned to smash this idyll. They came in their
huge, silvery space-ships and the Troxxt, barely warned in
time, just managed to rally under the blow and fight back in
kind. Even so, the Troxxt ship in the Ukraine was almost
immediately forced to flee to its base in the depths of space.
After three days, the only Troxxt on Earth were the devoted
members of a little band guarding the ship in Australia. They
proved, in three or more months, to be as difficult to remove
from the face of our planet as the continent itself; and since
there was now a state of close and hostile siege, with the Dendi
on one side of the globe, and the Troxxt on the other, the
battle assumed frightful proportions.

Seas boiled; whole steppes burned away; the climate itself
shifted and changed under the gruelling pressure of the
cataclysm. By the time the Dendi solved the problem, the
planet Venus had been blasted from the skies in the course of
a complicated battle maneuver, and Earth had wobbled over
as orbital substitute.

The solution was simple: since the Troxxt were too firmly
based on the small continent to be driven away, the numeri-
cally superior Dendi brought up enough firepower to disin-
tegrate all Australia into an ash that muddied the Pacific. This
occurred on the twenty-fourth of June, the Holy Day of First
Reliberation. A day of reckoning for what remained of the
human race, however.

How could we have been so naive, the Dendi wanted to
know, as to be taken in by the chauvinistic pro-protoplasm
propaganda? Surely, if physical characteristics were to be the
criteria of our racial empathy, we would not orient ourselves
on a narrow chemical basis! The Dendi life-plasma was based
on silicon instead of carbon, true, but did not vertebrates—

appendaged vertebrates, at that, such as we and the Dendi—
have infinitely more in common, in spite of a *minor* biochemi-
cal difference or two, than vertebrates and legless, armless,
slime-crawling creatures who happened, quite accidentally, to
possess an identical organic substance?

As for this fantastic picture of life in the galaxy. . . . *Well!*
The Dendi shrugged their quintuple shoulders as they went
about the intricate business of erecting their noisy weapons all
over the rubble of our planet. Had we ever seen a representative of these protoplasmic races the Troxxt were supposedly
protecting? No, nor would we. For as soon as a race—animal,
vegetable or mineral—developed enough to constitute even a
potential danger to the sinuous aggressors, its civilization was
systematically dismantled by the watchful Troxxt. We were in
so primitive a state that they had not considered it at all risky
to allow us the outward seeming of full participation.

Could we say we had learned a single useful piece of information about Troxxt technology—for all of the work we had
done on their machines, for all of the lives we had lost in the
process? No, of course not! We had merely contributed our
mite to the enslavement of far-off races who had done us no
harm.

There was much that we had cause to feel guilty about, the
Dendi told us gravely—once the few surviving interpreters of
the pre-Bengali dialect had crawled out of hiding. But our
collective onus was as nothing compared to that borne by
"vermicular collaborationists"—those traitors who had sup-
planted our martyred former leaders. And then there were the
unspeakable human interpreters who had had linguistic traffic
with creatures destroying a two-million-year-old galactic
peace! Why, killing was almost too good for them, the Dendi
murmured as they killed them.

When the Troxxt ripped their way back into possession of
Earth some eighteen months later, bringing us the sweet fruits
of the Second Reliberation—as well as a complete and most

convincing rebuttal of the Dendi—there were few humans found who were willing to accept with any real enthusiasm the responsibilities of newly opened and highly paid positions in language, science, and government.

Of course, since the Troxxt, in order to reliberate Earth, had found it necessary to blast a tremendous chunk out of the northern hemisphere, there were very few humans to be found in the first place. . . .

Even so, many of these committed suicide rather than as- sume the title of Secretary General of the United Nations when the Dendi came back for the glorious Re-Reliberation, a short time after that. This was the liberation, by the way, which swept the deep collar of matter off our planet, and gave it what our forefathers came to call a pear-shaped look.

Possibly it was at this time—possibly a liberation or so later —that the Troxxt and the Dendi discovered the Earth had become far too eccentric in its orbit to possess the minimum safety conditions demanded of a Combat Zone. The battle, therefore, zig-zagged coruscatingly and murderously away in the direction of Aldebaran.

That was nine generations ago, but the tale that has been handed down from parent to child, to child's child, has lost little in the telling. You hear it now from me almost exactly as I heard it. From my father I heard it as I ran with him from water puddle to distant water puddle, across the searing heat of yellow sand. From my mother I heard it as we sucked air and frantically grabbed at clusters of thick green weed, when- ever the planet beneath us quivered in omen of a geographical spasm that might bury us in its burned-out body, or a cosmic gyration threatened to fling us into empty space.

Yes, even as we do now did we do then, telling the same tale, running the same frantic race across miles of unendur- able heat for food and water; fighting the same savage battles with the giant rabbits for each other's carrion—and always, ever and always, sucking desperately at the precious air, which leaves our world in greater quantities with every mad twist of its orbit.

Naked, hungry, and thirsty came we into the world, and naked, hungry, and thirsty do we scamper our lives out upon it, under the huge and never-changing sun.

The same tale it is, and the same traditional ending it has as that I had from my father and his father before him. Suck air, grab clusters, and hear the last holy observation of our history:

"Looking about us, we can say with pardonable pride that we have been about as thoroughly liberated as it is possible for a race and a planet to be!"

A Bad Day for Sales

Fritz Leiber (1910-   )

FRITZ *Leiber is an eclectic science-fiction writer, capable of producing first-rate work in a wide variety of modes—heroic fantasy (the Grey Mouser series), hard science ("A Pail of Air"), straight fantasy (the classic* Conjure Wife, *1953),* high adventure (the Hugo winning The Wanderer, *1964 and* The Big Time, *1958), and thoughtful social science fiction like* Gather, Darkness *(1950),* The Green Millennium *(1953), and* The Silver Eggheads *(1959).*

In "A Bad Day for Sales" Leiber writes of a future based on the present—American business still shows no concern for anything other than the profit motive, even in the face of disaster. The impulse to sell is powerful in modern corporate man—and in his creations.

From *Galaxy Science Fiction*   1953

The big bright doors parted with a *whoosh* and Robie glided suavely onto Times Square. The crowd that had been watching the fifty-foot tall clothing-ad girl get dressed, or reading

156

the latest news about the Hot Truce scrawl itself in yard-high script, hurried to look.

Robie was still a novelty. Robie was fun. For a little while yet he could steal the show.

But the attention did not make Robie proud. He had no more vanity than the pink plastic giantess, and she did not even flicker her blue mechanical eyes.

Robie radared the crowd, found that it surrounded him solidly, and stopped. With a calculated mysteriousness, he said nothing.

"Say, ma, he doesn't look like a robot at all. He looks sort of like a turtle."

Which was not completely inaccurate. The lower part of Robie's body was a metal hemisphere hemmed with sponge rubber and not quite touching the sidewalk. The upper was a metal box with black holes in it. The box could swivel and duck.

A chromium-bright hoopskirt with a turret on top.

"Reminds me too much of the Little Joe Baratanks," a veteran of the Persian War muttered, and rapidly rolled himself away on wheels rather like Robie's.

His departure made it easier for some of those who knew about Robie to open a path in the crowd. Robie headed straight for the gap. The crowd whooped.

Robie glided very slowly down the path, deftly jogging aside whenever he got too close to ankles in skylon or sock-assins. The rubber buffer on his hoopskirt was merely an added safeguard.

The boy who had called Robie a turtle jumped in the middle of the path and stood his ground, grinning foxily.

Robie stopped two feet short of him. The turret ducked. The crowd got quiet.

"Hello, youngster," Robie said in a voice that was smooth as that of a TV star, and was in fact a recording of one.

The boy stopped smiling. "Hello," he whispered.

"How old are you?" Robie asked.

"Nine. No, eight."

"That's nice," Robie observed. A metal arm shot down from his neck, stopped just short of the boy. The boy jerked back.

"For you," Robie said gently.

The boy gingerly took the red polly-lop from the neatly-fashioned blunt metal claws. A gray-haired woman whose son was a paraplegic hurried on.

After a suitable pause Robie continued, "And how about a nice refreshing drink of Poppy Pop to go with your polly-lop?" The boy lifted his eyes but didn't stop licking the candy. Robie wiggled his claws ever so slightly. "Just give me a quarter and within five seconds—"

A little girl wriggled out of the forest of legs. "Give me a polly-lop too, Robie," she demanded.

"Rita, come back here," a woman in the third rank of the crowd called angrily.

Robie scanned the newcomer gravely. His reference silhouettes were not good enough to let him distinguish the sex of children, so he merely repeated, "Hello, youngster."

"Rita!"

"Give me a polly-lop!"

Disregarding both remarks, for a good salesman is single-minded and does not waste bait, Robie said winningly, "I'll bet you read *Junior Space Killers*. Now I have here—"

"Uh-hhh, I'm a girl. *He* got a polly-lop."

At the word "girl" Robie broke off. Rather ponderously he said, "Then—" After another pause he continued, "I'll bet you read *Gee-Gee Jones, Space Stripper*. Now I have here the latest issue of that thrilling comic, not yet in the stationary vending machines. Just give me fifty cents and within five—"

"Please let me through. I'm her mother."

A young woman in the front rank drawled over her powder-sprayed shoulder, "I'll get her for you," and slithered out on six-inch platforms. "Run away, children," she said nonchalantly and lifting her arms behind her head, pirouetted slowly before Robie to show how much she did for her bolero half-jacket and her form-fitting slacks that melted into skylon just above the knees. The little girl glared at her. She ended the pirouette in profile.

At this age-level Robie's reference silhouettes permitted him to distinguish sex, though with occasional amusing and embarrassing miscalls. He whistled admiringly. The crowd cheered.

Someone remarked critically to his friend. "It would go better if he was built more like a real robot. You know, like a man."

The friend shook his head. "This way it's subtler."

No one in the crowd was watching the newscript overhead as it scribbled, "Ice Pack for Hot Truce? Vanadin hints Russ may yield on Pakistan."

Robie was saying, ". . . in the savage new glamor-tint we have christened Mars Blood, complete with spray applicator and fit-all fingerstalls that mask each finger completely except for the nail. Just give me five dollars—uncrumpled bills may be fed into the revolving rollers you see beside my arm—and within five seconds,—"

"No thanks, Robie," the young woman yawned.

"Remember," Robie persisted, "for three more weeks seductivising Mars Blood will be unobtainable from any other robot or human vendor."

"No thanks."

Robie scanned the crowd resourcefully. "Is there any gentleman here . . ." he began just as a woman elbowed her way through the front rank.

"I told you to come back!" she snarled at the little girl.

"But I didn't get my polly-lop!"

". . . who would care to . . ."

"Rita!"

"Robie cheated. Ow!"

Meanwhile the young woman in the half-bolero had scanned the nearby gentlemen on her own. Deciding that there was less than a fifty per cent chance of any of them accepting the proposition Robie seemed about to make, she took advantage of the scuffle to slither gracefully back into the ranks. Once again the path was clear before Robie.

He paused, however, for a brief recapitulation of the more magical properties of Mars Blood, including a telling phrase about "the passionate claws of a Martian sunrise."

But no one bought. It wasn't quite time yet. Soon enough silver coins would be clinking, bills going through the rollers faster than laundry, and five hundred people struggling for the privilege of having their money taken away from them by America's only genuine mobile sales-robot.

But now was too soon. There were still some tricks that Robie did free, and one certainly should enjoy those before starting the more expensive fun.

So Robie moved on until he reached the curb. The variation in level was instantly sensed by his under-scanners. He stopped. His head began to swivel. The crowd watched in eager silence. This was Robie's best trick.

Robie's head stopped swiveling. His scanners had found the traffic light. It was green. Robie edged forward. But then it turned red. Robie stopped again, still on the curb. The crowd softly *ahhed* its delight.

Oh, it was wonderful to be alive and watching Robie on such a wonderful day. Alive and amused in the fresh, weather-controlled air between the lines of bright skyscrapers with their winking windows and under a sky so blue you could almost call it dark.

(But way, way up, where the crowd could not see, the sky was darker still. Purple-dark, with stars showing. And in that purple-dark, a silver-green something, the color of a bud, plunged downward at better than three miles a second. The silver-green was a paint that foiled radar.)

Robie was saying, "While we wait for the light there's time for you youngsters to enjoy a nice refreshing Poppy Pop. Or for you adults—only those over five feet are eligible to buy—to enjoy an exciting Poppy Pop fizz. Just give me a quarter or—I'm licensed to dispense intoxicating liquors—in the case of adults one dollar and a quarter and within five seconds . . ."

But that was not cutting it quite fine enough. Just three seconds later the silver-green bud bloomed above Manhattan into a globular orange flower. The skyscrapers grew brighter and brighter still, the brightness of the inside of the sun. The windows winked white fire.

The crowd around Robie bloomed too. Their clothes puffed into petals of flame. Their heads of hair were torches.

The orange flower grew, stem and blossom. The blast came. The winking windows shattered tier by tier, became black holes. The walls bent, rocked, cracked. A stony dandruff dribbled from their cornices. The flaming flowers on the sidewalk were all leveled at once. Robie was shoved ten feet. His metal hoopskirt dimpled, regained its shape.

The blast ended. The orange flower, grown vast, vanished overhead on its huge, magic beanstalk. It grew dark and very still. The cornice-dandruff pattered down. A few small fragments rebounded from the metal hoopskirt.

Robie made some small, uncertain movements, as if feeling for broken bones. He was hunting for the traffic light, but it no longer shone, red or green.

He slowly scanned a full circle. There was nothing anywhere to interest his reference silhouettes. Yet whenever he tried to move, his under-scanners warned him of low obstructions. It was very puzzling.

The silence was disturbed by moans and a crackling sound, faint at first as the scampering of rats.

A seared man, his charred clothes fuming where the blast had blown out the fire, rose from the curb. Robie scanned him.

"Good day, sir," Robie said. "Would you care for a smoke? A truly cool smoke? Now I have here a yet-unmarketed brand . . ."

But the customer had run away, screaming, and Robie never ran after customers, though he could follow them at a medium brisk roll. He worked his way along the curb where the man had sprawled, carefully keeping his distance from the low obstructions, some of which writhed now and then, forcing him to jog. Shortly he reached a fire hydrant. He scanned it. His electronic vision, though it still worked, had been somewhat blurred by the blast.

"Hello, youngster," Robie said. Then, after a long pause, "Cat got your tongue? Well, I've got a little present for you. A nice, lovely polly-lop." His metal arm snaked down.

"Take it, youngster," he said after another pause. "It's for you. Don't be afraid."

His attention was distracted by other customers, who began to rise up oddly here and there, twisting forms that confused his reference silhouettes and would not stay to be scanned properly. One cried, "Water," but no quarter clinked in Robie's claws when he caught the word and suggested, "How about a nice refreshing drink of Poppy Pop?"

The rat-crackling of the flames had become a jungle muttering. The blind windows began to wink fire again.

A little girl marched up, stepping neatly over arms and legs she did not look at. A white dress and the once taller bodies around her had shielded her from the brilliance and the blast. Her eyes were fixed on Robie. In them was the same imperious confidence, though none of the delight, with which she had watched him earlier.

"Help me, Robie," she said. "I want my mother."

"Hello, youngster," Robie said. "What would you like? Comics? Candy?"

"Where is she, Robie? Take me to her."

"Balloons? Would you like to watch me blow up a balloon?"

The little girl began to cry. The sound triggered off another of Robie's novelty circuits.

"Is something wrong?" he asked. "Are you in trouble? Are you lost?"

"Yes, Robie. Take me to my mother."

"Stay right here," Robie said reassuringly, "and don't be frightened. I will call a policeman." He whistled shrilly, twice.

Time passed. Robie whistled again. The windows flared and roared. The little girl begged, "Take me away, Robie," and jumped onto a little step in his hoopskirt.

"Give me a dime," Robie said. The little girl found one in her pocket and put it in his claws.

"Your weight," Robie said, "is fifty-four and one-half pounds, exactly."

"Have you seen my daughter, have you seen her?" a woman was crying somewhere. "I left her watching that thing while I stepped inside—Rita!"

"Robie helped me," the little girl was telling her moments later. "He knew I was lost. He even called a policeman, but he didn't come. He weighed me too. Didn't you, Robie?"

But Robie had gone off to peddle Poppy Pop to the members of a rescue squad which had just come around the corner, more robot-like than he in their fireproof clothing.

Saucer of Loneliness

Theodore Sturgeon (1916-   )

THEODORE *Sturgeon is a troublesome writer because although his great talent has been widely recognized (until recently, he was anthologized more often than any other writer), few can really say what it is about his stories that make them so memorable—indeed, his real contribution lies in the sense of mood and feeling that his works exhibit. His exploration of Gestalt psychology and of the nature and meaning of love are the themes that critics tend to emphasize, but what Sturgeon is really writing about is the nature of life.*

The fifties were a remarkable decade for him, with the publication of his novels The Dreaming Jewels *(1950),* The Cosmic Rape *(1958), and most notably* More Than Human *(1953), which won the International Fantasy Award in 1954. But it was his short stories and novelettes that won him his large and enthusiastic following, works like "Mr. Costello, Hero," "The Comedian's Children," "Bulkhead," "A Touch of Strange," "The Man Who Lost the Sea," and the taboo-breaking "The World Well Lost."*

164

"Saucer of Loneliness" beautifully captures the mood and feeling for which he is so famous—complete with a "touch of strange."

From *Galaxy Science Fiction*   February, 1953

If she's dead, I thought, I'll never find her in this white flood of moonlight on the white sea, with the surf seething in and over the pale, pale sand like a great shampoo. Almost always, suicides who stab themselves or shoot themselves in the heart carefully bare their chests; the same strange impulse generally makes the sea-suicide go naked.

A little earlier, I thought, or later, and there would be shadows for the dunes and the breathing toss of the foam. Now the only real shadow was mine, a tiny thing just under me, but black enough to feed the blackness of the shadow of a blimp.

A little earlier, I thought, and I might have seen her plodding up the silver shore, seeking a place lonely enough to die in. A little later and my legs would rebel against this shuffling trot through sand, the maddening sand that could not hold and would not help a hurrying man.

My legs did give way then and I knelt suddenly, sobbing—not for her; not yet—just for air. There was such a rush about me: wind, and tangled spray, and colors upon colors and shades of colors that were not colors at all but shifts of white and silver. If light like that were sound, it would sound like the sea on sand, and if my ears were eyes, they would see such a light.

I crouched there, gasping in the swirl of it, and a flood struck me, shallow and swift, turning up and outward like flower petals where it touched my knees, then soaking me to the waist in its bubble and crash. I pressed my knuckles to my eyes so they would open again. The sea was on my lips with the taste of tears and the whole white night shouted and wept aloud.

And there she was.

Her white shoulders were a taller curve in the sloping foam. She must have sensed me—perhaps I yelled—for she turned and saw me kneeling there. She put her fists to her temples and her face twisted, and she uttered a piercing wail of despair and fury, and then plunged seaward and sank.

I kicked off my shoes and ran into the breakers, shouting, hunting, grasping at flashes of white that turned to sea-salt and coldness in my fingers. I plunged right past her, and her body struck my side as a wave whipped my face and tumbled both of us. I gasped in solid water, opened my eyes beneath the surface and saw a greenish-white distorted moon hurtle as I spun. Then there was sucking sand under my feet again and my left hand was tangled in her hair.

The receding wave towed her away and for a moment she streamed out from my hand like steam from a whistle. In that moment I was sure she was dead, but as she settled to the sand, she fought and scrambled to her feet.

She hit my ear, wet, hard, and a huge, pointed pain lanced into my head. She pulled, she lunged away from me, and all the while my hand was caught in her hair. I couldn't have freed her if I had wanted to. She spun to me with the next wave, battered and clawed at me, and we went into deeper water.

"Don't . . . don't . . . I can't swim!" I shouted, so she clawed me again.

"Leave me alone," she shrieked. "Oh, dear God, why can't you *leave*" (said her fingernails) *"me* . . ." (said her finger-nails) *"alone!"* (said her small hard fist).

So by her hair I pulled her head down tight to her white shoulder; and with the edge of my free hand I hit her neck twice. She floated again, and I brought her ashore.

I carried her to where a dune was between us and the sea's

broad noisy tongue, and the wind was above us somewhere. But the light was as bright. I rubbed her wrists and stroked her face and said, "It's all right," and, "There!" and some names I used to have for a dream I had long, long before I ever heard of her.

She lay still on her back with the breath hissing between her teeth, with her lips in a smile which her twisted-tight, wrinkled-sealed eyes made not a smile but a torture. She was well and conscious for many moments and still her breath hissed and her closed eyes twisted.

"Why couldn't you leave me alone?" she asked at last. She opened her eyes and looked at me. She had so much misery that there was no room for fear. She shut her eyes again and said, "You know who I am."

"I know," I said.

She began to cry.

I waited, and when she stopped crying, there were shadows among the dunes. A long time.

She said, "You don't know who I am. Nobody knows who I am."

I said, "It was in all the papers."

"That!" She opened her eyes slowly and her gaze traveled over my face, my shoulders, stopped at my mouth, touched my eyes for the briefest second. She curled her lips and turned away her head. "Nobody knows who I am."

I waited for her to move or speak, and finally I said, "Tell *me.*"

"Who are you?" she asked, with her head still turned away.

"Someone who . . ."

"Well?"

"Not now," I said. "Later, maybe."

She sat up suddenly and tried to hide herself. "Where are my clothes?"

"I didn't see them."

"Oh," she said. "I remember. I put them down and kicked

sand over them, just where a dune would come and smooth them over, hide them as if they never were . . . I hate sand. I wanted to drown in the sand, but it wouldn't let me . . . You mustn't look at me!" she shouted. "I hate to have you looking at me!" She threw her head from side to side, seeking. "I can't stay here like this! What can I do? Where can I go?"

"Here," I said.

She let me help her up and then snatched her hand away, half-turned from me. "Don't touch me. Get away from me."

"Here," I said again, and walked down the dune where it curved in the moonlight, tipped back into the wind and down and became not dune but beach. "Here." I pointed behind the dune.

At last she followed me. She peered over the dune where it was chest-high, and again where it was knee-high. "Back there?"

I nodded.

"So dark . . ." She stepped over the low dune and into the aching black of those moon-shadows. She moved away cautiously, feeling tenderly with her feet, back to where the dune was higher. She sank down into the blackness and disappeared there. I sat on the sand in the light. "Stay away from me," she spat.

I rose and stepped back. Invisible in the shadows, she breathed, "Don't go away." I waited, then saw her hand press out of the clean-cut shadows. "There," she said, "over there. In the dark. Just be a . . . Stay away from me now . . . Be a—voice."

I did as she asked, and sat in the shadows perhaps six feet from her.

She told me about it. Not the way it was in the papers.

She was perhaps seventeen when it happened. She was in Central Park in New York. It was too warm for such an early spring day, and the hammered brown slopes had a dusting of green of precisely the consistency of that morning's hoar frost on the rocks. But the frost was gone and the grass was brave and tempted some hundreds of pairs of feet from the asphalt and concrete to tread on it.

Hers were among them. The sprouting soil was a surprise to her feet, as the air was to her lungs. Her feet ceased to be shoes as she walked, her body was consciously more than clothes. It was the only kind of day which in itself can make a city-bred person raise his eyes. She did.

For a moment she felt separated from the life she lived, in which there was no fragrance, no silence, in which nothing ever quite fit nor was quite filled. In that moment the ordered disapproval of the buildings around the pallid park could not reach her; for two, three clean breaths it no longer mattered that the whole wide world really belonged to images projected on a screen; to gently groomed goddesses in these steel and glass towers; that it belonged, in short, always, always to someone else.

So she raised her eyes, and there above her was the saucer.

It was beautiful. It was golden, with a dusty finish like that of an unripe Concord grape. It made a faint sound, a chord composed of two tones and a blunted hiss like the wind in tall wheat. It was darting about like a swallow, soaring and dropping. It circled and dropped and hovered like a fish, shimmering. It was like all these living things, but with that beauty it had all the loveliness of things turned and burnished, measured, machined, and metrical.

At first she felt no astonishment, for this was so different from anything she had ever seen before that it had to be a trick of the eye, a false evaluation of size and speed and distance that in a moment would resolve itself into a sun-flash on an airplane or the lingering glare of a welding arc.

She looked away from it and abruptly realized that many other people saw it—saw *something*—too. People all around her had stopped moving and speaking and were craning upward. Around her was a globe of silent astonishment, and outside it she was aware of the life-noise of the city, the hard-breathing giant who never inhales.

She looked up again, and at last began to realize how large and how far away the saucer was. No: rather, how small and how very near it was. It was just the size of the largest circle she might make with her two hands, and it floated not quite eighteen inches over her head.

Fear came then. She drew back and raised a forearm, but the saucer simply hung there. She bent far sideways, twisted away, leaped forward, looked back and upward to see if she had escaped it. At first she couldn't see it; then as she looked up and up, there it was, close and gleaming, quivering and croon-ing, right over her head.

She bit her tongue.

From the corner of her eye, she saw a man cross himself. *He did that because he saw me standing here with a halo over my head, she thought.* And that was the greatest single thing that had ever happened to her. No one had ever looked at her and made a respectful gesture before, not once, not ever. Through terror, through panic and wonderment, the comfort of that thought nestled into her, to wait to be taken out and looked at again in lonely times.

The terror was uppermost now, however. She backed away, staring upward, stepping a ludicrous cakewalk. She should have collided with people. There were plenty of people there, gasping and craning, but she reached none. She spun around and discovered to her horror that she was the center of a pointing, pressing crowd. Its mosaic of eyes all bulged and its inner circle braced its many legs to press back and away from her.

The saucer's gentle note deepened. It tilted, dropped an inch or so. Someone screamed, and the crowd broke away from her in all directions, milled about, and settled again in a new dynamic balance, a much larger ring, as more and more people raced to thicken it against the efforts of the inner circle to escape.

The saucer hummed and tilted, tilted . . .

She opened her mouth to scream, fell to her knees, and the saucer struck.

It dropped against her forehead and clung there. It seemed almost to lift her. She came erect on her knees, made one effort to raise her hands against it, and then her arms stiffened down and back, her hands not reaching the ground. For perhaps a second and a half the saucer held her rigid, and then it passed a single ecstatic quiver to her body and dropped it. She plumped to the ground, the backs of her thighs heavy and painful on her heels and ankles.

The saucer dropped beside her, rolled once in a small circle, once just around its edge, and lay still. It lay still and dull and metallic, different and dead.

Hazily, she lay and gazed at the gray-shrouded blue of the good spring sky, and hazily she heard whistles.

And some tardy screams.

And a great stupid voice bellowing "Give her air!" which made everyone press closer.

Then there wasn't so much sky because of the blueclad bulk with its metal buttons and its leatherette notebook. "Okay, okay, what's happened here stand back figods sake."

And the widening ripples of observation, interpretation and comment: "It knocked her down." "Some guy knocked her down." "He knocked her down." "Some guy knocked her down and—" "Right in broad daylight this guy . . ." "The park's gettin' to be . . ." onward and outward, the adulteration of fact until it was lost altogether because excitement is so much more important.

Somebody with a harder shoulder than the rest bulling close, a notebook here, too, a witnessing eye over it, ready to change ". . . a beautiful brunette . . ." to "an attractive brunette" for the afternoon editions, because "attractive" is as dowdy as any woman is allowed to get if she is a victim in the news.

The glittering shield and the florid face bending close: "You hurt bad, sister?" And the echoes, back and back through the crowd, "Hurt bad, hurt bad, badly injured, he beat the hell out of her, broad daylight . . ."

And still another man, slim and purposeful, tan gabardine, cleft chin and beard-shadow: "Flyin' saucer, hm? Okay, Officer, I'll take over here."

"And who the hell might you be, takin' over?"

The flash of a brown leather wallet, a face so close behind that its chin was pressed into the gabardine shoulder. The face said, awed: "F.B.I." and that rippled outward, too. The policeman nodded—the entire policeman nodded in one single bobbing genuflection.

"Get some help and clear this area," said the gabardine.

"Yes, *sir!*" said the policeman.

"F.B.I., F.B.I.," the crowd murmured and there was more sky to look at above her.

She sat up and there was glory in her face. "The saucer talked to me," she sang.

"You shut up," said the gabardine. "You'll have lots of chance to talk later."

"Yeah, sister," said the policeman. "My God, this mob could be full of Communists."

"You shut up, too," said the gabardine.

Someone in the crowd told someone else a Communist beat up this girl, while someone else was saying she got beat up because she was a Communist.

She started to rise, but solicitous hands forced her down again. There were thirty police there by that time.

"I can walk," she said.

"Now you just take it easy," they told her.

They put a stretcher down beside her and lifted her onto it and covered her with a big blanket.

"I can walk," she said as they carried her through the crowd.

A woman went white and turned away moaning, "Oh, my God, how awful!"

A small man with round eyes stared and stared at her and licked and licked his lips.

The ambulance. They slid her in. The gabardine was already there.

A white-coated man with very clean hands: "How did it happen, miss?"

"No questions," said the gabardine. "Security."

The hospital.

She said, "I got to get back to work."

"Take your clothes off," they told her.

She had a bedroom to herself then for the first time in her life. Whenever the door opened, she could see a policeman outside. It opened very often to admit the kind of civilians who were very polite to military people, and the kind of military people who were even more polite to certain civilians. She did not know what they all did nor what they wanted. Every single day they asked her four million, five hundred thousand questions. Apparently they never talked to each other because each of them asked her the same questions over and over.

"What is your name?"

"How old are you?"

"What year were you born?"

Sometimes they would push her down strange paths with their questions.

"Now your uncle. Married a woman from Middle Europe, did he? Where in Middle Europe?"

"What clubs or fraternal organizations did you belong to? Ah! Now about that Rinkeydinks gang on 63rd Street. Who was *really* behind it?"

But over and over again, "What did you mean when you said the saucer talked to you?"

And she would say, "It talked to me."

And they would say, "And it said—"

And she would shake her head.

There would be a lot of shouting ones, and then a lot of kind ones. No one had ever been so kind to her before, but she soon learned that no one was being kind to *her*. They were just getting her to relax, to think of other things, so they could suddenly shoot that question at her: "What do you mean it talked to you?"

Pretty soon it was just like Mom's or school or any place, and she used to sit with her mouth closed and let them yell. Once they sat her on a hard chair for hours and hours with a light in her eyes and let her get thirsty. Home, there was a transom over the bedroom door and Mom used to leave the kitchen light glaring through it all night, every night, so she wouldn't get the horrors. So the light didn't bother her at all.

They took her out of the hospital and put her in jail. Some ways it was good. The food. The bed was all right, too. Through the window she could see lots of women exercising in the yard. It was explained to her that they all had much harder beds.

"You are a very important young lady, you know."

That was nice at first, but as usual it turned out they didn't mean her at all. They kept working on her. Once they brought the saucer in to her. It was inside a big wooden crate with a padlock, and a steel box inside that with a Yale lock. It only weighed a couple of pounds, the saucer, but by the time they got it packed, it took two men to carry it and four men with guns to watch them.

They made her act out the whole thing just the way it happened with some soldiers holding the saucer over her head. It wasn't the same. They'd cut a lot of chips and pieces out of the saucer and, besides, it was that dead gray color. They asked her if she knew anything about that and for once she told them.

"It's empty now," she said.

The only one she would ever talk to was a little man with a fat belly who said to her the first time he was alone with her, "Listen, I think the way they've been treating you stinks. Now get this: I have a job to do. My job is to find out *why* you won't tell what the saucer said. I don't want to know what it said and I'll never ask you. I don't even want you to tell me. Let's just find out why you're keeping it a secret."

Finding out why turned out to be hours of just talking about having pneumonia and the flower pot she made in second grade that Mom threw down the fire escape and getting left back in school and the dream about holding a wine glass in both hands and peeping over it at some man.

And one day she told him why she wouldn't say about the saucer, just the way it came to her: "Because it was talking to *me*, and it's just nobody else's business."

She even told him about the man crossing himself that day. It was the only other thing she had of her own.

He was nice. He was the one who warned her about the trial. "I have no business saying this, but they're going to give you the full dress treatment. Judge and jury and all. You just say what you want to say, no less and no more, hear? And don't let 'em get your goat. You have a right to own something."

He got up and swore and left.

First a man came and talked to her for a long time about how maybe this Earth would be attacked from outer space by beings much stronger and cleverer than we are, and maybe she had the key to a defense. So she owed it to the whole world. And then even if the Earth wasn't attacked, just think of what an advantage she might give this country over its enemies. Then he shook his finger in her face and said that what she was doing amounted to working *for* the enemies of her country. And he turned out to be the man that was defending her at the trial.

The jury found her guilty of contempt of court and the judge recited a long list of penalties he could give her. He gave her one of them and suspended it. They put her back in jail for a few more days, and one fine day they turned her loose.

That was wonderful at first. She got a job in a restaurant, and a furnished room. She had been in the papers so much that Mom didn't want her back home. Mom was drunk most of the time and sometimes used to tear up the whole neighborhood, but all the same she had very special ideas about being respectable, and being in the papers all the time for spying was not her idea of being decent. So she put her maiden name on the mailbox downstairs and told her daughter not to live there any more.

At the restaurant she met a man who asked her for a date. The first time. She spent every cent she had on a red handbag to go with her red shoes. They weren't the same shade, but anyway they were both red. They went to the movies and afterward he didn't try to kiss her or anything, he just tried to find out what the flying saucer told her. She didn't say anything. She went home and cried all night.

Then some men sat in a booth talking and they shut up and glared at her every time she came past. They spoke to the boss, and he came and told her that they were electronics engineers working for the government and they were afraid to talk shop while she was around—wasn't she some sort of spy or something? So she got fired.

Once she saw her name on a juke box. She put in a nickel and punched that number, and the record was all about "the flyin' saucer came down one day, and taught her a brand new way to play, and what it was I will not say, but she took me out of this world." And while she was listening to it, someone in the juke-joint recognized her and called her by name. Four of them followed her home and she had to block the door shut.

Sometimes she'd be all right for months on end, and then someone would ask for a date. Three times out of five, she and the date were followed. Once the man she was with arrested the man who was tailing them. Twice the man who was tailing them arrested the man she was with. Five times out of five, the date would try to find out about the saucer. Sometimes she would go out with someone and pretend that it was a real date, but she wasn't very good at it.

So she moved to the shore and got a job cleaning at night in offices and stores. There weren't many to clean, but that just meant there weren't many people to remember her face from the papers. Like clockwork, every eighteen months, some feature writer would drag it all out again in a magazine or a Sunday supplement; and every time anyone saw a headlight on a mountain or a light on a weather balloon it had to be a flying saucer, and there had to be some tired quip about the saucer wanting to tell secrets. Then for two or three weeks she'd stay off the streets in the daytime.

Once she thought she had it whipped. People didn't want her, so she began reading. The novels were all right for a while until she found out that most of them were like the movies— all about the pretty ones who really own the world. So she learned things—animals, trees. A lousy little chipmunk caught in a wire fence bit her. The animals didn't want her. The trees didn't care.

Then she hit on the idea of the bottles. She got all the bottles she could and wrote on papers which she corked into the bottles. She'd tramp miles up and down the beaches and throw the bottles out as far as she could. She knew that if the right person found one, it would give that person the only thing in the world that would help. Those bottles kept her going for three solid years. Everyone's got to have a secret little something he does.

And at last the time came when it was no use any more. You can go on trying to help someone who *maybe* exists; but soon you can't pretend there is such a person any more. And that's it. The end.

"Are you cold?" I asked when she was through telling me.

The surf was quieter and the shadows longer.

"No," she answered from the shadows. Suddenly she said, "Did you think I was mad at you because you saw me without my clothes?"

"Why shouldn't you be?"

"You know, I don't care? I wouldn't have wanted . . . wanted you to see me even in a ball gown or overalls. You can't cover up my carcass. It shows; it's there whatever. I just didn't want you to *see* me. At all."

"Me, or anyone?"

She hesitated. "You."

I got up and stretched and walked a little, thinking. "Didn't the F.B.I. try to stop you throwing those bottles?"

"Oh, sure. They spent I don't know how much taxpayers' money gathering 'em up. They still make a spot check every once in a while. They're getting tired of it, though. All the writing in the bottles is the same." She laughed. I didn't know she could.

"What's funny?"

"All of 'em—judges, jailers, juke-boxes—people. Do you know it wouldn't have saved me a minute's trouble if I'd told 'em the whole thing at the very beginning?"

"No?"

"No. They wouldn't have believed me. What they wanted was a new weapon. Super-science from a super-race, to slap hell out of the super-race if they ever got a chance, or out of our own if they don't. All those brains," she breathed, with more wonder than scorn, "all that brass. They think 'super-race' and it comes out 'super-science.' Don't they ever imagine a super-race has super-feelings, too—super-laughter, maybe, or super-hunger?" She paused. "Isn't it time you asked me what the saucer said?"

"I'll tell you," I blurted.

> "There is in certain living souls
> A quality of loneliness unspeakable,
> So great it must be shared
> As company is shared by lesser beings.
> Such a loneliness is mine; so know by this
> That in immensity
> There is one lonelier than you."

"Dear Jesus," she said devoutly, and began to weep. "And how is it addressed?"

"To the loneliest one . . ."

"How did you know?" she whispered.

"It's what you put in the bottles, isn't it?"

"Yes," she said. "Whenever it gets to be too much, that no one cares, that no one ever did . . . you throw a bottle into the sea, and out goes a part of your own loneliness. You sit and think of someone somewhere finding it . . . learning for the first time that the worst there is can be understood."

The moon was setting and the surf was hushed. We looked up and out to the stars. She said, "We don't know what loneliness is like. People thought the saucer was a saucer, but it wasn't. It was a bottle with a message inside. It had a bigger ocean to cross—all of space—and not much chance of finding anybody. Loneliness? We don't know loneliness."

When I could, I asked her why she had tried to kill herself.

"I've had it good," she said, "with what the saucer told me. I wanted to . . . pay back. I was bad enough to be helped; I had to know I was good enough to help. No one wants me? Fine. But don't tell me no one, anywhere, wants my help. I can't stand that."

I took a deep breath. "I found one of your bottles two years ago. I've been looking for you ever since. Tide charts, current tables, maps and . . . wandering. I heard some talk about you and the bottles hereabouts. Someone told me you'd quit doing it, you'd taken to wandering the dunes at night. I knew why. I ran all the way."

I needed another breath now. "I got a club foot. I think right, but the words don't come out of my mouth the way they're inside my head. I have this nose. I never had a woman. Nobody ever wanted to hire me to work where they'd have to look at me. You're beautiful," I said. "You're beautiful."

She said nothing, but it was as if a light came from her, more light and far less shadow than ever the practiced moon could cast. Among the many things it meant was that even to loneliness there is an end, for those who are lonely enough, long enough.

Heirs Apparent

Robert Abernathy (1924–)

THE *Cold War hysteria which reached its peak in the early fifties was reflected in science fiction. The Soviets (or often unnamed Slavs or Eastern Europeans) were the villains who compete with "the free world" for dominance in outer space and on earth. The Soviet-American arms race also provided considerable material for the science-fiction writer, with "secret weapons" and the competition for them providing the backdrop for a number of stories.*

But not all the science-fiction works of the fifties portrayed the Soviets as evil with an "us and them" mentality. There were also stories that concentrated on the basic humanity of all sides in a conflict situation, focusing on what human beings have in common, rather than on the forces that separate them. "Heirs Apparent" is one of those stories, but one in which this realization comes too late.

Robert Abernathy was one of the most interesting minor stars of the forties and fifties. Although he produced no book-length works, his short fiction was consistently first-rate. Abernathy was another one of those who suddenly stopped writing science fiction, and the loss was the genre's. He holds a Ph.D. from Harvard in Slavic languages and teaches at the University of Colorado. Here he used his knowledge of the Russian language and Russian culture in a fascinating study of future history.

From *The Magazine of Fantasy and Science Fiction*   1954

Warily crouching, Bogomazov moved forward up the gentle slope. Above his head the high steppe-grass, the *kovýl'*, nodded its plumes in the chilly wind. He shivered.

All at once the wind brought again the wood-smoke smell, and his nostrils flared like a hunting animal's. With sudden recklessness he rose to his full height and looked eagerly across the grasslands that sloped to the river.

Down yonder, hugging the riverbank among scanty trees, was a cluster of crudely and newly built thatched huts. Bogomazov's hunger-keen eyes were quick to note the corral that held a few head of cattle, the pens that must mean poultry, as well as the brown swatches of plowed fields. The wanderer licked his lips, and his hand, almost of itself, unbuttoned the holster at his hip and loosened the pistol there.

But he controlled his urge to plunge ahead; he sank down to concealment in the grass again, and his tactician's glance swept over the scene, studying approaches, seeking human figures, signs of guards and readiness. He saw none, but still he did not move; only the habit of extreme caution had kept him alive this long and enabled him to travel a thousand miles across the chaos that had been Russia.

Presently two small figures emerged from one of the huts and went unhurriedly to the chicken pens, were busy there for a time, and returned. Bogomazov relaxed; it was almost certain now that he had not been seen. At last he obeyed his rumbling stomach and resumed his advance, though indirectly so as to take advantage of the terrain, stalking the village.

He was a strange, skulking figure—Nikolai Nikolayevich Bogomazov, onetime Colonel of the Red Army and Hero of the Soviet Union; now ragged and half naked, face concealed by a scraggly growth of beard, hair slashed awkwardly short across the forehead to prevent its falling into his eyes. His shoes had gone to pieces long ago and the rags he had wrapped around his feet in their place had worn through, leaving him barefoot; he did not know how to make shoes of bark, peasant-style. His army trousers flapped in shreds around his bony shanks. The torn khaki shirt he wore was of American manufacture, a trophy of the great offensive two years earlier that had carried the Russian armies halfway across Europe and through the Near East into Africa . . . those had been the great days: before the bitter realization that it would never be enough to defeat Western armies; after the destruction of the great cities and industries, to be sure, but before the really heavy bombardments had begun. . . .

Bogomazov wormed his way forward, mouth watering, thinking of chickens.

He was close enough to his objective to hear contented poultry noises, and was thinking of how best to deal with the plaited reeds of the enclosure, when a voice behind him cried startledly, *"Oho!"*

The stalker instinctively rolled to one side, his pistol in his hand; then he saw that the man who had shouted was some yards away and backing nervously toward the nearby hovels —a stocky, shabby figure, broad face richly bearded; most important, he had no weapon. Bogomazov came to a quick decision; sheathing his gun, he got to his feet and called sharply, "Halt!"

The other froze at the tone of command, and stared sullenly at the armed scarecrow confronting him. Farther off a door banged and there were footsteps hurrying nearer. Bogomazov watched without a tremor as a half dozen other men and boys approached and stopped beside the first man, as if he stood on an invisible line. A couple of them carried rifles, but the lone interloper did not flinch. Not for the first time, he was gambling everything on a bluff. And these were merely peasants.

"What place is this?" he demanded in the same crisp voice of authority.

"Novoselye," one answered hesitantly. "The New Settlement."

"I can see as much. Who is responsible here?"

"Wait a minute," rumbled the big bearded man who had first spotted him. "How about telling us who you are and what you want?" He shuffled uneasily from one foot to another as the stranger's cold eyes raked him, but succeeded in maintaining a halfhearted air of defiance.

"My name doesn't matter for the present," said Bogomazov slowly. "What does matter is that I am a Communist."

He felt and saw the stiffening, the electric rise of tension, the furtive crawling look that came into the score of eyes upon him; and outwardly Bogomazov was cool, relaxed, but inwardly he was like a coiled spring. His hand hovered unobtrusively close to the pistol butt.

This was the die-cast. He knew personally of too many cases of Communists beaten, assassinated, lynched by those who should have followed their orders, during the storm of madness and despair on the heels of the great disasters, the storm that still went on. . . . Bogomazov had been too clever to be caught, just as he had been clever enough to realize in time, when three months ago the total breakdown of the civil authority had commenced to envelop the military as well, that in the north where he then was the northern winter now setting in would finish what the bombardments had begun. A thousand miles of southward trek lay behind him—from the lands where the blizzards would soon sweep in from Asia to blanket the blackened relics of the Old and New Russias, where the river Moskvá was making a new marsh of the immense shallow depression that had been the site of Moscow, where scarcely a dead tree, let alone a building, stood on all the plain that had once been ruled by Great Novgorod and greater Leningrad.

The man with the beard said warily, "What do you want of us . . . Comrade?"

Bogomazov let out his breath in an inaudible sigh. He said curtly, "Are there any Communists among you?"

"No, Comrade."

"Then who is responsible?"

They looked at one another uneasily. The spokesman gulped and stammered, "The . . . the American is responsible."

Bogomazov's composure was sorely tested. He frowned searchingly at the speaker, "You said—*amerikanets?*"

"Da, tovarishch."

Bogomazov took a deep breath and two steps toward them. "All right. Take me to this American . . . at once!"

The peasants faltered briefly, then moved to obey. As Bogomazov strode up the straggling village street in their midst, he was very much aware that a man with a rifle walked on either side of him—like a guard of honor or a prisoner's escort. Bogomazov left his holster flap unbuttoned. From the hovels some women and children peered out to watch as they passed; a whisper fluttered from hut to hut: "*Kommunist prishól. . . .*"

They stopped in front of a shed, built roughly like the other buildings, of hand-hewn boards. From inside came a rhythmic clanging of metal, and when Bogomazov stepped boldly through the open doorway he was met by a hot blast of air. A stone forge glowed brightly, and a man turned from it, shirtless and sweating, hammer still raised above an improvised anvil.

As the blacksmith straightened, mopping his forehead, Bogomazov saw at first glance that he was in truth an American or at least a Westerner; he had the typical—and hated—

features, the long narrow face and jaw, the prominent nose like the beak of some predatory bird, the lanky loose-jointed build. The Russian word *amerikanets* means not only "American," but also, as a slang expression, "man who gets things done, go-getter"; and it had passed through Bogomazov's mind that these peasants might have applied the term as a fanciful sort of title to some energetic leader risen from among them—but, no: the man before him was really one of the enemy.

With a smooth motion Bogomazov drew and leveled his pistol. He said, "You are under arrest in the name of the Soviet Government."

The other stared at his unkempt menacing figure with a curious grimace, as if he were undecided whether to laugh or cry. The pistol moved in a short, commanding arc; the hammer fell from opened fingers, thudding dully on the earthen floor.

Bogomazov sensed rather than saw the painful uncertainty of the armed men in the doorway; he didn't turn his head. "Keep your hands in sight," he ordered. "Stand over there." The man obeyed carefully; evidently he understood Russian.

"Now," said the Communist, "explain. What kind of infiltration have you been carrying on here?"

The American blinked at him, still wearing that ambiguous expression. He said mildly, his speech fluent though heavily accented, "At the moment when I was so rudely interrupted, I was trying to beat part of a gun mounting into a plowshare. We put in the fall wheat with the old-style wooden plows; a couple of iron shares will make the spring sowing a lot easier and more rewarding, and we may even be able to break some more land this fall."

"Stop evading! I asked you . . . Wait." Feeling intuitively that the psychological moment had come, Bogomazov gestured brusquely at the men in the doorway. "You may go. I will call when you are needed."

They shuffled their feet, fingered the rifles they held, and melted away.

The American smiled wryly. "You know how to handle these people, don't you? . . . But I wish you'd quit pointing that gun now. You aren't going to shoot me in any case until after you've questioned me, and I wouldn't advise you to then. I'm not a very good blacksmith, I admit, but I am the only person here who knows anything about farm management . . . unless you happen to be a stray *agronóm*."

The Russian lowered the pistol and caressed its barrel with his other hand, his face expressionless. "Go on," he said. "I begin to see. You are a specialist who has turned his knowledge to account to obtain a position of leadership."

The other sighed. "You might say that, or you might say I was drafted. The original nucleus of this community was two light machine guns—abandoned after all the ammunition was used up in brushes with the *razbóiniki*. This group was footloose then; I persuaded them to strike south, since when winter came they'd have broken up or starved, and look for unblighted land to farm. As for me, I used to work for the United States Department of Agriculture; what I know about tractor maintenance doesn't do much good just now, but some of the rest is still applicable. I realized pretty early—after I walked away by myself from a crash landing near Tula—that my chances of survival alone, as an alien, would be practically zero. . . . My name, incidentally, is Leroy Smith—Smith means *kuznéts*, but I never thought I'd revert so far to type," he added with a glance at the smoldering forge.

"Go on, Smeet," said Bogomazov, still fondling the gun. "What have you accomplished?"

The American gave him a perplexed look. "Well . . . these people here aren't a very choice bunch. About half of them were factory hands—proletarians, you know—who've had to learn from the ground up. The rest were mostly low-grade collective farm workers—fair to mediocre at carrying out the foreman's orders, but lost when it comes to figuring out what to do next. That, of course, is where I come in." He eyed the Russian speculatively. "And you, as a lone survivor, must have talents that Novoselye can use. We ought to be able to make a deal."

"I," said Bogomazov flatly, "am a Communist."

Smith's eyes narrowed. "Oh, oh," he murmured under his breath. "I should have known it—the way he bulled in here, the way——"

"There will be no deal. As a specialist, you are useful. You will continue to be useful. You will remember that you are serving the Soviet State; any irregularity, any sabotage or wrecking activities—*I* will punish." He hefted the pistol.

The American said wearily, "Don't you realize that the Soviet State, the Communist Party, the war—all that's over and done with, *kapút?* And America too, I suppose—the last I heard our whole industrial triangle was a radioactive bonfire and Washington had been annexed to Chesapeake Bay. Here we're a handful of survivors trying to go on surviving."

"The war is not over. Did you think you could start a war and call it quits when you became nauseated with it?"

"We didn't start it."

In the light of the forge Bogomazov's eyes glittered with a color that matched the metal of the weapon he held. "You capitalists made your fundamental mistake through vulgar materialism. You thought you could destroy Communism by destroying the capital, the wealth and industry and military power we had built up as a base in the Soviet Union. You didn't realize that our real capital was always—ourselves, the Communists. That's why we will inherit the earth, now that your war has shattered the old world!"

Smith watched him talk with a sort of dazed fascination, and then, the spell breaking, smiled faintly. "Before you go about inheriting the earth, it will be necessary to worry about lasting out the winter."

"Naturally!" snapped Bogomazov. He stepped back to the doorway, and called, "You there! Come on in." He singled out one of the armed peasants. "You will stand guard, to see that this foreigner does not escape or commit any acts of sabotage, such as damaging tools. You will not listen to anything he may say. So long as he behaves properly, you will leave him strictly alone, understood?"

The man nodded violently. "Yes, Comrade."

"I am going to inspect the settlement. You, Smeet—back to making plowshares, and they had better be good!"

Winter closed down inexorably. Icy winds blew from the steppe—not the terrible fanged winds of the northern tundras, but freezing all the same; and on still days the smoke from the huts rose far into the bright frosty air, betraying the village's location to any chance marauders.

There was no help for that, but there was plenty of work to be done. Almost every day the forge was busy, and on the outskirts of Novoselye hammers rang, where new houses were going up to relieve the settlement's crowding. It would have been good to have a stockade, too; but on the almost treeless plain it had become necessary to go dangerously far to find usable timber.

Bogomazov, making one of his frequent circuits of the village in company with Ivanov, his silent and caninely devoted fellow Communist who had strayed in a few weeks after him, halted to watch the construction. The American Smith was lending a hand on the job—at the moment, he had paused to show a former urban clerk how to use a hammer without bending precious nails.

Bogomazov watched for a minute in silence, then called, "Smeet!"

The American looked round, straightened and came toward them without haste. "What is it now?"

"I have been looking for you. Some of the cattle are sick;

no one seems to know if it is serious. Do you know anything about veterinary medicine?"

"I've done a little cow doctoring—I was brought up on a farm. I'll take a look at them right away."

"Good." Watching the other turn to go, Bogomazov felt an uneasy though familiar surprise at the extent to which he and the settlement had come to rely on this outlander. Time and again, in greater or lesser emergencies calling for special skills, the only one who knew what to do—or the only one who would volunteer to try—had been this inevitable Smith.

There was an explanation for that, of course: from Smith's references to his prewar life in America, Bogomazov gathered that he had worked at one time or another at a remarkable variety of "specialties," moving from place to place and from job to job, in the chaotic capitalistic labor market, in a manner which would never have been tolerated in the orderly Soviet economic system. . . . As a result, he seemed to have done a little of everything and to know more than a little about everything.

And Bogomazov was aware that, behind his back, the villagers referred to the foreigner as "Comrade Specialist"— improperly giving him the title of honor, *tovarishch*, though he was not even a Soviet citizen, let alone a Party member. . . .

That train of thought was a reminder, and Bogomazov called, "Wait! Another matter, when you have time . . . I am told that the stove in Citizen Vrachov's hut will not draw."

Smith turned, smiling. "That's all right. Vrachov's wife complained to me about it, and I've already fixed the flue."

Bogomazov stiffened. "She should not have gone to you. She should have reported the matter to me first."

The American's smile faded. "Oh . . . discipline, eh?"

"Discipline is essential," said Bogomazov flatly. Ivanov, at his elbow, nodded emphatic agreement.

"I suppose it is." Smith eyed them thoughtfully. "I've got to admit that you've accomplished some things I probably couldn't have done—like redistributing the housing space and cooking up a system of rationing to take the village through the winter—and making it stick."

"You could not have done those things because you are not a Communist," said Bogomazov with energy. "You are used to the 'impossibilities' of a dying society; but we are strong in the knowledge that history is on our side. There is nothing that a real Bolshevik cannot achieve!"

Ivanov nodded again.

"History," Smith said reflectively, "is notorious for changing sides. I wonder if even a Bolshevik . . . But in the case of Vrachov's wife's chimney, your discipline seems rather petty."

The Russian drew visibly into himself. "Enough!" he said sharply. "You are to see to the cattle."

Smith shrugged slightly and turned away. "O.K.," he said. "*Volya vasha*—you're the boss."

A half-grown boy bolted headlong down the village street, feet ringing on the frost-hard ground. "*Razbóiniki!*" he shrieked. "*Razbo-o-oiniki!*"

At the feared cry—"Robbers!"—the inhabitants poured out of their dwellings like bees from a threatened hive, some snatching up axes, hoes, even sticks of firewood. No guns— one of Bogomazov's first acts after he had restored the Soviet authority in Novoselye had been to round up all the firearms, a motley collection of Russian and other makes, and store them safely in a stout shed under the protection of the village's only working padlock.

The villagers began to huddle together, hugging the shelter of their houses and staring anxiously eastward, at the farther banks of the frozen river. The boy who had given the alarm ran among them, pointing. Everyone saw the little black figures, men and horses, moving yonder, pacing up and down the snow-covered shore; and a concerted groan went up as one mounted man ventured testingly out onto the ice and, evidently, found it strong enough.

To make things worse, the penned cattle, upset by the

tumult, began bawling. That sound would carry clearly across the river, and would whet the appetites of the *razbóiniki*. The Novoselyane shivered, remembering all the tales of villages overrun and burned, the inhabitants driven off or slaughtered, remembering too their own collisions with such troops of marauders—remnants of revolted army units, of mobs that had escaped the cities' ruin, of dispersed Asian tribes—armed riffraff swept randomly together from Heaven knew where, *izzá granítsy*, from beyond the frontiers even. . . .

These *razbóiniki* were plainly numerous, and plainly, too, they were coming. Perhaps a hundred men, half of them mounted, were in sight, and on the skyline beyond the river the sharper-sighted glimpsed wagons, probably ox-drawn. The enemy were well organized, not merely casual looters. The Novoselyane gripped their improvised weapons—vaguely, frightenedly determined to show fight, but withal no more than sheep for the slaughter. A hulking young ex-factory worker mourned aloud, "*Bozhe moi*, if we only still had the machine guns . . ."

Then Bogomazov came striding down the street, flinging commands right and left as he went, commands that sent the villagers scurrying into an approximation of a defense line. He swore bitterly, wrestling with the frozen padlock on the shed where the guns had been stored; he got it open, and, together with Ivanov, began to run up and down the line passing out rifles and strict orders not to use them until word was given.

The mounted *razbóiniki* were approaching at a walk, in an uneven skirmish line across the ice.

Smith stood watching, hands tucked for warmth—he owned no mittens—into the pockets of the tattered flight jacket he still clung to. As Bogomazov hurried past, cradling a sniper's rifle equipped with telescopic sights, Smith remarked, "I used to be a pretty fair shot——"

"Keep out of the way!" snapped the Communist. He dropped to all fours, crept out onto the open slope beyond the row of houses, and lay sighting carefully. Behind the line

Ivanov scurried from point to point, repeating the orders: "Hold your fire, and when you do shoot, aim for the horses in front. They have fewer horses than men; and if an enemy can once be persuaded that the front line is too dangerous, he will shortly have no front line. . . ."

The hollow sound of the hooves came nearer, clear in the hush. Then Bogomazov's rifle cracked, and the lead horse reared, throwing its rider; the ice gave way beneath its hind feet, and it floundered. Guns began going off all along the line of houses as Bogomazov came wriggling back. The horsemen on the ice scattered, trotting and crouching low in the saddles, returning the fire. Bullets ricocheted screaming through the village, ripping splinters from walls and roofs.

Some of the *razbóiniki* were busied dragging their wounded or foundered comrades and their mounts back toward the farther shore, but off to the right a handful of horsemen broke into a reckless gallop across the groaning ice, making determinedly for the low bank above the village. Bogomazov, rifle slung, started in that direction, beckoning some of the defenders from the firing line and bellowing to the others: "Fire only at the ones still coming! Save your cartridges!"

The *razbóiniki* made the shore and bore down on Novoselye's flank, whooping, urging their unkempt ponies to a dead run. They were heading for the corral, hoping to smash the stockade around it and drive the cattle off; but when they were almost upon their objective bullets started snapping among them. One man spun from his saddle and went rolling along the frozen ground, and a horse sprawled headlong, pinning its rider. The others' nerve broke, and they wheeled and fled.

Bogomazov walked out, pistol ready, to inspect the casualties. The man who had been hit was already dead. Bogomazov fired twice with cool precision, finishing first the gasping, lung-shot horse and then the rider who lay stunned beneath it.

He told his men, "They may attack repeatedly. We will establish watches."

But the *razbóiniki* had had enough. After an anxious hour

of watching the movements on the far side of the river, the villagers became aware that the enemy, horse, foot, and wagons, had reassembled in marching order and was streaming away southward. The Novoselyane laughed, wept with relief, and embraced one another; someone did an impromptu clog dance in the street.

Bogomazov entered the sooty one-room dwelling which, because of his occupancy, was known as the *nachál'naya izbá*, the "primary hut." He breathed the warm close air gratefully, beginning to shed his mittens and padded coat. Then he stopped short as he saw Smith warming his hands by the stove, a rifle slung over his shoulder. "Where did you get that?"

The American grinned. "One of the proletariat developed combat fatigue about ten seconds after the shooting started, so I filled in."

Bogomazov hesitated imperceptibly, then thrust his hand out. "Give it to me."

Slowly Smith unslung the weapon and handed it over. Bogomazov unloaded it, stuffed the cartridges into his pocket, opened the door of the *izbá* and called to a passing boy, "Here. You are responsible for delivering this rifle to Comrade Ivanov."

The youth hugged the rifle to him, looking adoringly at Bogomazov. "Yes, sir, Comrade General!"

Bogomazov started to speak, checked himself, and closed the door.

"So you're putting the guns under lock and key again."

"Naturally. Ivanov is attending to that now."

The American raised an eyebrow quizzically. "In my country's Constitution there is, or used to be, a provision safeguarding the people's right to keep and bear arms."

"The Soviet Constitution contains no such provision."

"Today, though, we might have been overrun and massacred if the enemy had approached less openly, and hadn't been seen in time for you to break out the guns."

Bogomazov sank wearily onto a bench by the fire and began unwinding the rags that served him as leggings. He said heavily, "*Mister* Smeet, you are neither a Russian nor a Communist, and you do not understand these people as I do. You had better leave administration to me, and devote yourself to those matters which you are expert in. . . . How is your work with the radio?"

Smith shook his head impatiently. "Nothing there—I can't raise any signals, maybe because there aren't any. . . . But the question of the guns is a secondary one. The main thing is—what are we going to do now?"

The Russian eyed him wonderingly. "What do you mean?"

"I came here to speak to you because the attack today confirmed a suspicion that's been growing on me for some time, ever since the first bandits raided through here in November. . . . Did you notice the organization these *razbóiniki* seemed to have? They were fairly well disciplined; they attacked from and fell back on a mobile camp, with wagons no doubt carrying their women and children, and with driven cattle. The population of their whole camp must be two or three times that of Novoselye."

"So? We beat them off. You saw that they proceeded south; the winter is too much for them, whereas we will sit it out snugly in our houses, so long as order is maintained and rations are conserved."

"But they'll be back in the spring."

"Perhaps. If so, we will be stronger by then."

"How stronger? We've very little rifle ammunition left, and before the spring crop comes in there's going to be trouble with malnutrition."

"The marauders are subject to the same troubles. In Lipy, only fifty kilometers from here, there is a man who knows how to make gunpowder."

"I could make gunpowder, for that matter—but damned if I know where to find any sulfur. . . . You miss the point. The signs of organization we saw indicate that these people, wherever they came from originally, have succeeded in taking to a nomadic way of life—a permanently roving existence. They'll be on us again next spring, without 'perhaps.' "

Bogomazov shrugged impatiently. "So, there are dangers. I am not losing sight of them. You had better concentrate on trying to establish radio communication."

The American said hotly, "You're still blind to what this development means! You . . . Well, before this war some of our Western 'bourgeois' historians—naturally you wouldn't have read their writings—saw human history as a long struggle between two basically different ways of life, the two main streams of social evolution: Civilization and Nomadism. Civilization is a way of life based on agriculture—principally cereal crops—on fixed places of habitation, on comparatively stable social patterns whose highest form is the state. Nomadism, on the other hand, has as its economic foundation not fields, but herds; geographically, it rests not on settlements, villages, towns, cities, but on perpetual migration from pasture to pasture; socially, its typical higher form of organization is not the state, but the horde.

"Since written history began the boundary between Civilization and Nomadism has swayed back and forth as one or the other gained local advantage; but in general, during the historic period—really a very small part of the whole past of humanity—Civilization has been on the offensive. The last great onslaught from the nomad world was in the twelfth century—the Mongol conquests, which swept through this very region and brought about the period that your historians call the Tartar Yoke. By the eighteenth century the counterattack of Civilization had been so successful that the historian Gibbon—another bourgeois you probably haven't read—could rejoice that 'cannon and fortifications' had made Europe forever secure against any more such invasions. It looked as if Nomadism was through, due to disappear altogether. . . .

But Civilization went on to invent the means of destroying itself: weapons indefinitely effective against the fixed installations that civilized life depends on, but of little consequence to the rootless nomad.

"And now—where are your cannon, your fortifications, your coal mines and steel mills, your nitrogen-fixing and sulfuric-acid plants? When you discount these raiders as nuisances, you're still living in a world that just died a violent death. We no longer have the whole of Civilization backing us up; we're on our own!"

Bogomazov had listened with half-shut eyes, soaking up the fire's warmth. "Then you think Civilization is finished?"

"No! But I think that what's left of it will have to fall back and regroup. You and we, the Americans and Russians—we fought our war for the control of Civilization, and very nearly wrecked it in the process; but on both sides we were and are on the side of Civilization. That's what counts now. . . . What's our situation here? According to the scanty liaison we've achieved, there are a number of other settlements like this up and down the river, scattered seeds trying to take root again. From the east, toward the Caspian, there's no news at all, and westward, in the Ukraine, reports tell of nothing but wandering bands—the blights the planes spread interdicted agriculture throughout that region for some years to come.

"In spring the *razbóiniki* will be on us again—and perhaps in the meantime their fragmentary groups will have coalesced into bigger and more formidable hordes. With their rediscovered technique of nomadic life, they'll be expanding into the vacuum created by the internal collapse of the civilized world, as the Huns and their kindred did when the Roman Empire fell. . . . I think we have no choice but to migrate west as soon as the spring crop is in. This country here can no longer be held for Civilization; for one thing it's too badly devastated, and for another it's all one huge plain, natural nomad country. The Eurasian plain extends through northern Europe, clear across Germany and France; we should move south to look for a more favorable geography. It might be possible to make a stand in the Crimea, but it's said the radioactivity is very bad there; either the Balkans or Italy, with their mountains, should probably be our ultimate objective."

Bogomazov sat up straight, looking hard at Smith. He frowned. "You are suggesting—that Russia be abandoned to the *razbóiniki?*"

"Exactly. That will be the result in any case: I'm suggesting that we save ourselves while we've got time."

The Communist's eyes narrowed, with a peculiar glitter; he was motionless and silent for a moment, then he barked with humorless laughter. "You want to lecture a Marxist on history! I know history. Do you know that this is the very region where took place the events told in the *Tale of Igor's Host;* the same region where Prince Dmitri Donskói overthrew the Golden Horde? And you tell me to retreat from a handful of bandits! Do you know——"

"I don't see what the bygone glories of Holy Russia have to do either with Marxism or with preserving Civilization," Smith interrupted dryly.

The other rose to his feet, rocking on them like an undersized but infuriated bear, and glared hotly at the American's lanky figure. He shouted, "Will you be quiet, before I——"

The door slammed open, letting in a cold blast, and in it stood Ivanov breathing hard. He gasped, "Comrade Bogomazov! There are two rifles missing!"

In a flash Bogomazov was himself again, reaching for his coat. "Two? I'll investigate, and whoever is trying to hide——"

"Beg pardon, Comrade Bogomazov, but it's worse than that. Vasya and Mishka-the-Frog—that is, Citizens Rudin and Bagryanov—are gone with the rifles."

"The young fools . . ." Bogomazov plunged through the doorway, still struggling into his coat. Smith followed more slowly; when he caught up, the Communist was in the center of a knot of villagers, furiously interrogating a shawl-wrapped old woman who was bitterly weeping.

"Where did they go? Which way?" demanded Bogomazov.

The old woman, mother of one of the missing youths, only sniffled repeatedly: "*Ushlí v razbóiniki* . . . they went to the robbers. . . ."

The Communist wheeled from her in disgust, fists clenching uselessly at his sides. Smith said conversationally, "You'll never catch them now. There you see the effect of another weapon in Nomadism's arsenal."

"What in the devil's name are you talking about?"

"Psychological warfare. Those young fellows, finding guns in their hands and adventure in their hearts, deserted Civilization and its dreary chores for a more romantic-looking life."

Bogomazov grunted angrily, "Ideological nonsense! Russians have always run off to join the robbers. It's in their nature."

"Exactly. As boys in my country used to head West in hopes of becoming cowboys. I wonder what's happening in the American West now. . . . Men have always tended to rebel against civilized restraints and hanker after the nomad's free, picturesque existence; and when the restraints are loosened, they may bolt."

"We can do without that pair. And you——" Bogomazov eyed the American stonily and spoke with deliberate emphasis. "You'll not repeat these notions of yours to anyone else—understood?" Without awaiting any response, he turned on his heel and stalked away toward the *nachál'naya izbá*.

Smith gazed somberly after him, knowing that further argument would be useless. The decision was made—to stand and fight it out here.

Spring came with the thunderous breakup of the river ice, with the sluicing of thawed water that made the prairie a trackless wilderness of mud for a time, with the pushing of new green

everywhere on the vast rolling plains and, less densely, in the
fields that last fall had been so painfully broken and seeded.

Spring came with foreboding, that somehow waxed apace
with the hope that returning green life wakens in all living.
Smith had kept his ideas to himself; but the Novoselyane
whispered among themselves. Those who had been city dwellers had nothing but a formless and unfocused fear of the great
windy spaces, the silences, the night noises of birds and water
creatures along the marshy river brim; but the peasants had
their immemorial stories, raised up from the depths of a tradition as deep as race memory, given new and frightening meanings. Over their heads had come and gone serfdom, emancipa-
tion, serfdom again under the name of collectivization, and
finally the apocalyptic swallowing up of the world of cities that
they had never quite understood or trusted . . . and they
remembered other things.

They knew that in the old days the greening swells beyond
the river had been the edge of the world, the Tartar steppe,
out of which the khans had ridden to see the Russian princes
grovel and bring tribute before the horse-tail standards. The
grandiose half-finished works of the Fifth Five-Year Plan were
strewn wreckage there now, and it came to their mind that
perhaps it was the Tartar steppe again. They remembered the
ancient sorrows of the Slavs, the woes that are told in the
Russian Primary Chronicle. They spoke darkly of the Horde
of Mamai, which in Russian speech has passed into proverbs;
and of the *obry*, whose name now means "ogres," but who
historically were the nomad Avars, that took to herding
human cattle even into the heart of Europe. . . .

When the Communists were not watching them, they studied signs in the flight of migrating birds and the cries of night
fowl. Somehow all the portents were evil.

There were more tangible reasons for alarm. News filtered
in of settlements downriver raided and laid waste by wandering bands, whose numbers and ferocity no doubt grew might-

ily in the telling. Bogomazov succeeded in suppressing or minimizing most of these reports, but not all, nor could trailing smoke smudges in the southern sky one bright afternoon be concealed. . . .

Bogomazov sensed the slow rise of dark superstitious fear around him, and he moved about the village, the faithful Ivanov trotting at his heels, scolding, coaxing, exhorting, all to scant avail; to combat the villagers' fears was like wrestling with an amorphous thing in a nightmare. Once upon a time a local administrator could have reached for the telephone and conjured up an impressive caravan of Party officials in shiny automobiles, with uniforms, medals and manners which would leave the yokels for many weeks incapable of saying anything but "Yes, Comrade." Or he might have pointed to airplanes droning across the sky as visible signs of the omnipotence of the Soviet State. But now there was no telephone, and all that flew was the migrant birds, passing northward day after day as if fleeing from some terror in the south.

"We are on our own now," thought Bogomazov, then scowled as he remembered that the American had said it.

The end came suddenly.

Smith had gone out with half a dozen peasants to inspect the growing wheat. All at once they looked up and saw, across the narrow width of a field, a little group of horsemen, no more than their own number, quietly sitting their shaggy ponies, watching. How they had come up so silently and unseen was a mystery; it was as if the world had changed to that fairy-tale plenum of possibilities in which armed bands spring up from seed sown in the earth.

These watchers carried a bizarre mixture of modern and primitive armament; some had rifles, but cavalry sabers dangled against their thighs, and some bore spears whose hammered iron points flashed in the sun.

The two parties were motionless, confronting one another

for a minute or two like strangers from different worlds. Then the interlopers wheeled about without haste and trotted away over a rise.

"Come on!" said Smith quietly, and set out at a run for the village.

Bogomazov, face impassive, heard the news that the danger was again upon them. He produced his key and opened the padlocked shed door—and stood frozen in dismay, for the shed was empty. Someone had employed the winter's leisure to tunnel under a side wall and remove all the guns.

"Who did this?" shouted the Communist at the villagers assembling in the square.

"Not I, Comrade . . ."

"It wasn't I, Comrade . . ."

Uniformly, the peasant faces reflected the transparent guilt of naughty children.

"Very well!" said Bogomazov bitterly. "You're all in it. You've stolen the guns and hidden them, in the thatch, under the floor, no matter where. But now, bring them out—do you hear?"

They stirred uneasily, but did not move to obey.

"Apparently," said a sardonic voice, "the Soviet Constitution has been amended."

"You! . . . Were *you* behind this thievery?"

"Certainly not," said Smith. "They don't trust me too far either—they have a hazy notion that I'm one of your kind, one of the rulers they hate but haven't learned to do without."

He swung around and said, without raising his voice, to the men nearest: "You've taken the guns for your own protection —if you intend to use them that way, now's the time. The main body of the *razbóiniki* won't be far behind the scouting party we saw. Do you propose to defend yourselves, the houses you've built and the fields you've plowed?"

They murmured among themselves, and began to drift off by twos and threes. Presently men were emerging from all the huts, awkwardly carrying the missing rifles.

It was all of a taut hour before they had sight again of the enemy, but for a good part of that hour they heard the mournful creaking of wagons in the steppe, out of view beyond the higher ground. The sound was disembodied, sourceless, seeming to come from nowhere and everywhere.

The men of Novoselye clustered in uneasy groups, waiting, fingering their weapons unsteadily. Bogomazov took charge, ordering them here and there, lashing the village into a posture of defense; they obeyed him, but halfheartedly, with the look of dumb driven cattle on their faces.

One moment there was no sign of the foe save for the creaking of unseen wheels. The next, a dozen mounted figures were briefly silhouetted along the skyline, dipped down the green wave of the grassy slope toward the fields, and were followed by others and yet others, till—to eyes wavering in beginning panic—the whole hillside seemed sliding down in an avalanche of men and horses.

"Steady!" snapped Bogomazov. "Hold your fire——"

Abruptly one man let his rifle fall and turned, sobbing, to flee; it was Ivanov, the other Communist. Bogomazov intercepted him in two long strides and felled him with a full-armed blow, the pistol weighting his hand.

"Get up, get back to your post!" he spat into the dazed and bloody face.

But the villagers had already begun to fall back down the street, in a concerted tide of fear that threatened momentarily to become a total rout.

Smith, looming conspicuous by his height among them, shouted in a carrying voice, *"Don't drop your guns!* We'll make a stand in the square!" The American materialized at Bogomazov's side and wrenched urgently at his arm, dragging him, dazed with fury and disappointment, after the retreating mob. "Come on! If we can hold the men together for a few minutes, maybe we can still rally them."

The *razbóiniki* were jogging across the planted ground, trampling ruthlessly over the new wheat. From the street's other end rose a cry, "Here they come!" and almost simultaneously someone screamed and pointed across the river, where a third troop had come into view on the opposite bank, as if posted to cut off the last possible escape.

As the invaders, with jingling bridles and clattering hooves, swept from two sides into Novoselye, its able-bodied inhabitants huddled in the square; those who still clutched their weapons and those without wore the same look of hopeless waiting for an expected blow.

The *razbóiniki* closed in cautiously. Their leader, a squat leathery-looking man with a wide Kalmyk face, rode near; he reined in and looked down expressionlessly—at the Novoselyane. He said loudly, in stumbling Russian, "We—not want kill you. You give up—we burn village, go. Be peace." He repeated, "Peace!" watching for their response with almost a benevolent air, the while he tightened the strap of his slung rifle—it was his most prized possession, a German rifle that could hit targets at a thousand yards, and he had no intention of wasting his few remaining cartridges in close fighting. An old saber hung loose in its sheath at his side.

Smith pushed forward and spoke slowly and distinctly: "We too desire peace, between your people and ours. Why should we fight and waste lives, when so few are left after the great war? You are wanderers, we farm the land—only a little of the land, so there is room for both of us."

He watched the stolid Asiatic face keenly for any hint of response. Did the *razbóinik* leader realize that the villagers wouldn't fight, that—so far as this outpost was concerned—the resistance of Civilization was at an end?

"Village—bad," the Kalmyk declared, with unhelpful gestures. "Build houses, plow land—then, *boom!* No good . . ." He gave up, and half turned in the saddle, beckoning to a young man with Slavic features. The latter advanced a couple of paces, and said glibly in Russian:

"The *vozhd'* means that it is dangerous to live in towns. If people live in towns, sooner or later the American bombers come, many are killed and others sickened with burns and bowels turning to water; the death blows even across the steppes and kills animals and men. . . . We cannot allow you to live in such danger. So we will burn this town, and in return for the favor we do you we will take only half the cattle, and such ammunition as you may have that will fit the guns we possess; for the rest, you may keep your arms and movable property, and go freely where you like. Whoever may wish to join us is welcome."

"Your terms are too hard," said Smith steadily. "And you——"

He was interrupted. Bogomazov, pale with determination, thrust him aside and shouted in a voice of command, "That man is a traitor to the motherland! Citizens, follow me!"

The pistol in his hand roared, but in the instant as he aimed the young spokesman had thrown himself flat over his horse's neck. Simultaneously the Kalmyk leader leaned far out of the saddle, and his saber descended like a silent flash of lightning.

The villagers on one side, the raiders on the other, stared unmoving, unmoved, at the fallen man. Smith bent over him, almost under the nervously dancing feet of the Kalmyk's pony.

Bogomazov made a great effort to rise, and failed. His eyes looked unfocusedly up into the American's face; his expression was one of incredulity.

He strove to speak, choking on blood. Smith leaned close, and thought he understood the dying man's last words, uttered with that look of dazed wonder: *"Even a Bolshevik . . ."*

The nomad spokesman rode forward again, red in the face, and shouted fiercely, "Are there any more dissenters?"

Smith stood up and faced them. The game was lost and the enemy knew it now, but he still had to try the last card he possessed. He said tensely, "You are mistaken. The American bombers aren't coming any more."

"How can you know?"

"Because I myself am an American."

There was a dead hush, in which Smith heard clearly the noise of a carbine's hammer being drawn back. The Kalmyk's slanted eyes rested inscrutably upon him. Then the man grinned under his straggling mustache, and said something, a rapid string of Asiatic syllables.

"The *vozhd'* says: 'That may or may not be true. To him you seem to be a man much like other men.' "

"But——" Smith began.

"*But* we're taking no chances. We burn the village in half an hour; you have that long to assemble your goods. Those who wish to move on with us will signify by gathering in the field yonder. *Kryshka*—that's all!"

Smith let his hands fall to his sides. Some of the villagers had already begun to drift toward the indicated assembly point.

Some way out in the steppe there was a *kurgán*, an ancient grass-grown burial mound of some forgotten people. Civilizations, wars and disasters had passed it by and it was the same. It was the highest point for many miles. From it Smith watched the glowing embers of the New Settlement.

All around was the plain, immense and darkening in the spring twilight. Thousands of miles, months of footsore march, it must be to reach any place where there would be a doubtful security and a chance to begin anew. Time and space—once man had conquered them, but now man was a rare animal again in a world where time and space mocked him. Smith wondered: Would they be conquered again in his own lifetime, or that of his grandchildren? Bogomazov had been lucky in a way; his training had enabled him to disbelieve what he knew to be true, so that he had never been forced to recognize the meaning of what had happened—or had he, there at the end?

In the west the horizon was empty, or at least his eyes could no longer make out against the sunset the black specks of the westward-marching horde. About half of the uprooted villagers had gone with it—with few exceptions, those who had come originally from the cities, the factories; the peasants remained. They were encamped now about the ancient mound.

Behind Smith a voice asked plaintively, "Comrade American—what will we do? Some of us think we should go on south, toward . . ."

"Don't bother me now!" Smith said harshly; then, as the man drew back abashed: "Tomorrow . . . we'll see, tomorrow."

The retreating feet were soundless on the grassy slope. Down by the river the last sparks were dying. Somewhere far off in the steppe shuddered a mournful cry that Smith did not know—perhaps it was the howl of a wolf. In the west the light faded, and night fell with the darkness sweeping on illimitable wings out of Asia.

5, 271, 009

Alfred Bester (1913-   )

ALTHOUGH *his first science-fiction story—"The Broken Axiom"—was published in* Thrilling Wonder Stories *in 1939, Alfred Bester was one of the most important writers of the fifties. His two novels of that decade,* The Demolished Man *(1952) and* The Stars My Destination *(1956) became instant classics, the former book one of the first skillfully executed psychological science-fiction works to come out of the genre.*

Bester was also an important critic of the field as a reviewer for The Magazine of Fantasy and Science Fiction, *a man with few illusions concerning what he felt to be the limits and failures of most of the science fiction produced at that time. He was one of the pioneer "dropouts" from the field, but one who has come back home.*

From *The Magazine of Fantasy and Science Fiction*   March, 1954

Take two parts of Beelzebub, two of Israel, one of Monte Cristo, one of Cyrano, mix violently, season with mystery and you have Mr. Solon Aquila. He is tall, gaunt, sprightly in manner, bitter in expression, and when he laughs his dark eyes turn into wounds. His occupation is unknown. He is wealthy without visible means of support. He is seen everywhere and understood nowhere. There is something odd about his life.

This is what's odd about Mr. Aquila, and you can make what you will of it. When he walks he is never forced to wait on a traffic signal. When he desires to ride there is always a vacant taxi on hand. When he bustles into his hotel an elevator always happens to be waiting. When he enters a store, a salesclerk is always free to serve him. There always happens to be a table available for Mr. Aquila in restaurants. There are always last-minute ticket returns when he craves entertainment at sold-out shows.

You can question waiters, hack drivers, elevator girls, salesmen, box-office men. There is no conspiracy. Mr. Aquila does not bribe or blackmail for these petty conveniences. In any case, it would not be possible for him to bribe or blackmail the automatic clock that governs the city traffic signal system. These things, which make life so convenient for him, simply happen. Mr. Solon Aquila is never disappointed. Presently we shall hear about his first disappointment and see what it led to.

Mr. Aquila has been seen fraternizing in low saloons, in middle saloons, in high saloons. He has been met in bagnios, at coronations, executions, circuses, magistrates' courts and handbook offices. He has been known to buy antique cars, historic jewels, incunabula, pornography, chemicals, porro prisms, polo ponies and full-choke shotguns.

"HimmelHerrGottSeiDank! I'm crazy, man, crazy. Eclectic, by God," he told a flabbergasted department store president. "The Weltmann type, nicht wahr? My ideal: Goethe. Tout le monde. God damn."

He spoke a spectacular tongue of mixed metaphors and meanings. Dozens of languages and dialects came out in machine-gun bursts. Apparently he also lied *ad libitum*.

"Sacre bleu. Jeez!" he was heard to say once. "Aquila from

the Latin. Means aquiline. O tempora O mores. Speech by Cicero. My ancestor."

And another time: "My idol: Kipling. Took my name from him. Aquila, one of his heroes. God damn. Greatest Negro writer since *Uncle Tom's Cabin*."

On the morning that Mr. Solon Aquila was stunned by his first disappointment, he bustled into the atelier of Lagan & Derelict, dealers in paintings, sculpture and rare objects of art. It was his intention to buy a painting. Mr. James Derelict knew Aquila as a client. He had already purchased a Frederick Remington and a Winslow Homer some time ago when, by another odd coincidence, he had bounced into the Madison Avenue shop one minute after the coveted paintings went up for sale. Mr. Derelict had also seen Mr. Aquila boat a prize striper at Montauk.

"Bon soir, bel esprit, God damn, Jimmy," Mr. Aquila said. He was on first name terms with everyone. "Here's a cool day for color, oui! Cool. Slang. I have in me to buy a picture."

"Good morning, Mr. Aquila," Derelict answered. He had the seamed face of a cardsharp, but his blue eyes were honest and his smile was disarming. However, at this moment his smile seemed strained, as though the volatile appearance of Aquila had unnerved him.

"I'm in the mood for your man, by Jeez," Aquila said, rapidly opening cases, fingering ivories and testing the porcelains. "What's his name, my old? Artist like Bosch. Like Heinrich Kley. You handle him, parbleu, exclusive. O si sic omnia, by Zeus!"

"Jeffrey Halsyon?" Derelict asked timidly.

"Oeil de boeuf!" Aquila cried. "What a memory. Chryselephantine. Exactly the artist I want. He is my favorite. A monochrome, preferably. A small Jeffrey Halsyon for Aquila, bitte. Wrap her up."

"I wouldn't have believed it," Derelict muttered.

"Ah! Ah-ha? This is not 100 proof guaranteed Ming," Mr. Aquila exclaimed, brandishing an exquisite vase. "Caveat emptor, by damn. Well, Jimmy? I snap my fingers. No Halsyons in stock, old faithful?"

"It's extremely odd, Mr. Aquila." Derelict seemed to struggle with himself. "Your coming in like this. A Halsyon monochrome arrived not five minutes ago."

"You see? Tempo ist Richtung. Well?"

"I'd rather not show it to you. For personal reasons, Mr. Aquila."

"HimmelHerrGott! Pourquoi? She's bespoke?"

"N-no, sir. Not for my personal reasons. For your personal reasons."

"Oh? God damn. Explain myself to me."

"Anyway it isn't for sale, Mr. Aquila. It can't be sold."

"For why not? Speak, old fish & chips."

"I can't say, Mr. Aquila."

"Zut alors! Must I judo your arm, Jimmy? You can't show. You can't sell. Me, internally, I have pressurized myself for a Jeffrey Halsyon. My favorite. God damn. Show me the Halsyon or sic transit gloria mundi. You hear me, Jimmy?"

Derelict hesitated, then shrugged. "Very well, Mr. Aquila. I'll show you."

Derelict led Aquila past cases of china and silver, past lacquer and bronzes and suits of shimmering armor to the gallery in the rear of the shop where dozens of paintings hung on the gray velour walls, glowing under warm spotlights. He opened a drawer in a Goddard breakfront and took out a Manila envelope. On the envelope was printed BABYLON INSTITUTE. From the envelope Derelict withdrew a dollar bill and handed it to Mr. Aquila.

"Jeffrey Halsyon's latest," he said.

With a fine pen and carbon ink, a cunning hand had drawn another portrait over the face of George Washington on the dollar bill. It was a hateful, diabolic face set in a hellish background. It was a face to strike terror, in a scene to inspire loathing. The face was a portrait of Mr. Aquila.

"God damn," Mr. Aquila said.

"You see, sir? I didn't want to hurt your feelings."

"Now I must own him, big boy." Mr. Aquila appeared to be fascinated by the portrait. "Is she accident or for purpose? Does Halsyon know myself? Ergo sum."

"Not to my knowledge, Mr. Aquila. But in any event I can't sell the drawing. It's evidence of a felony . . . mutilating United States currency. It must be destroyed."

"Never!" Mr. Aquila returned the drawing as though he feared the dealer would instantly set fire to it. "Never, Jimmy. Nevermore quoth the raven. God damn. Why does he draw on money, Halsyon? My picture, pfui. Criminal libels but n'importe. But pictures on money? Wasteful. Joci causa."

"He's insane, Mr. Aquila."

"No! Yes? Insane?" Aquila was shocked.

"Quite insane, sir. It's very sad. They've had to put him away. He spends his time drawing these pictures on money."

"God damn, mon ami. Who gives him money?"

"I do, Mr. Aquila; and his friends. Whenever we visit him he begs for money for his drawings."

"Le jour viendra, by Jeez! Why you don't give him paper for drawings, eh, my ancient of days?"

Derelict smiled sadly. "We tried that, sir. When we gave Jeff paper, he drew pictures of money."

"HimmelHerrGott! My favorite artist. In the looney bin. Eh bien. How in the holy hell am I to buy paintings from same if such be the case?"

"You won't, Mr. Aquila. I'm afraid no one will ever buy a Halsyon again. He's quite hopeless."

"Why does he jump his tracks, Jimmy?"

"They say it's a withdrawal, Mr. Aquila. His success did it to him."

"Ah? Q.E.D. me, big boy. Translate."

"Well, sir, he's still a young man; in his thirties and very immature. When he became so very successful, he wasn't ready for it. He wasn't prepared for the responsibilities of his life and his career. That's what the doctors told me. So he turned his back on everything and withdrew into childhood."

"Ah? And the drawing on money?"

"They say that's his symbol of his return to childhood, Mr. Aquila. It proves he's too young to know what money is for."

"Ah? Oui. Ja. Astute, by crackey. And my portrait?"

"I can't explain that, Mr. Aquila, unless you have met him in the past and he remembers you somehow."

"Hmmm. Perhaps. So. You know something, my attic of Greece? I am disappointed. Je n'oublierai jamais. I am most severely disappointed. God damn. No more Halsyons ever? Merde. My slogan. We must do something about Jeffrey Halsyon. I will not be disappointed. We must do something."

Mr. Solon Aquila nodded his head emphatically, took out a cigarette, took out a lighter, then paused, deep in thought. After a long moment, he nodded again, this time with decision, and did an astonishing thing. He returned the lighter to his pocket, took out another, glanced around quickly and lit it under Mr. Derelict's nose.

Mr. Derelict appeared not to notice. Mr. Derelict appeared, in one instant, without transition, to be stuffed. Allowing the lighter to burn, Mr. Aquila placed it carefully on a ledge in front of the art dealer who stood before it without moving. The orange flame gleamed on his glassy eyeballs.

Aquila darted out into the shop, searched and found a rare Chinese crystal globe. He took it from its case, warmed it against his heart and peered into it. He mumbled. He nodded. He returned the globe to the case, went to the cashier's desk, took a pad and pencil and began ciphering in symbols that bore no relationship to any language or any graphology. He nodded again, tore up the sheet of paper and took out his wallet.

From the wallet he removed a dollar bill. He placed the bill on the glass counter, took an assortment of fountain pens from his vest pocket, selected one and unscrewed it. Carefully shielding his eyes, he allowed one drop to fall from the pen-point onto the bill. There was a blinding flash of light. There was a humming vibration that slowly died.

Mr. Aquila returned the pens to his pocket, carefully picked up the bill by a corner and ran back into the picture gallery where the art dealer still stood staring glassily at the orange flame. Aquila fluttered the bill before the sightless eyes.

"Listen, my ancient," Aquila whispered. "You will visit Jeffrey Halsyon this afternoon. N'est-ce-pas? You will give him this very own coin of the realm when he asks for drawing materials. Eh? God damn." He removed Mr. Derelict's wallet from his pocket, placed the bill inside and returned the wallet.

"And this is why you make the visit," Aquila continued. "It is because you have had an inspiration from le Diable Boiteux. Nolens volens, the lame devil has inspired you with a plan for healing Jeffrey Halsyon. God damn. You will show him samples of his great art of the past to bring him to his senses. Memory is the all-mother. HimmelHerrGott! You hear me, big boy? You do what I say. Go today and devil take the hindmost."

Mr. Aquila picked up the burning lighter, lit his cigarette and permitted the flame to go out. As he did so, he said: "No, my holy of holies! Jeffrey Halsyon is too great an artist to languish in durance vile. He must be returned to this world. He must be returned to me. L sempra l'ora. I will not be disappointed. You hear me, Jimmy? I will not!"

"Perhaps there's hope, Mr. Aquila," James Derelict said. "Something's just occurred to me while you were talking . . . a way to bring Jeff back to sanity. I'm going to try it this afternoon."

As he drew the face of the Faraway Fiend over George Washington's portrait on a bill, Jeffrey Halsyon dictated his autobiography to nobody.

"Like Cellini," he recited. "Line and literature simultaneously. Hand in hand, although all art is one art, holy brothers in barbiturate, near ones and dear ones in nembutal. Very well. I commence: I was born. I am dead. Baby wants a dollar. No——"

He arose from the padded floor and raged from padded wall to padded wall, envisioning anger as a deep purple fury running into the pale lavenders of recrimination by the magic of his brushwork, his chiaroscuro, by the clever blending of oil, pigment, light and the stolen genius of Jeffrey Halsyon torn from him by the Faraway Fiend whose hideous face——

"Begin anew," he muttered. "We darken the highlights. Start with the underpainting . . ." He squatted on the floor again, picked up the quill drawing pen whose point was warranted harmless, dipped it into carbon ink whose contents were warranted poisonless, and applied himself to the monstrous face of the Faraway Fiend which was replacing the first president on the dollar.

"I was born," he dictated to space while his cunning hand wrought beauty and horror on the banknote paper. "I had peace. I had hope. I had art. I had peace. Mama. Papa. Kin I have a glass a water? Oooo! There was a big bad bogey man who gave me a look; a big bad look and he fighta baby. Baby's afraid. Mama! Baby wantsa make pretty pictures onna pretty paper for Mama and Papa. Look, Mama. Baby makin' a picture of the bad bogey man who fighta baby with a mean look, a black look with his black eyes like pools of hell, like cold fires of terror, like faraway fiends from faraway fears—— Who's that!"

The cell door unbolted. Halsyon leaped into a corner and cowered, naked and squalling, as the door was opened for the Faraway Fiend to enter. But it was only the medicine man in his white jacket and a stranger man in black suit, black homburg, carrying a black portfolio with the initials J. D. lettered on it in a bastard gold Gothic with ludicrous overtones of Goudy and Baskerville.

"Well, Jeffrey?" the medicine man inquired heartily.

"Dollar?" Halsyon whined. "Kin baby have a dollar?"

"I've brought an old friend, Jeffrey. You remember Mr. Derelict?"

"Dollar," Halsyon whined. "Baby wants a dollar."

"What happened to the last one, Jeffrey? You haven't finished it yet, have you?"

Halsyon sat on the bill to conceal it, but the medicine man was too quick for him. He snatched it up and he and the stranger man examined it.

"As great as all the rest," Derelict sighed. "Greater. What a magnificent talent wasting away . . ."

Halsyon began to weep. "Baby wants a dollar!" he cried.

The stranger man took out his wallet, selected a dollar bill and handed it to Halsyon. As soon as he touched it, he heard it sing and he tried to sing with it, but it was singing him a private song so he had to listen.

It was a lovely dollar; smooth but not too new, with a faintly matte surface that would take ink like kisses. George Washington looked reproachful but resigned, as though he were used to the treatment in store for him. And indeed he might well be, for he was much older on this dollar. Much older than on any other for his serial number was 5,271,009 which made him 5,000,000 years old and more, and the oldest he had ever been before was 2,000,000.

As Halsyon squatted contentedly on the floor and dipped his pen in the ink as the dollar told him to, he heard the medicine man say, "I don't think I should leave you alone, Mr. Derelict."

"No, we must be, doctor. Jeff always was shy about his work. He could only discuss it with me when we were alone."

"How much time would you need?"

"Give me an hour."

"I doubt very much whether it'll do any good."

"But there's no harm trying?"

"I suppose not. All right, Mr. Derelict. Call the nurse when you're through."

The door opened; the door closed. The stranger man named Derelict put his hand on Halsyon's shoulder in a friendly, intimate way. Halsyon looked up at him and grinned cleverly, meanwhile waiting for the sound of the bolt in the door. It came; like a shot, like a final nail in a coffin.

"Jeff, I've brought some of your old work with me," Derelict said in a voice that was only approximately casual. "I thought you might like to look it over with me."

"Have you got a watch on you?" Halsyon asked.

Restraining his start of surprise at Halsyon's normal tone, the art dealer took out his pocket watch and displayed it.

"Lend it to me for a minute."

Derelict unchained the watch and handed it over. Halsyon took it carefully and said, "All right. Go ahead with the pictures."

"Jeff!" Derelict exclaimed. "This is you again, isn't it? This is the way you always———"

"Thirty," Halsyon interrupted. "Thirty-five, forty, forty-five, fifty, fifty-five, ONE." He concentrated on the flicking second hand with rapt expectation.

"No, I guess it isn't," the dealer muttered. "I only imagined you sounded—— Oh, well." He opened the portfolio and began sorting mounted drawings.

"Forty, forty-five, fifty, fifty-five, TWO."

"Here's one of your earliest, Jeff. Remember when you came into the gallery with the roughs and we thought you were the new polisher from the agency? Took you months to forgive us. You always claimed we bought your first picture just to apologize. Do you still think so?"

"Forty, forty-five, fifty, fifty-five, THREE."

"Here's that tempera that gave you so many heartaches. I was wondering if you'd care to try another? I really don't think tempera is as inflexible as you claim and I'd be interested to have you try again now that your technique's so much more matured. What do you say?"

"Forty, forty-five, fifty, fifty-five, FOUR."

"Jeff, put down that watch."

"Ten, fifteen, twenty, twenty-five . . ."

"What the devil's the point of counting minutes?"

"Well," Halsyon said reasonably, "sometimes they lock the door and go away. Other times they lock up and stay and spy on you. But they never spy longer than three minutes so I'm giving them five just to make sure. FIVE."

Halsyon gripped the small pocket watch in his big fist and drove the fist cleanly into Derelict's jaw. The dealer dropped without a sound. Halsyon dragged him to the wall, stripped him naked, dressed himself in his clothes, repacked the portfolio and closed it. He picked up the dollar bill and pocketed it. He picked up the bottle of carbon ink warranted non-poisonous and dashed the contents into his face.

Choking and shouting, he brought the nurse to the door.

"Let me out of here," Halsyon cried in a muffled voice. "That maniac tried to drown me. Threw ink in my face. I want out!"

The door was unbolted and opened. Halsyon shoved past the nurse man, cunningly mopping his blackened face with a hand that only smeared it more. As the nurse man started to enter the cell, Halsyon said, "Never mind Halsyon. He's all right. Get me a towel or something. Hurry!"

The nurse man locked the door again, turned and ran down the corridor. Halsyon waited until he disappeared into a supply room, then turned and ran in the opposite direction. He went through the heavy doors to the main wing corridor, still cleverly mopping, still sputtering with cunning indignation. He reached the main building. He was halfway out and still no alarm. He knew those brazen bells. They tested them every Wednesday noon.

It's like a Ringaleevio game, he told himself. It's fun. It's games. It's nothing to be scared of. It's being safely, sanely, joyously a kid again and when we quit playing I'm going home to mama and dinner and papa reading me the funnies and a I'm a kid again, really a kid again, forever.

There still was no hue and cry when he reached the main floor. He complained about his indignity to the receptionist. He complained to the protection guards as he forged James Derelict's name in the visitor's book, and his inky hand smeared such a mess on the page that the forgery went undetected. The guard buzzed the final gate open. Halsyon passed through into the street, and as he started away he heard the brass throats of the bells begin a clattering that terrified him.

He ran. He stopped. He tried to stroll. He could not. He lurched down the street until he heard the guards shouting. He darted around a corner, and another, tore up endless streets, heard cars behind him, sirens, bells, shouts, commands. It was a ghastly Catherine Wheel of flight. Searching desperately for a hiding place, Halsyon darted into the hallway of a desolate tenement.

Halsyon began to climb the stairs. He went up three at a clip, then two, then struggled step by step as his strength failed and panic paralyzed him. He stumbled at a landing and fell against a door. The door opened. The Faraway Fiend stood within, smiling briskly, rubbing his hands.

"Glückliche Reise," he said. "On the dot. God damn. You twenty-three skiddooed, eh? Enter, my old. I'm expecting you. Be it never so humble . . ."

Halsyon screamed.

"No, no, no! No Sturm und Drang, my beauty." Mr. Aquila clapped a hand over Halsyon's mouth, heaved him up, dragged him through the doorway and slammed the door.

"Presto-changeo," he laughed. "Exit Jeffrey Halsyon from mortal ken. Dieu vous garde."

Halsyon freed his mouth, screamed again and fought hysterically, biting and kicking. Mr. Aquila made a clucking noise, dipped into his pocket and brought out a package of cigarettes. He flipped one up expertly and broke it under Halsyon's nose. The artist at once subsided and suffered himself to be led to a couch, where Aquila cleaned the ink from his face and hands.

"Better, eh?" Mr. Aquila chuckled. "Non habit forming. God damn. Drinks now called for."

He filled a shot glass from a decanter, added a tiny cube of purple ice from a fuming bucket, and placed the drink in Halsyon's hand. Compelled by a gesture from Aquila, the artist drank it off. It made his brain buzz. He stared around, breathing heavily. He was in what appeared to be the luxurious waiting room of a Park Avenue physician. Queen Anne furniture. Axminster rug. Two Morlands and a Crome on the wall in gilt frames. They were genuine, Halsyon realized with amazement. Then, with even more amazement, he realized that he was thinking with coherence, with continuity. His mind was quite clear.

He passed a heavy hand over his forehead. "What's happened?" he asked faintly. "There's like . . . Something like a fever behind me. Nightmares."

"You have been sick," Aquila replied. "I am blunt, my old. This is a temporary return to sanity. It is no feat, God damn. Any doctor can do it. Niacin plus carbon dioxide. Id genus omne. We must search for something more permanent."

"What's this place?"

"Here? My office. Anteroom without. Consultation room within. Laboratory to left. In God we trust."

"I know you," Halsyon mumbled. "I know you from somewhere. I know your face."

"Oui. You have drawn and redrawn and redrawn me in your fever. Ecce homo. But you have the advantage, Halsyon. Where have we met? I ask myself." Aquila put on a brilliant speculum, tilted it over his left eye and let it shine into Halsyon's face. "Now I ask you. Where have we met?"

Blinded by the light, Halsyon answered dreamily. "At the Beaux Arts Ball . . . A long time ago . . . Before the fever . . ."

"Ah? Si. It was one-half year ago. I was there. An unfortunate night."

"No. A glorious night . . . Gay, happy, fun . . . Like a school dance . . . Like a prom in costume . . ."

"Always back to the childhood, eh?" Mr. Aquila murmured. "We must attend to that. Cetera desunt, young Lochinvar. Continue."

"I was with Judy . . . We realized we were in love that night. We realized how wonderful life was going to be. And then you passed and looked at me . . . Just once. You looked at me. It was horrible."

"Tk!" Mr. Aquila clicked his tongue in vexation. "Now I remember said incident. I was unguarded. Bad news from home. A pox on both my houses."

"You passed in red and black . . . Satanic. Wearing no mask. You looked at me . . . A red and black look I never forgot. A look from black eyes like pools of hell, like cold fires of terror. And with that look you robbed me of everything . . . of joy, of hope, of love, of life . . ."

"No, no!" Mr. Aquila said sharply. "Let us understand ourselves. My carelessness was the key that unlocked the door. But you fell into a chasm of your own making. Nevertheless, old beer & skittles, we must alter same." He removed the speculum and shook his finger at Halsyon. "We must bring you back to the land of the living. Auxilium ab alto. Jeez. That is for why I have arranged this meeting. What I have done I will undone, eh? But you must climb out of your own chasm. Knit up the ravelled sleave of care. Come inside."

He took Halsyon's arm, led him down a paneled hall, past a neat office and into a spanking white laboratory. It was all tile and glass with shelves of reagent bottles, porcelain filters, an electric oven, stock jars of acids, bins of raw materials. There was a small round elevation in the center of the floor, a sort of dais. Mr. Aquila placed a stool on the dais, placed Halsyon on the stool, got into a white lab coat and began to assemble apparatus.

"You," he chatted, "are an artist of the utmost. I do not

dorer le pilule. When Jimmy Derelict told me you were no longer at work, God damn! We must return him to his mut-tons, I said. Solon Aquila must own many canvases of Jeffrey Halsyon. We shall cure him. Hoc age."

"You're a doctor?" Halsyon asked.

"No. Let us say, a warlock. Strictly speaking, a witch-pathologist. Very highclass. No nostrums. Strictly modern magic. Black magic and white magic are passé, n'est-ce-pas? I cover entire spectrum, specializing mostly in the 15,000 angstrom band."

"You're a witch-doctor? Never!"

"Oh yes."

"In this kind of place?"

"Ah-ha? You too are deceived, eh? It is our camouflage. Many a modern laboratory you think concerns itself with science is devoted to magic. But we are scientific too. Parbleu! We move with the times, we warlocks. Witch's Brew now complies with Pure Food & Drug Act. Familiars 100 per cent sterile. Sanitary brooms. Cellophane-wrapped curses. Father Satan in rubber gloves. Thanks to Lord Lister; or is it Pas-teur? My idol."

The witch-pathologist gathered raw materials, consulted an ephemeris, ran off some calculations on an electronic com-puter and continued to chat.

"Fugit hora," Aquila said. "Your trouble, my old, is loss of sanity. Oui? Lost in one damn flight from reality and one damn desperate search for peace brought on by one un-guarded look from me to you. Hélas! I apologize for that, R.S.V.P." With what looked like a miniature tennis line-marker, he rolled a circle around Halsyon on the dais. "But your trouble is, to wit: You search for the peace of infancy. You should be fighting to acquire the peace of maturity, n'est-ce-pas? Jeez."

Aquila drew circles and pentagons with a glittering com-pass and rule, weighed out powders on a micro-beam balance, dropped various liquids into crucibles from calibrated burettes, and continued: "Many warlocks do brisk trade in potions from Fountains of Youths. Oh yes. Are many youths and many fountains; but none for you. No. Youth is not for artists. Age is the cure. We must purge your youth and grow you up, nicht wahr?"

"No," Halsyon argued. "No. Youth is the art. Youth is the dream. Youth is the blessing."

"For some, yes. For many, not. Not for you. You are cursed, my adolescent. We must purge you. Lust for power. Lust for sex. Injustice collecting. Escape from reality. Passion for revenges. Oh yes, Father Freud is also my idol. We wipe your slate clean at very small price."

"What price?"

"You will see when we are finished."

Mr. Aquila deposited liquids and powders around the helpless artist in crucibles and petri dishes. He measured and cut fuses, set up a train from the circle to an electric timer which he carefully adjusted. He went to a shelf of serum bottles, took down a small Woulff vial numbered 5-271-009, filled a syringe and meticulously injected Halsyon.

"We begin," he said, "the purge of your dreams. Voila!"

He tripped the electric timer and stepped behind a lead shield. There was a moment of silence. Suddenly black music crashed from a concealed loudspeaker and a recorded voice began an intolerable chant. In quick succession, the powders and liquids around Halsyon burst into flame. He was engulfed in music and fire fumes. The world began to spin around him in a roaring confusion . . .

The president of the United Nations came to him. He was tall and gaunt, sprightly but bitter. He was wringing his hands in dismay.

"Mr. Halsyon! Mr. Halsyon!" he cried. "Where have you been, my cupcake? God damn. Hoc tempore. Do you know what has happened?"

"No," Halsyon answered. "What's happened?"

"After your escape from the looney bin. Bango! H-bombs everywhere. The two-hour war. It is over. Hora fugit, old faithful. Virility is over."

"What!"

"Hard radiation, Mr. Halsyon, has destroyed the virility of the world. God damn. You are the only man left capable of engendering children. No doubt on account of a mysterious mutant strain in your makeup which it makes you different. Jeez."

"No."

"Oui. It is your responsibility to repopulate the world. We have taken for you a suite at the Odeon. It has three bedrooms. Three, my favorite. A prime number."

"Hot dog!" Halsyon said. "This is my big dream."

His progress to the Odeon was a triumph. He was garlanded with flowers, serenaded, hailed and cheered. Ecstatic women displayed themselves wickedly before him, begging for his attention. In his suite, Halsyon was wined and dined. A tall, gaunt man entered subserviently. He was sprightly but bitter. He had a list in his hand.

"I am World Procurer at your service, Mr. Halsyon," he said. He consulted his list. "God damn. Are 5,271,009 virgins clamoring for your attention. All guaranteed beautiful. Ewig-Weibliche. Pick a number from one to 5,000,000."

"We'll start with a redhead," Halyson said.

They brought him a redhead. She was slender, boyish, with a small hard bosom. The next was fuller with a rollicking rump. The fifth was Junoesque and her breasts were like African pears. The tenth was a voluptuous Rembrandt. The twentieth was wiry. The thirtieth was slender and boyish with a small hard bosom.

"Haven't we met before?" Halsyon inquired.

"No," she said.

The next was fuller with a rollicking rump.

"The body is familiar," Halsyon said.

"No," she answered.

The fiftieth was Junoesque with breasts like African pears.

"Surely?" Halsyon said.

"Never," she answered.

The World Procurer entered with Halsyon's morning aphrodisiac.

"Never touch the stuff," Halsyon said.

"God damn," the Procurer exlaimed. "You are a veritable giant. An elephant. No wonder you are the beloved Adam. Tant soit peu. No wonder they all weep for love of you." He drank off the aphrodisiac himself.

"Have you noticed they're all getting to look alike?" Halsyon complained.

"But no! Are all different. Parbleu! This is an insult to my office."

"Oh, they're different from one to another, but the types keep repeating."

"Ah? This is life, my old. All life is cyclic. Have you not, as an artist, noticed?"

"I didn't think it applied to love."

"To all things. Wahrheit und Dichtung."

"What was that you said about them weeping?"

"Oui. They all weep."

"Why?"

"For ecstatic love of you. God damn."

Halsyon thought over the succession of boyish, rollicking, Junoesque, Rembrandtesque, wiry, red, blonde, brunette, white, black and brown women.

"I hadn't noticed," he said.

"Observe today, my world father. Shall we commence?"

It was true. Halsyon hadn't noticed. They all wept. He was flattered but depressed.

"Why don't you laugh a little?" he asked.

They would not or could not.

Upstairs on the Odeon roof where Halsyon took his afternoon exercise, he questioned his trainer who was a tall, gaunt man with a sprightly but bitter expression.

"Ah?" said the trainer. "God damn. I don't know, old scotch & soda. Perhaps because it is a traumatic experience for them."

"Traumatic?" Halsyon puffed. "Why? What do I do to them?"

"Ah-ha? You joke, eh? All the world knows what you do to them."

"No, I mean . . . How can it be traumatic? They're all fighting to get to me, aren't they? Don't I come up to expectations?"

"A mystery. Tripotage. Now, beloved father of the world, we practice the push-ups. Ready? Begin."

Downstairs, in the Odeon restaurant, Halsyon questioned the headwaiter, a tall, gaunt man with a sprightly manner but bitter expression.

"We are men of the world, Mr. Halsyon. Suo jure. Surely you understand. These women love you and can expect no more than one night of love. God damn. Naturally they are disappointed."

"What do they want?"

"What every woman wants, my gateway to the west. A permanent relationship. Marriage."

"Marriage!"

"Oui."

"All of them?"

"Oui."

"All right. I'll marry all 5,271,009."

But the World Procurer objected. "No, no, no, young Lochinvar. God damn. Impossible. Aside from religious difficulties there are human also. God damn. Who could manage such a harem?"

"Then I'll marry one."

"No, no, no. Pensez à moi. How could you make the choice? How could you select? By lottery, drawing straws, tossing coins?"

"I've already selected one."

"Ah? Which?"

"My girl," Halsyon said slowly. "Judith Field."

"So. Your sweetheart?"

"Yes."

"She is far down on the list of 5,000,000."

"She's always been number one on my list. I want Judith." Halsyon sighed. "I remember how she looked at the Beaux Arts Ball . . . There was a full moon . . ."

"But there will be no full moon until the twenty-sixth."

"I want Judith."

"The others will tear her apart out of jealousy. No, no, no, Mr. Halsyon, we must stick to the schedule. One night for all, no more for any."

"I want Judith . . . or else."

"It will have to be discussed in council. God damn."

It was discussed in the U.N. council by a dozen delegates, all tall, gaunt, sprightly but bitter. It was decided to permit Jeffrey Halsyon one secret marriage.

"But no domestic ties," the World Procurer warned. "No faithfulness to your wife. That must be understood. We cannot spare you from our program. You are indispensable."

They brought the lucky Judith Field to the Odeon. She was a tall, dark girl with cropped curly hair and lovely tennis legs. Halsyon took her hand. The World Procurer tiptoed out.

"Hello, darling," Halsyon murmured.

Judith looked at him with loathing. Her eyes were wet, her face bruised from weeping.

"Hello, darling," Halsyon repeated.

"If you touch me, Jeff," Judith said in a strangled voice, "I'll kill you."

"Judy!"

"That disgusting man explained everything to me. He didn't seem to understand when I tried to explain to him . . . I was praying you'd be dead before it was my turn."

"But this is marriage, Judy."

"I'd rather die than be married to you."

"I don't believe you. We've been in love for——"

"For God's sake, Jeff, love's over for you. Don't you understand? Those women cry because they hate you. I hate you. The world loathes you. You're disgusting."

Halsyon stared at the girl and saw the truth in her face. In an excess of rage he tried to seize her. She fought him bitterly. They careened around the huge living room of the suite, overturning furniture, their breath hissing, their fury mounting. Halsyon struck Judith Field with his big fist to end the struggle once and for all. She reeled back, clutched at a drape, smashed through a french window and fell fourteen floors to the street like a gyrating doll.

Halsyon looked down in horror. A crowd gathered around the smashed body. Faces upturned. Fists shook. An ominous growl began. The World Procurer dashed into the suite.

"My old! My blue!" he cried. "What have you done? Per conto. It is a spark that will ignite savagery. You are in very grave danger. God damn."

"Is it true they all hate me?"

"Hélas, then you have discovered the truth? That indiscreet girl. I warned her. Oui. You are loathed."

"But you told me I was loved. The new Adam. Father of the new world."

"Oui. You are the father, but what child does not hate its father? You are also a legal rapist. What woman does not hate being forced to embrace a man . . . even by necessity for survival? Come quickly, my rock & rye. Passim. You are in great danger."

He dragged Halsyon to a back elevator and took him down to the Odeon cellar.

"The army will get you out. We take you to Turkey at once and effect a compromise."

Halsyon was transferred to the custody of a tall, gaunt, bitter army colonel who rushed him through underground passages to a side street where a staff car was waiting. The colonel thrust Halsyon inside.

"Jacta alea est," he said to the driver. "Speed, my corporal. Protect old faithful. To the airport. Alors!"

"God damn, sir," the corporal replied. He saluted and started the car. As it twisted through the streets at breakneck speed, Halsyon glanced at him. He was a tall, gaunt man, sprightly but bitter.

"Kulturkampf der Menschheit," the corporal muttered. "Jeez!"

A giant barricade had been built across the street, improvised of ash barrels, furniture, overturned cars, traffic stanchions. The corporal was forced to brake the car. As he slowed for a U-turn, a mob of women appeared from doorways, cellars, stores. They were screaming. Some of them brandished improvised clubs.

"Excelsior!" the corporal cried. "God damn." He tried to pull his service gun out of its holster. The women yanked open the car doors and tore Halsyon and the corporal out. Halsyon broke free, struggled through the wild clubbing mob, dashed to the sidewalk, stumbled and dropped with a sickening yaw through an open coal chute. He shot down and spilled out into an endless black space. His head whirled. A stream of stars sailed before his eyes . . .

And he drifted alone in space, a martyr, misunderstood, a victim of cruel injustice.

He was still chained to what had once been the wall of Cell 5, Block 27, Tier 100, Wing 9 of the Callisto Penitentiary until the unexpected gamma explosion had torn the vast fortress dungeon—vaster than the Chateau d'If—apart. That explosion, he realized, had been detonated by the Grssh.

His assets were his convict clothes, a helmet, one cylinder of O_2, his grim fury at the injustice that had been done him, and his knowledge of the secret of how the Grssh could be defeated in their maniacal quest for solar domination.

The Grssh, ghastly marauders from Omicron Ceti, space-degenerates, space-imperialists, cold-blooded, roachlike, depending for their metabolism upon the psychotic horrors which they engendered in man through mental control and upon which they fed, were rapidly conquering the Galaxy. They were irresistible, for they possessed the power of simul-kinesis . . . the ability to be in two places at the same time.

Against the vault of space, a dot of light moved, slowly, like a stricken meteor. It was a rescue ship, Halsyon realized, combing space for survivors of the explosion. He wondered whether the light of Jupiter, flooding him with rusty radiation, would make him visible to the rescuers. He wondered whether he wanted to be rescued at all.

"It will be the same thing again," Halsyon grated. "Falsely accused by Balorsen's robot . . . Falsely convicted by Judith's father . . . Repudiated by Judith herself . . . Jailed again . . . and finally destroyed by the Grssh as they destroy the last strongholds of Terra. Why not die now?"

But even as he spoke he realized he lied. He was the one man with the one secret that could save the earth and the very Galaxy itself. He must survive. He must fight.

With indomitable will, Halyson struggled to his feet, fighting the constricting chains. With the steely strength he had developed as a penal laborer in the Grssh mines, he waved and shouted. The spot of light did not alter its slow course away from him. Then he saw the metal link of one of his chains strike a brilliant spark from the flinty rock. He resolved on a desperate expedient to signal the rescue ship.

He detached the plasti-hose of the O_2 tank from his plasti-helmet, and permitted the stream of life-giving oxygen to spurt into space. With trembling hands, he gathered the links of his leg chain and dashed them against the rock under the oxygen. A spark glowed. The oxygen caught fire. A brilliant geyser of white flame spurted for half a mile into space.

Husbanding the last oxygen in his plasti-helmet, Halsyon twisted the cylinder slowly, sweeping the fan of flame back and forth in a last desperate bid for rescue. The atmosphere in his plasti-helmet grew foul and acrid. His ears roared. His sight flickered. At last his senses failed . . .

When he recovered consciousness he was in a plasti-cot in the cabin of a starship. The high frequency whine told him they were in overdrive. He opened his eyes. Balorsen stood before the plasti-cot, and Balorsen's robot, and High Judge Field, and his daughter Judith. Judith was weeping. The robot was in magnetic clamps and winced as General Balorsen lashed him again and again with a nuclear whip.

"Parbleu! God damn!" the robot grated. "It is true I framed Jeff Halsyon. Ouch! Flux de bouche. I was the space-pirate who space-hijacked the space-freighter. God damn. Ouch! The bartender in the Spaceman's Saloon was my accomplice. When Jackson wrecked the heli-cab I went to the space-garage and X-beamed the sonic *before* Tantial murdered O'Leary. Aux armes. Jeez. Ouch!"

"There you have the confession, Halsyon," General Balorsen grated. He was tall, gaunt, bitter. "By God. Ars est celare artem. You are innocent."

"I falsely condemned you, old faithful," Judge Field grated. He was tall, gaunt, bitter. "Can you forgive this God damn fool? We apologize."

"We wronged you, Jeff," Judith whispered. "How can you ever forgive us? Say you forgive us."

"You're sorry for the way you treated me," Halsyon grated. "But it's only because on account of a mysterious mutant strain in my makeup which it makes me different, I'm the one man with the one secret that can save the Galaxy from the Grssh."

"No, no, no, old gin & tonic," General Balorsen pleaded. "God damn. Don't hold grudges. Save us from the Grssh."

"Save us, faute de mieux, save us, Jeff," Judge Field put in.

"Oh please, Jeff, please," Judith whispered. "The Grssh are everywhere and coming closer. We're taking you to the U.N. You must tell the council how to stop the Grssh from being in two places at the same time."

The starship came out of overdrive and landed on Governors Island where a delegation of world dignitaries met the ship and rushed Halsyon to the General Assembly room of the U.N. They drove down the strangely rounded streets lined with strangely rounded buildings which had all been altered when it was discovered that the Grssh always appeared in corners. There was not a corner or an angle left on all Terra.

The General Assembly was filled when Halsyon entered. Hundreds of tall, gaunt, bitter diplomats applauded as he made his way to the podium, still dressed in convict plasti-clothes. Halsyon looked around resentfully.

"Yes," he grated. "You all applaud. You all revere me now; but where were you when I was framed, convicted and jailed . . . an innocent man? Where were you then?"

"Halsyon, forgive us. God damn!" they shouted.

"I will not forgive you. I suffered for seventeen years in the Grssh mines. Now it's your turn to suffer."

"Please, Halyson!"

"Where are your experts? Your professors? Your specialists? Where are your electronic calculators? Your super thinking machines? Let them solve the mystery of the Grssh."

"They can't, old whiskey & sour. Entre nous. They're stopped cold. Save us, Halsyon. Auf wiedersehen."

Judith took his arm. "Not for my sake, Jeff," she whispered. "I know you'll never forgive me for the injustice I did you. But for the sake of all the other girls in the Galaxy who love and are loved."

"I still love you, Judy."

"I've always loved you, Jeff."

"Okay. I didn't want to tell them but you talked me into it." Halsyon raised his hand for silence. In the ensuing hush he spoke softly. "The secret is this, gentlemen. Your calculators have assembled data to ferret out the secret weakness of the Grssh. They have not been able to find any. Consequently you have assumed that the Grssh have no secret weakness. *That was a wrong assumption.*"

The General Assembly held its breath.

"Here is the secret. *You should have assumed there was something wrong with the calculators.*"

"God damn!" the General Assembly cried. "Why didn't we think of that? God damn!"

"And I know what's wrong!"

There was a deathlike hush.

The door of the General Assembly burst open. Professor Deathhush, tall, gaunt, bitter, tottered in. "Eureka!" he cried. "I've found it. God damn. Something wrong with the thinking machines. Three comes *after* two, not before."

The General Assembly exploded into cheers. Professor Deathhush was seized and pummeled happily. Bottles were opened. His health was drunk. Several medals were pinned on him. He beamed.

"Hey!" Halsyon called. "That was my secret. I'm the one man who on account of a mysterious mutant strain in my——"

The ticker-tape began pounding:

Attention. Attention. Hushenkov in Moscow reports defect in calculators. 3 comes after 2 and not before. Repeat: after (underscore) not before.

A postman ran in. "Special delivery from Doctor Lifehush at Caltech. Says something's wrong with the thinking machines. Three comes after two, not before."

A telegraph boy delivered a wire: THINKING MACHINE WRONG STOP TWO COMES BEFORE THREE STOP NOT AFTER STOP. VON DREAMHUSH, HEIDELBERG.

A bottle was thrown through the window. It crashed on the floor revealing a bit of paper on which was scrawled: *Did you ever stopp to thinc that maibe the number 3 comes after 2 insted of in front? Down with the Grish. Mr. Hush-Hush.*

Halsyon buttonholed Judge Field. "What the hell is this?" he demanded. "I thought I was the one man in the world with that secret."

"HimmelHerrGott!" Judge Field replied impatiently. "You are all alike. You dream you are the one man with a secret, the one man with a wrong, the one man with an injustice, with a girl, without a girl, with or without anything. God damn. You bore me, you one-man dreamers. Get lost."

Judge Field shouldered him aside. General Balorsen shoved him back. Judith Field ignored him. Balorsen's robot sneakily tripped him into a corner where a Grssh, also in a corner on Neptune, appeared, did something unspeakable to Halsyon and disappeared with him, screaming, jerking and sobbing into a horror that was a delicious meal for the Grssh but an agonizing nightmare for Halsyon . . .

From which his mother awakened him and said, "This'll teach you not to sneak peanut-butter sandwiches in the middle of the night, Jeffrey."

"Mama?"

"Yes. It's time to get up, dear. You'll be late for school."

She left the room. He looked around. He looked at himself. It was true. True! The glorious realization came upon him. His dream had come true. He was ten years old again, in the flesh that was his ten-year-old body, in the home that was his boyhood home, in the life that had been his life in the nineteen thirties. And within his head was the knowledge, the experience, the sophistication of a man of thirty-three.

"Oh joy!" he cried. "It'll be a triumph. A triumph!"

He would be the school genius. He would astonish his parents, amaze his teachers, confound the experts. He would win scholarships. He would settle the hash of that kid Rennahan who used to bully him. He would hire a typewriter and write all the successful plays and stories and novels he remembered. He would cash in on that lost opportunity with Judy Field behind the memorial in Isham Park. He would steal inventions, discoveries, get in on the ground floor of new industries, make bets, play the stock market. He would own the world by the time he caught up with himself.

He dressed with difficulty. He had forgotten where his clothes were kept. He ate breakfast with difficulty. This was no time to explain to his mother that he'd gotten into the habit of starting the day with coffee laced with rye. He missed his morning cigarette. He had no idea where his schoolbooks were. His mother had trouble starting him out.

"Jeff's in one of his moods," he heard her mutter. "I hope he gets through the day."

The day started with Rennahan laying for him on the corner opposite the Boys' Entrance. Halsyon remembered him as a big tough kid with a vicious expression. He was astonished to discover that Rennahan was skinny, harassed and obviously compelled by some bedevilments to be omnivorously aggressive.

"Why, you're not hostile to me," Halsyon exclaimed. "You're just a mixed-up kid who's trying to prove something."

Rennahan punched him.

"Look, kid," Halsyon said kindly. "You really want to be friends with the world. You're just insecure. That's why you're compelled to fight."

Rennahan was deaf to spot analysis. He punched Halsyon harder. It hurt.

"Oh leave me alone," Halsyon said. "Go prove yourself on somebody else."

Rennahan, with two swift motions, knocked Halsyon's

books from under his arm and ripped his fly. There was nothing for it but to fight. Twenty years of watching films of the future Joe Louis did nothing for Halsyon. He was thoroughly licked. He was also late for school. Now was his chance to amaze his teachers.

"The fact is," he explained to Miss Ralph of the fifth grade, "I had a run-in with a neurotic. I can speak for his left hook but I won't answer for his Id."

Miss Ralph slapped him and sent him to the principal with a note, reporting unheard-of insolence.

"The only thing unheard of in this school," Halsyon told Mr. Snider, "is psychoanalysis. How can you pretend to be competent teachers if you don't——"

"Dirty little boy!" Mr. Snider interrupted angrily. He was tall, gaunt, bitter. "So you've been reading dirty books, eh?"

"What the hell's dirty about Freud?"

"And using profane language, eh? You need a lesson, you filthy little animal."

He was sent home with a note requesting an immediate consultation with his parents regarding the withdrawal of Jeffrey Halsyon from school as a degenerate in desperate need of correction and vocational guidance.

Instead of going home he went to a newsstand to check the papers for events on which to get a bet down. The headlines were full of the pennant race. But who the hell won the pennant in 1931? And the series? He couldn't for the life of him remember. And the stock market? He couldn't remember anything about that either. He'd never been particularly interested in such matters as a boy. There was nothing planted in his memory to call upon.

He tried to get into the library for further checks. The librarian, tall, gaunt, bitter, would not permit him to enter until chiildren's hour in the afternoon. He loafed on the streets. Wherever he loafed he was chased by gaunt and bitter adults. He was beginning to realize that ten-year-old boys had limited opportunities to amaze the world.

At lunch hour he met Judy Field and accompanied her home from school. He was appalled by her knobby knees and black corkscrew curls. He didn't like the way she smelled either. But he was rather taken with her mother who was the image of the Judy he remembered. He forgot himself with Mrs. Field and did one or two things that indeed confounded her. She drove him out of the house and then telephoned his mother, her voice shaking with indignation.

Halsyon went down to the Hudson River and hung around the ferry docks until he was chased. He went to a stationery store to inquire about typewriter rentals and was chased. He searched for a quiet place to sit, think, plan, perhaps begin the recall of a successful story. There was no quiet place to which a small boy would be admitted.

He slipped into his house at 4:30, dropped his books in his room, stole into the living room, sneaked a cigarette and was on his way out when he discovered his mother and father ambushing him. His mother looked shocked. His father looked gaunt and bitter.

"Oh," Halsyon said. "I suppose Snider phoned. I'd forgotten about that."

"*Mister* Snider," his mother said.

"And Mrs. Field," his father said.

"Look," Halsyon began. "We'd better get this straightened out. Will you listen to me for a few minutes? I have something startling to tell you and we've got to plan what to do about it. I——"

He yelped. His father had taken him by the ear and was marching him down the hall. Parents did not listen to children for a few minutes. They did not listen at all.

"Pop . . . Just a minute . . . Please! I'm trying to explain. I'm not really ten years old, I'm 33. There's been a freak in time, see? On account of a mysterious mutant strain in my makeup which——"

"Damn you! Be quiet!" his father shouted. The pain of his big hands, the suppressed fury in his voice silenced Halsyon.

He suffered himself to be led out of the house, four agonizing blocks to the school, and up one flight to Mr. Snider's office where a public school psychologist was waiting with the principal. He was a tall, gaunt, bitter man, but sprightly.

"Ah yes, yes," he said. "So this is our little degenerate. Our Scarface Al Capone, eh? Come, we take him to the clinic and there I shall take his journal intime. We will hope for the best. Nisi Prius. He cannot be all bad."

He took Halsyon's arm. Halsyon pulled his arm away and said, "Listen, you're an adult, intelligent man. You'll listen to me. My father's got emotional problems that blind him to the——"

His father gave him a tremendous box on the ear, grabbed his arm and thrust it back into the psychologist's grasp. Halsyon burst into tears. The psychologist led him out of the office and into the tiny school clinic. Halsyon was hysterical. He was trembling with frustration and terror.

"Won't anybody listen to me?" he sobbed. "Won't anybody try to understand? Is this what we're all like to kids? Is this what all kids go through?"

"Gently, my sausage," the psychologist murmured. He popped a pill into Halsyon's mouth and forced him to drink some water.

"You're all so damned inhuman," Halsyon wept. "You keep us out of your world, but you keep barging into ours. If you don't respect us why don't you leave us alone?"

"You begin to understand, eh?" the psychologist said. "We are two different breeds of animals, childrens and adults. God damn. I speak to you with frankness. Les absents ont toujours tort. There is no meetings of the minds. Jeez. There is nothing but war. It is why all childrens grow up hating their childhoods and searching for revenges. But there is never revenges. Pari mutuel. How can there be? Can a cat insult a king?"

"It's . . . S'hateful," Halsyon mumbled. The pill was taking effect rapidly. "Whole world's hateful. Full of conflicts'n'insults 'at can't be r'solved . . . or paid back . . . S'like a joke somebody's playin' on us. Silly joke without point. Isn't?"

As he slid down into darkness, he could hear the psychologist chuckle, but couldn't for the life of him understand what he was laughing at . . .

He picked up his spade and followed the first clown into the cemetery. The first clown was a tall man, gaunt, bitter, but sprightly.

"Is she to be buried in Christian burial that wilfully seeks her own salvation?" the first clown asked.

"I tell thee she is," Halsyon answered. "And therefore make her grave straight: the crowner hath sat on her, and finds it Christian burial."

"How can that be, unless she drowned herself in her own defense?"

"Why, 'tis found so."

They began to dig the grave. The first clown thought the matter over, then said, "It must be *se offendendo*; it cannot be else. For here lies the point: if I drown myself wittingly, it argues an act: and an act hath three branches; it is, to act, to do, to perform: argal, she drowned herself wittingly."

"Nay, but hear you, goodman delver——" Halsyon began.

"Give me leave," the first clown interrupted and went on with a tiresome discourse on quest-law. Then he turned sprightly and cracked a few professional jokes. At last Halsyon got away and went down to Yaughan's for a drink. When he returned, the first clown was cracking jokes with a couple of gentlemen who had wandered into the graveyard. One of them made quite a fuss about a skull.

The burial procession arrived; the coffin, the dead girl's brother, the king and queen, the priests and lords. They buried her, and the brother and one of the gentlemen began to quarrel over her grave. Halsyon paid no attention. There was a pretty girl in the procession, dark, with cropped curly hair and lovely long legs. He winked at her. She winked back. Halsyon edged over toward her, speaking with his eyes and she answered him saucily the same way.

Then he picked up his spade and followed the first clown into the cemetery. The first clown was a tall man, gaunt, with a bitter expression but a sprightly manner.

"Is she to be buried in Christian burial that wilfully seeks her own salvation?" the first clown asked.

"I tell thee she is," Halsyon answered. "And therefore make her grave straight: the crowner hath sat on her, and finds it Christian burial."

"How can that be, unless she drowned herself in her own defense?"

"Didn't you ask me that before?" Halsyon inquired.

"Shut up, old faithful. Answer the question."

"I could swear this happened before."

"God damn. Will you answer? Jeez."

"Why, 'tis found so."

They began to dig the grave. The first clown thought the matter over and began a long discourse on quest-law. After that he turned sprightly and cracked trade jokes. At last Halsyon got away and went down to Yaughan's for a drink. When he returned there were a couple of strangers at the grave and then the burial procession arrived.

There was a pretty girl in the procession, dark, with cropped curly hair and lovely long legs. Halsyon winked at her. She winked back. Halsyon edged over toward her, speaking with his eyes and she answering him the same way.

"What's your name?" he whispered.

"Judith," she answered.

"I have your name tattooed on me, Judith."

"You're lying, sir."

"I can prove it, Madam. I'll show you where I was tattooed."

"And where is that?"

"In Yaughan's tavern. It was done by a sailor off the *Golden Hind*. Will you see it with me tonight?"

Before she could answer, he picked up his spade and followed the first clown into the cemetery. The first clown was a tall man, gaunt, with a bitter expression but a sprightly manner.

"For God's sake!" Halsyon complained. "I could swear this happened before."

"Is she to be buried in Christian burial that wilfully seeks her own salvation?" the first clown asked.

"I just know we've been through all this."

"Will you answer the question!"

"Listen," Halsyon said doggedly. "Maybe I'm crazy; maybe not. But I've got a spooky feeling that all this happened before. It seems unreal. Life seems unreal."

The first clown shook his head. "HimmelHerrGott," he muttered. "It is as I feared. Lux et veritas. On account of a mysterious mutant strain in your makeup which it makes you different, you are treading on thin water. Ewigkeit! Answer the question."

"If I've answered it once, I've answered it a hundred times."

"Old ham & eggs," the first clown burst out, "you have answered it 5,271,009 times. God damn. Answer again."

"Why?"

"Because you must. Pot-au-feu. It is the life we must live."

"You call this life? Doing the same things over and over again? Saying the same things? Winking at girls and never getting any further?"

"No, no, no, my Donner und Blitzen. Do not question. It is a conspiracy we dare not fight. This is the life every man lives. Every man does the same things over and over. There is no escape."

"Why is there no escape?"

"I dare not say; I dare not. Vox populi. Others have questioned and disappeared. It is a conspiracy. I'm afraid."

"Afraid of what?"

"Of our owners."

"What? We are owned?"

"Si. Ach, ja! All of us, young mutant. There is no reality. There is no life, no freedom, no will. God damn. Don't you realize? We are . . . We are all characters in a book. As the book is read, we dance our dances; when the book is read again, we dance again. E pluribus unum. Is she to be buried in Christian burial that wilfully seeks her own salvation?"

"What are you saying?" Halsyon cried in horror. "We're puppets?"

"Answer the question."

"If there's no freedom, no free will, how can we be talking like this?"

"Whoever's reading our book is day-dreaming, my capitol of Dakota. Idem est. Answer the question."

"I will not. I'm going to revolt. I'll dance for our owners no longer. I'll find a better life . . . I'll find reality."

"No, no! It's madness, Jeffrey! Cul-de-sac!"

"All we need is one brave leader. The rest will follow. We'll smash the conspiracy that chains us!"

"It cannot be done. Play it safe. Answer the question."

Halsyon answered the question by picking up his spade and bashing in the head of the first clown who appeared not to notice. "Is she to be buried in Christian burial that wilfully seeks her own salvation?" he asked.

"Revolt!" Halsyon cried and bashed him again. The clown started to sing. The two gentlemen appeared. One said: "Has this fellow no feeling of business that he sings at grave-making?"

"Revolt! Follow me!" Halsyon shouted and swung his spade against the gentleman's melancholy head. He paid no attention. He chatted with his friend and the first clown. Halsyon whirled like a dervish, laying about him with his spade. The gentleman picked up a skull and philosophized over some person or persons named Yorick.

The funeral procession approached. Halsyon attacked it, whirling and turning, around and around with the clotted frenzy of a man in a dream.

"Stop reading the book," he shouted. "Let me out of the pages. Can you hear me? Stop reading the book! I'd rather be in a world of my own making. Let me go!"

There was a mighty clap of thunder, as of the covers of a mighty book slamming shut. In an instant Halsyon was swept spinning into the third compartment of the seventh circle of the Inferno in the fourteenth Canto of the *Divine Comedy* where they who have sinned against art are tormented by flakes of fire which are eternally showered down upon them. There he shrieked until he had provided sufficient amusement. Only then was he permitted to devise a text of his own . . . and he formed a new world, a romantic world, a world of his fondest dreams . . .

He was the last man on earth.

He was the last man on earth and he howled.

The hills, the valleys, the mountains and streams were his, his alone, and he howled.

5,271,009 houses were his for shelter. 5,271,009 beds were his for sleeping. The shops were his for the breaking and entering. The jewels of the world were his; the toys, the tools, the playthings, the necessities, the luxuries . . . all belonged to the last man on earth, and he howled.

He left the country mansion in the fields of Connecticut where he had taken up residence; he crossed into Westchester, howling; he ran south along what had once been the Hendrick Hudson Highway, howling; he crossed the bridge into Manhattan, howling; he ran downtown past lonely skyscrapers, department stores, amusement palaces, howling. He howled down Fifth Avenue, and at the corner of 50th Street he saw a human being.

She was alive, breathing; a beautiful woman. She was tall and dark with cropped curly hair and lovely long legs. She wore a white blouse, tiger-skin riding breeches and patent leather boots. She carried a rifle. She wore a revolver on her hip. She was eating stewed tomatoes from a can and she stared at Halsyon in unbelief. He howled. He ran up to her.

"I thought I was the last human on earth," she said.

"You're the last woman," Halsyon howled. "I'm the last man. Are you a dentist?"

"No," she said. "I'm the daughter of the unfortunate Professor Field whose well-intentioned but ill-advised experiment in nuclear fission has wiped mankind off the face of the earth with the exception of you and me who, no doubt on account of some mysterious mutant strain in our makeup which it makes us different, are the last of the old civilization and the first of the new."

"Didn't your father teach you anything about dentistry?" Halsyon howled.

"No," she said.

"Then lend me your gun for a minute."

She unholstered the revolver and handed it to Halsyon, meanwhile keeping her rifle ready. Halsyon cocked the gun.

"I wish you'd been a dentist," he howled.

"I'm a beautiful woman with an I.Q. of 141 which is more important for the propagation of a brave new beautiful race of men to inherit the good green earth," she said.

"Not with my teeth it isn't," Halsyon howled.

He clapped the revolver to his temple and blew his brains out.

He awoke with a splitting headache. He was lying on the tile dais alongside the stool, his bruised temple pressed against the cold floor. Mr. Aquila had emerged from the lead shield and was turning on an exhaust fan to clear the air.

"Bravo, my liver & onions," he chuckled. "The last one you did by yourself, eh? No assistance from yours truly required. Meglio tarde che mai. But you went over with a crack before I could catch you. God damn."

He helped Halsyon to his feet and led him into the consultation room where he seated him on a velvet chaise longue and gave him a glass of brandy.

"Guaranteed free of drugs," he said. "Noblesse oblige. Only the best spiritus frumenti. Now we discuss what we have done, eh? Jeez."

He sat down behind the desk, still sprightly, still bitter, and regarded Halsyon with kindliness. "Man lives by his decisions, n'est-ce-pas?" he began. "We agree, oui? A man has some five million two hundred seventy-one thousand and nine decisions to make in the course of his life. Peste! Is it a prime number? N'importe. Do you agree?"

Halsyon nodded.

"So, my coffee & doughnuts, it is the maturity of these decisions that decides whether a man is a man or a child. Nicht wahr? Malgré nous. A man cannot start making adult decisions until he has purged himself of the dreams of childhood. God damn. Such fantasies. They must go. Pfui."

"No," Halsyon said slowly. "It's the dreams that make my art . . . the dreams and fantasies that I translate into line and color . . ."

"God damn! Yes. Agreed. Maître d'hôtel! But adult dreams, not baby dreams. Baby dreams. Pfui! All men have them . . . To be the last man on earth and own the earth . . . To be the last fertile man on earth and own the women . . . To go back in time with the advantage of adult knowledge and win victories . . . To escape reality with the dream that life is make-believe . . . To escape responsibility with a fantasy of heroic injustice, of martyrdom with a happy ending . . . And there are hundreds more, equally popular, equally empty. God bless Father Freud and his merry men. He applies the quietus to such nonsense. Sic semper tyrannis. Avaunt!"

"But if everybody has those dreams, they can't be bad, can they?"

"For everybody read everybaby. Quid pro quo. God damn. Everybody in Fourteen century had lice. Did that make it good? No, my young, such dreams are for children. Too many adults are still childrens. It is you, the artists, who must lead them out as I have led you. I purge you; now you purge them."

"Why did you do this?"

"Because I have faith in you. Sic vos non vobis. It will not be easy for you. A long hard road and lonely."

"I suppose I ought to feel grateful," Halsyon muttered, "but I feel . . . well . . . empty. Cheated."

"Oh yes, God damn. If you live with one Jeez big ulcer long enough you miss him when he's cut out. You were hiding in an ulcer. I have robbed you of said refuge. Ergo: you feel cheated. Wait! You will feel even more cheated. There was a price to pay, I told you. You have paid it. Look."

Mr. Aquila held up a hand mirror. Halsyon glanced into it, then started and stared. A fifty-year-old face stared back at him: lined, hardened, solid, determined. Halsyon leaped to his feet.

"Gently, gently," Mr. Aquila admonished. "It is not so bad. It is damned good. You are still 33 in age of physique. You have lost none of your life—only all of your youth. What have you lost? A pretty face to lure young girls? Is that why you are wild?"

"Christ!" Halsyon cried.

"All right. Still, gently, my child. Here you are, purged, disillusioned, unhappy, bewildered, one foot on the hard road to maturity. Would you like this to have happened or not have happened? Si. I can do. This can never have happened. Spurlos versenkt. It is ten seconds from your escape. You can have your pretty young face back. You can be recaptured. You can return to the safe ulcer of the womb . . . a child again. Would you like same?"

"You can't!"

"Sauve qui peut, my Pike's Peak. I can. There is no end to the 15,000 angstrom band."

"Damn you! Are you Satan? Lucifer? Only the devil could have such powers."

"Or angels, my old."

"You don't look like an angel. You look like Satan."

"Ah? Ha? But Satan was an angel before he fell. He has many relations on high. Surely there are family resemblances. God damn." Mr. Aquila stopped laughing. He leaned across the desk and the sprightliness was gone from his face. Only the bitterness remained. "Shall I tell you who I am, my chicken? Shall I explain why one unguarded look from this phizz toppled you over the brink?"

Halsyon nodded, unable to speak.

"I am a scoundrel, a black sheep, a scapegrace, a blackguard. I am a remittance man. Yes. God damn! I am a remittance man." Mr. Aquila's eyes turned into wounds. "By your standards I am the great man of infinite power and variety. So was the remittance man from Europe to naive natives on the beaches of Tahiti. Eh? So am I to you as I comb the beaches of this planet for a little amusement, a little hope, a little joy to while away the weary desolate years of my exile . . .

"I am bad," Mr. Aquila said in a voice of chilling desperation. "I am rotten. There is no place in my home that can tolerate me. And there are moments, unguarded, when my sickness and my despair fill my eyes and strike terror into your waiting souls. As I strike terror into you now. Yes?"

Halsyon nodded again.

"Be guided by me. It was the child in Solon Aquila that destroyed him and led him into the sickness that destroyed his life. Oui. I too suffer from baby fantasies from which I cannot escape. Do not make the same mistake. I beg of you . . ." Mr. Aquila glanced at his wristwatch and leaped up. The sprightly returned to his manner. "Jeez. It's late. Time to make up your mind, old bourbon & soda. Which will it be? Old face or pretty face? The reality of dreams or the dream of reality?"

"How many decisions did you say we have to make in a lifetime?"

"Five million two hundred and seventy-one thousand and nine. Give or take a thousand. God damn."

"And which one is this for me?"

"Ah? Vérité sans peur. The two million six hundred and thirty-five thousand five hundred and fourth . . . off hand."

"But it's the big one."

"They are all big." Mr. Aquila stepped to the door, placed his hand on the buttons of a rather complicated switch and cocked an eye at Halsyon.

"Voilà tout," he said. "It rests with you."

"I'll take it the hard way," Halsyon decided.

There was a silver chime from the switch, a fizzing aura, a soundless explosion, and Jeffrey Halsyon was ready for his 2,635,505th decision.

Short in the Chest

Margaret St. Clair (1911–   )

MARGARET *St. Clair (under her own name and as "Idris Sea-*
bright") was a prolific science-fiction and fantasy author
during the fifties. Much of her best work can be found in her col-
lection Change the Sky and Other Stories *(1974). An uneven*
writer, she produced several memorable short stories during
the fifties: "The Pillows," "Thirsty God," "Brenda," and the
famous "An Egg a Month from All Over" (as Seabright). She
has become primarily a novelist since 1960.

"Short in the Chest" was a somewhat controversial story
for its time because of its portrayal of women and (as Pamela
Sargent has pointed out) its sexual allusions.

From *Fantastic Universe*   July, 1954

═══

The girl in the marine-green uniform turned up her hearing
aid a trifle—they were all a little deaf, from the cold-war
bombing—and with an earnest frown regarded the huxley that
was seated across the desk from her.

"You're the queerest huxley I ever heard of," she said flatly.
"The others aren't at all like you."

The huxley did not seem displeased at this remark. It took
off its windowpane glasses, blew on them, polished them on a

handkerchief, and returned them to its nose. Sonya's turning up the hearing aid had activated the short in its chest again; it folded its hands protectively over the top buttons of its dove-gray brocaded waistcoat.

"And in what way, my dear young lady, am I different from other huxleys?" it asked.

"Well—you tell me to speak to you frankly, to tell you exactly what is in my mind. I've only been to a huxley once before, but it kept talking about giving me the big, overall picture, and about using dighting* to transcend myself. It spoke about in-group love, and intergroup harmony, and it said our basic loyalty must be given to Defense, which in the cold-war emergency is the country itself.

"You're not like that at all, not at all philosophic. I suppose that's why they're called huxleys—because they're philosophic rob—I beg your pardon."

"Go ahead and say it," the huxley encouraged. "I'm not shy. I don't mind being called a robot."

"I might have known. I guess that's why you're so popular. I never saw a huxley with so many people in its waiting room."

"I *am* a rather unusual robot," the huxley said, with a touch of smugness. "I'm a new model, just past the experimental stage, with unusually complicated relays. But that's beside the point. You haven't told me yet what's troubling you."

---

* In the past, I have been accused of making up some of the unusual words that appear in my stories. Sometimes this accusation has been justified; sometimes, as in "Vulcan's Dolls," (see *Plant Life of the Pacific World*) it has not. For the record, therefore, be it observed that "dight" is a middle English word meaning, among other things, "to have intercourse with." (See *Poets of the English Language*, Auden and Pearson, Vol. 1, p. 173.) [See also *Webster's New International Dictionary*, unabridged version.—G.C.] "Dight" was reintroduced by a late twentieth-century philologist who disliked the "sleep with" euphemism, and who saw that the language desperately needed a transitive verb that would be "good usage."

—I.S.

The girl fiddled nervously with the control of her hearing aid. After a moment she turned it down; the almost audible sputtering in the huxley's chest died away.

"It's about the pigs," she said.

"The pigs!" The huxley was jarred out of its mechanical calm. "You know, I thought it would be something about dighting," it said after a second. It smiled winningly. "It usually is."

"Well . . . it's about that too. But the pigs were what started me worrying. I don't know whether you're clear about my rank. I'm Major Sonya Briggs, in charge of the Zone 13 piggery."

"Oh," said the huxley.

"Yes. . . . Like the other armed services, we Marines produce all our own food. My piggery is a pretty important unit in the job of keeping up the supply of pork chops. Naturally, I was disturbed when the newborn pigs refused to nurse.

"If you're a new robot, you won't have much on your memory coils about pigs. As soon as the pigs are born, we take them away from the sow—we use an aseptic scoop—and put them in an enclosure of their own with a big nursing tank. We have a recording of a sow grunting, and when they hear that they're supposed to nurse. The sow gets an oestric, and after a few days she's ready to breed again. The system is supposed to produce a lot more pork than letting the baby pigs stay with the sow in the old-fashioned way. But as I say, lately they've been refusing to nurse.

"No matter how much we step up the grunting record, they won't take the bottle. We've had to slaughter several litters rather than let them starve to death. And at that the flesh hasn't been much good—too mushy and soft. As you can easily see, the situation is getting serious."

"Um," the huxley said.

"Naturally, I made full reports. Nobody has known what to do. But when I got my dighting slip a couple of times ago, in the space marked 'Purpose,' besides the usual rubber-stamped

'To reduce interservice tension' somebody had written in: 'To find out from Air their solution of the neonatal pig nutrition problem.'

"So I knew my dighting opposite number in Air was not only supposed to reduce intergroup tension, but also I was supposed to find out from him how Air got its newborn pigs to eat." She looked down, fidgeting with the clasp of her musette bag.

"Go on," said the huxley with a touch of severity. "I can't help you unless you give me your full confidence."

"Is it true that the dighting system was set up by a group of psychologists after they'd made a survey of interservice tension? After they'd found that Marine was feuding with Air, and Air with Infantry, and Infantry with Navy, to such an extent that it was cutting down overall Defense efficiency? They thought that sex relations would be the best of all ways of cutting down hostility and replacing it with friendly feelings, so they started the dighting plan?"

"You know the answers to those questions as well as I do," the huxley replied frostily. "The tone of your voice when you asked them shows that they are to be answered with 'Yes.' You're stalling, Major Briggs."

"It's so unpleasant. . . . What do you want me to tell you?"

"Go on in detail with what happened after you got your blue dighting slip."

She shot a glance at him, flushed, looked away again, and began talking rapidly. "The slip was for next Tuesday. I hate Air for dighting, but I thought it would be all right. You know how it is—there's a particular sort of kick in feeling oneself change from a cold sort of loathing into being eager and excited and in love with it. After one's had one's Watson, I mean.

"I went to the neutral area Tuesday afternoon. He was in the room when I got there, sitting in a chair with his big feet spread out in front of him, wearing one of those loathsome leather jackets. He stood up politely when he saw me, but I knew he'd just about as soon cut my throat as look at me, since I was Marine. We were both armed, naturally."

"What did he look like?" the huxley broke in.

"I really didn't notice. Just that he was Air. Well, anyway, we had a drink together. I've heard they put cannabis in the drinks they serve you in the neutral areas, and it might be true. I didn't feel nearly so hostile to him after I'd finished my drink. I even managed to smile, and he managed to smile back. He said, 'We might as well get started, don't you think?' So I went in the head.

"I took off my things and left my gun on the bench beside the wash basin. I gave myself my Watson in the thigh."

"The usual Watson?" the huxley asked as she halted. "Oestric and anticoncipient injected subcutaneously from a sterile ampule?"

"Yes. He'd had his Watson too, the priapic, because when I got back. . . ." She began to cry.

"What happened after you got back?" the huxley queried after she had cried for a while.

"I just wasn't any good. No good at all. The Watson might have been so much water for all the effect it had. Finally he got sore. He said, 'What's the matter with you? I might have known anything Marine was in would get loused up.'

"That made me angry, but I was too upset to defend myself. 'Tension reduction!' he said. 'This is a fine way to promote interservice harmony. I'm not only not going to sign the checking-out sheet, I'm going to file a complaint against you to your group.' "

"Oh, my," said huxley.

"Yes, wasn't it terrible? I said, 'If you file a complaint, I'll file a countercharge. You didn't reduce *my* tension, either.'

"We argued about it for a while. He said that if I filed countercharges there'd be a trial and I'd have to take Pento-thal and then the truth would come out. He said it wasn't his fault! He'd been ready.

"I knew that was true, so I began to plead with him. I

reminded him of the cold war, and how the enemy were about to take Venus, when all we had was Mars. I talked to him about loyalty to Defense and I asked him how he'd feel if he was kicked out of Air. And finally, after what seemed like hours, he said he wouldn't file charges. I guess he felt sorry for me. He even agreed to sign the checking-out sheet.

"That was that. I went back to the head and put on my clothes and we both went out. We left the room at different times, though, because we were too angry to smile at each other and look happy. Even as it was, I think some of the neutral-area personnel suspected us."

"Is that what's been worrying you?" the huxley asked when she seemed to have finished.

"Well . . . I can trust you, can't I? You really won't tell?"

"Certainly I won't. Anything told to a huxley is a privileged communication. The first amendment applies to us, if to no other profession."

"Yes. I remember there was a Supreme Court decision about freedom of speech. . . ." She swallowed, choked, and swallowed again. "When I got my next dighting slip," she said bravely, "I was so upset I applied for a gyn. I hoped the doctor would say there was something physically wrong with me, but he said I was in swell shape. He said, 'A girl like you ought to be mighty good at keeping interservice tension down.' So there wasn't any help there.

"Then I went to a huxley, the huxley I was telling you about. It talked philosophy to me. That wasn't any help either. So—finally—well, I stole an extra Watson from the lab."

There was a silence. When she saw that the huxley seemed to have digested her revelation without undue strain, she went on, "I mean, an extra Watson beyond the one I was issued. I couldn't endure the thought of going through another dight like the one before. There was quite a fuss about the ampule's being missing. The dighting drugs are under strict control. But they never did find out who'd taken it."

"And did it help you? The double portion of oestric?" the

huxley asked. It was prodding at the top buttons of its waist-coat with one forefinger, rather in the manner of one who is not quite certain he feels an itch.

"Yes, it did. Everything went off well. He—the man—said I was a nice girl, and Marine was a good service, next to Infantry, of course. He was Infantry. I had a fine time myself, and last week when I got a request sheet from Infantry asking for some pig pedigrees, I went ahead and initialed it. That tension reduction does work. I've been feeling awfully jittery, though. And yesterday I got another blue dighting slip.

"What am I to do? I can't steal another Watson. They've tightened up the controls. And even if I could, I don't think one extra would be enough. This time I think it would take *two*."

She put her head down on the arm of her chair, gulping desperately.

"You don't think you'd be all right with just one Watson?" the huxley asked after an interval. "After all, people used to dight habitually without any Watsons at all."

"That wasn't interservice dighting. No, I don't think I'd be all right. You see, this time it's with Air again. I'm supposed to try to find out about porcine nutrition. And I've always particularly hated Air."

She twisted nervously at the control of her hearing aid. The huxley gave a slight jump. "Ah—well, of course you might resign," it said in a barely audible voice.

Sonya—in the course of a long-continued struggle there is always a good deal of cultural contamination, and if there were girls named Sonya, Olga, and Tatiana in Defense, there were girls named Shirley and Mary Beth to be found on the enemy's side—Sonya gave him an incredulous glance. "You must be joking. I think it's in very poor taste. I didn't tell you my difficulties for you to make fun of me."

The huxley appeared to realize that it had gone too far.

"Not at all, my dear young lady," it said placatingly. It pressed its hands to its bosom. "Just a suggestion. As you say, it was in poor taste. I should have realized that you'd rather die than not be Marine."

"Yes, I would."

She turned the hearing aid down again. The huxley relaxed. "You may not be aware of it, but difficulties like yours are not entirely unknown," it said. "Perhaps, after a long course of oestrics, antibodies are built up. Given a state of initial physiological reluctance, a forced sexual response might. . . . But you're not interested in all that. You want help. How about taking your troubles to somebody higher? Taking them all the way up?"

"You mean—the CO?"

The huxley nodded.

Major Briggs' face flushed scarlet. "I can't do that! I just can't! No nice girl would. I'd be too ashamed." She beat on her musette bag with one hand, and began to sob.

Finally she sat up. The huxley was regarding her patiently. She opened her bag, got out cosmetics and mirror, and began to repair emotion's ravages. Then she extracted an electronically powered vibro-needle from the depths of her bag and began crafting away on some indeterminate white garment.

"I don't know what I'd do without my crafting," she said in explanation. "These last few days, it's all that's kept me sane. Thank goodness it's fashionable to do crafting now. Well. I've told you all about my troubles. Have you any ideas?"

The huxley regarded her with faintly protruding eyes. The vibro-needle clicked away steadily, so steadily that Sonya was quite unaware of the augmented popping in the huxley's chest. Besides, the noise was of a frequency that her hearing aid didn't pick up any too well.

The huxley cleared its throat. "Are you sure your dighting difficulties are really your fault?" it asked in an oddly altered voice.

"Why—I suppose so. After all, there's been nothing wrong with the men either time." Major Briggs did not look up from her work.

"Yes, physiologically. But let's put it this way. And I want you to remember, my dear young lady, that we're both mature, sophisticated individuals, and that I'm a huxley, after all. Supposing your dighting date had been with . . . somebody in . . . Marine. Would you have had any difficulty with it?"

Sonya Briggs put down her crafting, her cheeks flaming. "With a group brother? You have no right to talk to me like that!"

"Now, now. You must be calm."

The sputtering in the huxley's chest was by now so loud that only Sonya's emotion could have made her deaf to it. It was so well-established that even her laying down the vibro-needle had had no effect on it.

"Don't be offended," the huxley went on in its unnatural voice. "I was only putting a completely hypothetical case."

"Then . . . supposing it's understood that it's completely hypothetical and I would never, never dream of doing a thing like that . . . then, I don't suppose I'd have had any trouble with it." She picked up the needle once more.

"In other words, it's not your fault. Look at it this way. You're Marine."

"Yes." The girl's head went up proudly. "I'm Marine."

"Yes. And that means you're a hundred times—a thousand times—better than any of these twerps you've been having to dight with. Isn't that true? Just in the nature of things. Because you're Marine."

"Why—I guess it is. I never thought of it before like that."

"But you can see it's true now, when you think of it. Take that date you had with the man from Air. How could it be your fault that you couldn't respond to him, somebody from *Air?* Why, it was his fault—it's as plain as the nose on your face—*his* fault for being from a repulsive service like Air!"

Sonya was looking at the huxley with parted lips and shining eyes. "I never thought of it before," she breathed. "But it's true. You're right. You're wonderfully, wonderfully right!"

"Of course I am," said the huxley smugly. "I was built to be right. Now, let's consider this matter of your next date."

"Yes, let's."

"You'll go to the neutral area, as usual. You'll be wearing your miniBAR won't you?"

"Yes, of course. We always go in armed."

"Good. You'll go to the head and undress. You'll give yourself your Watson. If it works—"

"It won't. I'm almost sure of that."

"Hear me out. As I was saying, if it works, you'll dight. If it doesn't you'll be carrying your miniBAR."

"Where?" asked Sonya, frowning.

"Behind your back. You want to give him a chance. But not too good a chance. If the Watson doesn't work—" the huxley paused for dramatic effect—*"get our your gun and shoot him. Shoot him through the heart.* Leave him lying up against a bulkhead. Why should you go through a painful scene like the one you just described for the sake of a yuk from Air?"

"Yes—but—" Sonya had the manner of one who, while striving to be reasonable, is none too sure that reasonableness can be justified. "That wouldn't reduce interservice tension effectively."

"My dear young lady, why should interservice tension be reduced at the expense of Marine? Besides, you've got to take the big overall view. Whatever benefits Marine, benefits Defense."

"Yes. . . . That's true. . . . I think you've given me good advice."

"Of course I have! One thing more. After you shoot him, leave a note with your name, sector, and identity number on it. You're not ashamed of it."

"No. . . . No. . . . But I just remembered. How can he give me the pig formula when he's dead?"

"He's just as likely to give it to you dead as when he was

alive. Besides, think of the humiliation of it. You, Marine, having to lower yourself to wheedle a thing like that out of Air! Why, he ought to be proud, honored, to give the formula to you."

"Yes, he ought." Sonya's lips tightened. "I won't take any nonsense from him," she said. "Even if the Watson works and I dight him, I'll shoot him afterwards. Wouldn't you?"

"Of course. Any girl with spirit would."

Major Briggs glanced at her watch. "Twenty past! I'm overdue at the piggery right now. Thank you so much." She beamed at him. "I'm going to take your advice."

"I'm glad. Good-bye."

"Good-bye."

She walked out of the room, humming, "From the halls of Montezuma. . . ."

Left alone, the huxley interchanged its eyes and nose absently a couple of times. It looked up at the ceiling speculatively, as if it wondered when the bombs from Air, Infantry, and Navy were going to come crashing down. It had had interviews with twelve young women so far, and it had given them all the same advice it had given Major Briggs. Even a huxley with a short in its chest might have foreseen that the final result of its counseling would be catastrophic for Marine.

It sat a little while longer, repeating to itself, "Poppoff, Poppoff. Papa, potatoes, poultry, prunes and prism, prunes and prism."

Its short was sputtering loudly and cheerfully; it hunted around on the broadcast sound band until it found a program of atonal music that covered the noise successfully. Though its derangement had reached a point that was not far short of insanity, the huxley still retained a certain cunning.

Once more it repeated "Poppoff Poppoff," to itself. Then it went to the door of its waiting room and called in its next client.

The Academy

Robert Sheckley (1928-   )

ROBERT *Sheckley was the prototype* Galaxy *writer of the fifties. He was incredibly prolific, writing under his own name and a large number of pseudonyms. His stories featured fast pacing, jolting endings, and often hilarious social extrapolation. But he was not always humorous; one of his specialties was tearing away the veneer of normality and community in his fictional societies to expose the fear, exploitation, and loss of identity that lurked beneath their surfaces. He was and is very much an anti-system writer.*

"The Academy" reflects one of his career-long interests: the role of the nonconformist in society and the way in which society defines normality. As usual, he comes down squarely on the side of the nonconformist and the relativity of what constitutes "normal" behavior. For Sheckley, the status quo is always an inviting target.

From *Worlds of If*   1954

INSTRUCTION SHEET FOR USE WITH THE CAHILL-THOMAS SANITY METER, SERIES JM-14(MANUAL):

The Cahill-Thomas Manufacturing Company is pleased to present our newest Sanity Meter. This beautiful, rugged instrument, small enough for any bedroom, kitchen or den, is in all respects an exact replica of the larger C-T Sanity Meters used in most places of business, recreation, transportation, etc. No pains have been spared to give you the best Sanity Meter possible, at the lowest possible price.

1. OPERATION. At the lower right-hand corner of your Meter is a switch. Turn it to *On* position, and allow a few seconds for warming up. Then switch from *On* position to *Operate* position. Allow a few seconds for reading.

2. READING. On the front of your Meter, above the operating switch, is a transparent panel, showing a straight-line scale numbered from zero to ten. The number at which the black indicator stops shows your Sanity Reading, in relation to the present statistical norm.

3. EXPLANATION OF NUMBERS ZERO TO THREE. On this model, as on all Sanity Meters, *zero* is the theoretically perfect sanity point. Everything above zero is regarded as a deviation from the norm. However, zero is a statistical rather than an actual idea. The normalcy range for our civilization lies between zero and three. Any rating in this area is considered normal.

4. EXPLANATION OF NUMBERS FOUR TO SEVEN. These numbers represent the sanity-tolerance limit. Persons registering in this area should consult their favorite therapy at once.

5. EXPLANATION OF NUMBERS EIGHT TO TEN. A person who registers above *seven* is considered a highly dangerous potential to his milieu. Almost certainly he is highly neurotic, prepsychotic or psychotic. This individual is *required by law* to register his rating, and to bring it below *seven* within a probationary period. (Consult your state laws for periods of probation.) Failing this, he must undergo Surgical Alteration, or may submit voluntarily to therapy at The Academy.

6. EXPLANATION OF NUMBER TEN. At *ten* on your Meter there is a red line. If a sanity-reading passes this line, the individual so registered can no longer avail himself of the regular commercial therapies. This individual must undergo Surgical Alteration immediately, or submit at once to therapy at The Academy.

WARNING:

A. THIS IS NOT A DIAGNOSTIC MACHINE. DO NOT ATTEMPT TO DETERMINE FOR YOURSELF WHAT YOUR AILMENT IS. THE NUMBERS ZERO TO TEN REPRESENT INTENSITY QUALITIES, NOT ARBITRARY CLASSIFICATIONS OF NEUROTIC, PRE-PSYCHOTIC, PSYCHOTIC, ETC. THE INTENSITY SCALE IS IN REFERENCE ONLY TO AN INDIVIDUAL'S POTENTIAL FOR HARM TO HIS SOCIAL ORDER. A PARTICULAR TYPE OF NEUROTIC MAY BE POTENTIALLY MORE DANGEROUS THAN A PSYCHOTIC, AND WILL SO REGISTER ON ANY SANITY METER. SEE A THERAPIST FOR FURTHER INSIGHT.

B. THE ZERO-TO-TEN READINGS ARE APPROXIMATE. FOR AN EXACT THIRTY DECIMAL RATING, GO TO A COMMERCIAL MODEL C-T METER.

C. REMEMBER—SANITY IS EVERYONE'S BUSINESS. WE HAVE COME A LONG WAY SINCE THE GREAT WORLD WARS, ENTIRELY BECAUSE WE HAVE FOUNDED OUR CIVILIZATION ON THE CONCEPTS OF SOCIAL SANITY, INDIVIDUAL RESPONSIBILITY, AND PRESERVATION OF THE STATUS QUO. THEREFORE, IF YOU RATE OVER THREE, GET HELP. IF YOU RATE OVER SEVEN, YOU MUST GET HELP. IF YOU RATE OVER TEN, DO NOT WAIT FOR DETECTION AND ARREST. GIVE YOURSELF UP VOLUNTARILY IN THE NAME OF CIVILIZATION.

Good Luck—
The Cahill-Thomas Company

After finishing his breakfast, Mr. Feerman knew he should leave immediately for work. Under the circumstances, any tardiness might be construed unfavorably. He went so far as to put on his neat gray hat, adjust his tie and start for the door. But, his hand on the knob, he decided to wait for the mail.

He turned away from the door, annoyed with himself, and began to pace up and down the living room. He had known he was going to wait for the mail; why had he gone through the pretense of leaving? Couldn't he be honest with himself, even now, when personal honesty was so important?

His black cocker spaniel Speed, curled up on the couch, looked curiously at him. Feerman patted the dog's head, reached for a cigarette, and changed his mind. He patted Speed again, and the dog yawned lazily. Feerman adjusted a lamp that needed no adjusting, shuddered for no reason, and began to pace the room again.

Reluctantly, he admitted to himself that he didn't want to leave his apartment, dreaded it in fact, although nothing was going to happen. He tried to convince himself that this was just another day, like yesterday and the day before. Certainly if a man could believe that, really believe it, events would defer indefinitely, and nothing would happen to him.

Besides, why should anything happen today? He wasn't at the end of his probationary period yet.

He thought he heard a noise outside his apartment, hurried over and opened the door. He had been mistaken; the mail hadn't arrived. But down the hall his landlady opened her door and looked at him with pale, unfriendly eyes.

Feerman closed the door and found that his hands were shaking. He decided that he had better take a sanity reading. He entered the bedroom, but his robutler was there, sweeping a little pile of dust toward the center of the room. Already his bed was made; his wife's bed didn't require making, since it had been unoccupied for almost a week.

"Shall I leave, sir?" the robutler asked.

Feerman hesitated before answering. He preferred taking his reading alone. Of course, his robutler wasn't really a person. Strictly speaking, the mechanical had no personality; but he had what *seemed* like a personality. Anyhow, it didn't matter whether he stayed or left, since all personal robots had sanity-reading equipment built into their circuits. It was required by law.

"Suit yourself," he said finally.

The robutler sucked up the little pile of dust and rolled noiselessly out of the room.

Feerman stepped up to the Sanity Meter, turned it on and set the operating control. He watched morosely as the black indicator climbed slowly through the normal twos and threes, through the deviant sixes and sevens, and rested finally on eight-point-two.

One tenth of a point higher than yesterday. One tenth closer to the red line.

Feerman snapped off the machine and lighted a cigarette. He left the bedroom slowly, wearily, as though the day were over, instead of just beginning.

"The mail, sir," the robutler said, gliding up to him. Feerman grabbed the letters from the robutler's outstretched hand and looked through them.

"She didn't write," he said involuntarily.

"I'm sorry, sir," the robutler responded promptly.

"You're sorry?" Feerman looked at the mechanical curiously. "Why?"

"I am naturally interested in your welfare, sir," the robutler stated. "As is Speed, to the extent of his intelligence. A letter from Mrs. Feerman would have helped your morale. We are sorry it didn't come."

Speed barked softly and cocked his head to one side. Sympathy from a machine, Feerman thought, pity from a beast. But he was grateful all the same.

"I don't blame her," he said. "She couldn't be expected to put up with me forever." He waited, hoping that the robot would tell him that his wife would return, that he would soon be well. But the robutler stood silently beside Speed, who had gone to sleep again.

Feerman looked through the mail again. There were several bills, an advertisement, and a small, stiff letter. The return address on it was The Academy, and Feerman opened it quickly.

Within was a card, which read, "Dear Mr. Feerman, your application for admission has been processed and found acceptable. We will be happy to receive you at any time. Thank You, the Directors."

Feerman squinted at the card. He had never applied for admission to The Academy. It was the last thing in the world he wanted to do. "Was this my wife's idea?" he asked.

"I do not know, sir," the robutler said.

Feerman turned the card over in his hand. He had always been vaguely aware of the existence of The Academy, of course. One couldn't help but be aware of it, since its presence affected every stratum of life. But actually, he knew very little about this important institution, surprisingly little.

"What is The Academy?" he asked.

"A large low gray building," his robutler answered. "It is situated in the Southwest corner of the city, and can be reached by a variety of public conveyances."

"But *what* is it?"

"A registered therapy," the robutler said, "open to anyone upon application, written or verbal. Moreover, The Academy exists as a voluntary choice for all people of plus ten rating, as an alternative to Surgical Personality Alteration."

Feerman sighed with exasperation. "I know all that. But what is their system? What kind of therapy?"

"I do not know, sir," the robutler said.

"What's their record of cures?"

"One hundred percent," the robutler answered promptly.

Feerman remembered something else now, something that struck him as rather strange. "Let me see," he said. "No one leaves The Academy. Is that right?"

"There has been no record of anyone leaving after physically entering," the robutler said.

"Why?"

"I do not know, sir."

Feerman crumpled the card and dropped it into an ashtray. It was all very strange. The Academy was so well known, so accepted, one never thought to ask about it. It had always been a misty place in his mind, far-away, unreal. It was the place you went to if you became plus ten, since you didn't want to undergo lobotomy, topectomy, or any other process involving organic personality loss. But of course you tried not to think of the possibility of becoming plus ten, since the very thought was an admission of instability, and therefore you didn't think of the choices open to you if it happened.

For the first time in his life, Feerman decided he didn't like the setup. He would have to do some investigating. Why didn't anyone leave The Academy? Why wasn't more known of their therapy, if their cures were really one hundred percent effective?

"I'd better get to work," Feerman said. "Make me anything at all for supper."

"Yes, sir. Have a good day, sir."

Speed jumped down from the couch and followed him to the door. Feerman knelt down and stroked the dog's sleek black head. "No, boy, you stay inside. No burying bones today."

"Speed does not bury bones," the robutler said.

"That's right." Dogs today, like their masters, rarely had a feeling of insecurity. No one buried bones today. "So long." He hurried past his landlady's door and into the street.

Feerman was almost twenty minutes late for work. As he entered the building, he forgot to present his probationary certificate to the scanning mechanism at the door. The gigantic commercial Sanity Meter scanned him, its indicator shot past the seven point, lights flashed red. A harsh metallic voice shouted over the loudspeaker, "Sir! Sir! Your deviation from the norm has passed the safety limit! Please arrange for therapy at once!"

Quickly Feerman pulled his probationary certificate out of his wallet. But perversely, the machine continued to bellow at him for a full ten seconds longer. Everyone in the lobby was staring at him. Messenger boys stopped dead, pleased at having witnessed a disturbance. Businessmen and office girls whispered together, and two Sanity Policemen exchanged meaningful glances. Feerman's shirt, soaked with perspiration, was plastered against his back. He resisted an urge to run from the building, instead walked toward an elevator. But it was nearly full, and he couldn't bring himself to enter.

He trotted up a staircase to the second floor, and then took an elevator the rest of the way up. By the time he reached the Morgan Agency he had himself under control. He showed his probationary certificate to the Sanity Meter at the door, mopped his face with a handkerchief, and walked in.

Everyone in the agency knew what had happened. He could tell by their silence, their averted faces. Feerman walked rapidly to his office, closed the door and hung up his hat.

He sat down at his desk, still slightly out of wind, filled with resentment at the Sanity Meter. If only he could smash all the damned things! Always prying, setting off their alarms in your ear, unstabilizing you . . .

Feerman cut off the thought quickly. There was nothing wrong with the Meters. To think of them as active persecuting agents was paranoidal, and perhaps a symptom of his present unsane status. The Meters were mere extensions of man's will. Society as a whole, he reminded himself, must be protected against the individual, just as a human body must be protected against malfunction of any of its parts. As fond as you might be of your gall bladder, you would sacrifice it mercilessly if it were going to impair the rest of you.

He sensed something shaky in this analogy, but decided not

to pursue it any farther. He had to find out more about The Academy.

After lighting a cigarette he dialed the Therapy Reference Service.

"May I help you, sir?" a pleasant-voiced woman answered.

"I'd like to get some information about The Academy," Feerman said, feeling a trifle foolish. The Academy was so well known, so much a part of everyday life, it was tantamount to asking what form of government your country had.

"The Academy is located—"

"I know where it's located," Feerman said. "I want to know what sort of therapy they administer."

"That information is not available, sir," the woman said, after a pause.

"No? I thought all data on commercial therapies was available to the public."

"Technically, it is," the woman answered slowly. "But The Academy is not, strictly, a commercial therapy. It does accept money; however, it admits charity cases as well, without quota. Also, it is partially supported by the government."

Feerman tapped the ash off his cigarette and said impatiently, "I thought all government projects were open to the public."

"As a general rule, they are. Except when such knowledge will be harmful to the public."

"Then such knowledge of The Academy *would* be harmful?" Feerman said triumphantly, feeling that he was getting to the heart of the matter.

"Oh, no sir!" The woman's voice became shrill with amazement. "I didn't mean to imply that! I was just stating the general rules for withholding of information. The Academy, although covered by the laws, is, to some extent, extra-legal. This status is allowed because of The Academy's one-hundred percent record of cures."

"Where can I see a few of these cures?" Feerman asked. "I understand that no one ever leaves The Academy."

He had them now, Feerman thought, waiting for an answer. Over the telephone he thought he heard a whispering. Suddenly a man's voice broke in, loud and clear. "This is the Section Chief. Is there some difficulty?"

Hearing the man's sharp voice, Feerman almost dropped the telephone. His feeling of triumph vanished, and he wished he had never made the call. But he forced himself to go on. "I want some information on The Academy."

"The location—"

"No! I mean real information!" Feerman said desperately.

"To what purpose do you wish to put this information?" the Section Chief asked, and his voice was suddenly the smooth, almost hypnotic voice of a therapist.

"Insight," Feerman answered quickly. "Since The Academy is a therapeutic alternative open to me at all times, I would like to know more about it, in order to judge—"

"Very plausible," the Section Chief said. "But consider. Are you asking for a useful, functional insight? One that will better your integration into society? Or are you asking merely for the sake of an overriding curiosity, thereby yielding to restlessness, and other, deeper drives?"

"I'm asking because—"

"What is your name?" the Section Chief asked suddenly.

Feerman was silent.

"What is your sanity rating?"

Still Feerman didn't speak. He was trying to decide if the call were already traced, and decided that it was.

"Do you doubt The Academy's essential benevolence?"

"No."

"Do you doubt that The Academy works for the preservation of the Status Quo?"

"No."

"Then what is your problem? Why won't you tell me your name and sanity rating? Why do you feel this need for more information?"

"Thank you," Feerman murmured, and hung up. He realized that the telephone call had been a terrible mistake. It had been the action of a plus-eight, not a normal man. The Section Chief, with his trained perceptions, had realized that at once. Of course the Section Chief wouldn't give information to a plus-eight! Feerman knew he would have to watch his actions far more closely, analyze them, understand them, if he ever hoped to return to the statistical norm.

As he sat, there was a knock; the door opened and his boss, Mr. Morgan, entered. Morgan was a big, powerfully built man with a full, fleshy face. He stood in front of Feerman's desk, drumming his fingers on the blotter, looking as embarrassed as a caught thief.

"Heard that report downstairs," he said, not looking at Feerman, tapping his fingers energetically.

"Momentary peak," Feerman said automatically. "Actually, my rating has begun to come down." He couldn't look at Morgan as he said this. The two men stared intently at different corners of the room. Finally, their eyes met.

"Look, Feerman, I try to stay out of people's business," Morgan said, sitting on the corner of Feerman's desk. "But damn it, man, Sanity is everyone's business. We're all in the game together." The thought seemed to increase Morgan's conviction. He leaned forward earnestly.

"You know, I'm responsible for a lot of people here. This is the third time in a year you've been on probation." He hesitated. "How did it start?"

Feerman shook his head. "I don't know, Mr. Morgan. I was just going along quietly—and my rating started to climb."

Morgan considered, then shook his head. "Can't be as simple as that. Have you been checked for brain lesions?"

"I've been assured it's nothing organic."

"Therapy?"

"Everything," Feerman said. "Electro-therapy, Analysis, Smith's Method, The Rannes School, Devio-Thought, Differentiation—"

"What did they say?" Morgan asked.

Feerman thought back on the endless line of therapists he had gone to. He had been explored from every angle that psychology had to offer. He had been drugged, shocked, explored. But it all boiled down to one thing.

"They don't know."

"Couldn't they tell you *anything?*" Morgan asked.

"Not much. Constitutional restlessness, deeply concealed drives, inability to accept the Status Quo. They all agree I'm a rigid type. Even Personality Reconstruction didn't take on me."

"Prognosis?"

"Not so good."

Morgan stood up and began to pace the floor, his hands clasped behind his back. "Feerman, I think it's a matter of attitude. Do you really want to be part of the team?"

"I've tried everything—"

"Sure. But have you *wanted* to change? Insight!" Morgan cried, smashing his fist into his hand as though to crush the word. "Do you have *insight?*"

"I don't suppose so," Feerman said with genuine regret.

"Take my case," Morgan said earnestly, standing in front of Feerman's desk with his feet widely and solidly planted. "Ten years ago, this agency was twice as big as it is now, and growing! I worked like a madman, extending my holdings, investing, expanding, making money and more money."

"And what happened?"

"The inevitable. My rating shot up from a two-point-three to plus-seven. I was in a bad way."

"No law against making money," Feerman pointed out.

"Certainly not. But there is a psychological law against making too much. Society today just isn't geared for that sort of thing. A lot of the competition and aggression have been bred out of the race. After all, we've been in the Status Quo for almost a hundred years now. In that time, there've been no new inventions, no wars, no major developments of any kind. Psychology has been normalizing the race, breeding out the irrational elements. So with my drive and ability, it was like— like playing tennis against an infant. I couldn't be stopped."

Morgan's face was flushed, and he had begun to breathe heavily. He checked himself, and went on in a quieter tone. "Of course, I was doing it for neurotic reasons. Power urge, a bad dose of competitiveness. I underwent Substitution Therapy."

Feerman said, "I don't see anything unsane about wanting to expand your business."

"Good Lord, man, don't you understand anything about Social Sanity, Responsibility, and Stasis? I was on my way to becoming *wealthy*. From there, I would have founded a *financial empire*. All quite legal, you understand, but *unsane*. After that, who knows where I would have gone? Into indirect control of the government, eventually. I'd want to change the psychological policies to conform to my own abnormalities. And you can see where that would lead."

"So you adjusted," Feerman said.

"I had my choice of Brain Surgery, The Academy, or adjustment. Fortunately, I found an outlet in competitive sports. I sublimated my selfish drives for the good of mankind. But the thing is this, Feerman. I was heading for that red line. I adjusted before it was too late."

"I'd gladly adjust," Feerman said, "if I only knew what was wrong with me. The trouble is, I really don't know."

Morgan was silent for a long time, thinking. Then he said, "I think you need a rest, Feerman."

"A rest?" Feerman was instantly on the alert. "You mean I'm fired?"

"No, of course not. I want to be fair, play the game. But I've got a team here." Morgan's vague gesture included the office, the building, the city. "Unsanity is insidious. Several ratings in the office have begun to climb in the last week."

"And I'm the infection spot."

"We must accept the rules," Morgan said, standing erectly in front of Feerman's desk. "Your salary will continue until— until you reach some resolution."

"Thanks," Feerman said dryly. He stood up and put on his hat.

Morgan put a hand on his shoulder. "Have you considered The Academy?" he asked in a low voice. "I mean, if nothing else seems to work—"

"Definitely and irrevocably not," Feerman said, looking directly into Morgan's small blue eyes.

Morgan turned away. "You seem to have an illogical prejudice against The Academy. Why? You know how our society is organized. You can't think that anything against the common good would be allowed."

"I don't suppose so," Feerman admitted. "But why isn't more known about The Academy?"

They walked through the silent office. None of the men Feerman had known for so long looked up from their work. Morgan opened the door and said, "You know all about The Academy."

"I don't know how it works."

"Do you know everything about any therapy? Can you tell me all about Substitution Therapy? Or Analysis? Or Olgivey's Reduction?"

"No. But I have a general idea how they work."

"Everyone does," Morgan said triumphantly, then quickly lowered his voice. "That's just it. Obviously, The Academy doesn't give out such information because it would interfere with the operation of the therapy itself. Nothing odd about that, is there?"

Feerman thought it over, and allowed Morgan to guide him into the hall. "I'll grant that," he said. "But tell me; why doesn't anyone ever leave The Academy? Doesn't that strike you as sinister?"

"Certainly not. You've got a very strange outlook." Morgan punched the elevator button as he talked. "You seem to be trying to create a mystery where there isn't one. Without prying into their professional business, I can assume that their therapy involves the patient's remaining at The Academy. There's nothing strange about a substitute environment. It's done all the time."

"If that's the truth, why don't they say so?"

"The fact speaks for itself."

"And where," Feerman asked, "is the proof of their hundred percent cures?"

The elevator arrived, and Feerman stepped in. Morgan said, "The proof is in their saying so. Therapists can't lie. They can't, Feerman!"

Morgan started to say something else, but the elevator doors slid shut. The elevator started down, and Feerman realized with a shock that his job was gone.

It was a strange sensation, not having a job any longer. He had no place to go. Often he had hated his work. There had been mornings when he had groaned at the thought of another day at the office. But now that he had it no longer, he realized how important it had been to him, how solid and reliable. A man is nothing, he thought, if he doesn't have work to do.

He walked aimlessly, block after block, trying to think. But he was unable to concentrate. Thoughts kept sliding out of reach, eluding him, and were replaced by glimpses of his wife's face. And he couldn't even think about her, for the city pressed in on him, its faces, sounds, smells.

The only plan of action that came to mind was unfeasible. Run away, his panicky emotions told him. Go where they'll never find you. Hide!

But Feerman knew this was no solution. Running away was sheer escapism, and proof of his deviation from the norm. Because what, really, would he be running from? From the sanest, most perfect society that Man had ever conceived. Only a madman would run from that.

Feerman began to notice the people he passed. They looked happy, filled with the new spirit of Responsibility and Social Sanity, willing to sacrifice old passions for a new era of peace. It was a good world, a hell of a good world. Why couldn't he live in it?

He *could*. With the first confidence he had felt in weeks, Feerman decided that he would conform, somehow.

If only he could find out how.

After hours of walking, Feerman discovered that he was hungry. He entered the first diner he saw. The place was crowded with laborers, for he had walked almost to the docks.

He sat down and looked at a menu, telling himself that he needed time to think. He had to assess his actions properly, figure out—

"Hey, mister!"

He looked up. The bald, unshaven counterman was glaring at him.

"What?"

"Get out of here."

"What's wrong?" Feerman asked, trying to control his sudden panic.

"We don't serve no madmen here," the counterman said. He pointed to the Sanity Meter on the wall, that registered everyone walking in. The black indicator pointed slightly past nine. "Get out."

Feerman looked at the other men at the counter. They sat in a row, dressed in similar rough brown clothing. Their caps were pulled down over their eyes, and every man seemed to be reading a newspaper.

"I've got a probationary—"

"Get out," the counterman said. "The law says I don't have to serve no plus-nines. It bothers my customers. Come on, move."

The row of laborers sat motionless, not looking at him.

Feerman felt the blood rush to his face. He had the sudden urge to smash in the counterman's bald, shiny skull, wade into the row of listening men with a meat cleaver, spatter the dirty walls with their blood, smash, kill. But of course, aggression was unsane, and an unsatisfactory response. He mastered the impulse and walked out.

Feerman continued to walk, resisting the urge to run, waiting for that train of logical thought that would tell him what to do. But his thoughts only became more confused, and by twilight he was ready to drop from fatigue.

He was standing on a narrow, garbage-strewn street in the slums. He saw a hand-lettered sign in a second-floor window, reading, J. J. FLYNN, PSYCHOLOGICAL THERAPIST. MAYBE I CAN HELP YOU. Feerman grinned wryly, thinking of all the high-priced specialists he had seen. He started to walk away, then turned, and went up the staircase leading to Flynn's office. He was annoyed with himself again. The moment he saw the sign he had known he was going up. Would he never stop deceiving himself?

Flynn's office was small and dingy. The paint was peeling from the walls, and the room had an unwashed smell. Flynn was seated behind an unvarnished wooden desk, reading an adventure magazine. He was small, middle-aged and balding. He was smoking a pipe.

Feerman had meant to start from the beginning. Instead he blurted out, "Look, I'm in a jam. I've lost my job, my wife's left me, I've been to every therapy there is. What can you do?"

Flynn took the pipe out of his mouth and looked at Feerman. He looked at his clothes, hat, shoes, as though estimating their value. Then he said, "What did the others say?"

"In effect, that I didn't have a chance."

"Of course they said that," Flynn said, speaking rapidly in a high, clear voice. "These fancy boys give up too easily. But there's always hope. The mind is a strange and complicated thing, my friend, and sometimes—" Flynn stopped abruptly and grinned with sad humor. "Ah, what's the use? You've got the doomed look, no doubt of it." He knocked the ashes from his pipe and stared at the ceiling. "Look, there's nothing I can do for you. You know it, I know it. Why'd you come up here?"

"Looking for a miracle, I suppose," Feerman said, wearily sitting down on a wooden chair.

"Lots of people do," Flynn said conversationally. "And this looks like the logical place for one, doesn't it? You've been to the fancy offices of the specialists. No help there. So it would be right and proper if an itinerant therapist could do what the famous men failed to do. A sort of poetic justice."

"Pretty good," Feerman said, smiling faintly.

"Oh, I'm not at all bad," Flynn said, filling his pipe from a shaggy green pouch. "But the truth of the matter is, miracles cost money, always have, always will. If the big boys couldn't help you, I certainly couldn't."

"Thanks for telling me," Feerman said, but made no move to get up.

"It's my duty as a therapist," Flynn said slowly, "to remind you that The Academy is always open."

"How can I go there?" Feerman asked. "I don't know anything about it."

"No one does," Flynn said. "Still I hear they cure every time."

"Death is a cure."

"But a non-functional one. Besides, that's too discordant with the times. Deviants would have to run such a place, and deviants just aren't allowed."

"Then why doesn't anyone ever leave?"

"Don't ask me," Flynn said. "Perhaps they don't want to." He puffed on his pipe. "You want some advice. OK. Have you any money?"

"Some," Feerman said warily.

"OK. I shouldn't be saying this, but . . . Stop looking for cures! Go home. Send your robutler out for a couple months' supply of food. Hole up for a while."

"Hole up? Why?"

Flynn scowled furiously at him. "Because you're running yourself ragged trying to get back to the norm, and all you're doing is getting worse. I've seen it happen a thousand times. Don't think about sanity or unsanity. Just lie around a couple months, rest, read, grow fat. Then see how you are."

"Look," Feerman said, "I think you're right. I'm sure of it! But I'm not sure if I should go home. I made a telephone call today. . . . I've got some money. Could you hide me here? Could you hide me?"

Flynn stood up and looked fearfully out the window at the dark street. "I've said too much as it is. If I were younger— but I can't do it! I've given you unsane advice! I can't commit an unsane action on top of that!"

"I'm sorry," Feerman said. "I shouldn't have asked you. But I'm really grateful. I mean it." He stood up. "How much do I owe you?"

"Nothing," Flynn said. "Good luck to you."

"Thanks." Feerman hurried downstairs and hailed a cab. In twenty minutes he was home.

The hall was strangely quiet as Feerman walked toward his apartment. His landlady's door was closed as he passed it, but he had the impression that it had been open until he came, and that the old woman was standing beside it now, her ear against the thin wood. He walked faster, and entered his apartment.

It was quiet in his apartment, too. Feerman walked into the kitchen. His robutler was standing beside the stove, and Speed was curled up in the corner.

"Welcome home, sir," the robutler said. "If you will sit, I will serve your supper."

Feerman sat down, thinking about his plans. There were a

lot of details to work out, but Flynn was right. Hole up, that was the thing. Stay out of sight.

"I'll want you to go shopping first thing in the morning," he said to the robutler.

"Yes sir," the robutler said, placing a bowl of soup in front of him.

"We'll need plenty of staples. Bread, meat. . . . No, buy canned goods."

"What kind of canned goods?" the robutler asked.

"Any kind, as long as it's a balanced diet. And cigarettes, don't forget cigarettes! Give me the salt, will you?"

The robutler stood beside the stove, not moving. But Speed began to whimper softly.

"Robutler. The salt please."

"I'm sorry, sir," the robutler said.

"What do you mean, you're sorry? Hand me the salt."

"I can no longer obey you."

"Why not?"

"You have just gone over the red line, sir. You are now plus ten."

Feerman just stared at him for a moment. Then he ran into the bedroom and turned on the Sanity Meter. The black indicator crept slowly to the red line, wavered, then slid decisively over.

He was plus ten.

But that didn't matter, he told himself. After all, it was a quantitative measurement. It didn't mean that he had suddenly become a monster. He would reason with the robutler, explain it to him.

Feerman rushed out of the bedroom. "Robutler! Listen to me—"

He heard the front door close. The robutler was gone.

Feerman walked into the living room and sat down on the couch. Naturally the robutler was gone. They had built-in sanity reading equipment. If their masters passed the red line, they returned to the factory automatically. No plus ten could command a mechanical.

But he still had a chance. There was food in the house. He would ration himself. It wouldn't be too lonely with Speed here. Perhaps he would just need a few days.

"Speed?"

There was no sound in the apartment.

"Come here, boy."

Still no sound.

Feerman searched the apartment methodically, but the dog wasn't there. He must have left with the robutler.

Alone, Feerman walked into the kitchen and drank three glasses of water. He looked at the meal his robutler had prepared, started to laugh, then checked himself.

He had to get out, quickly. There was no time to lose. If he hurried, he could still make it, to someplace, any place. Every second counted now.

But he stood in the kitchen, staring at the floor as the minutes passed, wondering why his dog had left him.

There was a knock on his door.

"Mr. Feerman!"

"No," Feerman said.

"Mr. Feerman, you must leave now."

It was his landlady. Feerman walked to the door and opened it. "Go? Where?"

"I don't care. But you can't stay here any longer, Mr. Feerman. You must go."

Feerman went back for his hat, put it on, looked around the apartment, then walked out. He left the door open.

Outside, two men were waiting for him. Their faces were indistinct in the darkness.

"Where do you want to go?" one asked.

"Where can I go?"

"Surgery or The Academy."

"The Academy, then."

They put him in a car and drove quickly away. Feerman

leaned back, too exhausted to think. He could feel a cool breeze on his face, and the slight vibration of the car was pleasant. But the ride seemed interminably long.

"Here we are," one of the men said at last. They stopped the car and led him inside an enormous gray building, to a barren little room. In the middle of the room was a desk marked RECEPTIONIST. A man was sprawled half across it, snoring gently.

One of Feerman's guards cleared his throat loudly. The receptionist sat up immediately, rubbing his eyes. He slipped on a pair of glasses and looked at them sleepily.

"Which one?" he asked.

The two guards pointed at Feerman.

"All right." The receptionist stretched his thin arms, then opened a large black notebook. He made a notation, tore out the sheet and handed it to Feerman's guards. They left immediately.

The receptionist pushed a button, then scratched his head vigorously. "Full moon tonight," he said to Feerman, with evident satisfaction.

"What?" Feerman asked.

"Full moon. We get more of you guys when the moon's full, or so it seems. I've thought of doing a study on it."

"More? More what?" Feerman asked, still adjusting to the shock of being within The Academy.

"Don't be dense," the receptionist said sternly. "We get more plus tens when the moon is full. I don't suppose there's any correlation, but—ah, here's the guard."

A uniformed guard walked up to the desk, still knotting his tie.

"Take him to 312AA," the receptionist said. As Feerman and the guard walked away, he removed his glasses and stretched out again on the desk.

The guard led Feerman through a complex network of corridors, marked off with frequent doors. The corridors seemed to have grown spontaneously, for branches shot off at all angles, and some parts were twisted and curved, like ancient city streets. As he walked, Feerman noticed that the doors were not numbered in sequence. He passed 3112, then 25P, and then 14. And he was certain he passed the number 888 three times.

"How can you find your way?" he asked the guard.

"That's my job," the guard said, not unpleasantly.

"Not very systematic," Feerman said, after a while.

"Can't be," the guard said in an almost confidential tone of voice. "Originally they planned this place with a lot fewer rooms, but then the rush started. Patients, patients, more every day, and no sign of a letup. So the rooms had to be broken into smaller units, and new corridors had to be cut through."

"But how do the doctors find their patients?" Feerman asked.

They had reached 312AA. Without answering, the guard unlocked the door, and, when Feerman had walked through, closed and locked it after him.

It was a very small room. There was a couch, a chair, and a cabinet, filling all the available space.

Almost immediately, Feerman heard voices outside the door. A man said, "Coffee then, at the cafeteria in half an hour." A key turned. Feerman didn't hear the reply, but there was a sudden burst of laughter. A man's deep voice said, "Yes, and a hundred more and we'll have to go underground for room!"

The door opened and a bearded man in a white jacket came in, still smiling faintly. His face became professional as soon as he saw Feerman. "Just lie on the couch, please," he said, politely, but with an unmistakable air of command.

Feerman remained standing. "Now that I'm here," he said, "would you explain what all this means?"

The bearded man had begun to unlock the cabinet. He

looked at Feerman with a wearily humorous expression, and raised both eyebrows. "I'm a doctor," he said, "not a lecturer."

"I realize that. But surely—"

"Yes, yes," the doctor said, shrugging his shoulders helplessly. "I know. You have a right to know, and all that. But they really should have explained it all before you reached here. It just isn't my job."

Feerman remained standing. The doctor said, "Lie down on the couch like a good chap, and I'll tell all." He turned back to the cabinet.

Feerman thought fleetingly of trying to overpower him, but realized that thousands of plus tens must have thought of it, too. Undoubtedly there were precautions. He lay down on the couch.

"The Academy," the doctor said as he rummaged in the cabinet, "is obviously a product of our times. To understand it, you must first understand the age we live in." The doctor paused dramatically, then went on with evident gusto. "Sanity! But there is a tremendous strain involved in sanity, you know, and especially in social sanity. How easily the mind becomes deranged! And once deranged, values change, a man begins to have strange hopes, ideas, theories, and a need for action. These things may not be abnormal in themselves, but they result inevitably in harm to society, for movement in any direction harms a static society. Now, after thousands of years of bloodshed, we have set ourselves the goal of protecting society against the unsane individual. Therefore—it is up to the individual to avoid those mental configurations, those implicit decisions which will make him a dangerous potential for change. This will to staticity which is our ideal required an almost superhuman strength and determination. If you don't have that, you end up here."

"I don't see—" Feerman began, but the doctor interrupted.

"The need for The Academy should now be apparent.

Today, brain surgery is the final effective alternative to sanity. But this is an unpleasant eventuality for a man to contemplate, a truly hellish alternative. Government brain surgery involves death to the original personality, which is death in its truest form. The Academy tries to relieve a certain strain by offering another alternative."

"But what *is* this alternative? Why don't you tell it?"

"Frankly, most people prefer not knowing." The doctor closed and locked the cabinet, but Feerman could not see what instruments he had selected. "Your reaction isn't typical, I assure you. You choose to think of us as something dark, mysterious, frightening. This is because of your unsanity. Sane people see us as a panacea, a pleasantly misty relief from certain grim certainties. They accept us on faith." The doctor chucked softly.

"To most people, we represent heaven."

"Then why not let your methods be known?"

"Frankly," the doctor said softly, "even the methods of heaven are best not examined too closely."

"So the whole thing is a hoax!" Feerman said, trying to sit up. "You're going to kill me!"

"Most assuredly not," the doctor said, restraining him gently until Feerman lay back again.

"Then what exactly are you going to do?"

"You'll see."

"And why doesn't anyone return?"

"They don't choose to," the doctor said. Before Feerman could move, the doctor had deftly inserted a needle into his arm, and injected him with a warm liquid. "You must remember," the doctor said, "society must be protected against the individual."

"Yes," Feerman said drowsily, "but who is to protect the individual against society?"

The room became indistinct and, although the doctor answered him, Feerman couldn't hear his words, but he was sure that they were wise, and proper, and very true.

When he recovered consciousness he found that he was standing on a great plain. It was sunrise. In the dim light, wisps of fog clung to his ankles, and the grass beneath his feet was wet and springy.

Feerman was mildly surprised to see his wife standing beside him, close to his right side. On his left was his dog Speed, pressed against his leg, trembling slightly. His surprise passed quickly, because this was where his wife and dog should be; at his side before the battle.

Ahead, misty movement resolved into individual figures, and as they approached Feerman recognized them.

They were the enemy! Leading the procession was his robutler, gleaming inhumanly in the half-light. Morgan was there, shrieking to the Section Chief that Feerman must die, and Flynn, that frightened man, hid his face but still advanced against him. And there was his landlady, screaming, "No home for him!" And behind her were doctors, receptionists, guards and behind them marched millions of men in rough laborer's clothing, caps jammed down over their faces, newspapers tightly rolled as they advanced.

Feerman tensed expectantly for this ultimate fight against the enemies who had betrayed him. But a doubt passed over his mind. Was this real?

He had a sudden sickening vision of his drugged body lying in a numbered room in The Academy, while his soul was here in the never-never land, doing battle with shadows.

There's nothing wrong with me! In a moment of utter clarity, Feerman understood that he had to escape. His destiny wasn't here, fighting dream-enemies. He had to get back to the real world. The Status Quo couldn't last forever. And what would mankind do, with all the toughness, inventiveness, individuality bred out of the race?

Did no one leave The Academy? He would! Feerman struggled with the illusions, and he could almost feel his discarded body stir on its couch, groan, move. . . .

But his dream-wife seized his arm and pointed. His dream-dog snarled at the advancing host.

The moment was gone forever, but Feerman never knew it. He forgot his decision, forgot earth, forgot truth, and drops of dew spattered his legs as he ran forward to engage the enemy in battle.

Nobody Bothers Gus

Algis Budrys (1931-   )

A. J. Budrys produced a string of excellent short stories and novels during the fifties, a period during which he spent his chronological twenties. His relative youth, while not unusual in the field of science fiction, is nevertheless significant because of the consistently high quality of his efforts in the handling of difficult material, as in his superior novel Who? (1958) and The Falling Torch (1959). After a long period of relative quiet since the late sixties, he is again writing both outstanding fiction and some of the most perceptive criticism of science fiction to be found anywhere.

Some of his best shorter fiction of the fifties such as "First to Serve," "The Executioner," "Riya's Foundling," and the lovely "The Edge of the Sea," can be found in his collections, especially The Unexpected Dimension (1960). The fact that he has never had a "Best of . . ." book is a major sin.

The individual with "special" or "wild" talents is a familiar character in science fiction, Olaf Stapledon's Odd John being a prominent example. "Gus" is perhaps the best short treatment of the type in modern science fiction, and his dilemmas

*and problems are those of everyone who society labels as
"different."*

From *Astounding Science Fiction*   November, 1955

Two years earlier, Gus Kusevic had been driving slowly
down the narrow back road into Boonesboro.

It was good country for slow driving, particularly in the late
spring. There was nobody else on the road. The woods were
just blooming into a deep, rich green as yet unburned by
summer, and the afternoons were still cool and fresh. And,
just before he reached the Boonesboro town line, he saw the
locked and weathered cottage standing for sale on its quarter-
acre lot.

He had pulled his roadcar up to a gentle stop, swung sideways in his seat, and looked at it.

It needed paint; the siding had gone from white to gray, and
the trim was faded. There were shingles missing here and there
from the roof, leaving squares of darkness on the sun-bleached
rows of cedar, and inevitably, some of the windowpanes had
cracked. But the frame hadn't slouched out of square, and the
roof hadn't sagged. The chimney stood up straight.

He looked at the straggled clumps and windrowed hay that
were all that remained of the shrubbery and the lawn. His
broad, homely face bunched itself into a quiet smile along its
well-worn seams. His hands itched for the feel of a spade.

He got out of the roadcar, walked across the road and up to
the cottage door, and copied down the name of the real estate
dealer listed on the card tacked to the doorframe.

Now it was almost two years later, early in April, and Gus was
top-dressing his lawn.

Earlier in the day he'd set up a screen beside the pile of
topsoil behind his house, shoveled the soil through the screen,

mixed it with broken peat moss, and carted it out to the lawn, where he left it in small piles. Now he was carefully raking it out over the young grass in a thin layer that covered only the roots, and let the blades peep through. He intended to be finished by the time the second half of the Giants-Kodiaks doubleheader came on. He particularly wanted to see it because Halsey was pitching for the Kodiaks, and he had something of an avuncular interest in Halsey.

He worked without waste motion or excess expenditure of energy. Once or twice he stopped and had a beer in the shade of the rose arbor he'd put up around the front door. Nevertheless, the sun was hot; by early afternoon, he had his shirt off.

Just before he would have been finished, a battered flivver settled down in front of the house. It parked with a flurry of its rotors, and a gangling man in a worn serge suit, with thin hair plastered across his tight scalp, climbed out and looked at Gus uncertainly.

Gus had glanced up briefly while the flivver was on its silent way down. He'd made out the barely-legible "Falmouth County Clerk's Office" lettered over the faded paint on its door, shrugged, and gone on with what he was doing.

Gus was a big man. His shoulders were heavy and broad; his chest was deep, grizzled with thick, iron-gray hair. His stomach had gotten a little heavier with the years, but the muscles were still there under the layer of flesh. His upper arms were thicker than a good many thighs, and his forearms were enormous.

His face was seamed by a network of folds and creases. His flat cheeks were marked out by two deep furrows that ran from the sides of his bent nose, merged with the creases bracketing his wide lips, and converged toward the blunt point of his jaw. His pale blue eyes twinkled above high cheekbones which were covered with wrinkles. His close-cropped hair was as white as cotton.

Only repeated and annoying exposure would give his body a tan, but his face was permanently browned. The pink of his body sunburn was broken in several places by white scar tissue. The thin line of a knife cut emerged from the tops of his pants and faded out across the right side of his stomach. The other significant area of scarring lay across the uneven knuckles of his heavy-fingered hands.

The clerk looked at the mailbox to make sure of the name, checking it against an envelope he was holding in one hand. He stopped and looked at Gus again, mysteriously nervous.

Gus abruptly realized that he probably didn't present a reassuring appearance. With all the screening and raking he'd been doing, there'd been a lot of dust in the air. Mixed with perspiration, it was all over his face, chest, arms, and back. Gus knew he didn't look very gentle even at his cleanest and best-dressed. At the moment, he couldn't blame the clerk for being skittish.

He tried to smile disarmingly.

The clerk ran his tongue over his lips, cleared his throat with a slight cough, and jerked his head toward the mailbox. "Is that right? You Mr. Kusevic?"

Gus nodded. "That's right. What can I do for you?"

The clerk held up the envelope. "Got a notice here from the County Council," he muttered, but he was obviously much more taken up by his effort to equate Gus with the rose arbor, the neatly edged and carefully tended flower beds, the hedges, the flagstoned walk, the small goldfish pond under the willow tree, the white-painted cottage with its window boxes and bright shutters, and the curtains showing inside the sparkling windows.

Gus waited until the man was through with his obvious thoughts, but something deep inside him sighed quietly. He had gone through this moment of bewilderment with so many other people that he was quite accustomed to it, but that is not the same thing as being oblivious.

"Well, come on inside," he said after a decent interval. "It's pretty hot out here, and I've got some beer in the cooler."

The clerk hesitated again. "Well, all I've got to do is deliver this notice—" he said, still looking around. "Got the place fixed up real nice, don't you?"

Gus smiled. "It's my home. A man likes to live in a nice place. In a hurry?"

The clerk seemed to be troubled by something in what Gus had said. Then he looked up suddenly, obviously just realizing he'd been asked a direct question. "Huh?"

"You're not in any hurry, are you? Come on in; have a beer. Nobody's expected to be a ball of fire on a spring afternoon."

The clerk grinned uneasily. "No . . . nope, guess not." He brightened. "O.K.! Don't mind if I do."

Gus ushered him into the house, grinning with pleasure. Nobody'd seen the inside of the place since he'd fixed it up; the clerk was the first visitor he'd had since moving in. There weren't even any delivery men; Boonesboro was so small you had to drive in for your own shopping. There wasn't any mail carrier service, of course—not that Gus ever received any mail.

He showed the clerk into the living room. "Have a seat. I'll be right back." He went quickly out to the kitchen, took some beer out of the cooler, loaded a tray with glasses, a bowl of chips and pretzels, and the beer, and carried it out.

The clerk was up, looking around the library that covered two of the living room walls.

Looking at his expression, Gus realized with genuine regret that the man wasn't the kind to doubt whether an obvious clod like Kusevic had read any of this stuff. A man like that could still be talked to, once the original misconceptions were knocked down. No, the clerk was too plainly mystified that a grown man would fool with books. Particularly a man like Gus; now, one of these kids that messed with college politics, that was something else. But a grown man oughtn't to act like that.

Gus saw it had been a mistake to expect anything of the clerk. He should have known better, whether he was hungry for company or not. He'd *always* been hungry for company, and it was time he realized, once and for all, that he just plain wasn't going to find any.

He set the tray down on the table, uncapped a beer quickly, and handed it to the man.

"Thanks," the clerk mumbled. He took a swallow, sighed loudly, and wiped his mouth with the back of his hand. He looked around the room again. "Cost you a lot to have all this put in?"

Gus shrugged. "Did most of it myself. Built the shelves and furniture; stuff like that. Some of the paintings I had to buy, and the books and records."

The clerk grunted. He seemed to be considerably ill at ease, probably because of the notice he'd brought, whatever it was. Gus found himself wondering what it could possibly be, but, now that he'd made the mistake of giving the man a beer, he had to wait politely until it was finished before he could ask.

He went over to the TV set. "Baseball fan?" he asked the clerk.

"Sure!"

"Giants-Kodiaks ought to be on." He switched the set on and pulled up a hassock, sitting on it so as not to get one of the chairs dirty. The clerk wandered over and stood looking at the screen, taking slow swallows of his beer.

The second game had started, and Halsey's familiar figure appeared on the screen as the set warmed up. The lithe young lefthander was throwing with his usual boneless motion, apparently not working hard at all, but the ball was whipping past the batters with a sizzle that the home plate microphone was picking up clearly.

Gus nodded toward Halsey. "He's quite a pitcher, isn't he?"

The clerk shrugged. "Guess so. Walker's their best man, though."

Gus sighed as he realized he'd forgotten himself again. The clerk wouldn't pay much attention to Halsey, naturally.

But he was getting a little irritated at the man, with his typical preconceptions of what was proper and what wasn't, of who had a right to grow roses and who didn't.

"Offhand," Gus said to the clerk, "could you tell me what Halsey's record was, last year?"

The clerk shrugged. "Couldn't tell you. Wasn't bad—I remember that much. 13–7, something like that."

Gus nodded to himself. "Uh-huh. How'd Walker do?"

"Walker! Why man, Walker just won something like twenty-five games, that's all. And three no-hitters. How'd Walker do? Huh!"

Gus shook his head. "Walker's a good pitcher, all right— but he didn't pitch any no-hitters. And he only won eighteen games."

The clerk wrinkled his forehead. He opened his mouth to argue and then stopped. He looked like a sure-thing bettor who'd just realized that his memory had played him a trick.

"Say—I think you're right! Huh! Now what the Sam Hill made me think Walker was the guy? And you know something —I've been talking about him all winter, and nobody once called me wrong?" The clerk scratched his head. "Now, *somebody* pitched them games! Who the dickens was it?" He scowled in concentration.

Gus silently watched Halsey strike out his third batter in a row, and his face wrinkled into a slow smile. Halsey was still young; just hitting his stride. He threw himself into the game with all the energy and enjoyment a man felt when he realized he was at his peak, and that, out there on the mound in the sun, he was as good as any man who ever had gone before him in this profession.

Gus wondered how soon Halsey would see the trap he'd set for himself.

Because it wasn't a contest. Not for Halsey. For Christy Mathewson, it had been a contest. For Lefty Grove and Dizzy Dean, for Bob Feller and Slats Gould, it had been a contest. But for Halsey it was just a complicated form of solitaire that always came out right.

Pretty soon, Halsey'd realize that you can't handicap yourself at solitaire. If you knew where all the cards are; if you knew that unless you deliberately cheated against yourself, you couldn't help but win—what good was it? One of these days, Halsey'd realize there wasn't a game on Earth he couldn't beat; whether it was a physical contest, organized and formally recognized as a game, or whether it was the billion-triggered pinball machine called Society.

What then, Halsey? What then? And if you find out, please, in the name of whatever kind of brotherhood we share, let me know.

The clerk grunted. "Well, it don't matter, I guess. I can always look it up in the record book at home."

Yes, you can, Gus commented silently. But you won't notice what it says, and, if you do, you'll forget it and never realize you've forgotten.

The clerk finished his beer, set it down on the tray, and was free to remember what he'd come here for. He looked around the room again, as though the memory were a cue of some kind.

"Lots of books," he commented.

Gus nodded, watching Halsey walk out to the pitcher's mound again.

"Uh . . . you read 'em all?"

Gus shook his head.

"How about that one by that Miller fellow? I hear that's a pretty good one."

So. The clerk had a certain narrow interest in certain aspects of certain kinds of literature.

"I suppose it is," Gus answered truthfully. "I read the first three pages, once." And, having done so, he'd known how the rest of it was going to go, who would do what when, and he'd lost interest. The library had been a mistake, just one of the dozen similar experiments. If he'd wanted an academic familiarity with human literature, he could just as easily have picked it up by browsing through bookstores, rather than buying the books and doing substantially the same thing at home. He couldn't hope to extract any emotional empathies, no matter what he did.

Face it, though; rows of even useless books were better than bare wall. The trappings of culture were a bulwark of sorts, even though it was a learned culture and not a *felt* one, and meant no more to him than the culture of the Incas. Try as he might, he could never be an Inca. Nor even a Maya or an Aztec, or any kind of kin, except by the most tenuous of extensions.

But he had no culture of his own. There was the thing; the emptiness that nevertheless ached; the rootlessness, the complete absence of a place to stand and say: "This is my own."

Halsey struck out the first batter in the inning with three pitches. Then he put a slow floater precisely where the next man could get the best part of his bat on it, and did not even look up as the ball screamed out of the park. He struck out the next two men with a total of eight pitches.

Gus shook his head slowly. That was the first symptom; when you didn't bother to be subtle about your handicapping any more.

The clerk held out the envelope. "Here," he said brusquely, having finally shilly-shallied his resolution up to the point of doing it despite his obvious nervousness at Gus' probable reaction.

Gus opened the envelope and read the notice. Then, just as the clerk had been doing, he looked around the room. A dark expression must have flickered over his face, because the clerk became even more hesitant. "I . . . I want you to know I regret this. I guess all of us do."

Gus nodded hastily. "Sure, sure." He stood up and looked

out the front window. He smiled crookedly, looking at the top-dressing spread carefully over the painstakingly rolled lawn, which was slowly taking form on the plot where he had plowed last year and picked out pebbles, seeded and watered, shoveled topsoil, laid out flower beds . . . ah, there was no use going into that now. The whole plot, cottage and all, was condemned, and that was that.

"They're . . . they're turnin' the road into a twelve-lane freight highway," the clerk explained.

Gus nodded absently.

The clerk moved closer and dropped his voice. "Look—I was told to tell you this. Not in writin'." He sidled even closer, and actually looked around before he spoke. He laid his hand confidentially on Gus' bare forearm.

"Any price you ask for," he muttered, "is gonna be O.K., as long as you don't get too greedy. The county isn't paying this bill. Not even the state, if you get what I mean."

Gus got what he meant. Twelve-lane highways aren't built by anything but national governments.

He got more than that. National governments don't work this way unless there's a good reason.

"Highway between Hollister and Farnham?" he asked.

The clerk paled. "Don't know for sure," he muttered.

Gus smiled thinly. Let the clerk wonder how he'd guessed. It couldn't be much of a secret, anyway—not after the grade was laid out and the purpose became self-evident. Besides, the clerk wouldn't wonder very long.

A streak of complete perversity shot through Gus. He recognized its source in his anger at losing the cottage, but there was no reason why he shouldn't allow himself to cut loose.

"What's your name?" he asked the clerk abruptly.

"Uh . . . Harry Danvers."

"Well, Harry, suppose I told you I could stop that highway, if I wanted to? Suppose I told you that no bulldozer could get near this place without breaking down, that no shovel could dig this ground, that sticks of dynamite just plain wouldn't explode if they tried to blast? Suppose I told you that if they did put in the highway, it would turn soft as ice cream if I wanted it to, and run away like a river?"

"Huh?"

"Hand me your pen."

Danvers reached out mechanically and handed it to him. Gus put it between his palms and rolled it into a ball. He dropped it and caught it as it bounced up sharply from the soft, thick rug. He pulled it out between his fingers, and it returned to its cylindrical shape. He unscrewed the cap, flattened it out into a sheet between two fingers, scribbled on it, rolled it back into a cap, and, using his fingernail to draw out the ink which was now part of it, permanently inscribed Danvers' name just below the surface of the metal. Then he screwed the cap on again and handed the pen back to the county clerk. "Souvenir," he said.

The clerk looked down at it.

"Well?" Gus asked. "Aren't you curious about how I did it and what I am?"

The clerk shook his head. "Good trick. I guess you magician fellows must spend a lot of time practicing, huh? Can't say I could see myself spendin' that much working time on a hobby."

Gus nodded. "That's a good, sound, practical point of view," he said. Particularly when all of us automatically put out a field that damps curiosity, he thought. What point of view *could* you have?

He looked over the clerk's shoulder at the lawn, and one side of his mouth twisted sadly.

Only God can make a tree, he thought, looking at the shrubs and flower beds. Should we all, then, look for our challenge in landscape gardening? Should we become the gardeners of the rich humans in their expensive houses, driving up in our old, rusty trucks, oiling our lawnmowers, kneeling on the humans' lawns with our clipping shears, coming to the kitchen door to ask for a drink of water on a hot summer day?

The highway. Yes, he could stop the highway. Or make it go around him. There was no way of stopping the curiosity damper, no more than there was a way of willing his heart to stop, but it could be stepped up. He could force his mind to labor near overload, and no one would ever even *see* the cottage, the lawn, the rose arbor, or the battered old man drinking his beer. Or rather, seeing them, would pay them absolutely no attention.

But the first time he went into town, or when he died, the field would be off, and then what? Then curiosity, then investigation, then, perhaps a fragment of theory here or there to be fitted to another somewhere else. And then what? Pogrom?

He shook his head. The humans couldn't win, and would lose monstrously. *That* was why he couldn't leave the humans a clue. He had no taste for slaughtering sheep, and he doubted if his fellows did.

His fellows. Gus stretched his mouth. The only one he could be sure of was Halsey. There had to be others, but there was no way of finding them. They provoked no reaction from the humans; they left no trail to follow. It was only if they showed themselves, like Halsey, that they could be seen. There was, unfortunately, no private telepathic party line among them.

He wondered if Halsey hoped someone would notice him and get in touch. He wondered if Halsey even suspected there were others like himself. He wondered if anyone had noticed *him*, when Gus Kusevic's name had been in the papers occasionally.

It's the dawn of my race, he thought. The first generation— or is it, and does it matter?—and I wonder where the females are.

He turned back to the clerk. "I want what I paid for the place," he said. "No more."

The clerk's eyes widened slightly, then relaxed, and he shrugged. "Suit yourself. But if it was me, I'd soak the government good."

Yes, Gus thought, you doubtless would. But I don't want to, because you simply don't take candy from babies.

So the superman packed his bags and got out of the human's way. Gus choked a silent laugh. The damping field. The damping field. The thrice-cursed, ever-benevolent, foolproof, autonomic, protective damping field.

Evolution had, unfortunately, not yet realized that there was such a thing as human society. It produced a being with a certain modification from the human stock, thereby arriving at practical psi. In order to protect this feeble new species, whose members were so terribly sparse, it gave them the perfect camouflage.

Result: When young Augustin Kusevic was enrolled in school, it was discovered that he had no birth certificate. No hospital recalled his birth. As a matter of brutal fact, his human parents sometimes forgot his existence for days at a time.

Result: When young Gussie Kusevic tried to enter high school, it was discovered that he had never entered grammar school. No matter that he could quote teachers' names, textbooks, or classroom numbers. No matter if he could produce report cards. They were misfiled, and the anguished interviews forgotten. No one doubted his existence—people remembered the fact of his being, and the fact of his having acted and being acted upon. But only as though they had read it in some infinitely boring book.

He had no friends, no girl, no past, no present, no love. He had no place to stand. Had there been such things as ghosts, he would have found his fellowship there.

By the time of his adolescence, he had discovered an absolute lack of involvement with the human race. He studied it, because it was the salient feature of his environment. He did not live with it. It said nothing to him that was of personal value; its motivations, morals, manners and morale did not find responsive reactions in him. And his, of course, made absolutely no impression on it.

The life of the peasant of ancient Babylon is of interest to only a few historical anthropologists, none of whom actually want to *be* Babylonian peasants.

Having solved the human social equation from his dispassionate viewpoint, and caring no more than the naturalist who finds that few are extremely fond of green aspen leaves, he plunged into physical release. He discovered the thrill of picking fights and winning them; of *making* somebody pay attention to him by smashing his nose.

He might have become a permanent fixture on the Manhattan docks, if another longshoreman hadn't slashed him with a carton knife. The cultural demand on him had been plain. He'd had to kill the man.

That had been the end of unregulated personal combat. He discovered, not to his horror but to his disgust, that he could get away with murder. No investigation had been made; no search was attempted.

So that had been the end of that, but it had led him to the only possible evasion of the trap to which he had been born. Intellectual competition being meaningless, organized sports became the only answer. Simultaneously regulating his efforts and annotating them under a mound of journalistic record-keeping, they furnished the first official continuity his life had ever known. People still forgot his accomplishments, but when they turned to the records, his name was undeniably there. A dossier can be misfiled. School records can disappear. But something more than a damping field was required to shunt aside the mountain of news copy and statistics that drags, ball-like, at the ankle of even the mediocre athlete.

It seemed to Gus—and he thought of it a great deal—that this chain of progression was inevitable for any male of his kind. When, three years ago, he had discovered Halsey, his hypothesis was bolstered. But what good was Halsey to another male? To hold mutual consolation sessions with? He had no intention of ever contacting the man.

The clerk cleared his throat. Gus jerked his head around to look at him, startled. He'd forgotten him.

"Well, guess I'll be going. Remember, you've only got two months."

Gus gestured noncommittally. The man had delivered his message. Why didn't he acknowledge he'd served his purpose, and go?

Gus smiled ruefully. What purpose did *homo nondescriptus* serve, and where was he going? Halsey was already walking downhill along the well-marked trail. *Were* there others? If so, then they were in another rut, somewhere, and not even the tops of their heads showed. He and his kind could recognize each other only by an elaborate process of elimination; they had to watch for the people no one noticed.

He opened the door for the clerk, saw the road, and found his thoughts back with the highway.

The highway would run from Hollister, which was a railroad junction, to the Air Force Base at Farnham, where his calculations in sociomathematics had long ago predicted the first starship would be constructed and launched. The trucks would rumble up the highway, feeding the open maw with men and material.

He cleaned his lips. Up there in space, somewhere; somewhere outside the Solar System, was another race. The imprint of their visits here was plain. The humans would encounter them, and again he could predict the result; the humans would win.

Gus Kusevic could not go along to investigate the challenges that he doubted lay among the stars. Even with scrapbooks full of notices and clippings, he barely made his career penetrate the public consciousness. Halsey, who had exuberantly broken every baseball record in the books, was known as a "pretty fair country pitcher."

What credentials could he present with his application to the Air Force? Who would remember them the next day if he had any? What would become of the records of his inoculations, his physical check-ups, his training courses? Who would remember to reserve a bunk for him, or stow supplies for him, or add his consumption to the total when the time came to allow for oxygen?

Stow away? Nothing easier. But, again; who would die so he could live within the tight lattice of shipboard economy? Which sheep would he slaughter, and to what useful purpose, in the last analysis?

"Well, so long," the clerk said.

"Good-by," Gus said.

The clerk walked down the flagstones and out to his flivver.

I think, Gus said to himself, it would have been much better for us if Evolution had been a little less protective and a little more thoughtful. An occasional pogrom wouldn't have done us any harm. A ghetto at least keeps the courtship problem solved.

Our seed has been spilt on the ground.

Suddenly, Gus ran forward, pushed by something he didn't care to name. He looked up through the flivver's open door, and the clerk looked down apprehensively.

"Danvers, you're a sports fan," Gus said hastily, realizing his voice was too urgent; that he was startling the clerk with his intensity.

"That's right," the clerk answered, pushing himself nervously back along the seat.

"Who's heavyweight champion of the world?"

"Mike Frazier. Why?"

"Who'd he beat for the title? Who used to be champion?"

The clerk pursed his lips. "Huh! It's been years—Gee, I

don't know. I don't remember. I could look it up, I guess."

Gus exhaled slowly. He half-turned and looked back toward the cottage, the lawn, the flower beds, the walk, the arbor, and the fish pond under the willow tree. "Never mind," he said, and walked back into the house while the clerk wobbled his flivver into the air.

The TV set was blaring with sound. He checked the status of the game.

It had gone quickly. Halsey had pitched a one-hitter so far, and the Giants' pitcher had done almost as well. The score was tied at 1–1, the Giants were at bat, and it was the last out in the ninth inning. The camera boomed in on Halsey's face.

Halsey looked at the batter with complete disinterest in his eyes, wound up, and threw the home-run ball.

Happy Birthday, Dear Jesus

Frederik Pohl (1919-   )

FREDERIK *Pohl was the most influential figure of the social
science fiction of the fifties. In three novels coauthored
with others, he systematically took apart three of the most
important institutions in American corporate life: the advertising industry in* The Space Merchants *(1953), written with
C. M. Kornbluth; the legal profession in* Gladiator-at-Law
(1955), also with Kornbluth; and the insurance industry in
Preferred Risk *(1955), written with Lester del Rey under the
name "Edson McCann." In addition, he produced a large number of short stories and novelettes on social themes, including
the classic "The Midas Plague." Indeed, he was the leading
critic of that aspect of American life known as the "admass
culture."*

*But Pohl's contribution encompassed much more than his
writing. He was one of the originators of the "original anthology" concept, which he pioneered with his* Star Science Fiction
*series. He was also the leading literary agent in science fiction
during the 1949–1953 period and was heavily responsible for
the first hardcover science-fiction books produced by major
publishers. In the sixties he would achieve fame as an award*

winning editor of Galaxy *and* Worlds of If. *In recognition of these and other contributions to science fiction, he was awarded the first H. G. Wells Award, designed to reflect excellence in the social satire tradition of science fiction.*

In "Happy Birthday, Dear Jesus" Pohl turned his attention once again to the production-consumption process and produced a superb example of social extrapolation carried out to its logical and terrifying conclusion.

From *Alternating Currents*   1956

It was the craziest Christmas I ever spent. Partly it was Heinemann's fault—he came up with a new wrinkle in gift-wrapping that looked good but like every other idea that comes out of the front office meant plenty of headaches for the rest of us. But what really messed up Christmas for me was the girl.

Personnel sent her down—after I'd gone up there myself three times and banged my fist on the table. It was the height of the season and when she told me that she had had her application in *three weeks* before they called her, I excused myself and got Personnel on the store phone from my private office. "Martin here," I said. "What the devil's the matter with you people? This girl is the Emporium type if I ever saw one, and you've been letting her sit around nearly a month while——"

Crawford, the Personnel head, interrupted me. "Have you talked to her very much?" he wanted to know.

"Well, no. But——"

"Call me back when you do," he advised, and clicked off.

I went back to the stockroom where she was standing patiently, and looked her over a little thoughtfully. But she looked all right to me. She was blond-haired and blue-eyed and not very big; she had a sweet, slow smile. She wasn't exactly beautiful, but she looked like a girl you'd want to know. She wasn't bold, and she wasn't too shy; and that's a perfect description of what we call "The Emporium Type."

So what in the world was the matter with Personnel?

Her name was Lilymary Hargreave. I put her to work on the gift-wrap spraying machine while I got busy with my paper work. I have a hundred forty-one persons in the department and at the height of the Christmas season I could use twice as many. But we do get the work done. For instance, Saul & Capell, the next biggest store in town, has a hundred and sixty in their gift and counseling department, and their sales run easily twenty-five per cent less than ours. And in the four years that I've headed the department we've yet to fail to get an order delivered when it was promised.

All through that morning I kept getting glimpses of the new girl. She was a quick learner—smart, too smart to be stuck with the sprayer for very long. I needed someone like her around, and right there on the spot I made up my mind that if she was as good as she looked I'd put her in a counseling booth within a week, and the devil with what Personnel thought.

The store was packed with last-minute shoppers. I suppose I'm sentimental, but I love to watch the thousands of people bustling in and out, with all the displays going at once, and the lights on the trees, and the loudspeakers playing *White Christmas* and *The Eighth Candle* and *Jingle Bells* and all the other traditional old favorites. Christmas is more than a mere selling season of the year to me; it *means* something.

The girl called me over near closing time. She looked distressed and with some reason. There was a dolly filled with gift-wrapped packages, and a man from Shipping looking annoyed. She said, "I'm sorry, Mr. Martin, but I seem to have done something wrong."

The Shipping man snorted. "Look for yourself, Mr. Martin," he said, handing me one of the packages.

I looked. It was wrong, all right. Heinemann's new wrinkle that year was a special attached gift card—a simple Yule scene and the printed message:

The very Merriest of Season's Greetings
From . . . .
To . . . .
$8.50

The price varied with the item, of course. Heinemann's idea was for the customer to fill it out and mail it, ahead of time, to the person it was intended for. That way, the person who got it would know just about how much he ought to spend on a present for the first person. It was smart, I admit, and maybe the smartest thing about it was rounding the price off to the nearest fifty cents instead of giving it exactly. Heinemann said it was bad-mannered to be too precise—and the way the customers were going for the idea, it had to be right.

But the trouble was that the gift-wrapping machines were geared to only a plain card; it was necessary for the operator to put the price in by hand.

I said, "That's all right, Joe; I'll take care of it." As Joe went satisfied back to Shipping, I told the girl: "It's my fault. I should have explained to you, but I guess I've just been a little too rushed."

She looked downcast. "I'm sorry," she said.

"Nothing to be sorry about." I showed her the routing slip attached to each one, which the Shipping Department kept for its records once the package was on its way. "All we have to do is go through these; the price is on every one. We'll just fill out the cards and get them out. I guess———" I looked at my watch—"I guess you'll be a little late tonight, but I'll see that you get overtime and dinner money for it. It wasn't your mistake, after all."

She said hesitantly, "Mr. Martin, couldn't it—well, can I let it go for tonight? It isn't that I mind working, but I keep house for my father and if I don't get there on time he just won't remember to eat dinner. Please?"

I suppose I frowned a little, because her expression was a little worried. But, after all, it was her first day. I said, "Miss Hargreave, don't give it a thought. I'll take care of it."

The way I took care of it, it turned out, was to do it myself; it was late when I got through, and I ate quickly and went home to bed. But I didn't mind, for oh! the sweetness of the smile she gave me as she left.

I looked forward to the next morning, because I was looking forward to seeing Lilymary Hargreave again. But my luck was out—for she was.

My number-two man, Johnny Furness, reported that she hadn't phoned either. I called Personnel to get her phone number, but they didn't have it; I got the address, but the phone company had no phone listed under her name. So I stewed around until the coffee break, and then I put my hat on and headed out of the store. It wasn't merely that I was interested in seeing her, I told myself; she was just too good a worker to get off on the wrong foot this way, and it was only simple justice for me to go to her home and set her straight.

Her house was in a nondescript neighborhood—not too good, not too bad. A gang of kids were playing under a fire hydrant at the corner—but, on the other hand, the houses were neat and nearly new. Middle-class, you'd have to say.

I found the address, and knocked on the door of a second-floor apartment.

It was opened by a tall, leathery man of fifty or so—Lilymary's father, I judged. "Good morning," I said. "Is Miss Hargreave at home?"

He smiled; his teeth were bright in a very sun-bronzed face. "Which one?"

"Blond girl, medium height, blue eyes. Is there more than one?"

"There are four. But you mean Lilymary; won't you come in?"

I followed him, and a six-year-old edition of Lilymary took my hat and gravely hung it on a rack made of bamboo pegs. The leathery man said, "I'm Morton Hargreave, Lily's father. She's in the kitchen."

"George Martin," I said. He nodded and left me, for the kitchen, I presumed. I sat down on an old-fashioned studio couch in the living room, and the six-year-old sat on the edge of a straight-backed chair across from me, making sure I didn't pocket any of the souvenirs on the mantel. The room was full of curiosities—what looked like a cloth of beaten bark hanging on one wall, with a throwing-spear slung over the cloth. Everything looked vaguely South-Seas, though I am no expert.

The six-year-old said seriously, "This is the man, Lilymary," and I got up.

"Good morning," said Lilymary Hargreave, with a smudge of flour and an expression of concern on her face.

I said, floundering, "I, uh, noticed you hadn't come in and, well, since you were new to the Emporium, I thought——"

"I *am* sorry, Mr. Martin," she said. "Didn't Personnel tell you about Sundays?"

"What about Sundays?"

"I must have my Sundays off," she explained. "Mr. Crawford said it was very unusual, but I really can't accept the job any other way."

"Sundays off?" I repeated. "But—but, Miss Hargreave, don't you see what that does to my schedule? Sunday's our busiest day! The Emporium isn't a rich man's shop; our customers work during the week. If we aren't staffed to serve them when they can come in, we just aren't doing the job they expect of us!"

She said sincerely, "I'm terribly sorry, Mr. Martin."

The six-year-old was already reaching for my hat. From the

doorway her father said heartily, "Come back again, Mr. Martin. We'll be glad to see you."

He escorted me to the door, as Lilymary smiled and nodded and headed back to the kitchen. I said, "Mr. Hargreave, won't you ask Lilymary to come in for the afternoon, at least? I hate to sound like a boss, but I'm really short-handed on weekends, right now at the peak of the season."

"Season?"

"The Christmas season," I explained. "Nearly ninety per cent of our annual business is done in the Christmas season, and a good half of it on weekends. So won't you ask her?"

He shook his head. "Six days the Lord labored, Mr. Martin," he boomed, "and the seventh was the day of rest. I'm sorry."

And there I was, outside the apartment and the door closing politely but implacably behind me.

Crazy people. I rode the subway back to the store in an irritable mood; I bought a paper, but I didn't read it, because every time I looked at it all I saw was the date that showed me how far the Christmas season already had advanced, how little time we had left to make our quotas and beat last year's record: the eighth of September.

I would have something to say to Miss Lilymary Hargreave when she had the kindness to show up at her job. I promised myself. But, as it turned out, I didn't. Because that night, checking through the day's manifolds when everyone else had gone home, I fell in love with Lilymary Hargreave.

Possibly that sounds silly to you. She wasn't even there, and I'd only known her for a few hours, and when a man begins to push thirty without ever being married, you begin to think he's a hard case and not likely to fall slambang, impetuously in love like a teenager after his first divorce. But it's true, all the same.

I almost called her up. I trembled on the brink of it, with

my hand on the phone. But it was close to midnight, and if she wasn't home getting ready for bed I didn't want to know it, so I went home to my own bed. I reached under the pillow and turned off my dreamster before I went to sleep; I had a full library for it, a de luxe model with five hundred dreams that had been a present from the firm the Christmas before. I had Haroun al Rashid's harem and three of Charles Second's favorites on tape, and I had rocketing around the moon and diving to Atlantis and winning a sweepstakes and getting elected king of the world; but what I wanted to dream about was not on anybody's tape, and its name was Lilymary Hargreave.

Monday lasted forever. But at the end of forever, when the tip of the nightingale's wing had brushed away the mountain of steel and the Shipping personnel were putting on their hats and coats and powdering their noses or combing their hair, I stepped right up to Lilymary Hargreave and asked her to go to dinner with me.

She looked astonished, but only for a moment. Then she smiled. . . . I have mentioned the sweetness of her smile. "It's wonderful of you to ask me, Mr. Martin," she said earnestly, "and I do appreciate it. But I can't."

"Please," I said.

"I *am* sorry."

I might have said please again, and I might have fallen to my knees at her feet, it was that important to me. But the staff was still in the shop, and how would it look for the head of the department to fall at the feet of his newest employee? I said woodenly, "That's too bad." And I nodded and turned away, leaving her frowning after me. I cleared my desk sloppily, chucking the invoices in a drawer, and I was halfway out the door when I heard her calling after me:

"Mr. Martin, Mr. Martin!"

She was hurrying toward me, breathless. "I'm sorry," she

said, "I didn't mean to scream at you. But I just phoned my father, and———"

"I thought you didn't have a phone," I said accusingly.

She blinked at me. "At the rectory," she explained. "Anyway, I just phoned him, and—well, we'd both be delighted if you would come and have dinner with us at home."

Wonderful words! The whole complexion of the shipping room changed in a moment. I beamed foolishly at her, with a soft surge at my heart; I felt happy enough to endow a home, strong enough to kill a cave bear or give up smoking or any crazy, mixed-up thing. I wanted to shout and sing; but all I said was: "That sounds great." We headed for the subway, and although I must have talked to her on the ride I cannot remember a word we said, only that she looked like the angel at the top of our tallest Christmas tree.

Dinner was good, and there was plenty of it, cooked by Lilymary herself, and I think I must have seemed a perfect idiot. I sat there, with the six-year-old on one side of me and Lilymary on the other, across from the ten-year-old and the twelve-year-old. The father of them all was at the head of the table, but he was the only other male. I understood there were a couple of brothers, but they didn't live with the others. I suppose there had been a mother at some time, unless Morton Hargreave stamped the girls out with a kind of cookie-cutter; but whatever she had been she appeared to be deceased. I felt overwhelmed. I wasn't used to being surrounded by young females, particularly as young as the median in that gathering.

Lilymary made an attempt to talk to me, but it wasn't altogether successful. The younger girls were given to fits of giggling, which she had to put a stop to, and to making what were evidently personal remarks in some kind of a peculiar foreign tongue—it sounded like a weird aboriginal dialect, and I later found out that it was. But it was disconcerting, especially from the lips of a six-year-old with the giggles. So I didn't make any very intelligent responses to Lilymary's overtures.

But all things end, even eating dinner with giggling girls. And then Mr. Hargreave and I sat in the little parlor, waiting for the girls to—finish doing the dishes? I said, shocked, "Mr. Hargreave, do you mean they *wash* them?"

"Certainly they wash them," he boomed mildly. "How else would they get them clean, Mr. Martin?"

"Why, *dishwashers*, Mr. Hargreave." I looked at him in a different way. Business is business. I said, "After all, this is the Christmas season. At the Emporium we put a very high emphasis on dishwashers as a Christmas gift, you know. We——"

He interrupted good-humoredly. "I already have my gifts, Mr. Martin. Four of them, and very fine dishwashers they are."

"But Mr. Hargreave——"

"Not Mister Hargreave." The six-year-old was standing beside me, looking disapproving. "*Doctor* Hargreave."

"Corinne!" said her father. "Forgive her, Mr. Martin. But you see we're not very used to the—uh, civilized way of doing things. We've been a long time with the Dyaks."

The girls were all back from the kitchen, and Lilymary was out of her apron and looking—unbelievable. "Entertainment," she said brightly. "Mr. Martin, would you like to hear Corinne play?"

There was a piano in the corner. I said hastily, "I'm crazy about piano music. But——"

Lilymary laughed. "She's good," she told me seriously. "Even if I do have to say it to her face. But we'll let you off that if you like. Gretchen and I sing a little bit, if you'd prefer it?"

Wasn't there any TV in this place? I felt as out of place as an Easterbunny-helper in the Santa Claus line, but Lilymary was still looking unbelievable. So I sat through Lilymary and the twelve-year-old named Gretchen singing ancient songs while the six-year-old named Corinne accompanied them on the piano. It was pretty thick. Then the ten-year-old, whose

name I never did catch, did recitations; and then they all
looked expectantly at me.

I cleared my throat, slightly embarrassed. Lilymary said
quickly, "Oh, you don't have to do anything, Mr. Martin. It's
just our custom, but we don't expect strangers to conform to
it!"

I didn't want that word "stranger" to stick. I said, "Oh, but
I'd like to. I mean, I'm not much good at public entertaining,
but——" I hesitated, because that was the truest thing I had
ever said. I had no more voice than a goat, and of course the
only instrument I had ever learned to play was a TV set. But
then I remembered something from my childhood.

"I'll tell you what," I said enthusiastically. "How would you
like something appropriate to the season? 'A Visit from Santa
Claus,' for instance?"

Gretchen said snappishly, "What season? *We* don't start
celebrating——"

Her father cut her off. "Please do, Mr. Martin," he said
politely. "We'd enjoy that very much."

I cleared my throat and started:

> 'Tis the season of Christmas, and all through the house
> St. Nick and his helpers begin their carouse.
> The closets are stuffed and the drawers overflowing
> With gift-wrapped remembrances, coming and going.
> What a joyous abandon of Christmastime glow!
> What a making of lists! What a spending of dough!
> So much for——

"Hey!" said Gretchen, looking revolted. "Daddy, *that* isn't
how——"

"Hush!" said Dr. Hargreave grimly. His own expression
wasn't very delighted either, but he said, "Please go on."

I began to wish I'd kept my face shut. They were all looking
at me very peculiarly, except for Lilymary, who was conscientiously studying the floor. But it was too late to back out;
I went on:

So much for the bedroom, so much for the bath,
So much for the kitchen—too little by half!
Come Westinghouse, Philco! Come Hotpoint, G.E.!
Come Sunbeam! Come Mixmaster! Come to the Tree!
So much for the wardrobe—how shine Daddy's eyes
As he reaps his Yule harvest of slippers and ties.
So much for the family, so much for the friends,
So much for the neighbors—the list never ends.
A contingency fund for the givers belated
Whose gifts must be hastily reciprocated.
And out of——

Gretchen stood up. "It's our bedtime," she said. "Good night, everybody."

Lilymary flared, "It is not! Now be still!" And she looked at me for the first time. "Please go on," she said, with a furrowed brow.

I said hoarsely:

And out of the shops, how they spring with a clatter,
The gifts and appliances words cannot flatter!
The robot dishwasher, the new Frigidaire,
The doll with the didy and curable hair!
The electrified hairbrush, the black lingerie,
The full-color stereoscopic TV!
Come, Credit Department! Come, Personal Loan!
Come, Mortgage, come Christmas Club, come——

Lilymary turned her face away. I stopped and licked my lips.

"That's all I remember," I lied. "I—I'm sorry if——"

Dr. Hargreave shook himself like a man waking from a nightmare. "It's getting rather late," he said to Lilymary. "Perhaps—perhaps our guest would enjoy some coffee before he goes."

I declined the coffee and Lilymary walked me to the subway. We didn't talk much.

At the subway entrance she firmly took my hand and shook it. "It's been a pleasant evening," she said.

A wandering group of carolers came by; I gave my contribution to the guitarist. Suddenly angry, I said, "Doesn't that *mean* anything to you?"

"What?"

I gestured after the carolers. "That. Christmas. The whole sentimental, lovable, warmhearted business of Christmas. Lilymary, we've only known each other a short time, but——"

She interrupted: "Please, Mr. Martin. I—I know what you're going to say." She looked terribly appealing there in the Christmassy light of the red and green lights from the Tree that marked the subway entrance. Her pale, straight legs, hardly concealed by the shorts, picked up chromatic highlights; her eyes sparkled. She said, "You see, as Daddy says, we've been away from—civilization. Daddy is a missionary, and we've been with the Dyaks since I was a little girl. Gretch and Marlene and Corinne were born there. We—we do things differently on Borneo." She looked up at the Tree over us, and sighed. "It's very hard to get used to," she said. "Sometimes I wish we had stayed with the Dyaks."

Then she looked at me. She smiled. "But sometimes," she said, "I am very glad we're here." And she was gone.

Ambiguous? Call it merely ladylike. At any rate, that's what I called it; I took it to be the beginning of the kind of feeling I so desperately wanted her to have; and for the second night in a row I let Haroun's harem beauties remain silent on their tapes.

Calamity struck. My number-two man, Furness, turned up one morning with a dismal expression and a letter in a government-franked envelope. "Greetings!" it began. "You are summoned to serve with a jury of citizens for the term——"

"Jury duty!" I groaned. "At a time like this! Wait a minute, Johnny, I'll call up Mr. Heinemann. He might be able to fix it if——"

Furness was shaking his head. "Sorry, Mr. Martin. I already asked him and he tried; but no go. It's a big case—blindfold sampling of twelve brands of filter cigarettes—and Mr. Heinemann says it wouldn't look right to try to evade it."

So there was breaking another man in, to add to my troubles.

It meant overtime, and that meant that I didn't have as much time as I would like for Lilymary. Lunch together, a couple of times; odd moments between runs of the gift-wrapping machines; that was about it.

But she was never out of my thoughts. There was something about her that appealed to me. A square, yes. Unworldly, yes. Her family? A Victorian horror; but they were *her* family. I determined to get them on my side, and by and by I began to see how.

"Miss Hargreave," I said formally, coming out of my office. We stepped to one side, in a corner under the delivery chutes. The rumble of goods overhead gave us privacy. I said, "Lilymary, you're taking this Sunday off, as usual? May I come to visit you?"

She hesitated only a second. "Why, of course," she said firmly. "We'd be delighted. For dinner?"

I shook my head: "I have a little surprise for you," I whispered. She looked alarmed. "Not for you, exactly. For the kids. Trust me, Lilymary. About four o'clock in the afternoon?"

I winked at her and went back to my office to make arrangements. It wasn't the easiest thing in the world—it was our busy season, as I say—but what's the use of being the boss if you can't pull rank once in a while? So I made it as strong as I could, and Special Services hemmed and hawed and finally agreed that they would work in a special Visit from Santa Claus at the Hargreave home that Sunday afternoon.

Once the kids were on my side, I plotted craftily, it would

be easy enough to work the old man around, and what kid could resist a Visit from Santa Claus?

I rang the bell and walked into the queer South-Seas living room as though I belonged there. "Merry Christmas!" I said genially to the six-year-old who let me in. "I hope you kiddies are ready for a treat!"

She looked at me incredulously, and disappeared. I heard her say something shrill and protesting in the next room, and Lilymary's voice being firm and low-toned. Then Lilymary appeared. "Hello, Mr. Martin," she said.

"George."

"Hello, George." She sat down and patted the sofa beside her. "Would you like some lemonade?" she asked.

"Thank you," I said. It was pretty hot for the end of September, and the place didn't appear to be air-conditioned. She called, and the twelve-year-old, Gretchen, turned up with a pitcher and some cookies. I said warningly:

"Mustn't get too full, little girl! There's a surprise coming."

Lilymary cleared her throat, as her sister set the tray down with a clatter and stamped out of the room. "I—I wish you'd tell me about this surprise, George," she said. "You know, we're a little, well, set in our ways, and I wonder——"

"Nothing to worry about, Lilymary," I reassured her. "What is it, a couple of minutes before four? They'll be here any minute."

"They?"

I looked around; the kids were out of sight. "Santa Claus and his helpers," I whispered.

She began piercingly: "Santa Cl——"

"Ssh!" I nodded toward the door. "I want it to be a surprise for the kids. Please don't spoil it for them, Lilymary."

Well, she opened her mouth; but she didn't get a chance to say anything. The bell rang; Santa Claus and his helpers were right on time.

"Lilymary!" shrieked the twelve-year-old, opening the door. "Look!"

You couldn't blame the kid for being excited. "Ho-ho-ho," boomed Santa, rolling inside. "Oh, hello, Mr. Martin. This the place?"

"Certainly, Santa," I said, beaming. "Bring it in, boys."

The twelve-year-old cried, "Corinne! Marlene! This you got to see!" There was an odd tone to her voice, but I didn't pay much attention. It wasn't my party any more. I retired, smiling, to a corner of the room while the Santa Claus helpers began coming in with their sacks of gear on their shoulders. It was "Ho-ho-ho, little girl!" and "Merry Christmas, everybody!" until you couldn't hear yourself think.

Lilymary was biting her lip, staring at me. The Santa tapped her on the shoulder. "Where's the kitchen, lady?" he asked. "That door? Okay, Wynken—go on in and get set up. Nod, you go down and hurry up the sound truck, then you can handle the door. The rest of you helpers—" he surveyed the room briefly—"start lining up your Christmas Goodies there, and there. Now hop to it, boys! We got four more Visits to make this afternoon yet."

You never saw a crew of Christmas Gnomes move as fast as them. Snap, and the Tree was up, complete with its tinsel stars and gray colored Order Forms and Credit Application Blanks. Snip, and two of the helpers were stringing the red and green lights that led from the Hargreave living room to the sound truck outside. Snip-snap, and you could hear the sound truck pealing the joyous strains of *All I Want for Christmas Is Two of Everything* in the street, and twos and threes of the neighborhood children were beginning to appear at the door, blinking and ready for the fun. The kitchen helpers were ladling out mugs of cocoa and colored-sugar Christmas cookies and collecting the dimes and quarters from the kids; the demonstrator helpers were showing the kids the toys and trinkets from their sacks; and Santa himself was seated on his glittering throne. "Ho-ho-ho, my boy," he was saying. "And where does your daddy work this merry Christmas season?"

I was proud of them. There wasn't a helper there who couldn't have walked into Saul & Cappell or any other store in town, and walked out a Santa with a crew of his own. But that's the way we do things at the Emporium, skilled hands and high paychecks, and you only have to look at our sales records to see that it pays off.

Well, I wanted to stay and watch the fun, but Sunday's a bad day to take the afternoon off; I slipped out and headed back to the store. I put in a hard four hours, but I made it a point to be down at the Special Services division when the crews came straggling in for their checkout. The crew I was interested in was the last to report, naturally—isn't that always the way? Santa was obviously tired; I let him shuck his uniform and turn his sales slips in to the cashier before I tackled him. "How did it go?" I asked anxiously. "Did Miss Hargreave—I mean the grown-up Miss Hargreave—did she say anything?"

He looked at me accusingly. "You," he whined. "Mr. Martin, you shouldn't have run out on us like that. How we supposed to keep up a schedule when you throw us that kind of a curve, Mr. Martin?"

It was no way for a Santa to be talking to a department head, but I overlooked it. The man was obviously upset. "What are you talking about?" I demanded.

"Those Hargreaves! Honestly, Mr. Martin, you'd think they didn't want us there, the way they acted! The kids were bad enough. But when the old man came home—wow! I tell you, Mr. Martin, I been eleven Christmases in the Department, and I never saw a family with less Christmas spirit than those Hargreaves!"

The cashier was yelling for the cash receipts so he could

lock up his ledgers for the night, so I let the Santa go. But I had plenty to think about as I went back to my own department, wondering about what he had said.

I didn't have to wonder long. Just before closing, one of the office girls waved me in from where I was checking out a new Counselor, and I answered the phone call. It was Lilymary's father. Mad? He was blazing. I could hardly make sense out of most of what he said. It was words like "perverting the Christian festival" and "selling out the Saviour" and a lot of stuff I just couldn't follow at all. But the part he finished up with, that I could understand. "I want you to know, Mr. Martin," he said in clear, crisp, emphatic tones, "that you are no longer a welcome caller at our home. It pains me to have to say this, sir. As for Lilymary, you may consider this her resignation, to be effective at once!"

"But," I said, "but——"

But I was talking to a dead line; he had hung up. And that was the end of that.

Personnel called up after a couple of days and wanted to know what to do with Lilymary's severance pay. I told them to mail her the check; then I had a second thought and asked them to send it up to me. I mailed it to her myself, with a little note apologizing for what I'd done wrong—whatever it was. But she didn't even answer.

October began, and the pace stepped up. Every night I crawled home, bone-weary, turned on my dreamster and slept like a log. I gave the machine a real workout; I even had the buyer in the Sleep Shoppe get me rare, out-of-print tapes on special order—Last Days of Petronius Arbiter, and Casanova's Diary, and The Polly Adler Story, and so on—until the buyer began to leer when she saw me coming. But it didn't do any good. While I slept I was surrounded with the loveliest of them all; but when I woke the face of Lilymary Hargreave was in my mind's eye.

October. The store was buzzing. National cost of living was up .00013, but our rate of sale was up .00021 over the previous year. The store bosses were beaming, and bonuses were in the air for everybody. November. The tide was at its full, and little wavelets began to ebb backward. Housewares was picked clean, and the manufacturers only laughed as we implored them for deliveries; but Home Appliances was as dead as the January lull. Our overall rate of sale slowed down microscopically, but it didn't slow down the press of work. It made things tougher, in fact, because we were pushing twice as hard on the items we could supply, coaxing the customers off the ones that were running short.

Bad management? No. Looking at my shipment figures, we'd actually emptied the store four times in seven weeks—better than fifty per cent turnover a week. Our July purchase estimates had been off only slightly—two persons fewer out of each hundred bought air-conditioners than we had expected, one and a half persons more out of each hundred bought kitchenware. Saul & Cappell had been out of kitchenware except for spot deliveries, sold the day they arrived, ever since late September!

Heinemann called me into his office. "George," he said, "I just checked your backlog. The unfilled order list runs a little over eleven thousand. I want to tell you that I'm surprised at the way you and your department have——"

"Now, Mr. Heinemann!" I burst out. "That isn't fair! We've been putting in overtime every night, every blasted one of us! Eleven thousand's pretty good, if you ask me!"

He looked surprised. "My point exactly, George," he said. "I was about to compliment you."

I felt *so* high. I swallowed. "Uh, thanks," I said. "I mean, I'm sorry I——"

"Forget it, George." Heinemann was looking at me thoughtfully. "You've got something on your mind, don't you?"

"Well——"

"Is it that girl?"

"Girl?" I stared at him. "Who said anything about a girl?"

"Come off it," he said genially. "You think it isn't all over the store?" He glanced at his watch. "George," he said, "I never interfere in employees' private lives. You know that. But if it's that girl that's bothering you, why don't you marry her for a while? It might be just the thing you need. Come on now, George, confess. When were you married last? Three years? Five years ago?"

I looked away. "I never was," I admitted.

That jolted him. "Never?" He studied me thoughtfully for a second. "You aren't——?"

"No, no, no!" I said hastily. "Nothing like that. It's just that, well, it's always seemed like a pretty big step to take."

He relaxed again. "Ah, you kids," he said genially. "Always afraid of getting hurt, eh? Well, I'll mind my own business, if that's the way you want it. But if I were you, George, I'd go get her."

That was that. I went back to work; but I kept right on thinking about what Heinemann had said.

After all . . . why not?

I called, "Lilymary!"

She faltered and half-turned. I had counted on that. You could tell she wasn't brought up in this country; from the age of six on, our girls learn Lesson One: When you're walking alone at night, *don't stop.*

She didn't stop long. She peered into the doorway and saw me, and her expression changed as though I had hit her with a club. "George," she said, and hesitated, and walked on. Her hair was a shimmering rainbow in the Christmas lights.

We were only a few doors from her house. I glanced, half-apprehensive, at the door, but no Father Hargreave was there to scowl. I followed her and said, "Please, Lilymary. Can't we just talk for a moment?"

She faced me. "Why?"

"To—" I swallowed. "To let me apologize."

She said gently, "No apology is necessary, George. We're different breeds of cats. No need to apologize for that."

"Please."

"Well," she said. And then, "Why not?"

We found a bench in the little park across from the subway entrance. It was late; enormous half-tracks from the Sanitation Department were emptying trash cans, sprinkler trucks came by and we had to raise our feet off the ground. She said once, "I really ought to get back. I was only going to the store." But she stayed.

Well, I apologized, and she listened like a lady. And like a lady she said, again, "There's nothing to apologize for." And that was that, and I still hadn't said what I had come for. I didn't know how.

I brooded over the problem. With the rumble of the trash trucks and the roar of their burners, conversation was difficult enough anyhow. But even under those handicaps, I caught a phrase from Lilymary. "—back to the jungle," she was saying. "It's home for us, George. Father can't wait to get back, and neither can the girls."

I interrupted her. "Get back?"

She glanced at me. "That's what I said." She nodded at the Sanitation workers, baling up the enormous drifts of Christmas cards, thrusting them into the site burners. "As soon as the mails open up," she said, "and Father gets his visa. It was mailed a week ago, they say. They tell me that in the Christmas rush it might take two or three weeks more to get to us, though."

Something was clogging up my throat. All I could say was, "Why?"

Lilymary sighed. "It's where we live, George," she explained. "This isn't right for us. We're mission brats and we belong out in the field, spreading the Good News. . . . Though Father says you people need it more than the Dyaks." She looked quickly into my eyes. "I mean——"

I waved it aside. I took a deep breath. "Lilymary," I said, all in a rush, "will you marry me?"

Silence, while Lilymary looked at me.

"Oh, George," she said, after a moment. And that was all; but I was able to translate it; the answer was no.

Still, proposing marriage is something like buying a lottery ticket; you may not win the grand award, but there are consolation prizes. Mine was a date.

Lilymary stood up to her father, and I was allowed in the house. I wouldn't say I was welcomed, but Dr. Hargreave was polite—distant, but polite. He offered me coffee, he spoke of the dream superstitions of the Dyaks and old days in the Long House, and when Lilymary was ready to go he shook my hand at the door.

We had dinner. . . . I asked her—but as a piece of conversation, not a begging plea from the heart—I asked her why they had to go back. The Dyaks, she said; they were Father's people; they needed him. After Mother's death, Father had wanted to come back to America . . . but it was wrong for them. He was going back. The girls, naturally, were going with him.

We danced. . . . I kissed her, in the shadows, when it was growing late. She hesitated, but she kissed me back.

I resolved to destroy my dreamster; its ersatz ecstasies were pale.

"There," she said, as she drew back, and her voice was gentle, with a note of laughter. "I just wanted to show you. It isn't all hymn-singing back on Borneo, you know."

I reached out for her again, but she drew back, and the laughter was gone. She glanced at her watch.

"Time for me to go, George," she said. "We start packing tomorrow."

"But——"

"It's time to go, George," she said. And she kissed me at her door; but she didn't invite me in.

I stripped the tapes off my dreamster and threw them away. But hours later, after the fiftieth attempt to get to sleep, and the twentieth solitary cigarette, I got up and turned on the light and looked for them again.

They were pale; but they were all I had.

Party Week! The store was nearly bare. A messenger from the Credit Department came staggering in with a load of files just as the closing gong sounded.

He dropped them on my desk. "Thank God!" he said fervently. "Guess you won't be bothering with these tonight, eh, Mr. Martin?"

But I searched through them all the same. He looked at me wonderingly, but the clerks were breaking out the bottles and the runners from the lunchroom were bringing up sandwiches, and he drifted away.

I found the credit check I had requested. *"Co-Maker Required!"* was stamped at the top, and triply underlined in red, but that wasn't what I was looking for. I hunted through the text until I found what I wanted to know: "Subject is expected to leave this country within forty-eight hours. Subject's employer is organized and incorporated under laws of State of New York as a religious mission group. No earnings record on file. *Caution:* Subject would appear a bad credit risk, due to——"

I read no farther. Forty-eight hours!

There was a scrawl at the bottom of the page, in the Credit Manager's own handwriting: "George, what the devil are you up to? This is the fourth check we made on these people!"

It was true enough; but it would be the last. In forty-eight hours they would be gone.

I was dull at the Christmas Party. But it had been a splendid Christmas for the store, and in an hour everyone was too drunk to notice.

I decided to skip Party Week. I stayed at home the next morning, staring out the window. It had begun to snow, and the cleaners were dragging away old Christmas trees. It's always a letdown when Christmas is over; but my mood had nothing to do with the season, only with Lilymary and the numbers of miles from here to Borneo.

I circled the date in red on my calendar: December 25th. By the 26th they would be gone. . . .

But I couldn't, repeat couldn't, let her go so easily. It wasn't that I wanted to try again, and be rebuffed again; it was not a matter of choice. I had to see her. Nothing else, suddenly, had any meaning. So I made the long subway trek out there, knowing it was a fool's errand. But what kind of an errand could have been more appropriate for me?

They weren't home, but I wasn't going to let that stop me. I banged on the door of the next apartment, and got a surly, suspicious, what-do-you-want-with-*them?* inspection from the woman who lived there. But she thought they might possibly be down at the Community Center on the next block.

And they were.

The Community Center was a big yellow-brick recreation hall; it had swimming pools and Ping-Pong tables and all kinds of odds and ends to keep the kids off the streets. It was that kind of a neighborhood. It also had a meeting hall in the basement, and there were the Hargreaves, all of them, along with a couple of dozen other people. None of them were young, except the Hargreave girls. The hall had a dusty, storeroom quality to it, as though it wasn't used much—and in fact, I saw, it still had a small Christmas tree standing in it. Whatever else they had, they did not have a very efficient cleanup squad.

I came to the door to the hall and stood there, looking

around. Someone was playing a piano, and they were having a
singing party. The music sounded familiar, but I couldn't recognize the words——

> Adeste fideles,
> Laeti triumphantes.
> Venite, venite in Bethlehem.

The girls were sitting together, in the front row; their father
wasn't with them, but I saw why. He was standing at a little
lectern in the front of the hall.

> Natum videte, regem angelorum.
> Venite adoremus, venite adoremus——

I recognized the tune then; it was a slow, draggy-beat steal
from that old-time favorite, *Christmas-Tree Mambo*. It didn't
sound too bad, though, as they finished with a big major chord
from the piano and all fifteen or twenty voices going. Then
Hargreave started to talk.

I didn't listen. I was too busy watching the back of Lilymary's head. I've always had pretty low psi, though, and she
didn't turn around.

Something was bothering me. There was a sort of glow
from up front. I took my eyes off Lilymary's blond head, and
there was Dr. Hargreave, radiant; I blinked and looked again,
and it was not so radiant. A trick of the light, coming through
the basement windows onto his own blond hair, I suppose, but
it gave me a curious feeling for a moment. I must have moved,
because he caught sight of me. He stumbled over a word, but
then he went on. But that was enough. After a moment Lilymary's head turned, and her eyes met mine.

She knew I was there. I backed away from the door and sat
down on the steps coming down from the entrance.

Sooner or later she would be out.

It wasn't long at all. She came toward me with a question in
her eye. She was all by herself; inside the hall, her father was
still talking.

I stood up straight and said it all. "Lilymary," I said, "I can't help it, I want to marry you. I've done everything wrong, but I didn't mean to. I—I don't even want it conditional, Lilymary, I want it for life. Here or Borneo, I don't care which. I only care about one thing, and that's you." It was funny—I was trying to tell her I loved her, and I was standing stiff and awkward, talking in about the same tone of voice I'd use to tell a stock boy he was fired.

But she understood. I probably didn't have to say a word, she would have understood anyhow. She started to speak, and changed her mind, and started again, and finally got out, "What would you do in Borneo?" And then, so soft that I hardly knew I was hearing it, she added, "Dear."

Dear! It was like the first time Heinemann came in and called me "Department Head!" I felt nine feet tall.

I didn't answer her. I reached out and I kissed her, and it wasn't any wonder that I didn't know we weren't alone until I heard her father cough, not more than a yard away.

I jumped, but Lilymary turned and looked at him, perfectly calm. "You ought to be conducting the service, Father!" she scolded him.

He nodded his big fair head. "Doctor Mausner can pronounce the Benediction without me," he said. "I should be there but—well, He has plenty of things to forgive all of us already; one more isn't going to bother Him. Now, what's this?"

"George has asked me to marry him."

"And?"

She looked at me. "I——" she began, and stopped. I said, "I love her."

He looked at me too, and then he sighed. "George," he said after a moment, "I don't know what's right and what's wrong, for the first time in my life. Maybe I've been selfish when I asked Lilymary to go back with me and the girls. I didn't mean it that way, but I don't deny I wanted it. I don't know. But——" He smiled, and it was a big, warm smile. "But there's something I do know. I know Lilymary; and I can trust her to make up her own mind." He patted her lightly.

"I'll see you after the service," he said to me, and left us. Back in the hall, through the door he opened, I could hear all the voices going at once.

"Let's go inside and pray, George," said Lilymary, and her whole heart and soul was on her face as she looked at me, with love and anxiousness.

I only hesitated a moment. Pray? But it meant Lilymary, and that meant—well, everything.

So I went in. And we were all kneeling, and Lilymary coached me through the words; and I prayed. And, do you know?—I've never regretted it.

A Work of Art

James Blish (1921–1975)

THE *late James Blish, like Alfred Bester, Damon Knight, and others represented in this book, was one of the first "serious" critics of science fiction, a man who was (and considered himself to be) an intellectual in the classic sense of the term who attempted to develop standards for the field. A major figure in British science-fiction circles after he moved to that country, he was more highly regarded there than in his native land.*

His accomplishments during the fifties were many: the magnificent A Case of Conscience *(1958);* They Shall Have Stars; *and* Year 2018 *(1956 and 1957), two of the novels of the* Cities in Flight *group;* Jack of Eagles *(1951); and* The Seedling Stars *(1957), which contained his justly famous "Pantropy" stories.*

The future of the arts was not a common theme in science fiction until quite recently. The best of the earlier stories were collected by Blish in his fine anthology New Dreams This Morning *(1968).*

From *Science Fiction Stories*   July, 1956

331

Instantly, he remembered dying. He remembered it, however, as if at two removes—as though he were remembering a memory, rather than an actual event; as though he himself had not really been there when he died.

Yet the memory was all from his own point of view, not that of some detached and disembodied observer which might have been his soul. He had been most conscious of the rasping, unevenly drawn movements of the air in his chest. Blurring rapidly, the doctor's face had bent over him, loomed, come closer, and then had vanished as the doctor's head passed below his cone of vision, turned sideways to listen to his lungs.

It had become rapidly darker, and then, only then, had he realized that these were to be his last minutes. He had tried dutifully to say Pauline's name, but his memory contained no record of the sound—only of the rattling breath and of the film of sootiness thickening in the air, blotting out everything for an instant.

Only an instant, and then the memory was over. The room was bright again, and the ceiling, he noticed with wonder, had turned a soft green. The doctor's head lifted again and looked down at him.

It was a different doctor. This one was a far younger man, with an ascetic face and gleaming, almost fey eyes. There was no doubt about it. One of the last conscious thoughts he had had was that of gratitude that the attending physician, there at the end, had not been the one who secretly hated him for his one-time associations with the Nazi hierarchy. The attending doctor, instead, had worn an expression amusingly proper for that of a Swiss expert called to the deathbed of an eminent man: a mixture of worry at the prospect of losing so eminent a patient, and complacency at the thought that, at the old man's age, nobody could blame this doctor if he died. At eighty-five, pneumonia is a serious matter, with or without penicillin.

"You're all right now," the new doctor said, freeing his patient's head of a whole series of little silver rods which had been clinging to it by a sort of network cap. "Rest a minute and try to be calm. Do you know your name?"

He drew a cautious breath. There seemed to be nothing at all the matter with his lungs now; indeed, he felt positively healthy. "Certainly," he said, a little nettled. "Do you know yours?"

The doctor smiled crookedly. "You're in character, it appears," he said. "My name is Barkun Kris; I am a mind sculptor. Yours?"

"Richard Strauss."

"Very good," Dr. Kris said, and turned away. Strauss, however, had already been diverted by a new singularity. *Strauss* is a word as well as a name in German; it has many meanings— an ostrich, a bouquet; von Wolzogen had had a high old time working all the possible puns into the libretto of *Feuersnot*. And it happened to be the first German word to be spoken either by himself or by Dr. Kris since that twice-removed moment of death. The language was not French or Italian, either. It was most like English, but not the English Strauss knew; nevertheless, he was having no trouble speaking it and even thinking in it.

Well, he thought, *I'll be able to conduct* The Love of Danae, *after all. It isn't every composer who can première his own opera posthumously.* Still, there was something queer about all this—the queerest part of all being that conviction, which would not go away, that he had actually been dead for just a short time. Of course, medicine was making great strides, but . . .

"Explain all this," he said, lifting himself to one elbow. The bed was different, too, and not nearly as comfortable as the one in which he had died. As for the room, it looked more like a dynamo shed than a sickroom. Had modern medicine taken to reviving its corpses on the floor of the Siemanns-Schukert plant?

"In a moment," Dr. Kris said. He finished rolling some

machine back into what Strauss impatiently supposed to be its place, and crossed to the pallet. "Now. There are many things you'll have to take for granted without attempting to understand them, Dr. Strauss. Not everything in the world today is explicable in terms of your assumptions. Please bear that in mind."

"Very well. Proceed."

"The date," Dr. Kris said, "is 2161 by your calendar—or, in other words, it is now two hundred and twelve years after your death. Naturally, you'll realize that by this time nothing remains of your body but the bones. The body you have now was volunteered for your use. Before you look into a mirror to see what it's like, remember that its physical difference from the one you were used to is all in your favor. It's in perfect health, not unpleasant for other people to look at, and its physiological age is about fifty."

A miracle? No, not in this new age, surely. It was simply a work of science. But what a science! This was Nietzsche's eternal recurrence and the immortality of the superman combined into one.

"And where is this?" the composer said.

"In Port York, part of the State of Manhattan, in the United States. You will find the country less changed in some respects than I imagine you anticipate. Other changes, of course, will seem radical to you, but it's hard for me to predict which ones will strike you that way. A certain resilience on your part will bear cultivating."

"I understand," Strauss said, sitting up. "One question, please; is it still possible for a composer to make a living in this century?"

"Indeed it is," Dr. Kris said, smiling. "As we expect you to do. It is one of the purposes for which we've—brought you back."

"I gather, then," Strauss said somewhat dryly, "that there is still a demand for my music. The critics in the old days—"

"That's not quite how it is," Dr. Kris said. "I understand

some of your work is still played, but frankly I know very little about your current status. My interest is rather—"

A door opened somewhere, and another man came in. He was older and more ponderous than Kris and had a certain air of academicism, but he, too, was wearing the oddly tailored surgeon's gown and looked upon Kris's patient with the glowing eyes of an artist.

"A success, Kris?" he said. "Congratulations."

"They're not in order yet," Dr. Kris said. "The final proof is what counts. Dr. Strauss, if you feel strong enough, Dr. Seirds and I would like to ask you some questions. We'd like to make sure your memory is clear."

"Certainly. Go ahead."

"According to our records," Kris said, "you once knew a man whose initials were R.K.L.; this was while you were conducting at the Vienna *Staatsoper*." He made the double "a" at least twice too long, as though German were a dead language he was striving to pronounce in some "classical" accent. "What was his name, and who was he?"

"That would be Kurt List—his first name was Richard, but he didn't use it. He was assistant stage manager."

The two doctors looked at each other. "Why did you offer to write a new overture to *The Woman Without a Shadow* and give the manuscript to the City of Vienna?"

"So I wouldn't have to pay the garbage removal tax on the Maria Theresa villa they had given me."

"In the back yard of your house at Garmisch-Partenkirchen there was a tombstone. What was written on it?"

Strauss frowned. That was a question he would be happy to be unable to answer. If one is to play childish jokes upon oneself, it's best not to carve them in stone and put the carving where you can't help seeing it every time you go out to tinker with the Mercedes. "It says," he replied wearily, " 'Sacred to the memory of Guntram, Minnesinger, slain in a horrible way by his father's own symphony orchestra.' "

"When was *Guntram* premièred?"

"In—let me see—1894, I believe."

"Where?"

"In Weimar."

"Who was the leading lady?"

"Pauline de Ahna."

"What happened to her afterwards?"

"I married her. Is she . . ." Strauss began anxiously.

"No," Dr. Kris said. "I'm sorry, but we lack the data to reconstruct more or less ordinary people."

The composer sighed. He did not know whether to be worried or not. He had loved Pauline, to be sure; on the other hand, it would be pleasant to be able to live the new life without being forced to take off one's shoes every time one entered the house, so as not to scratch the polished hardwood floors. And also pleasant, perhaps, to have two o'clock in the afternoon come by without hearing Pauline's everlasting, "Richard—*jetzt komponiert!*"

"Next question," he said.

For reasons which Strauss did not understand, but was content to take for granted, he was separated from Drs. Kris and Seirds as soon as both were satisfied that the composer's memory was reliable and his health stable. His estate, he was given to understand, had long since been broken up—a sorry end for what had been one of the principal fortunes of Europe— but he was given sufficient money to set up lodgings and resume an active life. He was provided, too, with introductions which proved valuable.

It took longer than he had expected to adjust to the changes that had taken place in music alone. Music was, he quickly began to suspect, a dying art, which would soon have a status not much above that held by flower arranging back in what he thought of as his own century. Certainly it couldn't be denied that the trend toward fragmentation, already visible back in his own time, had proceeded almost to completion in 2161.

He paid no more attention to American popular tunes than he had bothered to pay in his previous life. Yet it was evident that their assembly-line production methods—all the ballad composers openly used a slide-rule-like device called a Hit Machine—now had their counterparts almost throughout serious music.

The conservatives these days, for instance, were the twelve-tone composers—always, in Strauss's opinion, dryly mechanical but never more so than now. Their gods—Berg, Schoenberg, Webern—were looked upon by the concert-going public as great masters, on the abstruse side perhaps, but as worthy of reverence as any of the Three B's.

There was one wing of the conservatives, however, that had gone the twelve-tone procedure one better. These men composed what was called "stochastic music," put together by choosing each individual note by consultation with tables of random numbers. Their bible, their basic text, was a volume called *Operational Aesthetics*, which in turn derived from a discipline called information theory, and not one word of it seemed to touch upon any of the techniques and customs of composition which Strauss knew. The ideal of this group was to produce music which would be "universal"—that is, wholly devoid of any trace of the composer's individuality, wholly a musical expression of the universal Laws of Chance. The Laws of Chance seemed to have a style of their own, all right, but to Strauss it seemed the style of an idiot child being taught to hammer a flat piano, to keep him from getting into trouble.

By far the largest body of work being produced, however, fell into a category misleadingly called science-music. The term reflected nothing but the titles of the works, which dealt with space flight, time travel, and other subjects of a romantic or an unlikely nature. There was nothing in the least scientific about the music, which consisted of a mélange of clichés and imitations of natural sounds, in which Strauss was horrified to see his own time-distorted and diluted image.

The most popular form of science-music was a nine-minute composition called a concerto, though it bore no resemblance at all to the classical concerto form; it was instead a sort of free rhapsody after Rachmaninoff—long after. A typical one —"Song of Deep Space," it was called, by somebody named H. Valerion Krafft—began with a loud assault on the tam-tam, after which all the strings rushed up the scale in unison, followed at a respectful distance by the harp and one clarinet in parallel 6/4's. At the top of the scale cymbals were bashed together, *forte possibile*, and the whole orchestra launched itself into a major-minor wailing sort of melody; the whole orchestra, that is, except for the French horns, which were plodding back down the scale again in what was evidently supposed to be a countermelody. The second phrase of the theme was picked up by a solo trumpet with a suggestion of tremolo, the orchestra died back to its roots to await the next cloudburst, and at this point—as any four-year-old could have predicted—the piano entered with the second theme.

Behind the orchestra stood a group of thirty women, ready to come in with a wordless chorus intended to suggest the eeriness of Deep Space—but at this point, too, Strauss had already learned to get up and leave. After a few such experiences he could also count upon meeting in the lobby Sindi Noniss, the agent to whom Dr. Kris had introduced him and who was handling the reborn composer's output—what there was of it thus far. Sindi had come to expect these walkouts on the part of his client and patiently awaited them, standing beneath a bust of Gian-Carlo Menotti, but he liked them less and less, and lately had been greeting them by turning alternately red and white, like a totipotent barber pole.

"You shouldn't have done it," he burst out after the Krafft incident. "You can't just walk out on a new Krafft composition. The man's the president of the Interplanetary Society for Contemporary Music. How am I ever going to persuade them that you're a contemporary if you keep snubbing them?"

"What does it matter?" Strauss said. "They don't know me by sight."

"You're wrong; they know you very well, and they're watching every move you make. You're the first major composer the mind sculptors ever tackled, and the ISCM would be glad to turn you back with a rejection slip."

"Why?"

"Oh," said Sindi, "there are lots of reasons. The sculptors are snobs; so are the ISCM boys. Each of them wants to prove to the other that their own art is the king of them all. And then there's the competition; it would be easier to flunk you than to let you into the market. I really think you'd better go back in. I could make up some excuse—"

"No," Strauss said shortly. "I have work to do."

"But that's just the point, Richard. How are we going to get an opera produced without the ISCM? It isn't as though you wrote theremin solos, or something that didn't cost so—"

"I have work to do," he said, and left.

And he did, work which absorbed him as had no other project during the last thirty years of his former life. He had scarcely touched pen to music paper—both had been astonishingly hard to find—when he realized that nothing in his long career had provided him with touchstones by which to judge what music he should write *now*.

The old tricks came swarming back by the thousands, to be sure: the sudden, unexpected key changes at the crest of a melody, the interval stretching, the piling of divided strings, playing in the high harmonics, upon the already tottering top of a climax, the scurry and bustle as phrases were passed like lightning from one choir of the orchestra to another, the flashing runs in the brass, the chuckling in the clarinets, the snarling mixtures of colors to emphasize dramatic tension—all of them.

But none of them satisfied him now. He had been content with them for most of a lifetime and had made them do an astonishing amount of work. But now it was time to strike out afresh. Some of the tricks, indeed, actively repelled him: Where had he gotten the notion, clung to for decades, that violins screaming out in unison somewhere in the stratosphere were a sound interesting enough to be worth repeating inside a single composition, let alone in all of them?

And nobody, he reflected contentedly, ever approached such a new beginning better equipped. In addition to the past lying available in his memory, he had always had a technical armamentarium second to none; even the hostile critics had granted him that. Now that he was, in a sense, composing his first opera—his first after fifteen of them!—he had every opportunity to make it a masterpiece.

And every such intention.

There were, of course, many minor distractions. One of them was that search for old-fashioned score paper, and a pen and ink with which to write on it. Very few of the modern composers, it developed, wrote their music at all. A large bloc of them used tape, patching together snippets of tone and sound snipped from other tapes, superimposing one tape on another, and varying the results by twirling an elaborate array of knobs this way or that. Almost all the composers of 3-V scores, on the other hand, wrote on the sound track itself, rapidly scribbling jagged wiggly lines which, when passed through a photocell-audio circuit, produced a noise reasonably like an orchestra playing music, overtones and all.

The last-ditch conservatives who still wrote notes on paper did so with the aid of a musical typewriter. The device, Strauss had to admit, seemed perfected at last; it had manuals and stops like an organ, but it was not much more than twice as large as a standard letter-writing typewriter and produced a neat page. But he was satisfied with his own spidery, highly legible manuscript and refused to abandon it, badly though the one pen nib he had been able to buy coarsened it. It helped to tie him to his past.

Joining the ISCM had also caused him some bad moments, even after Sindi had worked him around the political road-blocks. The Society man who examined his qualifications as a member had run through the questions with no more interest than might have been shown by a veterinarian examining his four-thousandth sick calf.

"Had anything published?"

"Yes, nine tone poems, about three hundred songs, an—"

"Not when you were alive," the examiner said, somewhat disquietingly. "I mean since the sculptors turned you out again."

"Since the sculptors—ah, I understand. Yes, a string quartet, two song cycles, a—"

"Good. Alfie, write down, 'Songs.' Play an instrument?"

"Piano."

"Hmm." The examiner studied his fingernails. "Oh, well. Do you read music? Or do you use a Scriber, or tape clips? Or a Machine?"

"I read."

"Here." The examiner sat Strauss down in front of a viewing lectern, over the lit surface of which an endless belt of translucent paper was traveling. On the paper was an immensely magnified sound track. "Whistle me the tune of that, and name the instruments it sounds like."

"I don't read that *Musiksticheln*," Strauss said frostily, "or write it, either. I use standard notation, on music paper."

"Alfie, write down, 'Reads notes only.' " He laid a sheet of grayly printed music on the lectern above the ground glass. "Whistle me that."

"That" proved to be a popular tune called "Vangs, Snifters, and Store-Credit Snooky," which had been written on a Hit Machine in 2159 by a guitar-faking politician who sang it at campaign rallies. (In some respects, Strauss reflected, the United States had indeed not changed very much.) It had become so popular that anybody could have whistled it from the title alone, whether he could read the music or not. Strauss whistled it, and to prove his bona fides added, "It's in the key of B flat."

The examiner went over to the green-painted upright piano and hit one greasy black key. The instrument was horribly out of tune—the note was much nearer to the standard 440/cps A than it was to B flat—but the examiner said, "So it is. Alfie, write down, 'Also reads flats.' All right, son, you're a member. Nice to have you with us; not many people can read that old-style notation any more. A lot of them think they're too good for it."

"Thank you," Strauss said.

"My feeling is, if it was good enough for the old masters, it's good enough for us. We don't have people like them with us these days, it seems to me. Except for Dr. Krafft, of course. They were *great* back in the old days—men like Shilkrit, Steiner, Tiomkin, and Pearl . . . and Wilder and Janssen. Real goffin."

"Doch gewiss," Strauss said politely.

But the work went forward. He was making a little income now, from small works. People seemed to feel a special inter-est in a composer who had come out of the mind sculptors' laboratories, and in addition the material itself, Strauss was quite certain, had merits of its own to help sell it.

It was the opera that counted, however. That grew and grew under his pen, as fresh and new as his new life, as founded in knowledge and ripeness as his long, full memory. Finding a libretto had been troublesome at first. While it was possible that something existed that might have served among the current scripts for 3-V—though he doubted it—he found himself unable to tell the good from the bad through the fog cast over both by incomprehensibly technical production di-rections. Eventually, and for only the third time in his whole career, he had fallen back upon a play written in a language other than his own, and—for the first time—decided to set it in that language.

The play was Christopher Fry's *Venus Observed*, in all ways a perfect Strauss opera libretto, as he came gradually to realize. Though nominally a comedy, with a complex farcical plot, it was a verse play with considerable depth to it, and a number of characters who cried out to be brought by music into three dimensions, plus a strong undercurrent of autumnal tragedy, of leaf-fall and apple-fall—precisely the kind of contradictory dramatic mixture which von Hofmannsthal had supplied him with in *The Knight of the Rose*, in *Ariadne at Naxos*, and in *Arabella*.

Alas for von Hofmannsthal, but here was another long-dead playwright who seemed nearly as gifted, and the musical opportunities were immense. There was, for instance, the fire which ended Act II; what a gift for a composer to whom orchestration and counterpoint were as important as air and water! Or take the moment where Perpetua shoots the apple from the Duke's hand; in that one moment a single passing reference could add Rossini's marmoreal *William Tell* to the musical texture as nothing but an ironic footnote! And the Duke's great curtain speech, beginning:

> Shall I be sorry for myself? In Mortality's name
> I'll be sorry for myself. Branches and boughs,
> Brown hills, the valleys faint with brume,
> A burnish on the lake. . . .

There was a speech for a great tragic comedian, in the spirit of Falstaff: the final union of laughter and tears, punctuated by the sleepy comments of Reedbeck, to whose sonorous snore (trombones, no less than five of them, *con sordini*?) the opera would gently end. . . .

What could be better? And yet he had come upon the play only by the unlikeliest series of accidents. At first he had planned to do a straight knockabout farce, in the idiom of *The*

Silent Woman, just to warm himself up. Remembering that Zweig had adapted that libretto for him, in the old days, from a play by Ben Jonson, Strauss had begun to search out English plays of the period just after Jonson's, and had promptly run aground on an awful specimen in blank verse called *Venice Preserv'd*, by one Thomas Otway. The Fry play had directly followed the Otway in the card catalogue, and he had looked at it out of curiosity; why should a twentieth century playwright be punning on a title from the eighteenth?

After two pages of the Fry play, the minor puzzle of the pun disappeared entirely from his concern. His luck was running again; he had an opera.

Sindi worked miracles in arranging for the performance. The date of the première was set even before the score was finished, reminding Strauss pleasantly of those heady days when Fuerstner had been snatching the conclusion of *Elektra* off his work table a page at a time, before the ink was even dry, to rush it to the engraver before publication deadline. The situation now, however, was even more complicated, for some of the score had to be scribed, some of it taped, some of it engraved in the old way, to meet the new techniques of performance; there were moments when Sindi seemed to be turning quite gray.

But *Venus Observed* was, as usual, forthcoming complete from Strauss's pen in plenty of time. Writing the music in first draft had been hellishly hard work, much more like being reborn than had been that confused awakening in Barkun Kris's laboratory, with its overtones of being dead instead, but Strauss found that he still retained all of his old ability to score from the draft almost effortlessly, as undisturbed by Sindi's half-audible worrying in the room with him as he was by the terrifying supersonic bangs of the rockets that bulleted invisibly over the city.

When he was finished, he had two days still to spare before

the beginning of rehearsals. With those, furthermore, he would have nothing to do. The techniques of performance in this age were so completely bound up with the electronic arts as to reduce his own experience—he, the master *Kapellmeister* of them all—to the hopelessly primitive.

He did not mind. The music, as written, would speak for itself. In the meantime he found it grateful to forget the months-long preoccupation with the stage for a while. He went back to the library and browsed lazily through old poems, vaguely seeking texts for a song or two. He knew better than to bother with recent poets; they could not speak to him, and he knew it. The Americans of his own age, he thought, might give him a clue to understanding this America of 2161, and if some such poem gave birth to a song, so much the better.

The search was relaxing, and he gave himself up to enjoying it. Finally he struck a tape that he liked; a tape read in a cracked old voice that twanged of Idaho as that voice had twanged in 1910, in Strauss's own ancient youth. The poet's name was Pound; he said, on the tape:

>. . . the souls of all men great
> At times pass through us,
> And we are melted into them, and are not
> Save reflexions of their souls.
> Thus I am Dante for a space and am
> One François Villon, ballad-lord and thief,
> Or am such holy ones I may not write,
> Lest Blasphemy be writ against my name;
> This for an instant and the flame is gone.
> 'Tis as in midmost us there glows a sphere
> Translucent, molten gold, that is the "I"
> And into this some form projects itself:
> Christus, or John, or eke the Florentine;
> And as the clear space is not if a form's
> Imposed thereon,

> So cease we from all being for the time,
> And these, the Masters of the Soul, live on.

He smiled. That lesson had been written again and again, from Plato onward. Yet the poem was a history of his own case, a sort of theory for the metempsychosis he had undergone, and in its formal way it was moving. It would be fitting to make a little hymn of it, in honor of his own rebirth, and of the poet's insight.

A series of solemn, breathless chords framed themselves in his inner ear, against which the words might be intoned in a high, gently blending hush at the beginning . . . and then a dramatic passage in which the great names of Dante and Villon would enter ringing like challenges to Time. . . . He wrote for a while in his notebook before he returned the spool to its shelf.

These, he thought, are good auspices.

And so the night of the première arrived, the audience pouring into the hall, the 3-V cameras riding on no visible supports through the air, and Sindi calculating his share of his client's earnings by a complicated game he played on his fingers, the basic law of which seemed to be that one plus one equals ten. The hall filled to the roof with people from every class, as though what was to come would be a circus rather than an opera.

There were, surprisingly, nearly fifty of the aloof and aristocratic mind sculptors, clad in formal clothes which were exaggerated black versions of their surgeon's gowns. They had bought a block of seats near the front of the auditorium, where the gigantic 3-V figures which would shortly fill the "stage" before them (the real singers would perform on a small stage in the basement) could not but seem monstrously out of proportion, but Strauss supposed that they had taken this into account and dismissed it.

There was a tide of whispering in the audience as the sculptors began to trickle in, and with it an undercurrent of excite-

ment the meaning of which was unknown to Strauss. He did
not attempt to fathom it, however; he was coping with his own
mounting tide of opening-night tension, which, despite all the
years, he had never quite been able to shake.

The sourceless, gentle light in the auditorium dimmed, and
Strauss mounted the podium. There was a score before him,
but he doubted that he would need it. Directly before him,
poking up from among the musicians, were the inevitable 3-V
snouts, waiting to carry his image to the singers in the basement.

The audience was quiet now. This was the moment. His
baton swept up and then decisively down, and the prelude
came surging up out of the pit.

For a little while he was deeply immersed in the always tricky
business of keeping the enormous orchestra together and
sensitive to the flexing of the musical web beneath his hand.
As his control firmed and became secure, however, the task
became slightly less demanding, and he was able to pay more
attention to what the whole sounded like.

There was something decidedly wrong with it. Of course
there were the occasional surprises as some bit of orchestral
color emerged with a different *Klang* than he had expected;
that happened to every composer, even after a lifetime of experience. And there were moments when the singers, entering
upon a phrase more difficult to handle than he had calculated,
sounded like someone about to fall off a tightrope (although
none of them actually fluffed once; they were as fine a troupe
of voices as he had ever had to work with).

But these were details. It was the overall impression that
was wrong. He was losing not only the excitement of the
première—after all, that couldn't last at the same pitch all
evening—but also his very interest in what was coming from
the stage and the pit. He was gradually tiring, his baton arm
becoming heavier; as the second act mounted to what should
have been an impassioned outpouring of shining tone, he was

so bored as to wish he could go back to his desk to work on that song.

Then the act was over; only one more to go. He scarcely heard the applause. The twenty minutes' rest in his dressing room was just barely enough to give him the necessary strength.

And suddenly, in the middle of the last act, he understood.

There was nothing new about the music. It was the old Strauss all over again—but weaker, more dilute than ever. Compared with the output of composers like Krafft, it doubtless sounded like a masterpiece to this audience. But he knew.

The resolutions, the determination to abandon the old clichés and mannerisms, the decision to say something new— they had all come to nothing against the force of habit. Being brought to life again meant bringing to life as well all those deeply graven reflexes of his style. He had only to pick up his pen and they overpowered him with easy automatism, no more under his control than the jerk of a finger away from a flame.

His eyes filled; his body was young, but he was an old man, an old man. Another thirty-five years of this? Never. He had said all this before, centuries before. Nearly a half-century condemned to saying it all over again, in a weaker and still weaker voice, aware that even this debased century would come to recognize in him only the burnt husk of greatness?— no, never, never.

He was aware, dully, that the opera was over. The audience was screaming its joy. He knew the sound. They had screamed that way when *Day of Peace* had been premièred, but they had been cheering the man he had been, not the man that *Day of Peace* showed with cruel clarity he had become. Here the sound was even more meaningless: cheers of ignorance, and that was all.

He turned slowly. With surprise, and with a surprising sense of relief, he saw that the cheers were not, after all, for him.

They were for Dr. Barkun Kris.

Kris was standing in the middle of the bloc of mind sculptors, bowing to the audience. The sculptors nearest him were shaking his hand one after the other. More grasped at it as he made his way to the aisle and walked forward to the podium. When he mounted the rostrum and took the composer's limp hand, the cheering became delirious.

Kris lifted his arm. The cheering died instantly to an intent hush.

"Thank you," he said clearly. "Ladies and gentlemen, before we take leave of Dr. Strauss, let us again tell him what a privilege it has been for us to hear this fresh example of his mastery. I am sure no farewell could be more fitting."

The ovation lasted five minutes and would have gone another five if Kris had not cut it off.

"Dr. Strauss," he said, "in a moment, when I speak a certain formulation to you, you will realize that your name is Jerom Bosch, born in our century and with a life in it all your own. The superimposed memories which had made you assume the mask, the *persona*, of a great composer will be gone. I tell you this so that you may understand why these people here share your applause with me."

A wave of assenting sound.

"The art of mind sculpture—the creation of artificial personalities for aesthetic enjoyment—may never reach such a pinnacle again. For you should understand that as Jerom Bosch you had no talent for music at all; indeed, we searched a long time to find a man who was utterly unable to carry even the simplest tune. Yet we were able to impose upon such unpromising material not only the personality, but the genius, of a great composer. That genius belongs entirely to you—to the *persona* that thinks of itself as Richard Strauss. None of the credit goes to the man who volunteered for the sculpture. That is your triumph, and we salute you for it."

Now the ovation could no longer be contained. Strauss, with a crooked smile, watched Dr. Kris bow. This mind sculpturing was a suitably sophisticated kind of cruelty for this age, but the impulse, of course, had always existed. It was the same impulse that had made Rembrandt and Leonardo turn cadavers into art works.

It deserved a suitably sophisticated payment under the *lex talionis*: an eye for an eye, a tooth for a tooth—and a failure for a failure.

No, he need not tell Dr. Kris that the "Strauss" he had created was as empty of genius as a hollow gourd. The joke would always be on the sculptor, who was incapable of hearing the hollowness of the music now preserved on the 3-V tapes.

But for an instant a surge of revolt poured through his bloodstream. *I am I*, he thought. *I am Richard Strauss until I die, and will never be Jerom Bosch, who was utterly unable to carry even the simplest tune.* His hand, still holding the baton, came sharply up, though whether to deliver or to ward off a blow he could not tell.

He let it fall again, and instead, at last, bowed—not to the audience, but to Dr. Kris. He was sorry for nothing, as Kris turned to him to say the word that would plunge him back into oblivion, except that he would now have no chance to set that poem to music.

The Country of the Kind

Damon Knight (1922-   )

*S*HORT *story writer, novelist, critic, editor—Damon Knight has done it all, and done it well. Because he has been so eclectic, his contribution to science fiction is difficult to assess in detail, but there is little doubt that it has been great indeed. As a writer he has worked primarily with the short story, and his masterpieces of the fifties, especially "Not With a Bang," "Cabin Boy," and "Stranger Station" influenced a generation of writers. His 1955 novel,* Hell's Pavement, *is a superior example of the social science fiction of the fifties.*

And so is this story, a tale of alienation, of punishment, and of the modern condition.

From *The Magazine of Fantasy and Science Fiction*   February, 1956

The attendant at the car lot was daydreaming when I pulled up—a big, lazy-looking man in black satin checkered down the front. I was wearing scarlet, myself; it suited my mood. I got out, almost on his toes.

"Park or storage?" he asked automatically, turning around. Then he realized who I was, and ducked his head away.

"Neither," I told him.

There was a hand torch on a shelf in the repair shed right behind him. I got it and came back. I kneeled down to where I could reach behind the front wheel, and ignited the torch. I turned it on the axle and suspension. They glowed cherry red, then white, and fused together. Then I got up and turned the flame on both tires until the rubberoid stank and sizzled and melted down to the pavement. The attendant didn't say anything.

I left him there, looking at the mess on his nice clean concrete.

It had been a nice car, too, but I could get another any time. And I felt like walking. I went down the winding road, sleepy in the afternoon sunlight, dappled with shade and smelling of cool leaves. You couldn't see the houses; they were all sunken or hidden by shrubbery, or a little of both. That was the fad I'd heard about; it was what I'd come here to see. Not that anything the dulls did would be worth looking at.

I turned off at random and crossed a rolling lawn, went through a second hedge of hawthorn in blossom, and came out next to a big sunken games court.

The tennis net was up, and two couples were going at it, just working up a little sweat—young, about half my age, all four of them. Three dark-haired, one blonde. They were evenly matched, and both couples played well together; they were enjoying themselves.

I watched for a minute. But by then the nearest two were beginning to sense I was there, anyhow. I walked down onto the court, just as the blonde was about to serve. She looked at me frozen across the net, poised on tiptoe. The others stood.

"Off," I told them. "Game's over."

I watched the blonde. She was not especially pretty, as they go, but compactly and gracefully put together. She came down slowly, flatfooted without awkwardness, and tucked the racquet under her arm; then the surprise was over and she was trotting off the court after the other three.

I followed their voices around the curve of the path, between towering masses of lilacs, inhaling the sweetness, until I came to what looked like a little sunning spot. There was a sundial and a birdbath and towels lying around on the grass. One couple, the dark-haired pair, was still in sight farther down the path, heads bobbing along. The other couple had disappeared.

I found the handle in the grass without any trouble. The mechanism responded, and an oblong section of turf rose up. It was the stair I had, not the elevator, but that was all right. I ran down the steps and into the first door I saw, and was in the top-floor lounge, an oval room lit with diffused simulated sunlight from above. The furniture was all comfortably bloated, sprawling and ugly; the carpet was deep, and there was a fresh flower scent in the air.

The blonde was over at the near end with her back to me, studying the autochef keyboard. She was half out of her playsuit. She pushed it the rest of the way down and stepped out of it, then turned and saw me.

She was surprised again; she hadn't thought I might follow her down.

I got up close before it occurred to her to move; then it was too late. She knew she couldn't get away from me; she closed her eyes and leaned back against the paneling, turning a little pale. Her lips and her golden brows went up in the middle.

I looked her over and told her a few uncomplimentary things about herself. She trembled, but didn't answer. On impulse, I leaned over and dialed the autochef to hot cheese sauce. I cut the safety out of circuit and put the quantity dial all the way up. I dialed *soup tureen* and then *punch bowl*.

The stuff began to come out in about a minute, steaming hot. I took the tureens and splashed them up and down the wall on either side of her. Then when the first punch bowl came out, I used the empty bowls as scoops. I clotted the carpet with the stuff; I made streamers of it all along the walls, and dumped puddles into what furniture I could reach. Where it cooled it would harden, and where it hardened it would cling.

I wanted to splash it across her body, but it would've hurt, and we couldn't have that. The punch bowls of hot sauce were still coming out of the autochef, crowding each other around the vent. I punched *cancel*, and then *port wine*.

It came out well chilled in open bottles. I took the first one and had my arm back just about to throw a nice line of the stuff right across her midriff, when a voice said behind me:

"Watch out for cold wine."

My arm twitched and a little stream of the wine splashed across her thighs. She was ready for it; her eyes had opened at the voice, and she barely jumped.

I whirled around, fighting mad. The man was standing there where he had come out of the stairwell. He was thinner in the face than most, bronzed, wide-chested, with alert blue eyes. If it hadn't been for him, I knew it would have worked—the blonde would have mistaken the cold splash for a hot one.

I could hear the scream in my mind, and I wanted it.

I took a step toward him, and my foot slipped. I went down clumsily, wrenching one knee. I got up shaking and tight all over. I wasn't in control of myself. I screamed, "You—you—" I turned and got one of the punch bowls and lifted it in both hands, heedless of how the hot sauce was slopping over onto my wrists, and I had it almost in the air toward him when the sickness took me—that damned buzzing in my head, louder, louder, drowning everything out.

When I came to, they were both gone. I got up off the floor, weak as death, and staggered over to the nearest chair. My clothes were slimed and sticky. I wanted to die. I wanted to drop into that dark furry hole that was yawning for me and never come up, but I made myself stay awake and get out of the chair.

Going down in the elevator, I almost blacked out again. The blonde and the thin man weren't in any of the second-floor bedrooms—I made sure of that—then I emptied the closets and bureau drawers onto the floor, dragged the whole mess into one of the bathrooms and stuffed the tub with it, then turned on the water.

I tried the third floor: maintenance and storage. It was empty. I turned the furnace on and set the thermostat up as high as it would go. I disconnected all the safety circuits and alarms. I opened the freezer doors and dialed them to defrost. I propped the stairwell door open and went back up in the elevator.

On the second floor I stopped long enough to open the stairway door there—the water was halfway toward it, creeping across the floor—and then searched the top floor. No one was there. I opened book reels and threw them unwinding across the room; I would have done more, but I could hardly stand. I got up to the surface and collapsed on the lawn; that furry pit swallowed me up, dead and drowned.

While I slept, water poured down the open stairwell and filled the third level. Thawing food packages floated out into the rooms. Water seeped into wall panels and machine housings; circuits shorted and fuses blew. The air-conditioning stopped, but the pile kept heating. The water rose.

Spoiled food, floating supplies, grimy water surged up the stairwell. The second and first levels were bigger and would take longer to fill, but they'd fill. Rugs, furnishings, clothing, all the things in the house would be waterlogged and ruined. Probably the weight of so much water would shift the house, rupture water pipes and other fluid intakes. It would take a repair crew more than a day just to clean up the mess. The house itself was done for, not repairable. The blonde and the thin man would never live in it again.

Serve them right.

The dulls could build another house; they built like beavers. There was only one of me in the world.

The earliest memory I have is of some woman, probably the crechemother, staring at me with an expression of shock and horror. Just that. I've tried to remember what happened directly before or after, but I can't. Before, there's nothing but the dark formless shaft of no-memory that runs back to birth. Afterward, the big calm.

From my fifth year, it must have been, to my fifteenth, everything I can remember floats in a pleasant dim sea. Nothing was terribly important. I was languid and soft; I drifted. Waking merged into sleep.

In my fifteenth year it was the fashion in love-play for the young people to pair off for months or longer. "Loving steady," we called it. I remember how the older people protested that it was unhealthy, but we were all normal juniors, and nearly as free as adults under the law.

All but me.

The first steady girl I had was named Elen. She had blonde hair, almost white, worn long; her lashes were dark and her eyes pale green. Startling eyes; they didn't look as if they were looking at you. They looked blind.

Several times she gave me strange, startled glances, something between fright and anger. Once it was because I held her too tightly and hurt her; other times it seemed to be for nothing at all.

In our group a pairing that broke up sooner than four weeks was a little suspect—there must be something wrong with one partner or both, or the pairing would have lasted longer.

Four weeks and a day after Elen and I made our pairing, she told me she was breaking it.

I'd thought I was ready. But I felt the room spin half around me till the wall came against my palm and stopped.

The room had been in use as a hobby chamber; there was a rack of plasticraft knives under my hand. I took one without thinking, and when I saw it I thought, *I'll frighten her*.

And I saw the startled, half-angry look in her pale eyes as I went toward her, but this is curious: She wasn't looking at the knife. She was looking at my face.

The elders found me later with the blood on me, and put me into a locked room. Then it was my turn to be frightened, because I realized for the first time that it was possible for a human being to do what I had done. And if I could do it to Elen, I thought, surely they could do it to me.

But they couldn't. They set me free; they had to.

And it was then I understood that I was the king of the world.

Something else in me, that had been suppressed and forgotten, rose up with my first blow struck in anger. The sculpture began years afterward, as an accident, but in that moment I was free, and I was an artist.

One winter, in the AC Archives in Denver, I found a store-room full of old printed books. I spent months there, reading them, because until then I'd thought I had invented sculpture and drawing. The thing I chiefly wanted to know was, why had it stopped? There was no answer in so many words in any of the books. But reading the histories of those times before the Interregnum, I found one thing that might explain it. Whenever there was a long period of peace and plenty any-where in the ancient world, art grew poor—decoration, genre painting, imitations of imitations. And as for the great artists, they all belonged to violent periods—Praxiteles, da Vinci, Rembrandt, van Rijn, Renoir, Picasso. . . .

It had been bred out of the race, evidently. I don't suppose the genetic planners wanted to get rid of it, but they would have shed almost anything to make a homogeneous, rational, sane, and healthy world.

So there was only one man to carve the portrait of the Age of Reason. All right; I would have been content, only . . .

The sky was turning clear violet when I woke up, and shadow was spilling out from the hedges. I went down the hill until I saw the ghostly blue of photon tubes glowing in a big oblong, just outside the commerce area. I went that way, by habit.

Other people were lining up at the entrance to show their books and be admitted. I brushed by them, seeing the shocked faces and feeling their bodies flinch away, and went on into the robing chamber.

Straps, aqualungs, masks, and flippers were all for the taking. I stripped, dropping the clothes where I stood, and put the underwater equipment on. I strode out to the poolside, monstrous, like a being from another world. I adjusted the lung and the flippers and slipped into the water.

Underneath, it was all crystal blue, with the forms of swimmers sliding through it like pale angels. Schools of small fish scattered as I went down. My heart was beating with a painful joy.

Down, far down, I saw a girl slowly undulating through the motions of a sinuous underwater dance, writhing around and around a ribbed column of imitation coral. She had a suction-tipped fish lance in her hand, but she was not using it; she was only dancing, all by herself, down at the bottom of the water.

I swam after her. She was young, and delicately made, and when she saw the deliberately clumsy motions I made in imitation of hers, her eyes glinted with amusement behind her mask. She bowed to me in mockery, and slowly glided off with simple, exaggerated movements, like a child's ballet.

I followed. Around her and around I swam, stiff-legged, first more childlike and awkward than she, then subtly parodying her motions, then improvising on them until I was dancing an intricate, mocking dance around her.

I saw her eyes widen. She matched her rhythm to mine then, and together, apart, together again we coiled the wake of our dancing. At last, exhausted, we clung together where a bridge of plastic coral arched over us. Her cool body was in the bend of my arm; behind two thicknesses of vitrin—a world away!—her eyes were friendly and kind.

There was a moment when, two strangers, yet one flesh, we felt our souls speak to one another across that abyss of matter. It was a truncated embrace—we could not kiss, we could not speak—but her hands lay confidingly on my shoulders, and her eyes looked into mine.

That moment had to end. She gestured toward the surface and left me. I followed her up. I was feeling drowsy and almost at peace, after my sickness, I thought . . . I don't know what I thought.

We rose together at the side of the pool. She turned to me, removing her mask, and her smile stopped and melted away. She stared at me with a horrified disgust, wrinkling her nose.

"Pyah!" she said, and turned, awkward in her flippers. Watching her, I saw her fall into the arms of a white-haired man, and heard her hysterical voice tumbling over itself.

"But don't you remember?" the man's voice rumbled. "You should know it by heart." He turned. "Hal, is there a copy in the clubhouse?"

A murmur answered him, and in a few moments a young man came out holding a slender brown pamphlet.

I knew that pamphlet. I could even have told you what page the white-haired man opened it to, what sentences the girl was reading as I watched.

I waited. I don't know why.

I heard her voice rising: "To think that I let him *touch* me!" And the white-haired man reassured her, the words rumbling, too low to hear. I saw her back straighten. She looked across at me . . . only a few yards in that scented, blue-lit air; a world away . . . and folded up the pamphlet into a hard wad, threw it, and turned on her heel.

The pamphlet landed almost at my feet. I touched it with my toe, and it opened to the page I had been thinking of:

. . . sedation until his fifteenth year, when for sexual reasons it became no longer practicable. While the advisers and medical staff hesitated, he killed a girl of the group by violence.

And farther down:

The solution finally adopted was threefold.
1. *A sanction*—the only sanction possible to our humane, permissive society. Excommunication; not to speak to him, touch him willingly, or acknowledge his existence.
2. *A precaution*. Taking advantage of a mild predisposition to epilepsy, a variant of the so-called Kusko analogue technique was employed, to prevent by an epileptic seizure any future act of violence.
3. *A warning*. A careful alteration of his body chemistry was effected to make his exhaled and exuded wastes emit a strongly pungent and offensive odor. In mercy, he himself was rendered unable to detect this smell.
Fortunately, the genetic and environmental accidents which combined to produce this atavism have been fully explained, can never again . . .

The words stopped meaning anything, as they always did at that point. I didn't want to read any farther; it was all nonsense, anyway. I was the king of the world.

I got up and went away, out into the night, blind to the dulls who thronged the rooms I passed.

Two squares away was the commerce area. I found a clothing outlet and went in. All the free clothes in the display cases were drab: Those were for worthless floaters, not for me. I went past them to the specials and found a combination I could stand—silver and blue, with a severe black piping down the tunic. A dull would have said it was "nice." I punched for it. The automatic looked me over with its dull glassy eye, and croaked. "Your contribution book, please."

I could have had a contribution book, for the trouble of stepping out into the street and taking it away from the first passerby, but I didn't have the patience. I picked up the one-legged table from the refreshment nook, hefted it, and swung it at the cabinet door. The metal shrieked and dented opposite the catch. I swung once more to the same place, and the door sprang open. I pulled out clothing in handfuls till I got a set that would fit me.

I bathed and changed, and then went prowling in the big multioutlet down the avenue. All those places are arranged pretty much alike, no matter what the local managers do to them. I went straight to the knives, and picked out three in graduated sizes, down to the size of my fingernail. Then I had to take my chances. I tried the furniture department, where I had had good luck once in a while, but this year all they were using was metal. I had to have seasoned wood.

I knew where there was a big cache of cherry wood, in good-sized blocks, in a forgotten warehouse up north at a place called Kootenay. I could have carried some around with me—enough for years—but what for, when the world belonged to me?

It didn't take me long. Down in the workshop section, of all places, I found some antiques—tables and benches, all with wooden tops. While the dulls collected down at the other end of the room, pretending not to notice, I sawed off a good oblong chunk of the smallest bench, and made a base for it out of another.

As long as I was there, it was a good place to work, and I could eat and sleep upstairs, so I stayed.

I knew what I wanted to do. It was going to be a man, sitting, with his legs crossed and his forearms resting down along his calves. His head was going to be tilted back, and his eyes closed, as if he were turning his face up to the sun.

In three days it was finished. The trunk and limbs had a

shape that was not man and not wood, but something in between: something that hadn't existed before I made it.

Beauty. That was the old word.

I had carved one of the figure's hands hanging loosely, and
the other one curled shut. There had to be a time to stop and
say it was finished. I took the smallest knife, the one I had
been using to scrape the wood smooth, and cut away the handle and ground down what was left of the shaft to a thin spike.
Then I drilled a hole into the wood of the figurine's hand, in
the hollow between thumb and curled finger. I fitted the knife
blade in there; in the small hand it was a sword.

I cemented it in place. Then I took the sharp blade and
stabbed my thumb and smeared the blade.

I hunted most of that day and finally found the right place
—a niche in an outcropping of striated brown rock, in a little
triangular half-wild patch that had been left where two roads
forked. Nothing was permanent, of course, in a community
like this one that might change its houses every five years or
so, to follow the fashion, but this spot had been left to itself for
a long time. It was the best I could do.

I had the paper ready; it was one of a batch I had printed
up a year ago. The paper was treated, and I knew it would
stay legible a long time. I hid a little photo capsule in the back
of the niche and ran the control wire to a staple in the base of
the figurine. I put the figurine down on top of the paper and
anchored it lightly to the rock with two spots of all-cement. I
had done it so often that it came naturally; I knew just how
much cement would hold the figurine steady against a casual
hand, but yield to one that really wanted to pull it down.

Then I stepped back to look, and the power and the pity of
it made my breath come short, and tears start to my eyes.

Reflected light gleamed fitfully on the dark-stained blade
that hung from his hand. He was sitting alone in that niche
that closed him in like a coffin. His eyes were shut and his
head tilted back, as if he were turning his face up to the sun.

But only rock was over his head. There was no sun for him.

Hunched on the cool bare ground under a pepper tree, I was looking down across the road at the shadowed niche where my figurine sat.

I was all finished here. There was nothing more to keep me, and yet I couldn't leave.

People walked past now and then—not often. The community seemed half deserted, as if most of the people had flocked off to a surf party somewhere, or a contribution meeting, or to watch a new house being dug to replace the one I had wrecked. . . . There was a little wind blowing toward me, cool and lonesome in the leaves.

Up the other side of the hollow there was a terrace, and on that terrace, half an hour ago, I had seen a brief flash of color—a boy's head, with a red cap on it, moving past and out of sight.

That was why I had to stay. I was thinking how that boy might come down from his terrace and into my road, and passing the little wild triangle of land, see my figurine. I was thinking he might not pass by indifferently, but stop and go closer to look, and pick up the wooden man and read what was written on the paper underneath.

I believed that sometime it had to happen. I wanted it so hard that I ached.

My carvings were all over the world, wherever I had wandered. There was one in Congo City, carved of ebony, dusty-black; one on Cyprus, of bone; one in New Bombay, of shell; one in Changteh, of jade.

They were like signs printed in red and green in a color-blind world. Only the one I was looking for would ever pick one of them up and read the message I knew by heart.

TO YOU WHO CAN SEE, the first sentence said. I OFFER YOU A WORLD . . .

There was a flash of color up on the terrace. I stiffened. A minute later, here it came again, from a different direction: it was the boy, clambering down the slope, brilliant against the green, with his red sharp-billed cap like a woodpecker's head.

I held my breath.

He came toward me through the fluttering leaves, ticked off by pencils of sunlight as he passed. He was a brown boy, I could see at this distance, with a serious thin face. His ears stuck out, flickering pink with the sun behind them, and his elbow and knee pads made him look knobby.

He reached the fork in the road and chose the path on my side. I huddled into myself as he came nearer. *Let him see it, let him not see me*, I thought fiercely.

My fingers closed around a stone.

He was nearer, walking jerkily with his hands in his pockets, watching his feet mostly.

When he was almost opposite me, I threw the stone.

It rustled through the leaves below the niche in the rock. The boy's head turned. He stopped, staring. I think he saw the figurine then. I'm sure he saw it.

He took one step.

"Risha!" came floating down from the terrace.

And he looked up. "Here," he piped.

I saw the woman's head, tiny at the top of the terrace. She called something I didn't hear; I was standing up, squeezed tight with anger.

Then the wind shifted. It blew from me to the boy. He whirled around, his eyes big, and clapped a hand to his nose.

"Oh, what a stench!"

He turned to shout, "Coming!" and then he was gone, hurrying back up the road, into the unstable blur of green.

My one chance, ruined. He would have seen the image, I knew, if it hadn't been for that damned woman, and the wind shifting. . . . They were all against me, people, wind, and all.

And the figurine still sat, blind eyes turned up to the rocky sky.

There was something inside me that told me to take my disappointment and go away from there and not come back.

I knew I would be sorry. I did it, anyway: took the image out of the niche, and the paper with it, and climbed the slope. At the top I heard his clear voice laughing.

There was a thing that might have been an ornamental mound, or the camouflaged top of a buried house. I went around it, tripping over my own feet, and came upon the boy kneeling on the turf. He was playing with a brown-and-white puppy.

He looked up, with the laughter going out of his face. There was no wind, and he could smell me. I knew it was bad. No wind, and the puppy to distract him—everything about it was wrong. But I went to him blindly, anyhow, and fell on one knee, and shoved the figurine at his face.

"Look—" I said.

He went over backwards in his hurry; he couldn't even have seen the image, except as a brown blur coming at him. He scrambled up, with the puppy whining and yapping around his heels, and ran for the mound.

I was up after him, clawing up moist earth and grass as I rose. In the other hand I still had the image clutched, and the paper with it.

A door popped open and swallowed him and popped shut again in my face. With the flat of my hand I beat the vines around it until I hit the doorplate by accident and the door opened. I dived in, shouting, "Wait," and was in a spiral passage, lit pearl-gray, winding downward. Down I went, headlong, and came out at the wrong door—an underground conservatory, humid and hot under the yellow lights, with dripping rank leaves in long rows. I went down the aisle raging, overturning the tanks, until I came to a vestibule and an elevator.

Down I went again to the third level and a labyrinth of guest rooms, all echoing, all empty. At last I found a ramp leading upward, past the conservatory, and at the end of it voices.

The door was clear vitrin, and I paused on the near side of it, looking and listening. There was the boy, and a woman old enough to be his mother, just—sister or cousin, more likely—and an elderly woman in a hard chair holding the puppy. The room was comfortable and tasteless, like other rooms.

I saw the shock grow on their faces as I burst in; it was always the same; they knew I would like to kill them, but they never expected that I would come uninvited into a house. It was not done.

There was that boy, so close I could touch him, but the shock of all of them was quivering in the air, smothering, like a blanket that would deaden my voice. I felt I had to shout.

"Everything they tell you is lies!" I said. "See here—here, this is the truth!" I had the figurine in front of his eyes, but he didn't see.

"Risha, go below," said the young woman quietly. He turned to obey, quick as a ferret.

I got in front of him again. "Stay," I said, breathing hard. "Look—"

"Remember, Risha, don't speak," said the woman.

I couldn't stand any more. Where the boy went I don't know; I ceased to see him. With the image in one hand and the paper with it, I leaped at the woman. I was almost quick enough; I almost reached her, but the buzzing took me in the middle of a step, louder, louder, like the end of the world.

It was the second time that week. When I came to, I was sick and too faint to move for a long time.

The house was silent. They had gone, of course . . . the house had been defiled, having me in it. They wouldn't live here again, but would build elsewhere.

My eyes blurred. After a while I stood up and looked around at the room. The walls were hung with a gray close-woven cloth that looked as if it would tear, and I thought of ripping it down in strips, breaking furniture, stuffing carpets and bedding into the oubliette. . . . But I didn't have the heart for it. I was too tired.

At last I stooped and picked up the figurine and the paper that was supposed to go under it—crumpled now, with the forlorn look of a message that someone has thrown away unread.

I smoothed it out and read the last part.

YOU CAN SHARE THE WORLD WITH ME. THEY CAN'T STOP YOU. STRIKE NOW—PICK UP A SHARP THING AND STAB, OR A HEAVY THING AND CRUSH. THAT'S ALL. THAT WILL MAKE YOU FREE. ANY-ONE CAN DO IT.

Anyone. Anyone.

The Education of Tigress McCardle

C. M. Kornbluth (1923–1958)

C. M. Kornbluth is best known as a collaborator with Frederik Pohl, which is a shame because he was an outstanding talent in his own right, especially when working with the short story length. His solo novels, Not This August and The Syndic, the former a rather simple American-conquered-and-occupied tale, the latter a much more interesting story about a future U.S. where organized crime (compared to the disorganized crime of the present) runs the government, were inferior to his shorter fiction.

Kornbluth was a satiric, bitter, often black writer, reflecting to a large extent his personality. He died tragically at the age of thirty-four of a weak heart made weaker by carrying around a .50 caliber machine gun during World War II and his unwillingness to change his life style for the sake of his health.

"The Education of Tigress McCardle" was not one of his better known stories, but it is one of his best. It is representative of an interesting story category that flourished in the fifties —the "test story," in which a future society requires the passing of some form of test in order to either retain a natural right (as the right to life in Richard Matheson's "The Test") or to "earn" the right in the first place, as in this story. "The Education of Tigress McCardle" is interesting on many levels —it speculates about the future of the family, about solutions to population problems, and about what constitutes parental *"fitness." It was also (according to Fred Pohl) written in the same way that Kornbluth usually wrote—with a screaming child in the room, which probably accounts for its tone.*

From *Venture Science Fiction*   July, 1957

With the unanimity that had always characterized his fans, as soon as they were able to vote they swept him into office as President of the United States. Four years later the 28th Amendment was ratified, republican institutions yielded gracefully to the usages of monarchy, and King Purvis I reigned in the land.

Perhaps even then all would have gone well if it had not been for another major entertainment personage, the insidious Dr. Fu Manchu, squatting like some great evil spider in the center of his web of intrigue. The insidious doctor appeared to have so much fun on his television series, what with a lovely concubine to paw him and a dwarf to throw knives, that it quite turned the head of Gerald Wang, a hitherto-peaceable antique dealer of San Francisco. Gerald decided that he too would squat like some great evil spider in the center of a web of intrigue, and that he would *really* accomplish something. He grew a mandarin mustache, took to uttering cryptic quotations from the sages, and was generally addressed as "doctor" by the members of his organization, though he made no attempt to practice medicine. His wife drew the line at the concubine, but Gerald had enough to keep him busy.

His great coup occurred in 1986 when, after patient years of plotting, one of his most insidious ideas reached the attention of His Majesty via a recommendation ridered onto the annual population-resources report. The recommendation was implemented as the Parental Qualifications Program, or P.Q.P., by royal edict. "Ow rackon thet'll make um mahnd they P's and Q's," quipped His Majesty, and everybody laughed heartily—but none more heartily than the insidious

Dr. Wang, who was present in disguise as Tuner of the Royal Git-tar.

A typical P.Q.P. operation (at least when judged typical by the professor of Chronoscope History Seminar 201 given by Columbia University in 2756 A.D., who ought to know) involved George McCardle . . .

George McCardle had a *good* deal with his girl friend, Tigress Moone. He dined her and bought her pretties and had the freedom of the bearskin rug in front of her wood-burning fireplace. He had beaten the game; he had achieved a delightful combination of bachelor irresponsibility and marital gratification.

"George," Tigress said thoughtfully one day . . . so they got married.

With prices what they were in 1998, she kept her job, of course—at least until she again said thoughtfully: "George . . ."

She then had too much time on her hands; it was absurd for a healthy young woman to pretend that taking care of a two-room city apartment kept her occupied . . . so she thoughtfully said, "George?" and they moved to the suburbs.

George happened to be a rising young editor in the Civil War Book-of-the-Week Club. He won his spurs when he got MIGHTIER THAN THE SWORD: A STUDY OF PENS AND PENCILS IN THE ARMY OF THE POTOMAC, 1863–1865 whipped into shape for the printer. They then assigned him to the infinitely more difficult and delicate job of handling writers. A temperamental troll named Blount was his special trial. Blount was writing a novelized account of Corporal Piggott's Raid, a deservedly obscure episode which got Corporal Piggott of the 104th New York (Provisional) Heavy Artillery Regiment deservedly court-martialed in the summer of '63. It was George's responsibility to see that Blount novelized the verdict of guilty into a triumphant acquittal followed by an award of the Medal of Honor, and Blount was being unreasonable about it.

It was after a hard day of screaming at Blount, and being

screamed back at, that George dragged his carcass off the Long Island Rail Road and into the family car. "Hi, dear," he said to Mrs. McCardle, erstwhile tigress-Diana, and off they drove, and so far it seemed like the waning of another ordinary day. But in the car Mrs. McCardle said thoughtfully: "George . . ."

She told him what was on her mind, and he refrained from striking her in the face because they were in rather tricky traffic and she was driving.

She wanted a child.

It was necessary to have a child, she said. Inexorable logic dictated it. For one thing, it was absurd for just the two of them to live in a great barn of a six-room house.

For another thing, she needed a child to fulfill her womanhood. For a third, the brains and beauty of the Moone-McCardle strain should not die out; it was their duty to posterity.

(The students in Columbia's Chronoscope History Seminar 201 retched as one man at the words.)

For a fourth, everybody was having children.

George thought he had her there, but no. The statement was perfectly correct if for "everybody" you substituted "Mrs. Jacques Truro," their next-door neighbor.

By the time they reached their great six-room barn of a place she was consolidating her victory with a rapid drumfire of simple declarative sentences which ended with "Don't you?" and "Won't we?" and "Isn't it?" to which George, hanging onto the ropes, groggily replied: "We'll see . . . we'll see . . . we'll see . . ."

A wounded thing inside him was soundlessly screaming: *youth! joy! freedom! gone beyond recall, slain by wedlock, coffined by a mortgage, now to be entombed beneath a reeking Everest of diapers!*

"I believe I'd like a drink before dinner," he said. "Had quite a time with Blount today," he said as the martini curled quietly in his stomach. He was pretending nothing very bad had happened. "Kept talking about his integrity. Writers! They'll never learn. . . . Tigress? Are you with me?"

His wife noticed a slight complaining note in his voice, so she threw herself on the floor, began to kick and scream, went on to hold her breath until her face turned blue, and finished by letting George know that she had abandoned her career to assuage his bachelor misery, moved out to this dreary wasteland to satisfy his whim, and just once in her life requested some infinitesimal consideration in return for her ghastly drudgery and scrimping.

George, who was a kind and gentle person except with writers, dried her tears and apologized for his brutality. They would have a child, he said contritely. "Though," he added, "I hear there are some complications about it these days."

"For Motherhood," said Mrs. McCardle, getting off the floor, "no complications are too great." She stood profiled like a statue against their picture window, with its view of the picture window of the house across the street.

The next day George asked around at his office.

None of the younger men, married since the P.Q.P. went into effect, seemed to have had children.

A few of them cheerily admitted they had not had children and were not going to have children, for they had volunteered for D-Bal shots, thus doing away with a running minor expense and, more importantly, ensuring a certain peace of mind and unbroken continuity during tender moments.

"Ugh," thought George.

(The Columbia University professor explained to his students, "It is clearly in George's interest to go to the clinic for a painless, effective D-Bal shot and thus resolve his problem, but he does not go; he shudders at the thought. We cannot know what fear of amputation stemming from some early traumatic experience thus prevents him from action, but deep-rooted psychological reasons explain his behavior, we can be certain." The class bent over the chronoscope.)

And some of George's co-workers slunk away and would not submit to questioning. Young MacBirney, normally open and incisive, muttered vaguely and passed his hand across his brow when George asked him how one went about having a baby—red-tape-wise, that is.

It was Blount, come in for his afternoon screaming match, who spilled the vengeful beans. "You and your wife just phone P.Q.P. for an appointment," he told George with a straight face. "They'll issue you—everything you need." George in his innocence thanked him, and Blount turned away and grinned the twisted, sly grin of an author.

A glad female voice answered the phone on behalf of the P.Q.P. It assured George that he and Mrs. McCardle need only drop in any time at the Empire State Building and they'd be well on their way to parenthood.

The next day Mr. and Mrs. McCardle dropped in at the Empire State Building. A receptionist in the lobby was buffing her nails under a huge portrait of His Majesty. A beautifully lettered sign displayed the words with which His Majesty had decreed that P.Q.P. be enacted: "Ow Racken Theah's a Raht Smaht Ah-dee, Boys."

"Where do we sign up, please?" asked George.

The receptionist pawed uncertainly through her desk. "I *know* there's some kind of book," she said as she rummaged, but she did not find it. "Well, it doesn't matter. They'll give you everything you need in Room 100."

"Will I sign up there?" asked George nervously, conditioned by a lifetime of red tape and uncomfortable without it.

"No," said the receptionist.

"But for the tests—"

"There aren't any tests."

"Then the interviews, the deep probing of our physical and psychological fitness for parenthood, our heredity—"

"No interviews."

"But the evaluation of our financial and moral standing without which no permission can be—"

"No evaluation. Just Room 100." She resumed buffing her nails.

In Room 100 a cheerful woman took a Toddler out of a cabinet, punched the non-reversible activating button between its shoulder blades, and handed it to Mrs. McCardle with a cheery: "It's all yours, madame. Return with it in three months and, depending on its condition, you will or will not, be issued a breeding permit. Simple, isn't it?"

"The little darling!" gurgled Mrs. McCardle, looking down into the Toddler's pretty face.

It spit in her eye, punched her in the nose and sprang a leak.

"Gracious!" said the cheerful woman. "Get it out of our nice clean office, *if* you please."

"How do you work it?" yelled Mrs. McCardle, juggling the Toddler like a hot potato. "How do you turn it off?"

"Oh, you *can't* turn it off," said the woman. "And you'd better not swing it like that. Rough handling goes down on the tapes inside it and we read them in three months and now if you *please*, you're getting our nice office *all wet*—"

She shepherded them out.

"Do something, George!" yelled Mrs. McCardle. George took the Toddler. It stopped leaking and began a ripsaw scream that made the lighting fixtures tremble.

"Give the poor thing to me!" Mrs. McCardle shouted. "You're hurting it holding it like that—"

She took the Toddler back. It stopped screaming and resumed leaking.

It quieted down in the car. The sudden thought seized them both—*too* quiet? Their heads crashed together as they bent simultaneously over the glassy-eyed little object. It laughed delightedly and waved its chubby fists.

"Clumsy oaf!" snapped Mrs. McCardle, rubbing her head.

"Sorry, dear," said George. "But at least we must have got a good mark out of it on the tapes. I suppose it scores us good when it laughs."

Her eyes narrowed. "Probably," she said. "George, do you think if you fell heavily on the sidewalk—?"

"No," said George convulsively. Mrs. McCardle looked at him for a moment and held her peace.

("Note, young gentlemen," said the history professor, "the turning point, the seed of rebellion." They noted.)

The McCardles and the Toddler drove off down Sunrise Highway, which was lined with filling stations; since their '98 Landcruiser made only two miles to the gallon, it was not long before they had to stop at one.

The Toddler began its ripsaw shriek when they stopped. A hollow-eyed attendant shambled over and peered into the car. "Just get it?" he asked apathetically.

"Yes," said Mrs. McCardle, frantically trying to joggle the Toddler, to change it, to burp it, to do anything that would end the soul-splitting noise.

"Half pint of white 90-octane gas is what it needs," mumbled the attendant. "Few drops of SAE 40 oil. Got one myself. Two weeks to go. I'll never make it. I'll crack. I'll—I'll . . ." He tottered off and returned with the gasoline in a nursing bottle, the oil in an eyedropper.

The Toddler grabbed the bottle and began to gulp the gas down contentedly.

"Where do you put the oil?" asked Mrs. McCardle.

He showed her.

"Oh," she said.

"Fill her up," said George. "The car, I mean. I . . . ah . . . I'm going to wash my hands, dear."

He cornered the attendant by the cash register. "Look," he said. "What, ah, would happen if you just let it run out of gas? The Toddler, I mean?"

The man looked at him and put a compassionate hand on his shoulder. "It would *scream*, buddy," he said. "The main motors run off an atomic battery. The gas engine's just for a sideshow and for having breakdowns."

"Breakdowns? Oh, my God! How do you fix a break-down?"

"The best way you can," the man said. "And buddy, when you burp it, watch out for the fumes. I've seen some ugly explosions . . ."

They stopped at five more filling stations along the way when the Toddler wanted gas.

"It'll be better-behaved when it's used to the house," said Mrs. McCardle apprehensively as she carried it over the threshold.

"Put it down and let's see what happens," said George.

The Toddler toddled happily to the coffee table, picked up a large bronze ashtray, moved to the picture window and heaved the ashtray through it. It gurgled happily at the crash.

"You little—!" George roared, making for the Toddler with his hands clawed before him.

"George!" Mrs. McCardle screamed, snatching the Toddler away. "It's only a machine!"

The machine began to shriek.

They tried gasoline, oil, wiping with a clean lint-free rag, putting it down, picking it up and finally banging their heads together. It continued to scream until it was ready to stop screaming, and then it stopped and gave them an enchanting grin.

"Time to put it to—away for the night?" asked George.

It permitted itself to be put away for the night.

From his pillow George said later: "Think we did pretty well today. Three months? Pah!"

Mrs. McCardle said: "You were wonderful, George."

He knew that tone. "My Tigress," he said.

Ten minutes later, at the most inconvenient time in the world, bar none, the Toddler began its ripsaw screaming.

Cursing, they went to find out what it wanted. They found out. What it wanted was to laugh in their faces.

(The professor explained: "Indubitably, sadism is at work here, but harnessed in the service of humanity. Better a brutal

and concentrated attack such as we have been witnessing than long-drawn-out torments." The class nodded respectfully.)

Mr. and Mrs. McCardle managed to pull themselves together for another try, and there was an exact repeat. Apparently the Toddler sensed something in the air.

"Three months," said George, with haunted eyes.

"You'll live," his wife snapped.

"May I ask *just* what kind of a crack that was supposed to be?"

"If the shoe fits, my good *man*—"

So a fine sex quarrel ended the day.

Within a week the house looked as if it had been liberated by a Mississippi National Guard division. George had lost ten pounds because he couldn't digest anything, not even if he seasoned his food with powdered Equanil instead of salt. Mrs. McCardle had gained fifteen pounds by nervous gobbling during the moments when the Toddler left her unoccupied. The picture window was boarded up. On George's salary, and with glaziers' wages what they were, he couldn't have it replaced twice a day.

Not unnaturally, he met his next-door neighbor, Jacques Truro, in a bar.

Truro was rye and soda, he was dry martini; otherwise they were identical.

"It's the little whimper first that gets me, when you know the big screaming's going to come next. I could jump out of my skin when I hear that whimper."

"Yeah. The waiting. Sometimes one second, sometimes five. I count."

"I forced myself to stop. I was throwing up."

"Yeah. Me too. And nervous diarrhea?"

"All the time. Between me and that goddam thing the house is awash. Cheers." They drank and shared hollow laughter.

"My stamp collection. Down the toilet."

"My fishing pole. Three clean breaks and peanut butter in the reel."

"One thing I'll never understand, Truro. *What* decided you two to have a baby?"

"Wait a minute, McCardle," Truro said. "Marguerite told me that *you* were going to have one, so *she* had to have one—"

They looked at each other in shared horror.

"Suckered," said McCardle in an awed voice.

"Women," breathed Truro.

They drank a grim toast and went home.

"It's beginning to talk," Mrs. McCardle said listlessly, sprawled in a chair, her hand in a box of chocolates. "Called me 'old pig-face' this afternoon." She did look somewhat piggish with fifteen superfluous pounds.

George put down his briefcase. It was loaded with work from the office which these days he was unable to get through in time. He had finally got the revised court-martial scene from Blount, and would now have to transmute it into readable prose, emending the author's stupid lapses of logic, illiterate blunders of language and raspingly ugly style.

"I'll wash up," he said.

"Don't use the toilet. Stopped up again."

"Bad?"

"He said he'd come back in the morning with an eight-man crew. Something about jacking up a corner of the house."

The Toddler toddled in with a bottle of bleach, made for the briefcase, and emptied the bleach into it before the exhausted man or woman could comprehend what was going on, let alone do anything about it.

George incredulously spread the pages of the court-martial scene on the gouged and battered coffee table. His eyes bulged as he watched the thousands of typed words vanishing before his eyes, turning pale and then white as the paper.

Blount kept no carbons. Keeping carbons called for a minimal quantity of prudence and brains, but Blount was an author and so he kept no carbons. The court-martial scene, the product of six months' screaming, was *gone*.

The Toddler laughed gleefully.

George clenched his fists, closed his eyes and tried to ignore the roaring in his ears.

The Toddler began a whining chant:

> "*Da*-dy's an *au*-thor!
> *Da*-dy's an *au*-thor!"

"*That did it!*" George shrieked. He stalked to the door and flung it open.

"Where are you going?" Mrs. McCardle quavered.

"To the first doctor's office I find," said her husband in sudden icy calm. "There I will request a shot of D-Bal. When I have had a D-Bal shot, a breeding permit will be of no use whatever to us. Since a breeding permit will be useless, we need not qualify for one by being tortured for another eleven weeks by that obscene little monster, which we shall return to P.Q.P. in the morning. And unless it behaves, it will be returned in a basket, for them to reassemble at their leisure."

"I'm so glad," his wife sighed.

The Toddler said: "May I congratulate you on your decision. By voluntarily surrendering your right to breed, you are patriotically reducing the population pressure, a problem of great concern to His Majesty. We of the P.Q.P. wish to point out that your decision has been arrived at not through coercion but through education; i.e., by presenting you in the form of a Toddler with some of the arguments against parenthood."

"I didn't know you could talk that well," marveled Mrs. McCardle.

The Toddler said modestly: "I've been with the P.Q.P. from the very beginning, ma'am; I'm a veteran Toddler operator, I may say, working out of Room 4567 of the Empire State. And the improved model I'm working through has reduced the breakdown time an average thirty-five percent. I foresee a time, ma'am, when we experienced operators and ever-improved models will do the job in one day!"

The voice was fanatical.

Mrs. McCardle turned around in sudden vague apprehension. George had left for his D-Bal shot. . . .

The Cage

A. Bertram Chandler (1912–)

A. Bertram Chandler is an Australian ship captain who has written excellent adventure science fiction for more than thirty years. He is perhaps best known for his Rim Worlds series. But Chandler is also a very thoughtful writer, interested in the cultures of those beings who inhabit the edge of his fictional galaxy.

One of the best examples is this fine story which asks a number of important questions: what is it that constitutes human behavior as distinct from non-human behavior? What constitutes rational behavior? The humans in this story find themselves in an interesting and dangerous predicament—they must convince those with superior (or perhaps just different) intelligence that they are rational creatures. In their efforts to accomplish this difficult task they find that the culture which produced them is more helpful than the technological manifestations of that culture. And in overcoming the dilemma that faces them the protagonists give us an important lesson about ourselves, our penal system, and our culture.

From *The Magazine of Fantasy and Science Fiction* 1957

Imprisonment is always a humiliating experience, no matter how philosophical the prisoner. Imprisonment by one's own kind is bad enough—but one can, at least, talk to one's captors, one can make one's wants understood; one can, on occasion, appeal to them man to man.

Imprisonment is doubly humiliating when one's captors, in all honesty, treat one as a lower animal.

The party from the survey ship could, perhaps, be excused for failing to recognize the survivors from the interstellar liner *Lode Star* as rational beings. At least two hundred days had passed since their landing on the planet without a name—an unintentional landing made when *Lode Star*'s Ehrenhaft generators, driven far in excess of their normal capacity by a breakdown of the electronic regulator, had flung her far from the regular shipping lanes to an unexplored region of Space. *Lode Star* had landed safely enough; but shortly thereafter (troubles never come singly) her Pile had got out of control and her captain had ordered his First Mate to evacuate the passengers and such crew members not needed to cope with the emergency, and to get them as far from the ship as possible.

Hawkins and his charges were well clear when there was a flare of released energy, a not very violent explosion. The survivors wanted to turn to watch, but Hawkins drove them on with curses and at times, blows. Luckily they were up wind from the ship and so escaped the fall-out.

When the fireworks seemed to be over Hawkins, accompanied by Dr. Boyle, the ship's surgeon, returned to the scene of the disaster. The two men, wary of radioactivity, were cautious and stayed a safe distance from the shallow, still smoking crater that marked where the ship had been. It was all too obvious to them that the Captain, together with his officers and technicians, was now no more than an infinitesimal part of the incandescent cloud that had mushroomed up into the low overcast.

Thereafter the fifty-odd men and women, the survivors of *Lode Star*, had degenerated. It hadn't been a fast process—Hawkins and Boyle, aided by a committee of the more responsible passengers, had fought a stout rearguard action. But it had been a hopeless sort of fight. The climate was against them, for a start. Hot it was, always in the neighborhood of 85° Fahrenheit. And it was wet—a thin, warm drizzle falling all the time. The air seemed to abound with the spores of fungi—luckily these did not attack living skin but throve on dead organic matter, on clothing. They throve to an only slightly lesser degree on metals and on the synthetic fabrics that many of the castaways wore.

Danger, outside danger, would have helped to maintain morale. But there were no dangerous animals. There were only little smooth-skinned things, not unlike frogs, that hopped through the sodden undergrowth, and, in the numerous rivers, fishlike creatures ranging in size from the shark to the tadpole, and all of them possessing the bellicosity of the latter.

Food had been no problem after the first few hungry hours. Volunteers had tried a large, succulent fungus growing on the boles of the huge fern-like trees. They had pronounced it good. After a lapse of five hours they had neither died nor even complained of abdominal pains. That fungus was to become the staple diet of the castaways. In the weeks that followed other fungi had been found, and berries, and roots—all of them edible. They provided a welcome variety.

Fire—in spite of the all-pervading heat—was the blessing most missed by the castaways. With it they could have supplemented their diet by catching and cooking the little frog things of the rain forest, the fishes of the streams. Some of the hardier spirits did eat these animals raw, but they were frowned upon by most of the other members of the community. Too, fire would have helped to drive back the darkness of the long nights, would, by its real warmth and light, have dispelled the illusion of cold produced by the ceaseless dripping of water from every leaf and frond.

When they fled from the ship most of the survivors had possessed pocket lighters—but the lighters had been lost when the pockets, together with the clothing surrounding them, had disintegrated. In any case, all attempts to start a fire in the days when there were still pocket lighters had failed—there was not, Hawkins swore, a single dry spot on the whole accursed planet. Now the making of fire was quite impossible: even if there had been present an expert on the rubbing together of two dry sticks he could have found no material with which to work.

They made their permanent settlement on the crest of a low hill. (There were, so far as they could discover, no mountains.) It was less thickly wooded there than the surrounding plains, and the ground was less marshy underfoot. They succeeded in wrenching fronds from the fern-like trees and built for themselves crude shelters—more for the sake of privacy than for any comfort that they afforded. They clung, with a certain desperation, to the governmental forms of the worlds that they had left, and elected themselves a council. Boyle, the ship's surgeon, was their chief. Hawkins, rather to his surprise, was returned as a council member by a majority of only two votes—on thinking it over he realized that many of the passengers must still bear a grudge against the ship's executive staff for their present predicament.

The first council meeting was held in a hut——if so it could be called—especially constructed for the purpose. The council members squatted in a rough circle. Boyle, the president, got slowly to this feet. Hawkins grinned wryly as he compared the surgeon's nudity with the pomposity that he seemed to have assumed with his elected rank, as he compared the man's dignity with the unkempt appearance presented by his uncut, uncombed gray hair, his uncombed and straggling gray beard.

"Ladies and gentlemen," began Boyle.

Hawkins looked around him at the naked, pallid bodies, at the stringy, lusterless hair, the long, dirty fingernails of the men and the unpainted lips of the women. He thought, I don't suppose I look much like an officer and a gentleman myself.

"Ladies and gentlemen," said Boyle, "we have been, as you know, elected to represent the human community upon this planet. I suggest that at this, our first meeting, we discuss our chances of survival—not as individuals, but as a race—"

"I'd like to ask Mr. Hawkins what our chances are of being picked up," shouted one of the two women members, a dried-up, spinsterish creature with prominent ribs and vertebrae.

"Slim," said Hawkins. "As you know, no communication is possible with other ships, or with planet stations when the Interstellar Drive is operating. When we snapped out of the Drive and came in for our landing we sent out a distress call—but we couldn't say where we were. Furthermore, we don't know that the call was received—"

"Miss Taylor," said Boyle huffily, "Mr. Hawkins, I would remind you that I am the duly elected president of this council. There will be time for a general discussion later.

"As most of you may already have assumed, the age of this planet, biologically speaking, corresponds roughly with that of Earth during the Carboniferous Era. As we already know, no species yet exists to challenge our supremacy. By the time such a species does emerge—something analogous to the giant lizards of Earth's Triassic Era—we should be well established—"

"*We* shall be dead!" called one of the men.

"We should be dead," agreed the doctor, "but our descendants will be very much alive. We have to decide how to give them as good a start as possible. Language we shall bequeath to them—"

"Never mind the language, Doc," called the other woman member. She was a small blonde, slim, with a hard face. "It's just this question of descendants that I'm here to look after. I represent the women of childbearing age—there are, as you must know, fifteen of us here. So far the girls have been very, very careful. We have reason to be. Can you, as a medical man, guarantee—bearing in mind that you have no drugs, no instruments—safe deliveries? Can you guarantee that our children will have a good chance of survival?"

Boyle dropped his pomposity like a worn-out garment.

"I'll be frank," he said. "I have not, as you, Miss Hart, have pointed out, either drugs or instruments. But I can assure you, Miss Hart, that your chances of a safe delivery are far better than they would have been on Earth during, say, the Eighteenth Century. And I'll tell you why. On this planet, so far as we know (and we have been here long enough now to find out the hard way), there exist no microorganisms harmful to Man. Did such organisms exist, the bodies of those of us still surviving would be, by this time, mere masses of suppuration. Most of us, of course, would have died of septicemia long ago. And that, I think, answers *both* your questions."

"I haven't finished yet," she said. "Here's another point. There are fifty-three of us here, men and women. There are ten married couples—so we'll count them out. That leaves thirty-three people, of whom twenty are men. Twenty men to thirteen (aren't we girls always unlucky?) women. All of us aren't young—but we're all of us women. What sort of marriage set-up do we have? Monogamy? Polyandry?"

"Monogamy, of course," said a tall, thin man sharply. He was the only one of those present who wore clothing—if so it could be called. The disintegrating fronds lashed around his waist with a strand of vine did little to serve any useful purpose.

"All right, then," said the girl. "Monogamy. I'd rather prefer it that way myself. But I warn you that if that's the way we play it there's going to be trouble. And in any murder involving passion and jealousy the woman is as liable to be a victim as either of the men—and I don't want *that*."

"What do you propose, then, Miss Hart?" asked Boyle.

"Just this, Doc. When it comes to our matings we leave love out of it. If two men want to marry the same woman, then let them fight it out. The best man gets the girl—and keeps her."

"Natural selection . . ." murmured the surgeon. "I'm in favor—but we must put it to the vote."

At the crest of the low hill was a shallow depression, a natural arena. Round the rim sat the castaways—all but four of them.

One of the four was Dr. Boyle—he had discovered that his duties as president embraced those of a referee; it had been held that he was best competent to judge when one of the contestants was liable to suffer permanent damage. Another of the four was the girl Mary Hart. She had found a serrated twig with which to comb her long hair, she had contrived a wreath of yellow flowers with which to crown the victor. Was it, wondered Hawkins as he sat with the other council members, a hankering after an Earthly wedding ceremony, or was it a harking back to something older and darker?

"A pity that these blasted molds got our watches," said the fat man on Hawkins' right. "If we had any means of telling the time we could have rounds, make a proper prizefight of it."

Hawkins nodded. He looked at the four in the center of the arena—at the strutting, barbaric woman, at the pompous old man, at the two dark-bearded young men with their glistening white bodies. He knew them both—Fennet had been a Senior Cadet of the ill-fated *Lode Star*; Clemens, at least seven years Fennet's senior, was a passenger, had been a prospector on the frontier worlds.

"If we had anything to bet with," said the fat man happily, "I'd lay it on Clemens. That cadet of yours hasn't a snowball's chance in hell. He's been brought up to fight clean—Clemens has been brought up to fight dirty."

"Fennet's in better condition," said Hawkins. "He's been taking exercise, while Clemens has just been lying around sleeping and eating. Look at the paunch on him!"

"There's nothing wrong with good healthy flesh and muscle," said the fat man, patting his own paunch.

"No gouging, no biting!" called the doctor. "And may the best man win!"

He stepped back smartly away from the contestants, stood with the Hart woman.

There was an air of embarrassment about the pair of them as they stood there, each with his fists hanging at his sides.

Each seemed to be regretting that matters had come to such a pass.

"Go *on!*" screamed Mary Hart at last. "Don't you want me? You'll live to a ripe old age here—and it'll be lonely with no woman!"

"They can always wait around until your daughters grow up, Mary!" shouted one of her friends.

"If I ever have any daughters!" she called. "I shan't at this rate!"

"Go on!" shouted the crowd. "Go on!"

Fennet made a start. He stepped forward almost diffidently, dabbed with his right fist at Clemens' unprotected face. It wasn't a hard blow, but it must have been painful. Clemens put his hand up to his nose, brought it away and stared at the bright blood staining it. He growled, lumbered forward with arms open to hug and crush. The cadet danced back, scoring twice more with his right.

"Why doesn't he *hit* him?" demanded the fat man.

"And break every bone in his fist? They aren't wearing gloves, you know," said Hawkins.

Fennet decided to make a stand. He stood firm, his feet slightly apart, and brought his right into play once more. This time he left his opponent's face alone, went for his belly instead. Hawkins was surprised to see that the prospector was taking the blows with apparent equanimity—he must be, he decided, much tougher in actuality than in appearance.

The cadet sidestepped smartly . . . and slipped on the wet grass. Clemens fell heavily on to his opponent; Hawkins could hear the *whoosh* as the air was forced from the lad's lungs. The prospector's thick arms encircled Fennet's body—and Fennet's knee came up viciously to Clemens' groin. The prospector squealed, but hung on grimly. One of his hands was around Fennet's throat now, and the other one, its fingers viciously hooked, was clawing for the cadet's eyes.

"No gouging!" Boyle was screaming. "No gouging!"

He dropped down to his knees, caught Clemens' thick wrist with both his hands.

Something made Hawkins look up then. It may have been a sound, although this is doubtful; the spectators were behaving like boxing fans at a prizefight. They could hardly be blamed —this was the first piece of real excitement that had come their way since the loss of the ship. It may have been a sound that made Hawkins look up, it may have been the sixth sense possessed by all good spacemen. What he saw made him cry out.

Hovering about the arena was a helicopter. There was something about the design of it, a subtle oddness, that told Hawkins that this was no Earthly machine. Suddenly, from its smooth, shining belly, dropped a net, seemingly of dull metal. It enveloped the struggling figures on the ground, trapped the doctor and Mary Hart.

Hawkins shouted again—a wordless cry. He jumped to his feet, ran to the assistance of his ensnared companions. The net seemed to be alive. It twisted itself around his wrists, bound his ankles. Others of the castaways rushed to aid Hawkins.

"Keep away!" he shouted. "Scatter!"

The low drone of the helicopter's rotors rose in pitch. The machine lifted. In an incredibly short space of time the arena was to the First Mate's eyes no more than a pale green saucer in which little white ants scurried aimlessly. Then the flying machine was above and through the base of the low clouds, and there was nothing to be seen but drifting whiteness.

When, at last, it made its descent Hawkins was not surprised to see the silvery tower of a great spaceship standing among the low trees on a level plateau.

The world to which they were taken would have been a marked improvement on the world they had left had it not been for the mistaken kindness of their captors. The cage in which the three men were housed duplicated, with remarkable fidelity, the climatic conditions of the planet upon which *Lode*

Star had been lost. It was glassed in, and from sprinklers in its roof fell a steady drizzle of warm water. A couple of dispirited tree ferns provided little shelter from the depressing precipitation. Twice a day a hatch at the back of the cage, which was made of a sort of concrete, opened, and slabs of a fungus remarkably similar to that on which they had been subsisting were thrown in. There was a hole in the floor of the cage; this the prisoners rightly assumed was for sanitary purposes.

On either side of them were other cages. In one of them was Mary Hart—alone. She could gesture to them, wave to them, and that was all. The cage on the other side held a beast built on the same general lines as a lobster, but with a strong hint of squid. Across the broad roadway they could see other cages, but could not see what they housed.

Hawkins, Boyle and Fennet sat on the damp floor and stared through the thick glass and the bars at the beings outside who stared at them.

"If only they were humanoid," sighed the doctor. "If only they were the same shape as we are we might make a start towards convincing them that we, too, are intelligent beings."

"They aren't the same shape," said Hawkins. "And we, were the situations reversed, would take some convincing that three six-legged beer barrels were men and brothers. . . . Try Pythagoras' Theorem again," he said to the cadet.

Without enthusiasm the youth broke fronds from the nearest tree fern. He broke them into smaller pieces, then on the mossy floor laid them out in the design of a right-angled triangle with squares constructed on all three sides. The natives —a large one, one slightly smaller and a little one—regarded him incuriously with their flat, dull eyes. The large one put the tip of a tentacle into a pocket—the things wore clothing—and pulled out a brightly colored packet, handed it to the little one. The little one tore off the wrapping, started stuffing pieces of some bright blue confection into the slot on its upper side that, obviously, served it as a mouth.

"I wish they were allowed to feed the animals," sighed Hawkins. "I'm sick of that damned fungus."

"Let's recapitulate," said the doctor. "After all, we've nothing else to do. We were taken from our camp by the helicopter —six of us. We were taken to the survey ship—a vessel that seemed in no way superior to our own interstellar ships. You assure us, Hawkins, that the ship used the Ehrenhaft Drive or something so near to it as to be its twin brother. . . ."

"Correct," agreed Hawkins.

"On the ship we're kept in separate cages. There's no ill treatment, we're fed and watered at frequent intervals. We land on this strange planet, but we see nothing of it. We're hustled out of cages like so many cattle into a covered van. We know that we're being driven *somewhere*, that's all. The van stops, the door opens and a couple of these animated beer barrels poke in poles with smaller editions of those fancy nets on the end of them. They catch Clemens and Miss Taylor, drag them out. We never see them again. The rest of us spend the night and the following day and night in individual cages. The next day we're taken to this . . . zoo . . ."

"Do you think they were vivisected?" asked Fennet. "I never liked Clemens, but . . ."

"I'm afraid they were," said Boyle. "Our captors must have learned of the difference between the sexes by it. Unluckily there's no way of determining intelligence by vivisection—"

"The filthy brutes!" shouted the cadet.

"Easy, son," counseled Hawkins. "You can't blame them, you know. We've vivisected animals a lot more like us than we are to these things."

"The problem," the doctor went on, "is to convince these things—as you call them, Hawkins—that we are rational beings like themselves. How would they define a rational being? How would *we* define a rational being?"

"Somebody who knows Pythagoras' Theorem," said the cadet sulkily.

"I read somewhere," said Hawkins, "that the history of

Man is the history of the fire-making, tool-using animal . . ."

"Then make fire," suggested the doctor. "Make us some tools, and use them."

"Don't be silly. You know that there's not an artifact among the bunch of us. No false teeth even—not even a metal filling. Even so . . ." He paused. "When I was a youngster there was, among the cadets in the interstellar ships, a revival of the old arts and crafts. We considered ourselves in a direct line of descent from the old windjammer sailormen, so we learned how to splice rope and wire, how to make sennit and fancy knots and all the rest of it. Then one of us hit on the idea of basketmaking. We were in a passenger ship, and we used to make our baskets secretly, daub them with violent colors and then sell them to passengers as genuine souvenirs from the Lost Planet of Arcturus VI. There was a most distressing scene when the Old Man and the Mate found out. . . ."

"What are you driving at?" asked the doctor.

"Just this. We will demonstrate our manual dexterity by the weaving of baskets—I'll teach you how."

"It might work. . . ." said Boyle slowly. "It might just work. . . . On the other hand, don't forget that certain birds and animals do the same sort of thing. On Earth there's the beaver, who builds quite cunning dams. There's the bower bird, who makes a bower for his mate as part of the courtship ritual . . ."

The Head Keeper must have known of creatures whose courting habits resembled those of the Terran bower bird. After three days of feverish basketmaking, which consumed all the bedding and stripped the tree ferns, Mary Hart was taken from her cage and put in with the three men. After she had got over her hysterical pleasure at having somebody to talk to again she was rather indignant.

It was good, thought Hawkins drowsily, to have Mary with them. A few more days of solitary confinement must surely have driven the girl crazy. Even so, having Mary in the same cage had its drawbacks. He had to keep a watchful eye on young Fennet. He even had to keep a watchful eye on Boyle —the old goat!

Mary screamed.

Hawkins jerked into complete wakefulness. He could see the pale form of Mary—on this world it was never completely dark at night—and, on the other side of the cage, the forms of Fennet and Boyle. He got hastily to his feet, stumbled to the girl's side.

"What is it?" he asked.

"I . . . I don't know. . . . Something small, with sharp claws . . . It ran over me. . . ."

"Oh," said Hawkins, "that was only Joe."

"*Joe?*" she demanded.

"I don't know exactly what he—or she—is," said the man.

"I think he's definitely *he*," said the doctor.

"What is Joe?" she asked again.

"He must be the local equivalent to a mouse," said the doctor, "although he looks nothing like one. He comes up through the floor somewhere to look for scraps of food. We're trying to tame him—"

"You encourage the brute?" she screamed. "I demand that you do something about him—at once! Poison him, or trap him. Now!"

"Tomorrow," said Hawkins.

"Now!" she screamed.

"Tomorrow," said Hawkins firmly.

The capture of Joe proved to be easy. Two flat baskets, hinged like the valves of an oyster shell, made the trap. There was bait inside—a large piece of the fungus. There was a cunningly arranged upright that would fall at the least tug at the bait. Hawkins, lying sleepless on his damp bed, heard the tiny click and thud that told him that the trap had been sprung. He heard Joe's indignant chitterings, heard the tiny claws scrabbling at the stout basket-work.

Mary Hart was asleep. He shook her.

"We've caught him," he said.

"Then kill him," she answered drowsily.

But Joe was not killed. The three men were rather attached to him. With the coming of daylight they transferred him to a cage that Hawkins had fashioned. Even the girl relented when she saw the harmless ball of multi-colored fur bouncing indignantly up and down in its prison. She insisted on feeding the little animal, exclaimed gleefully when the thin tentacles reached out and took the fragment of fungus from her fingers.

For three days they made much of their pet. On the fourth day beings whom they took to be keepers entered the cage with their nets, immobilized the occupants, and carried off Joe and Hawkins.

"I'm afraid it's hopeless," Boyle said. "He's gone the same way . . ."

"They'll have him stuffed and mounted in some museum," said Fennet glumly.

"No," said the girl. "They couldn't!"

"They could," said the doctor.

Abruptly the hatch at the back of the cage opened.

Before the three humans could retreat to the scant protection supplied by a corner a voice called, "It's all right, come on out!"

Hawkins walked into the cage. He was shaved, and the beginnings of a healthy tan had darkened the pallor of his skin. He was wearing a pair of trunks fashioned from some bright red material.

"Come on out," he said again. "Our hosts have apologized very sincerely, and they have more suitable accommodation prepared for us. Then, as soon as they have a ship ready, we're to go to pick up the other survivors."

"Not so fast," said Boyle. "Put us in the picture, will you? What made them realize that we were rational beings?"

Hawkins' face darkened.

"Only rational beings," he said, "put other beings in cages."

The Last of the Deliverers

Poul Anderson (1926–   )

POUL *Anderson has been writing first-rate science fiction since 1948, a large percentage of which has featured hard-nosed, classical liberal viewpoints. One of his principle series characters is Nicholas Van Rijn, a trader who brings the "fruits" of private enterprise and entrepreneurship to the far reaches of the galaxy.*

During the fifties Anderson's Dominic Flandry, an intelligence agent type who specialized in problems of intergalactic politics, was featured, but it is his novel, Brain Wave *(1954) that will be long remembered. In it, he skillfully examined the social and psychological effects of raised intelligence levels on all living creatures on earth.*

Anderson's realistic portrayal of the factors which drive and motivate human beings, as well as his presentation of the manifestations of those drives, has led some to label him as "right-wing," "ultraconservative," and "libertarian." But these labels are largely meaningless and he has consistently opposed fanaticism under any name, rejecting utopian societal arrangements because human beings themselves are not perfect. This

attitude can clearly be seen in "The Last of the Deliverers"—
perhaps the definitive "end of ideology" story.

From *The Magazine of Fantasy and Science Fiction*   1958

When I was nine years old, we still had a crazy man living in our town. He was very old, almost a hundred I suppose, and all his kin were dead. But in those days every town still had a few people who did not belong to any family.

Uncle Jim was wrong in the head, but harmless. He cobbled for us. His shop was in the front room of his house, always prim and neat, and when you stood there among the good smells of leather and oil, you could see his living room beyond. He did not have many books, but shelf after shelf was loaded with tall bright sheafs cased in plastic—old as himself, and as cracked and yellow with their age. He called them his magazines, and if we children were good he sometimes let us look at the pictures in them, but we had to be very careful. After he was dead I had a chance to read the texts, which didn't make sense. Nobody would worry about the things the people in those magazines made such a fuss over. He also had a big antique television set, though why he kept it when there was nothing to receive but official calls and the town had a perfectly good set for them, I don't know. But he was crazy.

Every morning his long stiff figure went for a walk down Main Street. The Trees there were mostly elms, grown tall enough to overshadow it and speckle the pavement with cool bright sunflecks. Uncle Jim was always dressed in his ancient clothes, no matter how hot the day, and summer in Ohio can get plenty hot. He wore frayed white shirts with scratchy, choky collars, and long trousers and a clumsy kind of jacket, and narrow shoes that pinched his feet. They were ugly, but he kept them painfully clean. We children, being young and therefore cruel, thought at first that because we never saw him unclothed he must be hiding some awful deformity, and teased him about it. But my aunt's brother John made us stop, and Uncle Jim never held it against us. He even used to give us candy he had made himself, till the town dentist complained; then all of us had solemn talks with our fathers and found out that sugar rots the teeth.

Finally we decided that Uncle Jim—we called him that, without saying on which side he was anyone's uncle, because he wasn't really—wore all those clothes as a sort of background for his button that said WIN WITH WILLARD. He told me once, when I asked, that Willard had been the last Republican President of the United States and a very great man who tried to avert disaster but was too late because the people were already far gone in sloth and decadence. That was a big lading for a nine-year-old head, and I still don't really understand it, except that once the towns did not govern themselves and the country was divided between two big groups who were not even clans but who more or less took turns furnishing a President; and the President was not an umpire between towns and states, but ran everything.

Uncle Jim used to creak down Main Street past Townhall and the sunpower plant, then turn at the fountain and go by my fathergreatuncle Conrad's house to the edge of town where the fields and Trees rolled to the blue rim of the world. At the airport he would turn and come back to Joseph Arakelian's, where he always looked in at the hand looms and sneered with disgust and talked about automatic machinery; though what he had against the looms I don't know, because Joseph's weavery was famous. He also made harsh remarks about our ratty little airport and the town's half-dozen flitters. That wasn't fair: we had a very good airport, surfaced with concrete block ripped out of the old highway, and there were enough flitters for all our longer trips. You'd never get more than six groups going anywhere at any one time in a town this size.

But I wanted to tell about the Communist.

This was in the spring. The snow had melted and the ground begun to dry and our farmers were out planting. The rest of our town bustled with preparations for the Fete, cooking and baking, oh such a smell as filled the air, women trading recipes from porch to porch, artisans hammering and sawing and welding, the washlines afire with Sundaybest clothes taken out of winter chests, lovers hand in hand whispering of the festivals to come. Red and Bob and Stinky and I were playing marbles by the airport. It used to be mumbletypeg, but some of the kids flipped their knives into Trees and the Elders made a rule that no kid could carry a knife unless a grownup was with him.

So it was a fair sweet morning, the sky a dizzy-high arch of blue, sunlight bouncing off puffy white clouds and down to the earth, and the first pale whisper of green had been breathed across the hills. Dust leaped where our marbles hit, a small wind blew up from the south and slid across my skin and rumpled my hair, the world and the season and we were young.

We were about to quit, fetch our guns and take into the woods after rabbit, when a shadow fell across us and we saw Uncle Jim and my mothercousin Andy. Uncle Jim wore a long coat above all his other clothes, and still shivered as he leaned on his cane, and the shrunken hands were blue with cold. Andy wore a kilt, for the pockets, and sandals. He was our town engineer, a stocky man of forty, but once in the prehistoric past before I was born he had been on an expedition to Mars, and this made him a hero for us kids. We never understood why he was not a swaggering corsair. He owned three thousand books at least, more than twice the average in our town. He spent a lot of time with Uncle Jim too, and I didn't know why. Now I see that he was trying to learn about the past from him, not the dead past mummified in the history books but the people who had once been alive.

The old man looked down at us and said: "You boys aren't wearing a stitch. You'll catch your death of cold." He had a high, thin voice, but it was steady. In all the years alone, he must have learned how to be firm with himself.

"Oh, nonsense," said Andy. "I'll bet it's sixty in the sun."

"We are going after rabbits," I said importantly. "I'll bring mine to your place and your wife can make us a stew." Like all children, I spent as much time with kinfolk as I did with my orthoparents, but I favored Andy's home. His wife was a wonderful cook, his oldest son was better than most on the guitar, and his daughter's chess was just about my speed, neither too good nor too bad.

I'd won most of the marbles this game, so now I gave them back. "When I was a boy," said Uncle Jim, "we played for keeps."

"What happened after the best shooter had won all the marbles in town?" asked Stinky. "It's hard work making a good marble, Uncle Jim. I can't hardly replace all I lose anyway."

"You could have bought some more," he told him. "There were stores where you could buy anything."

"But who made all those marbles?"

"There were factories—"

Imagine that! Big grown men spending their lives making colored glass balls!

We were almost ready to leave when the Communist showed up. We saw him as he rounded the clump of Trees at the north quarter-section, which was pasture that year. He was on the Middleton road, and dust scuffed up from his bare feet.

A stranger in town is always big news, and we kids started running to meet him till Andy recalled us with a sharp word and reminded us that he was entitled to proper courtesy. So we waited, with our eyes bugging out, till he reached us.

But this was a woebegone stranger. He was tall and thin, like Uncle Jim, but his cape hung in rags about a narrow chest where you could count all the ribs, and under a bald dome of a head was a dirty white beard down to his waist. He walked heavily, leaning on a staff, heavy as Time, and even then I sensed the loneliness like a weight on his thin shoulders.

Andy stepped forward and bowed. "Greetings and welcome, Freeborn," he said. "I am Andrew Jackson Welles, town engineer, and on behalf of the Folks I bid you stay, rest, and refresh yourself." He didn't just rattle the words off as he would for someone he knew, but declaimed them with great care.

Uncle Jim smiled then, a smile like thawing after a nine year's winter, for this man was as old as himself and born in the same forgotten world. He trod forth and held out his hand. "Hello, sir," he said. "My name is Robbins. Pleased to meet you." They didn't have very good manners in his day.

"Thank you, Comrade Welles, Comrade Robbins," said the stranger. His smile was lost somewhere in that tangled mold of whiskers. "I'm Harry Miller."

"Comrade?" Uncle Jim spoke it slowly, like a word out of a nightmare, and his hand crept back again. "What do you mean?"

The newcomer wanderer straightened and looked at us in a way that frightened me. "I meant what I said," he answered. "I don't make any bones about it. Harry Miller, of the Communist Party of the United States of America!"

Uncle Jim sucked in a long breath. "But—" he stammered, "but I thought . . . at the very least, I thought all you rats were dead."

"Now hold on," said Andy. "Your pardon, Freeborn Miller. Our friend isn't, uh, isn't quite himself. Don't take it personally, I beg you."

There was a grimness in Miller's chuckle. "Oh, I don't mind. I've been called worse than that."

"And deserved it!" I had never seen Uncle Jim angry before. His face got red and he stamped his cane in the dust. "Andy, this, this man is a traitor. D'you hear? He's a foreign agent!"

"You mean you come clear from Russia?" murmured

Andy, and we boys clustered near with our ears stiff in the breeze, because a foreigner was a seldom sight.

"No," said Miller. "No, I'm from Pittsburgh. Never been to Russia. Wouldn't want to go. Too awful there—they *had* Communism once."

"Didn't know anybody was left in Pittsburgh," said Andy. "I was there last year with a salvage crew, after steel and copper, and we never saw anything but birds."

"A few. A few. My wife and I—But she died, and I couldn't stay in that rotting empty shell of a city, so I went out on the road."

"And you can go back on the road," snarled Uncle Jim.

"Now, please be quiet," said Andy. "Come on into town, Freeborn Miller—Comrade Miller, if you prefer. May I invite you to stay with me?"

Uncle Jim grabbed Andy's arm. He shook like a dead leaf in fall, under the heartless fall winds. "You can't!" he shrieked. "Don't you see, he'll poison your minds, he'll subvert you, we'll end up slaves to him and his gang of bandits!"

"It seems you've been doing a little mind-poisoning of your own, Mr. Robbins," said Miller.

Uncle Jim stood for a moment, head bent to the ground, and the quick tears of an old man glimmered in his eyes. Then he lifted his face and pride rang in the words: "I am a Republican."

"I thought so." The Communist glanced around and nodded to himself. "Typical bourgeois pseudo-culture. Look at those men, each out on his own little tractor in his own field, hugging his own little selfishness to him."

Andy scratched his head. "What are you talking about, Freeborn?" he asked. "Those are town machines. Who wants to be bothered with keeping his own tractor and plow and harvester?"

"Oh . . . you mean—" I could see a light of wonder in the Communist's eyes, and he half stretched out his hands. They were aged hands, I could see the bones just under the dried-out skin. "You mean you *do* work the land collectively?"

"Why, no. What on earth would be the point of that?" replied Andy. "A man's entitled to what he raises himself, isn't he?"

"So the land, which should be the property of all the people, is parceled among those kulaks!" flared Miller.

"How in hell's name can land be anybody's property? It's . . . it's land! You can't put forty acres in your pocket and walk off with them." Andy took a long breath. "You must have been pretty well cut off from things in Pittsburgh—ate the ancient canned stuff, didn't you? I thought so. It's easy enough to explain. Look, that section out there is being planted in corn by my mothercousin Glenn. It's his corn, that he swaps for whatever else he needs. But next year, to conserve the soil, it'll be put in alfalfa, and my sisterson Willy takes care of it then. As for garden truck and fruit, most of us raise our own, just to get outdoors each day."

The light faded in our visitor. "It doesn't make sense," said Miller, and I could hear how tired he was. It must have been a long hike from Pittsburgh, living off handouts from gypsies and the Lone Farmers.

"I quite agree," said Uncle Jim with a stiff kind of smile. "In my father's day—" He closed his mouth. I knew his father had died in Korea, in some war when he was just a baby, and Uncle Jim had been left to keep the memory and the sad barren pride of it. I remembered my history, which Freeborn Levinsohn taught in our town because he knew it best, and a shiver crept in my skin. A *Communist!* Why, they had killed and tortured Americans . . . only this was a faded rag of a man, he couldn't kill a puppy. It was very odd.

We started toward Townhall. People saw us and began to crowd around, staring and whispering as much as decorum allowed. I strutted with Red and Bob and Stinky, right next to the stranger, the real live Communist, under the eyes of all the other kids.

We passed Joseph's weavery, and his family and apprentices came out to join the goggle eyes. Miller spat in the street. "I imagine those people are hired!" he said.

"You don't expect them to work for nothing, do you?" asked Andy.

"They should work for the common good."

"But they do. Every time somebody needs a garment or a blanket, Joseph gets his boys together and they make one. You can buy better stuff from him than most women can make at home."

"I knew it. The bourgeois exploiter—"

"I only wish that were the case," said Uncle Jim, tight-lipped.

"You would," snapped Miller.

"But it isn't. People don't have any drive these days. No spirit of competition. No desire to improve their living standard. No . . . they buy what they need, and wear it while it lasts—and it's made to last damn near forever." Uncle Jim waved his cane in the air. "I tell you, Andy, the country's gone to hell. The economy is stagnant. Business has become a bunch of miserable little shops and people making for themselves what they used to buy!"

"I think we're pretty well fed and clothed and housed," said Andy.

"But where's your . . . your drive? Where's the get-up-and-go, the hustling, that made America great? Look—your wife wears the same model of gown her mother wore. You use a flitter that was built in your father's time. Don't you want anything *better?*"

"Our machinery works well enough," said Andy. He spoke in a bored voice, this was an old argument to him while the Communist was new. I saw Miller's tattered cape swirl into Si Johansen's carpenter shop and followed.

Si was making a chest of drawers for George Hulme, who was getting married this spring. He put down his tools and answered politely.

"Yes . . . yes, Freeborn . . . sure, I work here . . . Organize? What *for*? Social-like, you mean? But my apprentices got too damn much social life as it is. Every third day a holiday, damn near . . . No, they *ain't* oppressed. Hell, they're my own kin! . . . But there ain't any people who haven't got good furniture. Not unless they're lousy carpenters and too uppity to get help—"

"But the people all over the world!" screamed Miller. "Don't you have any heart, man? What about the Mexican peons?"

Si Johansen shrugged. "What about them? If they want to run things different down there, it's their own business." He put away his electric sander and hollered to his apprentices that they could have the rest of the day off. They'd have taken it anyway, of course, but Si was a little bit bossy.

Andy got Miller out in the street again, and at Townhall the Mayor came in from the fields and received him. Since good weather was predicted for the whole week, we decided there was no hurry about the planting and we'd spend the afternoon welcoming our guest.

"Bunch of bums!" snorted Uncle Jim. "Your ancestors stuck by a job till it was finished."

"This'll get finished in time," said the Mayor, like he was talking to a baby. "What's the rush, Jim?"

"Rush? To get on with it—finish it and go on to something else. Better things for better living!"

"For the benefit of your exploiters," cackled Miller. He stood on the Townhall steps like a starved and angry rooster.

"What exploiters?" The Mayor was as puzzled as me.

"The . . . the big businessmen, the—"

"There aren't any more businessmen," said Uncle Jim, and a little more life seemed to trickle out of him as he admitted it. "Our shopkeepers . . . no. They only want to make a living. They've never heard of making a profit. They're too lazy to expand."

"Then why haven't you got socialism?" Miller's red eyes

glared around as if looking for some hidden enemy. "It's every family for itself. Where's your solidarity?"

"We get along pretty well with each other, Freeborn," said the Mayor. "We got courts to settle any arguments."

"But don't you want to go on, to advance, to—"

"We got enough," declared the Mayor, patting his belly. "I couldn't eat any more than I do."

"But you could wear more!" said Uncle Jim. He jittered on the steps, the poor crazy man, dancing before all our eyes like the puppets in a traveling show. "You could have your own car, a new model every year with beautiful chrome plate all over it, and new machines to lighten your labor, and—"

"—and to buy those shoddy things, meant only to wear out, you would have to slave your lives away for the capitalists," said Miller. "The People must produce for the People."

Andy traded a glance with the Mayor. "Look, Freeborns," he said gently, "you don't seem to get the point. We don't *want* all those gadgets. We have enough. It isn't worthwhile scheming and working to get more than we have, not while there are girls to love in springtime and deer to hunt in the fall. And when we do work, we'd rather work for ourselves, not for somebody else, whether you call the somebody else a capitalist or the People. Now let's go sit down and take it easy before lunch."

Wedged between the legs of the Folks, I heard Si Johansen mutter to Joseph Arakelian: "I don't get it. What would we do with all this machinery? If I had some damn machine to make furniture for me, what'd I do with my hands?"

Joseph lifted his shoulders. "Beats me, Si. Personally, I'd go nuts watching two people wear the same identical pattern."

"It might be kind of nice at that," said Red to me. "Having a car like they show in Uncle Jim's ma-gazines."

"Where'd you go in it?" asked Bob.

"Gee, I dunno. To Canada, maybe. But shucks, I can go to Canada any time I can talk my dad into borrowing a flitter."

"Sure," said Bob. "And if you're going less than a hundred miles, you got a horse, haven't you? Who wants an old car?"

I wriggled through the crowd toward the Plaza, where the women were setting up outdoor tables and bringing food for a banquet. The crowd was so thick around our guest where he sat that I couldn't get near, but Stinky and I skun up into the Plaza Tree, a huge gray oak, and crawled along a branch till we hung just above his head. It was a bare and liver-spotted head, wobbling on a thread of neck, but he darted it around and spoke shrill.

Andy and the Mayor sat near him, puffing their pipes, and Uncle Jim was there too. The Folks had let him in so they could watch the fireworks. That was perhaps a cruel and thoughtless thing to do, but how could we know? Uncle Jim had always been so peaceful, and we'd never had two crazy men in town.

"I was still young," Comrade Miller was saying, "I was only a boy, and there were still telecasts. I remember how my mother cried, when we knew the Soviet Union was dissolved. On that night she made me swear to keep faith, and I have, I have, and now I'm going to show you the truth and not a pack of capitalist lies."

"Whatever did happen to Russia?" wondered Ed Mulligan. He was the town psychiatrist, he'd trained at Menninger clear out in Kansas. "I never would have thought the Communists would let their people go free, not from what I've read of them."

"The Communists were corrupted," said Miller fiercely. "Filthy bourgeois lies and money."

"Now that isn't true," said Uncle Jim. "They simply got corrupt and easygoing of their own accord. Any tyrant will. And so they didn't foresee what changes the new technology would make, they blithely introduced it, and in the course of one generation their Iron Curtain rusted away. Nobody *listened* to them any more."

"Pretty correct, Jim," said Andy. He saw my face among the twigs, and winked at me. "There was some violence, it was more complicated than you think, but that's essentially what happened. Trouble is, you can't seem to realize that it happened in the U.S.A. also."

Miller shook his withered head. "Marx proved that technological advances mean inevitable progress toward socialism," he said. "Oh, the cause has been set back, but the day is coming."

"Why, maybe you're right up to a point," said Andy. "But you see, science and society went beyond that point. Maybe I can give you a simple explanation."

"If you wish," said Miller, grumpy-like.

"Well, I've studied the period. Technology made it possible for a few people and acres to feed the whole country, so there were millions of acres lying idle; you could buy them for peanuts. Meanwhile the cities were overtaxed, underrepresented, and choked by their own traffic. Along came the cheap sunpower unit and the high-capacity accumulator. Those made it possible for a man to supply most of his wants, not work his heart out for someone else to pay the inflated prices demanded by an economy where every single business was subsidized or protected at the taxpayer's expense. Also, by living in the new way, a man cut down his money income to the point where he had to pay almost no taxes—so he actually lived better on a shorter work week.

"More and more, people tended to drift out and settle in small country communities. They consumed less, so there was a great depression, and that drove still more people out to fend for themselves. By the time big business and organized labor realized what was happening and tried to get laws passed against what they called un-American practices, it was too late; nobody was interested. It all happened so gradually, you see . . . but it happened, and I think we're happier now."

"Ridiculous!" said Miller. "Capitalism went bankrupt, as

Marx foresaw two hundred years ago, but its vicious influence was still so powerful that instead of advancing to collectivism you went back to being peasants."

"Please," said the Mayor. I could see he was annoyed, and thought that maybe peasants were somebody not Freeborn. "Uh, maybe we can pass the time with a little singing."

Though he had no voice to speak of, courtesy demanded that Miller be asked to perform first. He stood up and quavered out something about a guy named Joe Hill. It had a nice tune, but even a nine-year-old like me knew it was lousy poetics. A childish *a-b-c-b* scheme of masculine rhymes and not a double metaphor anywhere. Besides, who cares what happened to some little tramp when there are hunting songs and epics about interplanetary explorers to make? I was glad when Andy took over and gave us some music with muscle in it.

Lunch was called, and I slipped down from the Tree and found a seat nearby. Comrade Miller and Uncle Jim glowered at each other across the table, but nothing was said till after the meal, a couple of hours later. People had kind of lost interest in the stranger as they learned he'd spent his life huddled in a dead city, and wandered off for the dancing and games. Andy hung around, not wanting to but because he was Miller's host.

The Communist sighed and got up. "You've been nice to me," he said.

"I thought we were all a bunch of capitalists," sneered Uncle Jim.

"It's man I'm interested in, wherever he is and whatever conditions he has to live under," said Miller.

Uncle Jim lifted his voice with his cane: "Man! You claim to care for man, you who only killed and enslaved him?"

"Oh, come off it, Jim," said Andy. "That was a long time ago. Who cares at this late date?"

"*I* do!" Uncle Jim started crying, but he looked at Miller and walked up to him, stiff-legged, hands clawed. "They killed my father! Men died by the tens of thousands—for an ideal! And you don't care! The whole damn country has lost its guts!"

I stood under the Tree, one hand on the cool rough comfort of its bark. I was a little afraid, because I did not understand. Surely Andy, who had been sent by the United Townships Research Foundation all the long black way to Mars, just to gather knowledge, was no coward. Surely my father, a gentle man and full of laughter, did not lack guts. What was it we were supposed to want?

"Why, you bootlicking belly-crawling lackey," yelled Miller, "it was you who gutted them! It was you who murdered workingmen, and roped their sons into your dummy unions, and . . . and . . . what about the Mexican peons?"

Andy tried to come between them. Miller's staff clattered on his head. Andy stepped back, wiping the blood off, looking helpless, as the old crazy men howled at each other. He couldn't use force—he might hurt them.

Perhaps, in that moment, he realized. "It's all right, Freeborns," he said quickly. "It's all right. We'll listen to you. Look, you can have a nice debate tonight, right in Townhall, and we'll all come and—"

He was too late. Uncle Jim and Comrade Miller were already fighting, thin arms locked and dim eyes full of tears because they had no strength left to destroy what they hated. But I think, now, that the hate arose from a baffled love. They both loved us in a queer maimed fashion, and we did not care, we did not care.

Andy got some men together and separated the two and they were led off to different houses for a nap. But when Dr. Simmons looked in on Uncle Jim a few hours later, he was gone. The doctor hurried off to find the Communist, and he was gone too.

I only learned that afterward, since I went off to play tag and pom-pom-pullaway with the other kids down where the river flowed cool and dark. It was in the same river, next morning, that Constable Thompson found the Communist and the Republican. Nobody knew what had happened. They met under the Trees, alone, at dusk when bonfires were being lit and the Elders making merry around them and lovers stealing off into the woods. That's all anybody knows. We gave them a nice funeral.

It was the talk of the town for a week, and in fact the whole state of Ohio heard about it, but then the talk died and the old crazy men were forgotten. That was the year the Brotherhood came into power in the north, and men worried what it could mean. The next spring they learned, and there was an alliance made and war went across the hills. For the Brotherhood gang, just as it had threatened, planted no Trees at all, and such evil cannot go unpunished.

Adrift on the Policy Level

Chan Davis (1926-   )

ALTHOUGH *Dr. Chandler Davis is a Ph.D. in mathematics, during the fifties he produced a small number of science-fiction gems on sociopolitical themes, including this story.*

In some respects it is similar to Beaumont's "The Vanishing American" since it speaks so dramatically of the rise of large, complex bureaucratic structures and the resulting alienation of the individual attempting to cope with them. One of the most depressing aspects of Davis's story is the need for outside assistance—in this case an agent who accompanies the protagonist through the various levels of the bureaucracy in a desperate search for someone who can make a decision. In Davis's science-fictional world it is the fittest salesmen *who survive, not the fittest ideas. While the issue of bureaucratization has been discussed before, most notably in the work of Franz Kafka, it has been rarely done with as fine a cutting edge as in this tale, which anticipated one of the major social issues of the sixties and seventies.*

From *Star Science Fiction Stories*   1959

I

J. Albert LaRue was nervous, but you couldn't blame him. It was his big day. He looked up for reassurance at the big,

410

bass-voiced man sitting so stolidly next to him in the hissing subway car, and found what he sought.

There was plenty of reassurance in having a man like Calvin Boersma on your side.

Albert declared mildly but firmly: "One single thought is uppermost in my mind."

Boersma inclined his ear. "What?"

"Oxidase epsilon!" cried Albert.

Cal Boersma clapped him on the shoulder and answered, like a fight manager rushing last-minute strategies to his boxer: "The one single thought that *should* be uppermost in your mind is *selling* oxidase epsilon. Nothing will be done unless The Corporation is sold on it. And when you deal with Corporation executives you're dealing with experts."

LaRue thought that over, swaying to the motion of the car.

"We do have something genuinely important to sell, don't we?" he ventured. He had been studying oxidase epsilon for three years. Boersma, on the other hand, was involved in the matter only because he was LaRue's lab-assistant's brother-in-law, an assistant sales manager of a plastics firm . . . and the only businessman LaRue knew.

Still, today—the big day—Cal Boersma was the expert. The promoter. The man who was right in the thick of the hard, practical world outside the University's cloistered halls—the world that terrified J. Albert LaRue.

Cal was all reassurance. "Oxidase epsilon *is* important, all right. That's the only reason we have a chance."

Their subway car gave a long, loud whoosh, followed by a shrill hissing. They were at their station. J. Albert LaRue felt a twinge of apprehension. This, he told himself, was it! They joined the file of passengers leaving the car for the luxurious escalator.

"Yes, Albert," Cal rumbled, as they rode up side by side, "we have something big here, if we can reach the top men— say, the Regional Director. Why, Albert, this could get you an assistant section managership in The Corporation itself!"

"Oh, thank you! But of course I wouldn't want—I mean, my devotion to research—" Albert was flustered.

"But of course I could take care of that end of it for you," Boersma said reassuringly. "Well, here we are, Albert."

The escalator fed them into a sunlit square between twenty-story buildings. A blindingly green mall crossed the square to the Regional Executive Building of The Corporation. Albert could not help being awed. It was a truly impressive structure —a block wide, only three stories high.

Cal said, in a reverent growl: "Putting up a building like that in the most heavily taxed area of Detroit—you know what that symbolizes, Albert? *Power.* Power and salesmanship! That's what you're dealing with when you deal with The Corporation."

The building was the hub of the Lakes Region, and the architecture was appropriately monumental. Albert murmured a comment, impressed. Cal agreed. "Superbly styled," he said solemnly.

Glass doors extending the full height of the building opened smoothly at the touch of Albert's hand. Straight ahead across the cool lobby another set of glass doors, equally tall, were a showcase for dramatic exhibits of The Corporation's activities. Soothing lights rippled through an enchanted twilight. Glowing letters said, "Museum of Progress."

Several families on holiday wandered delighted among the exhibits, basking in the highest salesmanship the race had produced.

Albert started automatically in that direction. Cal's hand on his arm stopped him. "This way, Albert. The corridor to the right."

"Huh? But—I thought you said you couldn't get an appointment, and we'd have to follow the same channels as any member of the public." Certainly the "public" was the delighted wanderer through those gorgeous glass doors.

"Oh, sure, that's what we're doing. But I didn't mean *that* public."

"Oh." Apparently the Museum was only for the herd. Albert humbly followed Cal (not without a backward glance) to the relatively unobtrusive door at the end of the lobby—the initiate's secret passage to power, he thought with deep reverence.

But he noticed that three or four new people just entering the building were turning the same way.

A waiting room. But it was not a disappointing one; evidently Cal had directed them right; they had passed to a higher circle. The room was large, yet it looked like a sanctum.

Albert had never seen chairs like these. All of the twenty-five or so men and women who were there ahead of them were distinctly better dressed than Albert. On the other hand Cal's suit—a one-piece wooly buff-colored outfit, fashionably loose at the elbows and knees—was a match for any of them. Albert took pride in that.

Albert sat and fidgeted. Cal's bass voice gently reminded him that fidgeting would be fatal, then rehearsed him in his approach. He was to be, basically, a professor of plant metabolism; it was a poor approach, Cal conceded regretfully, but the only one Albert was qualified to make. Salesmanship he was to leave to Cal; his own appeal was to be based on his position—such as it was—as a scientific expert; therefore he was to be, basically, himself. His success in projecting the role might possibly be decisive—although the main responsibility, Cal pointed out, was Cal's.

While Cal talked, Albert fidgeted and watched the room. The lush chairs, irregularly placed, still managed all to face one wall, and in that wall were three plain doors. From time to time an attendant would appear to call one of the waiting supplicants to one of the doors. The attendants were liveried young men with flowing black hair. Finally, one came their way! He summoned them with a bow—an eye-flashing, head-tossing, flourishing bow, like a dancer rather than a butler.

Albert followed Cal to the door. "Will this be a junior executive? A personal secretary? A—"

But Cal seemed not to hear.

Albert followed Cal through the door and saw the most beautiful girl in the world.

He couldn't look at her, not by a long way. She was much too beautiful for that. But he knew exactly what she looked like. He could see in his mind her shining, ringleted hair falling gently to her naked shoulders, her dazzling bright expressionless face. He couldn't even think about her body; it was terrifying.

She sat behind a desk and looked at them.

Cal struck a masterful pose, his arms folded. "We have come on a scientific matter," he said haughtily, "not familiar to The Corporation, concerning several northern colonial areas."

She wrote deliberately on a small plain pad. Tonelessly, sweetly, she asked, "Your name?"

"Calvin Boersma."

Her veiled eyes swung to Albert. He couldn't possibly speak. His whole consciousness was occupied in not looking at her.

Cal said sonorously: "This is J. Albert LaRue, Professor of Plant Metabolism." Albert was positively proud of his name, the way Cal said it.

The most beautiful girl in the world whispered meltingly: "Go out this door and down the corridor to Mr. Blick's office. He'll be expecting you."

Albert chose this moment to try to look at her. And *she* smiled! Albert, completely routed, rushed to the door. He was grateful she hadn't done *that* before! Cal, with his greater experience and higher position in life, could linger a moment, leaning on the desk, to leer at her.

But all the same, when they reached the corridor, he was sweating.

Albert said carefully, "*She* wasn't an executive, was she?"

"No," said Cal, a little scornfully. "She's an Agency Model, what else? Of course, you probably don't see them much at the University, except at the Corporation Representative's Office and maybe the President's Office." Albert had never been near either. "She doesn't have much to do except to impress visitors, and of course stop the ones that don't belong here."

Albert hesitated. "She *was* impressive."

"She's impressive, all right," Cal agreed. "When you consider the Agency rates, and then realize that any member of the public who comes to the Regional Executive Building on business sees an Agency Model receptionist—then you know you're dealing with power, Albert."

Albert had a sudden idea. He ventured: "Would we have done better to have brought an Agency Model with us?"

Cal stared. "To go through the whole afternoon with us? Impossible, Albert! It'd cost you a year's salary."

Albert said eagerly: "No, that's the beauty of it, Cal! You see, I have a young cousin—I haven't seen her recently, of course, but she was drafted by the Agency, and I might have been able to get her to—" He faltered. Boersma was looking scandalized.

"Albert—excuse me. If your cousin had so much as walked into any business office with makeup on, she'd have had to collect Agency rates—or she'd have been out of the Agency like *that*. And owing them plenty." He finished consolingly, "A Model wouldn't have done the trick anyway."

II

Mr. Blick looked more like a scientist than a businessman, and his desk was a bit of a laboratory. At his left hand was an elaborate switchboard, curved so all parts would be in easy reach; most of the switches were in rows, the handles color-coded. As he nodded Cal to a seat his fingers flicked over three switches. The earphones and microphone clamped on his head had several switches too, and his right hand quivered beside a stenotype machine of unfamiliar complexity.

He spoke in an undertone into his mike, then his hand whizzed almost invisibly over the stenotype.

"Hello, Mr. Boersma," he said, flicking one last switch but not removing the earphones. "Please excuse my idiosyncrasies, it seems I actually work better this way." His voice was firm, resonant and persuasive.

Cal took over again. He opened with a round compliment for Mr. Blick's battery of gadgets, and then flowed smoothly on to an even more glowing series of compliments—which Albert realized with a qualm of embarrassment referred to *him*.

After the first minute or so, though, Albert found the talk less interesting than the interruptions. Mr. Blick would raise a forefinger apologetically but fast; switches would tumble; he would listen to the earphones, whisper into the mike, and perform incredibly on the absolutely silent stenotype. Shifting lights touched his face, and Albert realized the desk top contained at least one TV screen, as well as a bank of blinking colored lights. The moment the interruption was disposed of, Mr. Blick's faultless diction and pleasant voice would return Cal exactly to where he'd been. Albert was impressed.

Cal's peroration was an urgent appeal that Mr. Blick consider the importance to The Corporation, financially, of what he was about to learn. Then he turned to Albert, a little too abruptly.

"One single thought is uppermost in my mind," Albert stuttered, caught off guard. "Oxidase epsilon. I am resolved that The Corporation shall be made to see the importance—"

"Just a moment, Professor LaRue," came Mr. Blick's smooth Corporation voice. "You'll have to explain this to *me*. I don't have the background or the brains that you people in the academic line have. Now in layman's terms, just what *is* oxidase epsilon?" He grinned handsomely.

"Oh, don't feel bad," said Albert hastily. "Lots of my colleagues haven't heard of it, either." This was only a half-truth. Every one of his colleagues that Albert met at the University in a normal working month had certainly heard of oxidase epsilon—from Albert. "It's an enzyme found in many plants but recognized only recently. You see, many of the laboratory species created during the last few decades have been unable to produce ordinary oxidase, or oxidase alpha, but surprisingly enough some of these have survived. This is due to the presence of a series of related compounds, of which oxidases beta, gamma, delta, and epsilon have been isolated, and beta and epsilon have been prepared in the laboratory."

Mr. Blick shifted uncertainly in his seat. Albert hurried on so he would see how simple it all was. "I have been studying the reactions catalyzed by oxidase epsilon in several species of *Triticum*. I found quite unexpectedly that none of them produce the enzyme themselves. Amazing, isn't it? All the oxidase epsilon in those plants comes from a fungus, *Puccinia triticina*, which infects them. This, of course, explains the failure of Hinshaw's group to produce viable *Triticum kaci* following—"

Mr. Blick smiled handsomely again. "Well now, Professor LaRue, you'll have to tell me what this means. In *my* terms—you understand."

Cal boomed portentously, "It may mean the saving of the economies of three of The Corporation's richest colonies." Rather dramatic, Albert thought.

Mr. Blick said appreciatively, "Very good. *Very* good. Tell me more. Which colonies—and why?" His right hand left its crouch to spring restlessly to the stenotype.

Albert resumed, buoyed by this flattering show of interest. "West Lapland in Europe, and Great Slave and Churchill on this continent. They're all Corporation colonies, recently opened up for wheat-growing by *Triticum witti*, and I've been told they're extremely productive."

"Who is Triticum Witti? One of our vice-presidents?"

Albert, shocked, explained patiently, "*Triticum witti* is one of the new species of wheat which depend on oxidase epsilon.

And if the fungus *Puccinia triticina* on that wheat becomes a pest, sprays may be used to get rid of it. And a whole year's wheat crop in those colonies may be destroyed."

"Destroyed," Mr. Blick repeated wonderingly. His forefinger silenced Albert like a conductor's baton; then both his hands danced over keys and switches, and he was muttering into his microphone again.

Another interruption, thought Albert. He felt proper reverence for the undoubted importance of whatever Mr. Blick was settling, still he was bothered a little, too. Actually (he remembered suddenly) he had a reason to be so presumptuous: oxidase epsilon was important, too. Over five hundred million dollars had gone into those three colonies already, and no doubt a good many people.

However, it turned out this particular interruption must have been devoted to West Lapland, Great Slave, and Churchill after all. Mr. Blick abandoned his instrument panel and announced his congratulations to them: "Mr. Boersma, the decision has been made to assign an expediter to your case!" And he smiled heartily.

This was a high point for Albert.

He wasn't sure he knew what an expediter was, but he was sure from Mr. Blick's manner that an unparalleled honor had been given him. It almost made him dizzy to think of all this glittering building, all the attendants and Models and executives, bowing to *him,* as Mr. Blick's manner implied they must.

A red light flicked on and off on Mr. Blick's desk. As he turned to it he said, "Excuse me, gentlemen." Of course, Albert pardoned him mentally, you have to work.

He whispered to Cal, "Well, I guess we're doing pretty well."

"Huh? Oh, yes, very well," Cal whispered back. "So far."

"So far? Doesn't Mr. Blick understand the problem? All we have to do is give him the details now."

"Oh, no, Albert! I'm sure *he* can't make the decision. He'll have to send us to someone higher up."

Higher up? "Why? Do we have to explain it all over again?"

Cal turned in his chair so he could whisper to Albert less conspicuously. "Albert, an enterprise the size of The Corporation can't give consideration to every crackpot suggestion anyone tries to sell it. There have to be regular channels. Now the Plant Metabolism Department doesn't have any connections here (maybe we can do something about that), so we have to run a sort of obstacle course. It's survival of the fittest, Albert! Only the most worthwhile survive to see the Regional Director. Of course the Regional Director selects which of those to accept, but he doesn't have to sift through a lot of crackpot propositions."

Albert could see the analogy to natural selection. Still, he asked humbly: "How do you know the best suggestions get through? Doesn't it depend a lot on how good a salesman is handling them?"

"Very much so. Naturally!"

"But then— Suppose, for instance, I hadn't happened to know you. My good idea wouldn't have got past Mr. Blick."

"It wouldn't have got past the Model," Cal corrected. "Maybe not that far. But you see in that case it wouldn't have been a very important idea, because it wouldn't have been *put into effect.*" He said it with a very firm, practical jawline. "Unless of course someone else had had the initiative and resourcefulness to present the same idea better. Do you see now? *Really important ideas attract the sales talent to put them across.*"

Albert didn't understand the reasoning, he had to admit. It was such an important point, and he was missing it. He reminded himself humbly that a scientist is no expert outside his own field.

So all Mr. Blick had been telling them was that they had not yet been turned down. Albert's disappointment was sharp.

420

Still, he was curious. How had such a trivial announcement given him such euphoria? Could you produce that kind of effect just by your delivery? Mr. Blick could, apparently. The architecture, the Model, and all the rest had been build-up for him; and certainly they had helped the effect; but they didn't explain it.

What was the key? *Personality*, Albert realized. This was what businessmen meant by their technical term "personality." Personality was the asset Mr. Blick had exploited to rise to where he was—rather than becoming, say, a scientist.

The Blicks and Boersmas worked hard at it. Wistfully, Albert wondered how it was done. Of course the experts in this field didn't publish their results, and anyhow he had never studied it. But it was the most important field of human culture, for on it hinged the policy decisions of government—even of The Corporation!

He couldn't estimate whether Cal was as good as Mr. Blick, because he assumed Cal had never put forth a big effort on him, Albert. He wasn't worth it.

He had one other question for Cal. "What is an expediter?"

"Oh, I thought you knew," boomed Cal. "They can be a big help. That's why we're doing well to be assigned one. We're going to get into the *top levels*, Albert, where only a salesman of true merit can hope to put across an idea. An expediter can do it if anyone can. The expediters are too young to hold Key Executive Positions, but they're Men On The Way Up. They—"

Mr. Blick turned his head toward a door on his left, putting the force of his personality behind the gesture. "Mr. Demarest," he announced as the expediter walked into the room.

III

Mr. Demarest had captivating red curly sideburns, striking brown eyes, and a one-piece coverall in a somewhat loud pattern of black and beige. He almost trembled with excess energy. It was contagious; it made you feel as if you were as abnormally fit as he was.

He grinned his welcome at Albert and Cal, and chuckled merrily: "How do you do, Mr. Boersma."

It was as if Mr. Blick had been turned off. Albert hardly knew he was still in the room. Clearly Mr. Demarest was a Man On The Way Up indeed.

They rose and left the room with him—to a new corridor, very different from the last: weirdly lighted from a strip two feet above the floor, and lined with abstract statuary.

This, together with Mr. Demarest, made a formidable challenge.

Albert rose to it recklessly. "Oxidase epsilon," he proclaimed, "may mean the saving of three of The Corporation's richest colonies!"

Mr. Demarest responded with enthusiasm. "I agree one hundred percent—our Corporation's crop of *Triticum witti* must be saved! Mr. Blick sent me a playback of your explanation by interoffice tube, Professor LaRue. You've got me on your side one hundred per cent! I want to assure you both, very sincerely, that I'll do my utmost to sell Mr. Southfield. Professor, you be ready to fill in the details when I'm through with what I know."

There was no slightest condescension or reservation in his voice. He would take care of things, Albert knew. What a relief!

Cal came booming in: "Your Mr. Blick seems like a competent man."

What a way to talk about a Corporation executive! Albert decided it was not just a simple faux pas, though. Apparently Cal had decided he had to be accepted by Mr. Demarest as an equal, and this was his opening. It seemed risky to Albert. In fact, it frightened him.

"There's just one thing, now, about your Mr. Blick," Cal was saying to Mr. Demarest, with a tiny wink that Albert was proud of having spotted. "I couldn't help wondering how he

manages to find so much to do with those switches of his."
Albert barely restrained a groan.

But Mr. Demarest grinned! "Frankly, Cal," he answered,
"I'm not just sure how many of old Blick's switches are dummies."

Cal had succeeded! That was the main content of Mr.
Demarest's remark.

But *were* Mr. Blick's switches dummies? Things were much
simpler back—way back—at the University, where people
said what they meant.

They were near the end of the corridor. Mr. Demarest said
softly, "Mr. Southfield's Office." Clearly Mr. Southfield's presence was enough to curb even Mr. Demarest's boyishness.

They turned through an archway into a large room, lighted
like the corridor, with statuary wilder still.

Mr. Southfield was at one side, studying papers in a vast
easy chair: an elderly man, fantastically dressed but with a
surprisingly ordinary face peeping over the crystal ruff on his
magenta leotards. He ignored them. Mr. Demarest made it
clear they were supposed to wait until they were called on.

Cal and Albert chose two of the bed-sized chairs facing Mr.
Southfield, and waited expectantly.

Mr. Demarest whispered, "I'll be back in time to make the
first presentation. Last-minute brush-up, you know." He
grinned and clapped Cal smartly on the shoulder. Albert was
relieved that he didn't do the same to him, but just shook his
hand before leaving. It would have been too upsetting.

Albert sank back in his chair, tired from all he'd been
through and relaxed by the soft lights.

It was the most comfortable chair he'd ever been in. It was
more than comfortable, it was a deliciously irresistible invitation to relax completely. Albert was barely awake enough to
notice that the chair was rocking him gently, tenderly massag-
ing his neck and back.

He lay there, ecstatic. He didn't quite go to sleep. If the
chair had been designed just a little differently, no doubt, it

could have put him to sleep, but this one just let him rest carefree and mindless.

Cal spoke (and even Cal's quiet bass sounded harsh and urgent): "Sit up straighter, Albert!"

"Why?"

"Albert, any sales resistance you started with is going to be completely *gone* if you don't sit up enough to shut off that chair!"

"Sales resistance?" Albert pondered comfortably. "What have we got to worry about? Mr. Demarest is on our side, isn't he?"

"Mr. Demarest," Cal pointed out, "is *not* the Regional Director."

So they still might have problems! So the marvelous chair was just another trap where the unfit got lost! Albert resolved to himself: "From now on, one single thought will be uppermost in my mind: defending my sales resistance."

He repeated this to himself.

He repeated it again. . . .

"Albert!" There was genuine panic in Cal's voice now.

A fine way to defend his sales resistance! He had let the chair get him again. Regretfully he shifted his weight forward, reaching for the arms of the chair.

"Watch it!" said Cal. "Okay now, but don't use the arms. Just lean yourself forward. There." He explained, "The surface on the arms is rough and moist, and I can't think of any reason it should be—unless it's to give you narcotic through the skin! Tiny amounts, of course. But we can't afford any. First time I've ever seen that one in actual use," he admitted.

Albert was astonished, and in a moment he was more so. "Mr. Southfield's chair is the same as ours, and *he's* leaning back in it. Why, he's even stroking the arm while he reads!"

"I know." Cal shook his head. "Remarkable man, isn't he? Remarkable. Remember this, Albert. The true salesman, the man on the very pinnacle of achievement, is also—a connoisseur. Mr. Southfield is a connoisseur. He wants to be presented with the most powerful appeals known, for the sake of the pleasure he gets from the appeal itself. Albert, there is a strong strain of the sensuous, the self-indulgent, in every really successful man like Mr. Southfield. Why? Because to be successful he must have the most profound understanding of self-indulgence."

Albert noticed in passing that, just the same, Cal wasn't self-indulgent enough to trust himself to that chair. He didn't even make a show of doing so. Clearly in Mr. Southfield they had met somebody far above Cal's level. It was unnerving. Oxidase epsilon seemed a terribly feeble straw to outweigh such a disadvantage.

Cal went on, "This is another reason for the institution of expediters. The top executive can't work surrounded by inferior salesmanship. He needs the stimulus and the luxury of receiving his data well packaged. The expediters can do it." He leaned over confidentially. "I've heard them called back-scratchers for that reason," he whispered.

Albert was flattered that Cal admitted him to this trade joke.

Mr. Southfield looked up at the archway as someone came in—not Mr. Demarest, but a black-haired young woman. Albert looked inquiringly at Cal.

"Just a minute. I'll soon know who she is."

She stood facing Mr. Southfield, against the wall opposite Albert and Cal. Mr. Southfield said in a drowsy half-whisper, "Yes, Miss Drury, the ore-distribution pattern. Go on."

"She must be another expediter, on some other matter," Cal decided. "Watch her work. Albert. You won't get an opportunity like this often."

Albert studied her. She was not at all like an Agency Model; she was older than most of them (about thirty); she was fully dressed, in a rather sober black and gray business suit, snug around the hips; and she wasn't wearing makeup. She couldn't be even an ex-Model, she wasn't the type. Heavier in build, for one thing, and though she was very pretty it wasn't that unhuman blinding beauty. On the contrary, Albert enjoyed looking at her (even lacking Mr. Southfield's connoisseurship). He found Miss Drury's warm dark eyes and confident posture very pleasant and relaxing.

She began to talk, gently and musically, something about how to compute the most efficient routing of metallic ore traffic in the Great Lakes Region. Her voice became a chant, rising and falling, but with a little catch in it now and then. Lovely!

Her main device, though, sort of snuck up on him, the way the chair had. It had been going on for some time before Albert was conscious of it. It was like the chair.

Miss Drury moved.

Her hips swung. Only a centimeter each way, but very, very sensuously. You could follow the motion in detail, because her dress was more than merely snug around the hips, you could see every muscle on her belly. The motion seemed entirely spontaneous, but Albert knew she must have worked hard on it.

The knowledge, however, didn't spoil his enjoyment.

"Gee," he marveled to Cal, "how can Mr. Southfield hear what she's saying?"

"Huh? Oh—she lowers her voice from time to time on purpose so we won't overhear Corporation secrets, but he's much nearer her than we are."

"That's not what I mean!"

"You mean why doesn't her delivery distract him from the message? Albert," Boersma said wisely, "if you were sitting in his chair you'd be getting the message, too—with crushing force. A superior presentation *always* directs attention to the message. But in Mr. Southfield's case it actually stimulates critical consideration as well! Remarkable man. An expert and a connoisseur."

Meanwhile Albert saw that Miss Drury had finished. Maybe she would stay and discuss her report with Mr. Southfield? No, after just a few words he dismissed her.

IV

In a few minutes the glow caused by Miss Drury had changed to a glow of excited pride.

Here was he, plain old Professor LaRue, witnessing the drama of the nerve center of the Lakes Region—the interplay of titanic personalities, deciding the fate of millions. Why, he was even going to be involved in one of the decisions! He hoped the next expediter to see Mr. Southfield would be Mr. Demarest!

Something bothered him. "Cal, how can Mr. Demarest possibly be as—well—persuasive as Miss Drury? I mean—"

"Now, Albert, you leave that to him. Sex is not the only possible vehicle. Experts can make strong appeals to the weakest and subtlest of human drives—even altruism! Oh yes, I know it's surprising to the layman, but even altruism can be useful."

"Really?" Albert was grateful for every tidbit.

"Real masters will sometimes prefer such a method out of sheer virtuosity," whispered Cal.

Mr. Southfield stirred a little in his chair, and Albert snapped to total alertness.

Sure enough, it was Mr. Demarest who came through the archway.

Certainly his entrance was no let down. He strode in even more eagerly than he had into Mr. Blick's office. His costume glittered, his brown eyes glowed. He stood against the wall beyond Mr. Southfield; not quite straight, but with a slight wrestler's crouch. A taut spring.

He gave Albert and Cal only half a second's glance, but that glance was a tingling communication of comradeship and joy of battle. Albert felt himself a participant in something heroic.

Mr. Demarest began releasing all that energy slowly. He gave the background of West Lapland, Great Slave, and Churchill. Maps were flashed on the wall beside him (exactly how, Albert didn't follow), and the drama of arctic colonization was recreated by Mr. Demarest's sportscaster's voice. Albert would have thought Mr. Demarest was the overmodest hero of each project if he hadn't known all three had been done simultaneously. No, it was hard to believe, but all these vivid facts must have been served to Mr. Demarest by some research flunky within the last few minutes. And yet, how he had transfigured them!

The stirring narrative was reaching Mr. Southfield, too. He had actually sat up out of the easy chair.

Mr. Demarest's voice, like Miss Drury's, dropped in volume now and then. Albert and Cal were just a few feet too far away to overhear Coporation secrets.

As the saga advanced, Mr. Demarest changed from Viking to Roman. His voice, by beautifully controlled stages, became bubbling and hedonistic. Now, he was talking about grandiose planned expansions—and, best of all, about how much money The Corporation expected to make from the three colonies. The figures drooled through loose lips. He clapped Mr. Southfield on the shoulder. He stroked Mr. Southfield's arm; when he came to the estimated trade balances, he tickled his neck. Mr. Southfield showed his appreciation of the change in mood by lying back in his chair again.

This didn't stop Mr. Demarest.

It seemed almost obscene. Albert covered his embarrassment by whispering, "I see why they call them back-scratchers."

Cal frowned, waved him silent, and went on watching.

Suddenly Mr. Demarest's tone changed again: it became bleak, bitter, desperate. A threat to the calculated return on The Corporation's investment—even to the capital investment itself!

Mr. Southfield sat forward attentively to hear about this danger. Was that good? He hadn't done that with Miss Drury.

What Mr. Demarest said about the danger was, of course, essentially what Albert had told Mr. Blick, but Albert realized that it sounded a lot more frightening Mr. Demarest's way.

When he was through, Albert felt physically chilly. Mr. Southfield sat saying nothing. What was he thinking? Could he fail to see the tragedy that threatened?

After a moment he nodded and said, "Nice presentation." He hadn't said that to Miss Drury, Albert exulted!

Mr. Demarest looked dedicated.

Mr. Southfield turned his whole body to face Albert, and looked him straight in the eyes. Albert was too alarmed to look away. Mr. Southfield's formerly ordinary jaw now jutted, his chest swelled imposingly. "*You*, I understand, are a well-informed worker on plant metabolism." His voice seemed to grow too, until it rolled in on Albert from all sides of the room. "Is it *your* opinion that the danger is great enough to justify taking up the time of the Regional Director?"

It wasn't fair. Mr. Southfield against J. Albert LaRue was a ridiculous mismatch anyway! And now Albert was taken by surprise—after too long a stretch as an inactive spectator—and hit with the suggestion that he had been *wasting Mr. Southfield's time* . . . that his proposition was not only not worth acting on, it was a *waste of the Regional Director's time.*

Albert struggled to speak.

Surely, after praising Mr. Demarest's presentation, Mr. Southfield would be lenient; he would take into account Albert's limited background; he wouldn't expect too much. Albert struggled to say anything.

He couldn't open his mouth.

As he sat staring at Mr. Southfield, he could feel his own shoulders drawing inward and all his muscles going limp.

Cal said, in almost a normal voice, "Yes."

That was enough, just barely. Albert whispered, "Yes," terrified at having found the courage.

Mr. Southfield glared down at him a moment more.

Then he said, "Very well, you may see the Regional Director. Mr. Demarest, take them there."

Albert followed Mr. Demarest blindly. His entire attention was concentrated on recovering from Mr. Southfield.

He had been one up, thanks to Mr. Demarest. Now, how could he have stayed one up? How should he have resisted Mr. Southfield's dizzying display of personality?

He had played the episode back mentally over and over, trying to correct it to run as it should have. Finally he succeeded, at least in his mind. He saw what his attitude *should* have been. He *should* have kept his shoulders squared and his vocal cords loose, and faced Mr. Southfield confidently. Now he saw how to do it.

He walked erectly and firmly behind Mr. Demarest, and allowed a haughty half-smile to play on his lips.

He felt armed to face Mr. Southfield all by himself—or, since it seemed Mr. Southfield was not the Regional Director after all, even to face the Regional Director!

They stopped in front of a large double door guarded by an absolutely motionless man with a gun.

"Men," said Mr. Demarest with cheerful innocence, "I wish you luck. I wish you all the luck in the world."

Cal looked suddenly stricken but said, with casualness that didn't fool even Albert, "Wouldn't you like to come in with us?"

"Oh, no. Mr. Southfield told me only to bring you here. I'd be overstepping my bounds if I did any more. But all the good luck in the world, men!"

Cal said hearty goodbyes. But when he turned back to Albert he said, despairing: "The brushoff."

Albert could hardly take it in. "But— we get to make our presentation to the Regional Director, don't we?"

Boersma shrugged hopelessly, "Don't you see, Albert? Our presentation won't be good enough, without Demarest. When Mr. Southfield sent us on alone he was giving us the brushoff."

"Cal—are *you* going to back out too?"

"I should say not! It's a feather in our cap to have got this far, Albert. We have to follow up just as far as our abilities will take us!"

Albert went to the double door. He worried about the armed guard for a moment, but they weren't challenged. The guard hadn't even blinked, in fact.

Albert asked Cal, "Then we do still have a chance?"

"No, we haven't got a chance."

He started to push the door open, then hesitated again. "But you'll do your best?"

"I should say so! You don't get to present a proposition to the Regional Director *every* day."

With determination, Albert drew himself even straighter, and prepared himself to meet an onslaught twice as overbearing as Mr. Southfield's. One single thought was uppermost in his mind: defending his sales resistance. He felt inches taller than before; he even slightly looked down at Cal and his pessimism.

Cal pushed the door open and they went in.

The Regional Director sat alone in a straight chair, at a plain desk in a very plain office about the size of most offices.

The Regional Director was a woman.

She was dressed about as any businesswoman might dress; as conservatively as Miss Drury. As a matter of fact, she looked like Miss Drury, fifteen years older. Certainly she had the same black hair and gentle oval face.

What a surprise! A *pleasant* surprise. Albert felt still bigger and more confident than he had outside. He would certainly get on well with this motherly, unthreatening person!

She was reading from a small microfilm viewer on an otherwise bare desk. Obviously she had only a little to do before she would be free. Albert patiently watched her read. She read very conscientiously, that was clear.

After a moment she glanced up at them briefly, with an apologetic smile, then down again. Her shy dark eyes showed so much! You could see how sincerely she welcomed them, and how sorry she was that she had so much work to do—how much she would prefer to be talking with *them*. Albert pitied her. From the bottom of his heart, he pitied her. Why, that small microfilm viewer, he realized, could perfectly well contain volumes of complicated Corporation reports. Poor woman! The poor woman who happened to be Regional Director read on.

Once in a while she passed one hand, wearily but determinedly, across her face. There was a slight droop to her shoulders. Albert pitied her more all the time. She was not too strong—she had such a big job—and she was so courageously trying to do her best with all those reports in the viewer!

Finally she raised her head.

It was clear she was not through; there was no relief on her face. But she raised her head to them.

Her affection covered them like a warm bath. Albert realized he was in a position to do the kindest thing he had ever done. He felt growing in himself the resolution to do it. He would!

He started toward the door.

Before he left she met his eyes once more, and her smile showed *such* appreciation for his understanding!

Albert felt there could be no greater reward.

Out in the park again he realized for the first time that Cal was right behind him.

They looked at each other for a long time

Then Cal started walking again, toward the subway. "The brushoff," he said.

"I thought you said you'd do your best," said Albert. But he knew that Cal's "I did" was the truth.

They walked on slowly. Cal said, "Remarkable woman. . . . A real master. Sheer virtuosity!"

Albert said, "Our society certainly rewards its most deserving members."

That one single thought was uppermost in his mind, all the long way home.

AFTERWORD:
Barry N. Malzberg

LOVE O CARELESS LOVE

TENN's "The Liberation of Earth," appeared in *Future Science Fiction*, however. This has to be noted; the fact is not insignificant. *Future* was among the shortest-lived of the thirty or forty science-fiction magazines that were born to perish within the decade; it paid a penny a word sometime around publication and had a circulation of, say, thirty-five thousand as opposed to the one hundred thousand that *Galaxy* and *Astounding*, the leading magazines, achieved. "The Liberation of Earth," the most savage and perhaps most sophisticated anti-war story of its generation in science fiction, a story which has been reprinted subsequently many times and which seems to totally encapsulate our Vietnam experience, appeared in a bottom-line, penny-a-word pulp magazine, presumably because none of the better markets within science fiction wanted any part of it and because the magazines *outside* of science fiction would not even take it seriously. Genre trappings, you know.

Three other stories in this anthology—"Short in the Chest" by St. Clair, "A Work of Art" by Blish, "The Education of Tigress McCardle" by Kornbluth—fit into a similar category. It is true that as the tragic Kornbluth became better his work drifted out of the high paying markets. His last appearance in *Astounding* alone or in collaboration was in 1952; although his collaborative novels with Fred Pohl appeared in *Galaxy* until the very end, his byline was virtually absent after *The*

Altar at Midnight. The Syndic, his best uncollaborative novel, was rescued for serial publication by Harry Harrison for the staggering *Science Fiction Adventures.* Sturgeon appeared frequently in *Galaxy* in the fifties, less frequently in *Fantasy and Science Fiction* and with the exception of "Will You Walk" in January, 1956, not at all in *Astounding.* Even Mark Clifton, whose psionics stories fused so well with John Campbell's obsessions in mid-decade, wound up selling his last short stories to *Amazing* and his last novel had no serial sale whatsoever.

The point of this rather grim sub-history is that although the fifties were a period of adventure and experimentation for science fiction they were also characterized by a good deal of caution and as the decade wandered its sad way through the waters of political repression and the steady compartmentalization of American life science fiction, no less than popular music or American automotive design, began to indicate decadence. Too much too fast becomes too little too late. In a 1972 interview (with Gerald Jonas for a long *New Yorker* profile of the field) Robert Silverberg remembered why, in 1959, he left science fiction for several years. "The great magazine washout of 1958 left only a few markets," Silverberg said. "One of them would let you say only cheerful, encouraging things about science. Another would only let you say downbeat things about science. And the rest of them wouldn't let you say anything at all."

This anthology is a festival, but it is, then, important to note that in its wake, as is true of many traveling enterprises of shaky economic base, the carnival left a largely empty landscape, a fair accumulation of litter, a mass of unpaid bills and rather queasy digestions for many of those who had come to try their luck at the wheel or carry confections high, ever higher, into the sky. The two leading editors presiding at decade's end, Horace Gold and John W. Campbell, had become increasingly locked into parodies of their original editorial personae; the other leading editor, Anthony Boucher, had left altogether. Campbell came to celebrate man's ability to use science for transcendent purposes; by 1959 his conception of "science" had become debased toward the magical and the characters in control could barely, by standards of literary technique, be called human. Gold had come to question science and man's perfectability; he had ended in mockery which drained complexity from characters or extrapolation. Cynical contributors knew by the late nineteen fifties that they could sell *Galaxy* by deliberate evocation of Gold's phobias (he wanted to read about characters in physical isolation who could not break out) and contributors even more cynical than Gold's knew the way to John Campbell's payout book was to make John Campbell, barely disguised, the hero of a novelette. Meanwhile *Fantasy and Science Fiction* and *Venture* were trying to slip a little sex into the format, a magazine other than the big three was giving up the ghost every month and Phillip Klass and A. J. Budrys had decided that editing or the academy was steadier and less humiliating than attempting to do serious work for editors who did not want it or readers who could not tell the difference. The fifties ended dismally for most of its science-fiction writers. There is no other way to put this.

Still, the work remains and in the very long run it may be decided that science fiction, as a genre, both became an art form and contributed most of its best examples during this decade. The quality of the top ten percent was very high, higher than it was before or since. What does not remain, overall, are the writers. Of those in this volume, only three, Fred Pohl, Algis J. Budrys and Katherine MacLean can be said to have significant careers within science fiction today and all of them were virtually out of the field between 1960–72—Pohl editing *Galaxy* but doing almost no fiction, Budrys editing and doing public relations but committing only one novel and a scattering of short stories, MacLean out entirely. The others have made no significant contribution to science fiction after that decade. (MacDonald, a major writer, has published no science fiction in decades; Sturgeon's case might be argued but he has, since the early sixties, published no more than a dozen stories and a third of a major novel which he never completed.) The decade burned them out, one might speculate. On the other hand, decades burn writers out simply by *being* decades; the working span of a creative literary career seems to be for most of us around ten years and one does not want to make the sociologist's error of retrospectively constructing a system that simply did not exist. There are no literary movements, someone has pointed out, merely a lot of writers doing their work. Still, and to add a little more complexity, science-fiction writers and editors are an incestuous bunch. It is historically a close field. In the nineteen fifties no more than fifty editors and writers must have been responsible for nine tenths of the work published in books and the major magazines and they all knew each other and hung tight, as the expression goes. Married the same women at different times, roomed together, bought and reviewed each other's work. And so on. Science fiction is amazingly complicated for small business; about as complicated (and for roughly the same reasons) as the New York Racing Association. Leave those social paradigms, anyway, to the sociologists and welcome are they to it.

Let us be unsentimental, however; let us not idealize. Golden ages look like brass while lived in; only the survivors call them golden and then only because retrospective falsification is not only the sociologist's, it is the human condition. It was a hard time, ladies and gents. Good work got rejected, careers got broken, writers lost their way, marriages lost their way, editors lost their way, the country lost its way. The fifties set us up for disaster; by the end almost *any* call to arms would have sounded good—*pace* JFK. For my children the fifties are the lovable Fonz and lovable *Grease*; to me it was Francis E. Walters and the Rosenbergs and Senator Pat McCarran's Act. Still, Presley blew it open and Sturgeon wrote like mad. It is a mystery.

23 June 1978—New Jersey

SELECTED BIBLIOGRAPHY

Poul Anderson. BRAIN WAVE. New York: Ballantine Books, 1954.

Isaac Asimov. FOUNDATION. New York: Gnome Press, 1951; The Foundation Stories were written in the forties.

————. *FOUNDATION AND EMPIRE.* New York: Gnome Press, 1952.

————. *SECOND FOUNDATION.* New York: Gnome Press, 1953.

————. *THE CAVES OF STEEL.* New York: Doubleday & Company, Inc., 1954.

————. *THE CAVES OF STEEL.* New York: Doubleday & Company, Inc., 1954.

————. *THE NAKED SUN.* New York: Doubleday & Company, Inc., 1957.

James Blish. A CASE OF CONSCIENCE. New York: Ballantine Books, 1958.

Leigh Brackett. THE LONG TOMORROW. New York: Doubleday & Company, Inc., 1955.

Ray Bradbury. FAHRENHEIT 451. New York: Ballantine Books, 1953.

Fredric Brown. ANGELS AND SPACESHIPS. New York: E. P. Dutton & Company, Inc., 1954.

Algis Budrys. WHO? New York: Pyramid Books, 1958.

John Christopher. NO BLADE OF GRASS. New York: Simon & Schuster, Inc., 1957.

Arthur C. Clarke. CHILDHOOD'S END. New York: Ballantine Books, 1953.

————. *AGAINST THE FALL OF NIGHT.* New York: Gnome Press, 1953.

Edmund Cooper. DEADLY IMAGE. New York: Ballantine Books, 1958.

Kendall Foster Crossen. *YEAR OF CONSENT.* New York: Dell Publishing Company, Inc., 1954.

L. Sprague de Camp. *ROGUE QUEEN.* New York: Doubleday & Company, Inc., 1951.

Philip K. Dick. *SOLAR LOTTERY.* New York: Ace Books, 1955.

———. *THE MAN WHO JAPED.* New York: Ace Books, 1955.

———. *THE WORLD JONES MADE.* New York: Ace Books, 1956.

———. *EYE IN THE SKY.* New York: Ace Books, 1957.

———. *TIME OUT OF JOINT.* Philadelphia: J. B. Lippincott Company, 1959.

Philip Jose Farmer. *STRANGE RELATIONS.* New York: Ballantine Books, 1960.

Howard Fast. *THE EDGE OF TOMORROW.* New York: Bantam Books, 1961.

James Gunn. *THIS FORTRESS WORLD.* New York: Gnome Press, 1955.

———. *THE JOYMAKERS.* New York: Bantam Books, 1961.

Robert A. Heinlein. *STARSHIP TROOPERS.* New York: G. P. Putnam's Sons, 1959.

Raymond F. Jones. *RENAISSANCE.* New York: Gnome Press, 1951.

Fritz Lieber. *GATHER, DARKNESS!* New York: Pellegrini & Cudahy, 1950.

———. *THE GREEN MILLENNIUM.* New York: Abelard, 1953.

———. *THE SILVER EGGHEADS.* New York: Ballantine Books, 1961, shorter version appeared in 1959.

C. M. Kornbluth. *THE SYNDIC.* New York: Doubleday & Company, Inc., 1953.

———. *NOT THIS AUGUST.* New York: Doubleday & Company, Inc., 1955.

———. *THE MARCHING MORONS.* New York: Ballantine Books, 1959.

J. T. McIntosh. *WORLD OUT OF MIND.* Doubleday & Company, Inc., 1957.

Walter M. Miller, Jr. *A CANTICLE FOR LEIBOWITZ.* Philadelphia: J. B. Lippincott Company, 1959.

C. L. Moore. *DOOMSDAY MORNING.* New York: Doubleday & Company, Inc., 1957.

Ward Moore. *BRING THE JUBILEE.* New York: Farrar, 1953.

Chad Oliver. *SHADOWS IN THE SUN.* New York: Ballantine Books, 1954.

————. *THE WINDS OF TIME.* New York: Ballantine Books, 1957.

Frederik Pohl. ALTERNATING CURRENTS. New York: Ballantine Books, 1956.

————. *SLAVE SHIP.* New York: Ballantine Books, 1957.

————. *THE CASE AGAINST TOMORROW.* New York: Ballantine Books, 1957.

————. *TOMORROW TIMES SEVEN.* New York: Ballantine Books, 1959.

————. *THE MAN WHO ATE THE WORLD.* New York: Ballantine Books, 1960.

Frederik Pohl and Lester del Rey (as "Edson McCann"). PREFERRED RISK. New York: Simon & Schuster Inc., 1955.

Frederik Pohl and C. M. Kornbluth. THE SPACE MERCHANTS. New York: Ballantine Books, 1953.

————. *SEARCH THE SKY.* New York: Ballantine Books, 1954.

————. *GLADIATOR-AT-LAW.* New York: Ballantine Books, 1955.

Robert Sheckley. UNTOUCHED BY HUMAN HANDS. New York: Ballantine Books, 1954.

————. *CITIZEN IN SPACE.* New York: Ballantine Books, 1956.

————. *STORE OF INFINITY.* New York: Bantam Books, 1960.

————. *NOTIONS, UNLIMITED.* New York: Bantam Books, 1960.

Robert Silverberg. INVADERS FROM EARTH. New York: Ace Books, 1958.

Clifford D. Simak. CITY. New York: Gnome Press, 1952.

Theodore Sturgeon. MORE THAN HUMAN. New York: Ballantine Books, 1953.

William Tenn. OF ALL POSSIBLE WORLDS. New York: Ballantine Books, 1955.

————. *THE HUMAN ANGLE.* New York: Ballantine Books, 1956.

————. *THE SQUARE ROOT OF MAN.* New York: Ballantine Books, 1968.

————. *THE WOODEN STAR.* New York: Ballantine Books, 1968.

Wilson Tucker. THE LONG LOUD SILENCE. New York: Rinehart, 1952.

Jack Vance. TO LIVE FOREVER. New York: Ballantine Books, 1956.

Kurt Vonnegut, Jr. PLAYER PIANO. New York: Charles Scribner's Sons, Inc., 1951.

Richard Wilson. THE GIRLS FROM PLANET 5. New York: Ballantine Books, 1955.

John Wyndham. RE-BIRTH. New York: Ballantine Books, 1955.

SCIENCE FICTION
OF THE 40's

Edited, with historical commentary, by
FREDERIK POHL, MARTIN HARRY GREENBERG, and
JOSEPH OLANDER

These twenty-one remarkable stories, never before
collected in one volume, represent the most outstanding work of the phenomenal forties—when
magazines like *Amazing, Astounding,* and *Astonishing* were in their heyday. Included are writers whose
works are classics of the genre: Isaac Asimov,
James Blish, Ray Bradbury, Arthur C. Clark, Robert
Heinlein, Lester del Rey, A. E. van Vogt, and others.
Here is a marvelous collection that offers an insider's view into the exciting years and flamboyant
personalities that brought science fiction to a
gleaming, fantastic art.

WITH AN INTRODUCTION BY FREDERIK POHL

AVON   40097 / $4.95

SCIENCE FICTION OF THE 30's

Edited, with historical commentary, by
DAMON KNIGHT

Eighteen stories, long out of print and available only
in the rare original magazines and special collections in which they appeared, are assembled in this
extraordinary volume. Accompanying the stories
are the actual illustrations from those original magazines and Damon Knight's candid, insider's commentary on the men, the editors, and the publishers
of SF's first great decade. Included are stories by
such early masters of the genre as: John W. Campbell, Jr., Murray Leinster, L. Sprague de Camp, Eric
Frank Russell, and many more.

SELECTED BY THE SCIENCE FICTION BOOK CLUB

AVON  31708 / $4.95

SFT 9-78